THICK FOG IN PACHECO PASS

R.P. McCabe

Pen & Ink Publishing, Ltd.

Thick Fog In Pacheco Pass is a work of fiction. Names, characters, places, and incidents are products of the author's imagination or are used fictitiously. Any resemblance to actual events, locales, or persons, living or dead, is entirely coincidental.

Printed in the United States of America

Cover art and design: Yevinn Graphics

Also by R.P. McCabe

Betrayed

Coming Soon

Slaughtered

For my father, O.P. McCabe

My father always used to say that when you die, if you've got five real friends, then you've had a great life—
Lee Iacocca

My father had many real friends when he left this place...I am one of them.

Thanks

I was encouraged and assisted in a multitude of ways during my year's work on this project. I'm not certain the significance is always apparent to friends and colleagues; the profound contribution that is made whenever those kernels of reinforcement are proffered. Devan Mullins is one such voice who is constant in his interest, reassuring kindness and support of my work. Fellow writer and friend, Bobbi Hughes-Millman inspired boldness in my work on this novel and taught me a good deal about sentence structure. My editor, Natascha Jaffa, deserves special recognition since as we were attempting to birth this novel, she was quite literally in the process of birthing her first child. I thought it particularly poignant she should hold her child off long enough to finish this manuscript with me. What dissimilarity, loyalty!

My dear friend and sister, Ann Clark, remains the steady voice of "can do" in my life. She seemingly never tires of listening patiently to my insecurities, then offering just the right measure of reassurance that I can, and will, prevail if I just keep toeing the mark.

And finally, I want to thank all of you who have supported my work by purchasing my debut novel, Betrayed. Special thanks to the hundreds of readers who've taken the time to communicate with me and express their appreciation of my work and offer encouragement to send them a new novel. Here you are. And thank you all for your patience.

CHAPTER 1

AT SIX-THIRTY on a cool Wednesday morning in April 1972, I was awake and dressed and shifting along the sidewalk past sleepy storefronts up the wide, mostly deserted, main street of Divina, California. The aura of contentment was in blatant contrast to the fires of dissent burning high across America over the Vietnam War, the Feminist Movement and Civil Rights. The town was slowly waking itself like a puppy stretching and yawning from a long nap. I'd grown up here; graduated high school ten years earlier. The heavy, humid air of the spring morning still held the scent of freshly cut, damp alfalfa, which is always at some stage of maturation on the outskirts of town. Experience told me it would be a hot day.

Several months earlier, the US Army cut me loose after what was euphemistically referred to as a rough second combat tour in Vietnam. I'd made promises to three men who were my brothers. They didn't come home. That's a nice way of saying they'd been zapped. What happened was a lot worse than that, actually, but who needs to hear that shit, right? I'd occupied my time since being back stateside keeping my word to them. War had taught me some things. Two stood out: We are woefully fragile creatures, we humans. And death is profoundly final. Tough, but useful lessons to learn early in life.

We'd promised each other if one of us didn't make it back, whoever among us did would do the deed; sit before mothers and fathers and sisters and aunts and close friends—tell them all the things we'd never be able to say to them ourselves. The way we spoke about, even contemplated, death, as if it were inevitable, a foregone conclusion to what was happening to us was weirdly serene. It would've been bad enough to have to keep that promise to one of them. But when you come up the sole survivor of a squad, the Brass pins a bronze star on your chest, designating you some kind of hero, calls it a rough tour and cuts you loose. Then you're free to figure out how to become a fucking human being again. My first step was keeping the promise I'd made to the guys I fought next to, the ones who died helping *me* stay alive. I constantly have to live with that; why I made it back and they didn't.

I'd decided it was a mistake to allow pride to stand in the way of telling the few people I cared anything about in this world how I felt about them. There was only one person I needed to see and talk to. Then I figured to be gone again—for good I imagined.

While I stared into the huge front window of Viera's Five & Dime, I could still hear the cruel voice of the uppity cashier buzzing in my ears across nearly twenty years. *If your father took his paycheck home instead of to the bar, you'd be able to buy that yo-yo, Charlie Caldwell.* Divina was that kind of nasty little town where everybody knew everybody else's business or made it their business to pass judgment. Kids were easy targets for pettiness toward a parent somebody had it in for or simply felt superior to. My old man seemed to relish making it easy for them to hold him in contempt.

In the reflection of the glass window, I stalked a police car as it crept by, its occupant eyeing me

2

suspiciously. I recognized Jorge Olivera. He was a pimple-faced punk the last I knew. Here he was wearing a police uniform and driving a shiny 1970 black and white Plymouth Fury with a chromed swivel spotlight hanging on the driver's side door above the emblem of a gold badge. The car slowed to a crawl and he ogled me through his side view mirror.

Once the cop car was a block up the street I moved on to the next storefront, which was a place called The Sweet Shop. It was closed, too. A fat orange and white tuxedo cat pondered me with large yellow, curious eyes, lying on its belly in the front window between ruffled pink percale curtains and the glass. I traced a circle on the window with my finger and the cat followed with its nose.

"Name's Simon." The woman's gravelly voice startled me and I spun. She withdrew a key from a worn leather purse and slid it into the locked door. The cat jumped down to greet her.

"You want some breakfast?"

Whether she was talking to the cat or me was hard to tell.

"Won't be open for another hour, but I'll put some coffee on if you'd like."

The morning air was crisp and damp with an edge to it. Why not, I figured? The cat rubbed between my legs, then bounded off after its owner. The dark-haired, middle-aged woman moved purposefully behind the counter.

The inside of The Sweet Shop seemed preserved in a time-warp just the way I remembered it; lipstick-red vinyl covered booths against a worn white linoleum floor. Everything was bright, clean looking, uncluttered, with sharp distinct lines. The counter seats matched and were set atop shiny chrome pedestals like large, juicy, flaming-red lollypops. Each booth table was perched on a matching chrome pedestal. Even the edging around the white Formica tabletops was shiny chrome. Though it was accidental, the décor was 50s retro, including the miniature jukeboxes sitting on each table at the wall end of all four booths. The jukeboxes were strategically located at convenient intervals along the long white countertop as well. The place was as authentic as it gets.

"Don't see many new faces 'round these parts." The woman mumbled the words while turning on the water over a long sink.

"Passing through," I lied, intending to avoid any probing invasion.

I minded the fifty-something-year-old woman while she worked with her back to me. Should've recognized her, but I didn't.

The cat meowed to be fed and rubbed against her legs while she sprinkled coffee grounds into the filter and turned on the tall polished commercial coffeemaker glinting from the far end of the counter. *Shiny* would've been the one word to describe the place.

"Health Department cited me for having him in here last year."

I glanced around the quaint parlor, recalling times I'd spent here in my youth. "Not worried they'll catch him in here again?" I asked, spinning in her direction.

She turned slowly from the coffeepot and locked her dark, puffy eyes onto me. "Not unless some do-gooder turns me in." The way she cocked her head, the grave demeanor of her body language; it was a threat.

Rocking backward from the counter, I held my hands against my chest. "Nothing to worry about from me." My assurance was truth.

"Never know," she went on, dropping her hands from her hips. "Local busy-body turned me in last time." The woman went back to what she was doing, but carried on about being reported. "Before that it'd been a couple years since the inspector even bothered to come out—and then she called first," she said, sliding behind the pass-through window to the grill. "Long drive over here from Merced. That's the county seat."

"People are funny," I agreed. "Some'll let a puppy lick 'em in the face. Others…"

The strong smell of fresh coffee filled the space. A spatula slapped against hard metal at the stove and I heard the sound of gas whooshing into flame.

"Gal 'at turned me in got more'n even she deserved for her troubles, though." The woman's head and shoulders momentarily disappeared from view like a jack-in-the-box.

"How so?" I wondered aloud.

"Found her murdered," she told me as if it were a quotidian announcement. "'Bout a month back now. Bad— real bad." Potatoes rumbled into a metal sink echoing inside the inner kitchen and I heard water splash. She paused as if to consider what she was saying. "Found her necked as an 'ole J-bird. Layin' dead along the edge of a field. Say she was raped and strangled. "Whole town took it real hard."

The profound heaviness of the words *murder* and *rape* caught my full attention. The details hit me in my guts. "Hard to imagine a thing like that in such a quiet little town."

The red light flashed on the coffee machine and a buzzer sounded. "Coffee," the woman announced, tossing a hand towel across her shoulder. "Lemme grab ya a cup." She swung out from the back kitchen, her apron now showing wet handprints.

"Both of 'em," she said, "from right here in town. They was in here same night it all happened. Him sittin' 'bout where you are now. She was over yonder." She pointed to a corner table. "Got into a big fight—everybody heard him threaten her." She held a second mug under the spigot of the coffeemaker. "'Course, like I say, she was as bad with her language as any o' the men she chased around with." She flipped the spigot closed and dabbed at a spill

5

before taking a sip from one of the cups. Sliding the other cup in front of me, she continued her tale. "Still, nobody deserves to die like she did…so young. Pretty girl, too."

The topic of young people dying before their time was a sore subject with me, but this woman couldn't know that. I let it pass. Clearly, we were coming at the death of young people from two different places.

"Daddy's a big shot here in town. Owns the mercantile," she said.

That last revelation made me go queasy and I cut her off mid-thought. "You talking about Sal DeCosta?"

"His oldest daughter Miranda that was killed," she affirmed, looking up at me. The woman must have seen into me because she stopped speaking and touched my hand gently before she asked, "You know the DeCosta family?"

"Yeah," I said, more to myself than in answer to her. "I know them—knew them—all of them…the DeCostas." But I had no interest in revealing any more to her about what was gripping me inside. "Jesus. Miranda dead. How can that be?" I whispered.

"Sounds like you knew 'em pretty well." She was niggling after details by that point.

I ignored her. Memories drifted like grey clouds across an ominous November sky. "I went to school with her," I heard myself droning. Maybe I was just thinking it, I'm not sure. It felt as if I'd slipped down a long constricted tunnel; a VC warren. I was back in the jungle. Steven lay dead beside me. What was left of Randy's life was oozing out of him thirty yards away. No way I could get to him. Ray's remains were unrecognizable the way the grenade blew his face and chest wide open. One moment we were there, giving each other a raft of shit. I could hear them, feel them, smell them. In the next instant, nothingness. And it could never be undone. Whatever was left unsaid between us, between everyone they ever knew, would remain unsaid forever. Life became appallingly finite in an instant.

The nightmare was happening again. I'd come here to speak to one person—Miranda DeCosta. Not for the first time, I found the cruelty of life overwhelming.

"You don't look familiar," the woman on the other side of the counter said.

"I gotta go." As I stepped away from the counter and opened the door, the big orange cat slipped by. I lunged for him, but just touched his tail as he broke free.

"It's okay," the woman assured me. "He usually goes out about now anyway."

"You said they were both from here. Was there more than one person killed?"

"Meant Miranda and the guy who killed her. Both from right here in town."

I stood in the doorway, holding it half open. "They caught who did it?"

"Had to know him too you went to school here." The woman had pulled the bottom edge of her apron up, wrung her hands nervously. She studied my six-foot frame thoroughly. I'd filled out a lot since high school; wore my hair longer now, down over my ears and to my collar in the back. I didn't want people to recognize me as a Vet. None of what she saw answered the question in her mind; who was it she was talking to?

The phone rang before she could dig further. I let the door swing closed in front of me while she went to answer the call. "No, Jorge," she said. "Everything's fine. Just didn't know what time I opened." She shook her head a few times and thanked the caller. She walked back toward me. "Local deputy checking up on me." She jabbed her thumb over her shoulder in the direction of the phone. "Not normally open this hour."

I grabbed the handle to the door once more and began to push.

7

"Fella name o' Caputo—Vinny Caputo—guy who murdered Miranda."

The revelation stunned me and I stood with my head buried down the front of my chest. "Knew him, too," I confessed.

"And you say you went to school right here in town." The woman went on probing the depths of her memory. The unanswered question of my identity was grinding on her. "Been around these parts thirty-five years. Oughtta know who you are."

Suddenly I just didn't give a shit about anonymity any longer. "Charlie Caldwell."

"Oh, my goodness," she bellowed, drawing both hands up to her mouth. "I woulda never recognized you." She stepped back to survey me closely. "Why, you seem—taller?" She hesitated. "You remember me, Charlie? You went to school with both o' my boys, too. Jeffery and Dennis Ponder. I'm Dorothy—Dorothy Ponder." She smiled up at me, reaching over to run her hands down the full length of my arm as though she were caressing something venerable or expensive.

The instant she told me her name, I knew who she was. "Sure, Mrs. Ponder. Now that you remind me, I do remember you."

"How long has it been?" Dorothy Ponder dithered, trying to recall things from the past. "You left town right after high school graduation back in…'62. People talked about that. You just up and left."

Too much information coming in, going out. "Another time, Mrs. Ponder," I said, pushing out the door.

"Dorothy," she called after me. "Call me Dorothy."

I turned to face her. "Okay…Dorothy. Another time." This time I gave her no opportunity to corral me and moved up the street, headed back to the Trail's End Motel.

Why I didn't immediately check out of my room and return to Mexico, I can't tell you. But I didn't.

I wasn't surprised to learn Dorothy Ponder had gone straight to her telephone and dialed her closest friend. By the end of the day, nearly all of Divina, California, population two-thousand-plus, knew Charlie Caldwell was back in town.

CHAPTER 2

ON THE EASTERN SLOPE of California's Diablo Mountains, perched well above the floor of the sprawling San Joaquin Valley along side Pacheco Pass, sits the tiny rural town of Divina. State Route 152 is the closest highway.

In 1769, a Spanish Monk by the name of Junipero Serra began establishing a string of missions stretching from Baja California all the way north to Monterey.

Serra built a mission at San Juan Bautista, close to a well-worn footpath over the mountains leading to the interior valley. Mission San Juan Bautista was situated at the trailhead, about half the distance between the path over the mountains that would later come to be called Pacheco Pass and the larger settlement at Monterey. The southern tip of San Francisco Bay lay close to the north of the pass where the Mission of San Jose was a burgeoning settlement.

As religious zealots since the time of Christ are given to do, Fr. Serra and his small army of brown-habited crusaders for the Lord went on to enslave the local heathens to do the work of God so they might know the salvation of heaven; a destination they were generally dispatched to in fairly short order. Those Ausaymus Indians had been the first to use the goat and deer path over the mountains into the great valley lying beyond to the east.

During the early 1800's, Don Francisco Perez Pacheco—whose land grant from Mexico stretched from Mission San Juan Bautista to Gilroy, California—established his Rancho Divina at the eastern trailhead exiting the pass into the San Joaquin Valley. One should not be surprised to learn the pass carries his name.

By about 1848, immigrants who arrived in San Francisco hoping to unearth their fortunes in the California gold fields poured over the coastal range mountains like ants out of a nest.

Among those heading east over Pacheco Pass in route to Angels Camp along the banks of the Columbia River were two Portuguese immigrants who'd survived the historically brutal trek across the Isthmus of Panama.

History teaches these men were skilled livestock handlers. Work would have been easy for them to find at Rancho Divina, which by then had spawned a small settlement nearby. Both men needed to earn enough money to fit-out for their mining expedition to the Sierra Nevada.

In late winter, California's coastal fog would roll in and creep up the western slope of the pass, finally spilling over onto Rancho Divina where it condensed and dripped in a fine mist over the rolling foothills, turning them into a verdant paradise. Each day as the misty shroud of fog receded, the two Portuguese immigrants stood in the open grassland of the foothills, gazed wistfully out across the vast valley stretching before them to see the towering, snow-covered peaks of the Sierra Nevada. Their will to leave the place receded permanently with the fog about early June that year as the rolling foothill grasses began to turn golden. California would take its name, "The Golden State," from those yellowed grasses and fields of golden poppies as much as it would from the gold rush itself.

By the end of the nineteenth century, Rancho Divina, having been divided into many smaller ranches and sold off, had become simply Divina, the small settlement now a township. The only remaining trace of Divina's Mexican origins lay in the pronunciation of its name. The Portuguese, speaking little English, pronounced both "i's" in Divina like two hard "ee's", and by that quirk of language, the beauty of the Mexican name of Don Francisco Perez Pacheco's *Devine Ranch* was saved.

What would attract and bring the extended families and friends of those early founding settlers to immigrate to Divina would come to be the same reason I had to get the hell out of the place the summer I graduated high school. Funny isn't it? One man's paradise—another's hell.

R.P. McCabe

CHAPTER 3

BY 1952, MY FAMILY had been living in the town more than five years. The high school and elementary school defined the north-south limits of downtown with the high school located at the far north end of Main Street and the elementary school at the south.

Souza's Market was the grocery store clearinghouse for fresh produce supplied by nearby farms and represented roughly the center of town. When the wind was right, the pungent odor of fresh cow shit and fermenting overripe fruits and vegetables amplified the source of the town's commerce.

On an opposite corner from the market was the post office and next to that a small branch of Bank of America. On the other corner was a disagreeable looking baby blue two-story office building with a beauty salon on the bottom and the accounting office of Duke Matta above. Moving up one side of Main Street, you come to Mattos' Hardware, Rodrigues' Cleaners and Paulo Cotta's clothing store where high school kids ordered their letter jackets and sweaters every fall for the past twenty-five years.

When Sal DeCosta's father passed away and Sal took over the family mercantile, he built a movie theater next to Cotta's. Called it the *Westside Cinema*. I saw my first

Tarzan movie there with Johnny Weissmuller and Maureen O'Sullivan. The Saturday matinee cost twenty-five cents. Didn't matter it was a rerun of the 1932 episode, Tarzan the Ape Man. Sal DeCosta never paid to get first-run films. None of us could have afforded it if he had. On the other side of the theater was Viera's Five & Dime, The Sweet Shop and Bambino's Pool Hall. Mortimer's Pharmacy was directly across the street on the corner.

The citizens of Divina, like so many other out of the way towns around America dominated by one ethnic group or another, harbor suspicion, fear and prejudice. Anyone not of their own ethnicity—a trait America seems doomed to preserve, bigotry and racism are alive and well nearly everywhere I go—becomes an outcast.

Beyond the pharmacy at the edge of town is DeMartino's Filling Station where just about every boy of high school age works at one time or another in his life assuming, of course, he was Portuguese or Italian. The police station is located in a grimy little building behind the post office that was once a feed store.

West of Main Street there's a small cluster of municipal buildings; City Hall, a city park with public swimming pool, public library, courthouse and fire department. A bit further along are the elite neighborhoods, such that they are. If your family didn't own one of the huge dairies, farming operations or ranches in the area, this is where you would *want* to live. Few could actually afford that privilege. This is where Divina's *old money* resides.

The spacious homes of those neighborhoods display the exotic essence of the places that inspired them: Portugal, the Azores Islands, Italy and perhaps even Spain, northwestern Mediterranean. Natural stone masonry facades grown over by large, leafy green ivy and shaded by giant oak trees, old enough to have provided a cool respite to the Indians who originally hunted and lived here.

Divina is inclined to the old ways. Cultural protocols prevail here. When the DeCosta family migrated from Italy in 1902, the Portuguese in the community welcomed them. Their European roots offering familiarity, a binding between them.

No such connection, however, was shared with the coarse speaking, hard drinking, Anglo Saxon southerners who began showing up in the labor camps around Bakersfield, California in the 1930's.

My own grandparents were one consequence of the Great Depression, the devastating drought and dust storms that swept across the southern Great Plains until about 1940. The white trash dust-bowlers had little in common with the established European settlers of Divina, who by then claimed rights of community dominance dating back to the mid 1800's.

Took moving away for me to learn being a minority is largely dictated by where you live in America. In the south, blacks are the minority. In Colorado, Democrats. In Divina, California, Okies & Arkies were white trash. And the majority of people living there made damn sure they didn't forget it.

Like I said, my family was one of those itinerant farm-laboring families who found their way to Divina by the early 1950's.

The Portuguese and Italian majority who came to dominate the small town didn't welcome us. My parents and a few other farm laborers, for reasons that remain a mystery to me, decided to settle here. They found places to live in rundown neighborhoods of tiny houses on the east side of town, virtually buttressing the railroad tracks. Along with the trembling clatter of steam locomotives, we all learned to accept the strong stench of cow shit as normal.

My parents and other poor whites became the labor class supporting agricultural endeavor, the exact inverse of other small towns along California's border with Mexico.

15

Mexican *"Braceros"* in great numbers dominated the agricultural fieldwork around Salinas, but they hadn't yet moved to the San Joaquin Valley.

When I left in 1962, families like mine were still picking the fruits and vegetables, chopping weeds in the fields and cleaning the homes of the wealthy. White Trash as we were called, no matter how hard working, would never become any meaningful class component of Divina, but we'd remain indispensable for doing the menial labor the upper crust needed performed.

CHAPTER 4

LUNCH HOUR WAS winding down and my prediction of a hot afternoon was being born out. I'd been wandering around town aimlessly, trying to process what I'd learned from Dorothy Ponder. I found myself standing on an adjacent corner from my old high school, absorbing the pensive melancholy of the first days of spring. The faces of the kids trudging reluctantly across the street onto the campus lawn seemed innocent, oblivious to the gravity of life going on outside of their trivial cocoon. Perhaps that was a harsh assessment. Miranda was in my head.

These kids streaming into the classrooms might have been from my own high school class ten years earlier—dark, olive-skinned youths with bright green eyes and black curly hair; portraits of their ethnicity. They were a handsome bunch, just as my schoolmates had been.

Deputy Jorge Olivera pulled his black and white Plymouth to a screeching stop at the curb in front of me. "Well, well," he belched acidly. "Old Lady Ponder was right." Olivera threw a half-smoked, wooden-tipped Cheroot toward my feet. "Wouldn't o' recognized your white trash ass unless I knew it was you. Now that I do, what the hell you doin' 'round here?"

I smiled at the jerk and crushed out the short cigar. "Been a while, Jorge."

A snarl curled off of Olivera's thin lips. "This ain't gonna' be old home week, Caldwell," the deputy snorted. "You ain't no more welcome now'n the day you left."

I picked up the nasty crushed cigar between my index finger and thumb, held it out to him. "Haven't you heard, Jorge? Littering's against the law now...most towns anyway."

"Don't smart ass me," Olivera warned. "I don't know what you're up to, but you better damn well stay out of my way." The tires squealed when the surly deputy punched the gas and shot away. Smarmy prick. The stench of burned rubber and cheap cigar assaulted me while I watched the cop car disappear around the corner.

Mine had been a childhood trapped by small-minded people, stuck in a small-minded existence, living closeted, inconsequential lives, which for some vague reason led them to feel puffed up and important. Most were born, raised and now, like Miranda DeCosta, buried in Divina and proud to make the claim they'd never lived further away than fifty miles of the place.

Walking west from the high school, I trudged into the upward sweep of the foothills a few blocks before turning south toward the city park. I wandered tiny side streets, recalling one event or another from my childhood until I found myself standing next to the empty community swimming pool in the center of the park.

I found a wooden bench and wasted the rest of the afternoon letting my mind cruise down memory lane, the Portuguese celebrations that return each year around Catholic Holy days. Still love those Portuguese and Italian foods I grew up with.

Small traveling carnivals would creep into town late some Friday nights. They'd be set up in the park bright and early Saturday morning to rip off parents and adolescent

18

boys who'd invest as much as ten dollars in some hopeless scam of a game to win a child or girlfriend a twenty-five cent trinket. We'd ride the beat up buckets of some jury-rigged enterprise that would spin us in circles until we threw up the cotton candy and peanuts we'd gorged on.

All afternoon I labored to put it all together, the innocence and promise I'd naively felt certain would eventually come my way. And now to accept the idea that others my own age, people I'd known and cared about who would have held those same hopes and dreams, were no more. It was as if the pitiless flank of life had appropriated a deep gasp and obliterated the light that was once the engine of hope. They simply no longer existed. Of course, there was nothing *simple* about it. The tacit actuality of death confronted me even here. I found myself wanting to run from it, but I'd tried that. The demon always seeks the same refuge you think you've discovered.

CHAPTER 5

TOWARD THE END of the following day, Thursday, I paid a visit to Frankie DeCosta. Frankie was Miranda's cousin of my same age. He'd been a childhood friend. Well...maybe friend isn't what he'd been, but I'd done my best to be *his* friend. The young brunette at the front desk turned down the Moody Blues working their way through *Nights in White Satin* long enough to show me into his office.

"Wondered how long it would be before you'd come around," Frankie said from his throne behind a large birds-eye-maple desk. The office smelled of stale cigarettes and heavily perfumed air freshener; something hovering between Swiss Alps and Patchouli. He didn't appear happy to see me, but neither did he seem particularly annoyed. He swiveled his heavy leather chair sideways and stood.

Ten years looked good on Frankie. The last time I saw him, July '62, he was still wearing braces on his teeth. They were reasonably straight now, but not quite piano keys. The brown stains that had persisted like rust around the edges of the metal had been bleached away. He'd broadened some in the shoulders. Still kept his hair cropped in an old fashioned butch cut. My hair hadn't been that short since the day after I'd reported to boot camp.

"Sorry I didn't make it by sooner." There was an awkward silence between us for a moment. "You look good, Frankie."

"You, too." He came around the end of his desk, tentative at first, and then extended his hand. I shook it and in an instant I knew Frankie'd developed no more spine as a man than he had when we were kids.

"Sit with me," he said motioning toward a leather couch against the far wall. Frankie sat in an antique wooden chair across from me. The carvings of a dragon across the backrest reminded me of a Saigon whorehouse.

Watching him squirm uncomfortably, I remembered playing toy soldiers with him when we were kids, the carefree years before high school. We were nine—maybe eleven—at the time. Ours was a friendship that began by accident one early spring morning when I stumbled onto Frankie crouched down in a bermed up irrigation ditch separating the alfalfa fields between the houses where we lived. At first I thought something was wrong.

He was hiding behind a mound of chunky dirt clods, launching one clod after the other toward a second mound several yards away. Between throws he seemed to be yelling at someone. I squatted down and worked my way up the ditch behind him and whispered, "You okay?"

"Yeah!" he yelled. "Grab some ammo and let 'em have it." With that he rose full onto his knees and unleashed another barrage of dirt rocks at the other mound. "Bombs away," he roared, letting the word 'away' trail off. "Gotcha, you stinkin' Krauts."

Spent and in a febrile huff, he'd fallen backward against the angle of the berm and lay totally silent. The 'zoom...zoom' Doppler sounds of a distant crop duster trilled the morning air like the whir of a nighthawk's wings. The sweet, pungent smell of fresh-cut alfalfa and the faint odor of DDT permeated our senses with the promise of summer vacation just around the corner. I'd never met

21

Frankie DeCosta before that morning. He attended *Sacred Heart of Madonna,* Divina's private Catholic school. I attended the Union Elementary.

I rolled onto the side of the berm next to him and asked what it was he was up to.

"Don't you know how to play soldiers?" He was incredulous at the idea I might not. My ignorance of what he was engaged in was ludicrous to him.

"Never played it before," I admitted. "What's your name?"

"Frankie DeCosta. What's yours?"

"Charlie Caldwell," I told him. "Live right over there." I pointed to the tiny, rundown shack across the field.

"I live back that way," Frankie said, looking toward the fancy ranch house across the road opposite the adjacent alfalfa field.

Then came high school and suddenly we were together every day. It didn't take me long to figure out there was no parity of value in our friendship. I'd do about anything for Frankie, who was a pudgy kid of maybe five feet two inches. He had droopy shoulders and his belly and chest sagged like the cartoon character Wimpy. That's what the other kids began calling him. He was frequently the object of their cruelty. But I never failed to stick up for him. Frankie, on the other hand, had to measure what he was getting himself into before deciding to back me against other kids and especially around adults. I sought acceptance, so I ignored the breach between us.

"Heard about Miranda," I said, glancing down at my entwined fingers.

Silence.

"Yeah," Frankie echoed, his tone somber. He stood slowly and crossed back behind his desk taking his time lighting up a Marlboro. Tilting the pack in my direction, he offered me a smoke. Then he spoke into his desk. "Been ugly." He exhaled a long stream of smoke and sucked a lot of it back into his nostrils.

Longer silent moment.

"How are your folks doing?" I asked.

He shifted in his chair, leaned forward onto his elbows then exhaled another long breath of cigarette smoke. "You know...gettin' older," he said. "Old man's got high blood pressure. Ma', she keeps on top of him to take care of himself." He drew hard on the cigarette. "What you been up to? Been what…ten years?"

Now he was getting down to it. He was curious. The whole town was curious because outside of one regrettable phone conversation with Miranda not long after I'd settled in Denver, I'd never spoken to anyone from the time I'd escaped this claustrophobic piss hole ten years earlier.

"Moved around some—Colorado, New Mexico," I told him.

"Home?"

"Not sure for now," I told him honestly. "Been living down in Old Mexico this past year."

"What the hell you doin' in Old Mexico? You hidin' from the law or somethin'?" He guffawed. "No. I got it," he went on, attempting what he might have thought of as humor. "You're runnin' from a broad."

"Neither." I cocked my head sideways and looked Frankie right in the eyes.

"What?" he protested.

I waited a beat then started in a new direction. "So, how's your Uncle Sal taking things?"

"Hard. You know Uncle Sal." Suddenly Frankie became fidgety.

"Yeah. Uncle Sal," I said. We locked eyes. There was no shortage of enmity between Sal DeCosta and me; something Frankie understood.

Frankie moved on. "Sometimes hard to figure if he's hurt over losing her, or pissed off somebody would destroy something belonged to him. Know what I mean?"

"Miranda was pretty close with her dad way I remember."

"Yeah, well, that was then. You know she graduated Fresno State?"

I shook my head. "Nope. One brief phone conversation with her that summer I moved away. No contact with anyone from here since."

Frankie leaned back in his chair. He studied me for several seconds. "What're you doin' back, Charlie? Whaddaya want?"

I engaged his arrogant stare. "Not a thing, Frankie. Nothing."

"Then, what? Why now?"

"Take it easy. I found myself with some time to kill and got curious. Started wondering about people, things…you know. Just curious."

Sitting there in his office I felt no connection with Frankie DeCosta. Any conversation about the profound thoughts buzzing around in my brain, what happened to me in Nam; not the kind of shit I was about to take up with this guy.

"Miranda," he hissed. "You got curious about Miranda. I remember how you took it when she dumped your ass our senior year."

"Just curious about…things. Been ten years. Nothing more." I couldn't stop myself turning to look out the window next to the couch where I sat. "When I heard what happened to her—" That part of what I felt, the confusion, the mixed emotions pounding away inside me over her death—that I'd share with him. "I've seen death, Frankie. But I just can't wrap my mind around Miranda being dead."

"When she got home," he said, "from college—found out Uncle Sal wasn't gonna' let her into the business—things got shitty. I mean, Uncle Sal, women workin'. Uncle Sal, he don't go for that shit. Jesus, not to mention his own daughter. Way Uncle Sal sees it, women belong at home." Frankie spoke with his hands, making gestures in the air with the cigarette between his fingers. "She started drinkin', sleepin' 'round. I think she did it to piss him off at first. Then she got into the habit. Seemed to like it. Know what I mean?" He brushed a fallen ash pile from his desk onto the floor. "Real pain in Uncle Sal's ass. The rest of us, too, for that matter." He leaned all the way back in his chair, rocked backward and exhaled a long stream of smoke toward the ceiling.

All I could do was look away toward the honeysuckle flowers hanging around the edges of the big window.

"You're thinkin' about her, ain't' ya'?" Frankie accused, interrupting my thoughts.

"I didn't come back because of Miranda, Frankie," I lied. "I really just wanted to see how the place changed. Seems to me it hasn't." The whole of the conversation helped me decide I'd had enough of Frankie DeCosta and Divina and I stood to leave.

Frankie remained seated. "Look, Charlie, I might as well tell you. You ain't exactly gonna' be met with open arms around here. I mean, Uncle Sal, he don't forget things. Know what I'm sayin'?"

I tried to maintain my composure. "You give your whole family my condolences, Frankie. You let them know I didn't come looking for anything from the DeCostas. Nothing. We straight?"

"Shit. I didn't mean it like that," he offered lamely. "You gonna' stick around a while?" He walked around the corner of the desk and proffered his hand.

"No plans," I said dryly.

25

"You need anything, you let me know. Anything. You hear?" he emphasized, shaking my hand too vigorously.

"If I need anything."

Outside I stood for a moment on the small stoop regarding the panorama of the San Joaquin Valley stretching eastward before me. Summer would come creeping on soon. Pacheco Pass was as beautiful as I'd ever remembered. Great day for a long jog. Even a place like Divina had its appeal, however limited.

The scene back in Frankie's office must have been frenetic. Wouldn't be wrong by much if I was wrong at all: he'd be reporting to his uncle immediately. The likely conversation played in my head.

"He's gone, Uncle Sal."

"What'd he want?"

"Says nothin', Uncle Sal."

"Let me know you find out anything different. Understand?"

"Sure, Uncle Sal. Sure!"

Frankie was as big a suck-up as he'd always been. He hadn't earned his way to the position he now enjoyed. Nepotism was a word the DeCostas understood.

As I gained the opposite side of the street I glanced over my shoulder. He stared out the window at me. I stared back until he stepped away. Sure bet Frankie was praying he'd never hear from me again.

****

Souza's market was a two-block walk from the DeCosta Mercantile. The place was possessed of a cornucopic aura; angled troughs filled with fresh vegetables in splashes of brilliant red and yellow and orange—shades of green—informing their various stages of ripeness. All of it enriched by the delicate scent of fresh earth and the sweet

26

aroma of warm, yeasty bread. The place was one of the town's great assets. The hour was close to five o'clock and the store was fairly busy. Shoppers recognized neighbors and visited in small clusters. No one paid attention to the stranger among them.

I bought a bottle of red wine, a small stick of hard salami, a block of sharp cheddar and a fresh baguette that felt warm and smelled as though it just came from someone's oven. Then I headed back to the Trail's End Motel.

As soon as I entered my room, I noticed the red message light blinking on the telephone. When I picked it up the clerk answered. "Yes, Mr. Caldwell," the man replied. "A friend left a note in the office for you."

"Up in a minute." Who else had discovered I was in town? More to the point, who would bother tracking me down?

Back in my room I popped the cork from the bottle of wine, poured myself half a water glass and took a healthy slug. I eyed the unopened pale blue envelope I'd tossed on the nightstand. There was no question the handwriting was female. "Now what?"

Settling the glass of wine on the table, I opened the cheese and salami first. I pulled my trench knife from the leather holster on the back of my hip. Since the jungle, it never left my side. The blade didn't look like much of a weapon at a little over three inches folded. But its snubbed, wide vane sharpened to the precision of a surgeon's scalpel was designed at the exact perfect length to drive upward into a man's sternum and rip a lethal hole in the bottom of his heart. For a split second, I thought about the last time I'd had to use it that way. The thick blade hacked through a piece of the tough salami like it was a stick of butter. I popped a chunk into my mouth. What I was going to call dinner lay before me. Then I tore off a piece of the baguette. Having ignored my curiosity long enough, I retrieved the envelope from the nightstand.

Sliding the trench blade along the sealed edge made a clean, surgical cut. A single page flipped out from inside. The note read: *Buy you a drink at the Cross Street tomorrow night, 7:30?* Signed, *Natalie Silva-Bettencourt*— nothing more.

Natalie Silva was a year behind me in high school. She was also Miranda DeCosta's best friend. Married now it seemed. I tossed the note back onto the table. Slumping into the uncomfortable chair that furnished my room, I hung my feet on the side of the bed and helped myself to more wine and cheese.

The *Cross Street Club* was on the corner of Cross Street and Railroad Avenue, a block over from the police station. When I was a kid, my father hung out there as if it was his second home. There were two town whores, Diamond Lil and Francis something-or-other who held court there.

My mind flashed on a time I'd stumbled onto Father Parry, Divina's Catholic priest and moral conscience, out on a canal bank in the back seat of his big yellow Cadillac with Diamond Lil, his pasty, corpulent, ass visible, bobbing up and down.

My mother would send me into the Cross Street on Friday nights to drag the old man out before he spent half his week's paycheck buying beers for the two old whores and anybody else who'd stand him drink for drink. He was genetically predisposed to the afflictions of the Irish, though we are as much Scotch, which I suppose doesn't gain me much.

On most of those occasions, my old man was deep enough in the bottle he'd put his arm around me and insist I have a Shirley Temple; Seven-Up with a little maraschino cherry juice and a couple of whole cherries. "Make the boy a drank!" he'd yodel to the bartender as if he owned the joint. Then the bragging would start. "This here's my boy, Charlie. Football star." My old man would clench me around the neck, pull me to him, his breath acrid with the stench of stale beer and freshly licked pussy, and yell across the entire place, "He's the whole reason this here high school team is doin' as good as they are. Hell, without him you got nothin'."

Invariably, some other kid's old man would take exception. "Bullshit!" the insulted father would assert acerbically. "My boy's every bit as good as yours," and the barney was on.

After all the years, I still winced at the recollection. It was a tough position to be in and he did it to me often. I'd pull and shove on him, trying to get him out of the place before things actually turned into a fight or the bartender called the cops. I came to understand it was too many episodes like that over the years which gradually led to me being resented by some adults; sins of the father, as it were. My old man's carrying on hung like a yoke about my neck.

Take Prado Mendoza for example. He was the local deputy then, newly elevated to Chief of Police in `60. I was just a junior in high school. He detested my old man, constantly harassed him. Mendoza would catch him being loud and mouthy at the bar and threaten to run him in. But the old man was smart enough not to get himself arrested. Still, Mendoza ached for the opportunity to get at him and finally began to use me as a means. Anything went wrong or came up missing around town; Mendoza would show up on our doorstep. If he didn't outright accuse me of something, he made it clear he was suspicious I'd done the deed. I was branded a white trash troublemaker by the part of the community in which I wanted to be accepted.

What the hell, I figured, rereading Natalie's invitation. The thought struck me this would be the first time I'd be setting foot in the joint being of legal age. A visit with Natalie would mean delaying my departure another day, but so what. I was drifting in a slow current anyway. Time, for the moment, mattered little.

CHAPTER 6

EARLY FRIDAY MORNING I rolled out of bed, stretched and ran my fingers through my rumpled hair. Shuffling into the tiny bathroom, I leaned against the wall behind the toilet and relieved myself. Backing out of the tight space, I turned the tap water on in the sink, let it run until it was as hot as it would get. The foul tasting instant shit I'd picked up at Souza's Market would have to serve as coffee. Combat makes many things possible in a life going forward—including drinking shit like this—assuming you survive—combat, I mean. Surviving the vile brew I was drinking just then would no doubt prepare me for even greater inconveniences in life.

The visit with Frankie DeCosta the day before set a fractured web of memories loose in my brain. I hadn't slept well. Then there was the note from Natalie Silva to gnaw on. A piece of dry bread and some small chunks of cheese I'd hacked off to go with the sludge passed for breakfast.

I decided to suffer a second cup of the vile concoction. As I say, the military taught me not to be overly judgmental about such things. Stumbling listlessly around the room, I took up a position on my unmade bed with a copy of James Michener's book, Caravans. This wasn't my normal routine, but I felt constrained, like wearing a t-shirt that's too tight in the armpits. You can wear it; you just can't get comfortable in it. That's what being in Divina was doing to me.

Around eleven I set the book aside and did what I could to make myself presentable for public viewing. I decided to walk back to the north end of town to the high school, maybe take a closer look around during lunch hour.

The walk was rejuvenating, got the blood pumping. By the time I reached the campus I was feeling nostalgic.

The front lawn was littered with kids in small clusters, laughing, a few holding hands, several talking enthusiastically, gestures flying behind shrieks and giggles. Some were actually eating. Routines weren't much different from my time.

The double doors to the main building were thrown open. I walked in and down the wide central hallway toward the lockers. Mine had been in the upper row. Flower decals stuck all over the surface—girl.

Further down the hall, toward the auditorium, several classroom doors were blocked open. Metal clanged against metal. As I walked by an open doorway, a janitor was adjusting a liner in a trash can inside the math room where I'd studied geometry. Well, study isn't an accurate word for what I did in this room. I'd come to regret I hadn't actually studied math or any other subject for that matter during high school. They graduated me just to get rid of me. I was ineligible to play football any longer.

Without intending, I found myself standing in front of the school's long glass trophy cabinet. Above the case were senior class pictures of every graduating class since 1913. Glancing from one to the other, I stopped at my own, the class of `62. Examining the picture of me felt as though I were looking at someone I had known once but lost track of.

I shifted my attention back to the trophy case, sought out the 1962 football championship trophy. My name was etched just below Duke Matta's. I'd finally placed the absurdity surrounding that night into perspective. Vietnam did that for me.

Even so, I still recalled the event in vivid detail. There must have been more attached to what happened than I understood. That was the only logical explanation. Whatever the hidden truth was, I was positive Sal DeCosta was at the root of it.

In retrospect, I should view the whole damn episode as the best thing that ever happened to me. What occurred that night became the epicenter of what pushed me to escape this town. At the time, I guess it amounted to running away—from everything—everyone; the game that night, my teammates, Sal DeCosta, *my* parents—Miranda. Mostly Miranda if I'm honest with myself. An experience like I had with her taints the well. But the sum of it all had inspired in me the notion if I didn't value myself, no one else would either. And it'd become painfully obvious; nobody in Divina placed much value on Charlie Caldwell.

Although I didn't understand until much later, that was the moment I grew to be a man. We are, after all, the sum of the consequences of the choices we make in life. In Vietnam I forfeited any pretense of innocence that may have remained.

Preparation for that championship game had begun unlike the groundwork for all the others.

"All right," Coach Davenport had begun, "take a knee. Helmets off." All of us were winded, our chests heaving. Sweat, blood and snot dripped from noses. Coach appeared calm, contemplative.

"Listen up, gentlemen," he went on, his voice subdued. "This is the last football game most of you seniors will ever play." He paused and looked around from one player to another. "For a few of you though, this could be just the beginning. Scouts from a lot of colleges are going to be here."

His voice became stern, almost angry. "Make no mistake, gentlemen, you will have achieved *nothing* if you do not close the deal. This isn't just another game." He spoke then in machinegun-like staccato, his intensity and voice rising together. "Lose this one and you may as well not have won any of the others. Nobody remembers *almost* perfect. Nobody remembers *almost* outstanding. Nobody remembers anybody who *almost* achieves anything!" He left off that nobody would remember the guy who coached them either, but his own motivation had not escaped me.

We were so quiet you could nearly hear the sweat dripping off our faces onto the grass. Assistant Coach DeGregorio popped a bubble in his gum as if to punctuate the statement.

Davenport continued haranguing us. "Nine and one won't matter—ten and 0 is history and that, gentlemen, is what you are about to make."

Sal DeCosta had gone to a great deal of effort and expense to ensure a scout from Army would be there to watch *me* play. Yeah...that Army. West Point. The problem was nobody bothered to ask what I wanted. And the last thing on my mind was a military career.

Coach DeGregorio stopped at the end of the long bench where I sat and rested one foot on the seat. Leaning his elbow on his knee, he said, "Might as well spill it, Champ. What's on your mind?"

I almost couldn't bring myself to speak the words. But if there was any person on earth I could confide in, it was Coach DeGregorio. "I don't want to go to West Point," I admitted.

DeGregorio was deliberate, thoughtful when he spoke. "What do you have in mind, Champ?" he asked in that calm, even tone he'd affect with me when he wanted me to give serious consideration to what we were talking about.

I thought I might vomit trying to explain to this man, whom I deeply respected, how I felt. "I don't want to spend the rest of my life in the Army," I whispered apologetically. "I've read all the pamphlets they sent me. If I go to The Point, I'll have to be in the Army the rest of my life." That last bit was an exaggeration, but it made my argument against a military career.

DeGregorio hung his head, spoke softly but firmly. "Some of the most important men in American history have attended West Point, Charlie. Right now, at your age— Champ, look, I understand how it might not seem—" He was the only adult in my life who ever spoke to me like who *I* was mattered, that the decisions I made would follow me forever. I've wished many times since I'd had the maturity and wisdom to have listened to the man better than I did.

I cut him off mid-sentence. "Coach, I don't want a career in the Army. Couldn't Mr. DeCosta get me into a regular college just as easy, or easier, even?"

"Look, Charlie," he pointed out bluntly. "Even if you had the grades to get into a private or state university, and I doubt that, where would you get the money? Frankly, son," and then his voice softened a bit, "you haven't been the best student. You're going to be lucky to have a shot at West Point. It's the military service side of it that gives you any chance at all. It's a long shot at best, Charlie."

"Excuse me, sir." The voice pulling me back was that of the janitor. "I need to close this part of the building."

"Just leaving." I looked into his eyes for a second, but I didn't recognize him.

The sunlight was bright and it was warm as I emerged from the building. I navigated the four steps of the main entrance, walked out onto the sprawling lawn at the front of the school and surveyed the scene. Kids reluctantly answered the call of buzzers. Where Main Street merged into the school parking lot at the east corner was the shortcut I used to take to get to the burger joint for lunch.

While I stood waiting for a car full of laughing teenagers to pass, I heard a rustling of branches in the huge cottonwood tree at the edge of the lot. A male form appeared high up in the branches.

The man looked down and saw me eyeing him. "I ain't hurtin' nothin'," he shouted down.

"What?"

"Honest. I ain't hurtin' nothin'!" the man repeated over and over. He rappelled down from the upper branches, babbling apologetically the entire way. "I-I-I-I didn't hurt nothin'. Didn't hurt nothin'. Didn't hurt nothin'." He dropped the final few feet to the ground.

Jeff Ponder stood before me. The backward boy was now a man in his early thirties. He hadn't changed much; stockier maybe, a grown up face with a man's stubble of whiskers—that was it. He still wore Coke-bottle-thick glasses that magnified his eyeballs, giving him something of a bug-eyed look. His left eye wandered continually and the right one was lazy so the pupil would periodically sink to the bottom of its socket and roll inward as if inspecting his large, black-head-pocked nose. You could never be quite certain where Jeff was looking. His mother kept his hair cropped short in a butch; same as she had when he was a kid.

Jeff was a few years older than me, but hadn't been admitted to elementary school until the same year I was. In a different time and place Jeff might have lived a more normal existence. But the time was late 1950s and the place was Divina, California. I learned what happened to him when I'd overheard my parents talking about Jack Ponder, Jeff's father. Ponder worked construction jobs all over the San Joaquin Valley. Jeff arrived on the scene one night while his father was out on a job and Dorothy was home alone. She went into labor early. Had trouble finding help.

36

By the time neighbors got her to the hospital both she and Jeff nearly died. Jeff was born prematurely, suffered severe oxygen deprivation and was brain damaged. My parents concluded it was nobody's fault. Things like that just happened sometimes. I expect that was the case in 1942 rural America because it's still not all that uncommon even now.

"You gonna tell my mom? Gonna tell? Gonna tell `er, huh?" he demanded.

"Tell her what?" His agitation confused me.

I placed my hand on his shoulder. His muscles were rock solid. He was strong like that even when we were kids. In fact, Jeff was so strong as a child the other kids had to be careful not to rile him to the point of violence because he could hurt you.

One day in the sixth grade Duke Matta tormented Jeff, telling him at recess he was going to pull Jeff's pants down and let the girls see his pecker. That horrified Jeff and just as the bell rang, Jeff stabbed Duke in the back with a lead pencil that had to be removed at the hospital. There was a big flap over the incident, how dangerous Jeff was to the other kids. But several kids confessed about how Duke scared Jeff and how far Jeff had been pushed. The principal and faculty finally decided to let it go and he was allowed to continue in school with the rest of us.

"Remember me, Jeff?"

He inspected my face closely. "Nymphs are getting ready to hatch," he replied.

"Charlie Caldwell. Remember me? We used to go to school together."

"Don't look like Charlie Caldwell," Jeff evaluated. He made a clucking kind of chuckle while he wiped sweat from his face. "You gonna tell my mom I was up that tree? Not supposed to be up in the trees."

"No," I assured him. "I'm not going to tell your mom."

"Good man, Caldwell. Good man. Good man." Jeff laughed out loud at nothing. He searched my face in earnest once more, cocked his head, a crinkle burrowing across his forehead as though perhaps there was a glimmer of recollection. "Cicadas," he announced abruptly. "Get real big now, Caldwell. Hey, Caldwell. You ever seen a seventeen-year cicada?"

"Jeff, I hardly know what an ordinary cicada is. I have to go. Be careful climbing the tree." I stepped off the curb.

"Wanna see some snakes? I know where there's some real nice bull snakes…fat, too."

"No thanks. Be careful."

"Don't look like old Charlie Caldwell. Don't tell my mom." His plea was an emphatic order. Jeff headed off across the lawn in front of the high school with his eyes to the ground like a bloodhound's nose.

He looked happy, content in his attenuated world. I thought briefly about the two of us—Jeff and me. My life in Divina had been troubling. Life here had proven a refuge for him.

Life is like that, isn't it? Anachronistic for some, punitive for others. You might argue life is what you make of it. But it's only after you *can* make of it what you will one can legitimately make that argument.

CHAPTER 7

WHEN I WALKED into the Cross Street Club a little past seven thirty that evening, everyone in the place turned toward me. Edgy ambulation. In these kinds of hometown watering holes strangers don't *just* walk in. Natalie Silva sat at the far end of the room. She hadn't changed a lot. A bit thicker, maybe, but she wore it well. Maturity looked better on her than some I recognized around town in the last two days.

She slid out of the booth and ran to greet me. Heads along the bar bobbed back to their previous occupations.

Natalie was a traditional beauty in a tribal sense; satiny olive complexion, soft beige eyes, black curly hair; the classic physical attributes of her ethnicity. At eighteen she weighed roughly a hundred pounds and stood about five feet three inches tall. She looked to have added about two inches to her height and twenty pounds, mostly in her hips. Natalie's face was pleasant, maybe even pretty, with thick, full eyebrows and a delicate nose. Her eyes were actually a light shade of coffee, like cappuccino and contrasted in a unique, muted way against her olive skin and wavy jet-black hair flowing over her shoulders.

The hug was genuine, warm. "Wow," she said, stepping back. "You look great, Charlie!"

"You too, Natalie. You haven't aged since high school."

"I wish! Come on. Want you to meet someone." She took my hand and led me to the booth toward the back of the long narrow room. "You remember Johnny Bettencourt?"

"Don't think I'd know you on the street." I leaned in and shook Johnny's hand. "Sure, I remember you. How are you, Johnny?" I'd never really known Johnny Bettencourt, but in a town of less than two thousand, you come to *know of* every soul.

"Good. I'm good. Tanks for aksin'," Johnny said, a little reticent, I thought.

"Me'n Johnny been married eight years this October." Natalie squeezed his hand, smiled at him.

"Congratulations." I was already uncomfortable with the small talk and I'd just sat down.

"Got two little girls. Miranda Antonia and Kathy Eloisa, seven and five," Natalie announced, beaming.

"That's great, Natalie." I nodded toward Johnny.

"Let's have a beer," she suggested. "What are you drinkin', Charlie?"

"They stock any Mexican beers?"

"Hey, Tony," Natalie shouted. "Got any Mexican beer?"

The bartender yelled back, "Yeah…Coors and Bud!" He pronounced Coors—Kers.

"Coors is fine," I said to Natalie.

"Make it three Coors," Natalie shouted back. "Johnny'n me, we don't know the difference anyways." She elbowed Johnny gently in the side.

"You know, Charlie, when I heard you was in town, I says to Johnny, 'I'd really like to see, Charlie.' I don't know…old times. Somethin'. I really wanted to see ya." She shrugged, dropped her head to the side. Johnny smiled at her, patted her affectionately between the shoulders.

"You and Dorothy Ponder are about the only people in the last two days who seemed interested one way or the other in talking to me." I chuckled.

Natalie fidgeted with her fingers as she spoke. "I would o' invited you to the house, but I wasn't sure you'd come. I mean, we was just friends through Miranda. You and me... we—"

The beers arrived. I leaned back in the booth and slid my hand into a front pocket of my jeans.

"Just run a tab, Tony." Natalie turned back to me. "Was me invited you, remember?"

I nodded again toward Natalie and Johnny and tipped the long neck of the bottle at them before taking a healthy swig.

"I have happy memories, Natalie." I set my longneck on the table. "You, me, Miranda...couple of the other cheerleaders. Root Beer floats after football practice. Cheerleading practice...burgers at The Sweet Shop—"

"You see," Johnny said, "I tol' use, he's gonna be glad to say hello." Johnny grinned. "She worries too much 'bout tings. Know what I mean?"

I took another pull from my beer. Conditions were as bad inside the Cross Street Club as I remembered. The stale smell of sour beer soaked into the same grungy red carpet from ten years earlier—stubbed out cigarette butts permeated everything—flooded my conscious along with images of brawling with my old man. My clothes would reek from the stench of the joint.

"You heard 'bout Miranda, I guess?" Natalie poured herself another half glass of beer. Johnny shifted uncomfortably in his seat.

"By accident," I said. "I'm trying to..." I had no fucking idea what I was trying to do with the trauma of that reality. "Sorry...still find it hard to accept."

Long pause.

"I went to see Frankie yesterday. Told me Miranda changed quite a bit."

"Well, she wasn't perfect or nothin' like that," Natalie said, jumping to the defense of her friend. "Even when we was in high school. You remember. But..."

None of us made eye contact.

"I have a hard time picturing Miranda with Vinny Caputo," I said.

"Miranda wasn't *with Vinny*," Natalie instantly shot back. The words '*with*' and '*Vinny*' dripped with disdain. "I should know; she was my best friend. I named my daughter after her. Miranda is her Godmother. Miranda and Miranda. Johnny's ma' dint like it too much. But she was my best friend, you know, since we was little girls." Natalie appeared defiant when she looked at Johnny.

Johnny shook his head and looked away.

"Johnny dint like her much neither." Natalie took another sip of her beer.

"Dorothy Ponder made it sound like there was some kind of lover's squabble." That wasn't the truth, but I could see the idea of it provoked Natalie. Suddenly I wanted her to talk about Miranda. "Told me they had a big fight in The Sweet Shop the night...that night."

The inflection in Natalie's voice when she used Vinny Caputo's name said it all. That anyone would think Miranda, no matter her reputation, would be involved with a guy like Vinny Caputo really pissed her off.

That made sense to me based on my memories of Vinny Caputo.

Natalie leaned forward. Her ample breasts rested on the table with her elbows. In a lowered voice, she said, "That fat pig, Caputo, killed Miranda 'cause she wouldn't give him the time o' day much less the piece o' ass he was lookin' for."

Natalie held up her bottle. "Tony, three more!" She paused, looked backward at Johnny slouched down in the booth, head leaning back, staring into the ceiling as though he'd heard this once too often. "She was my best friend, Charlie." Tears welled in her cappuccino eyes and overflowed in two single shiny streams down each side of her kind face.

"I'm sorry, Nat. I understand how you feel." And I did understand. I reached across the table and squeezed her hand.

"She could o' done somethin' with her life. Know what I mean?" After some delay she answered the question herself. "O' course you don't. You wasn't here. After she graduated Fresno State—you know she graduated from Fresno?"

"Frankie told me."

Listening to Natalie, something in how she glanced up at me as she spoke, it was becoming evident she, Frankie, maybe others, figured I'd come back seeking somehow to reconnect with Miranda. She *was* at the center of why I was here; one of the monkeys on my back I determined to stop carrying around. A lesson I'd learned so vividly in a death-filled Vietnamese jungle—the things you might never get the chance to say to someone until it was too late—and there it was.

Natalie went on with her tale. "Anyways, after Miranda graduated she was sure she could talk her father into letting her into the family business. She was crushed when he refused. Even worse, Sal picks Frankie over his own daughter to take over after him 'n his brothers are gone." Natalie stopped and took another sip of her beer. "They say Sal had to buy Frankie's degree. Now that's when things really got crazy. Miranda was so much smarter than Frankie, but he was the oldest boy. Girls don't count for shit with the DeCostas. This is 1972 for Christ sake!"

Natalie shifted in her seat, then reached over and ran her hand over Johnny's affectionately. She paused and looked down into her glass as though searching. "Miranda moved out of her parents' house and got her own place," she went on musing. "You remember how skinny she was in high school?"

"The guys nicknamed her Stork—really pissed her off."

"You should o' seen her after college," Natalie argued. "She filled out everywhere. I wish you could o' seen her, Charlie." She was emphatic and animated. "She was the prettiest girl anywhere around, ain't that right, Johnny? One o' the smartest, too." Natalie paused again. "That was a lot of the problem. Pretty, smart…way too smart for the single guys in this town. No place to go, nothin' to do.

"She was drinkin' way too much. More than once Jorge Olivera, he's town deputy now, dragged her out of this place, drove her home." Natalie caught her breath, took another drink of beer and glanced around the room. She brought her eyes back to mine, lowered her voice once more and went on with what she had to say. "Miranda told me she thought that creepy bastard, Olivera, fucked her once, but she was too drunk to remember for sure." Natalie had a disgusted look on her face when she checked to see Johnny's reaction. "Nobody would o' believed her anyways." Natalie looked directly at her husband.

I found myself improbably interested in what Natalie said. I figured this was likely to be the most I'd ever learn about how Miranda's life went on after I moved away.

"Too many men," she continued, shrugging and casting another reproachful glance at Johnny. "It was like she was out to prove something to her father. Sal argued with her; women belonged in their place. Miranda decided to take her place all right—in the bedroom—with just about anybody who wanted to take her there. Married, single— didn't matter much to her."

Considering how her life turned out, it was beginning to sound like what I wanted to say to Miranda wouldn't have meant much.

"She got real ugly about men in general," Natalie said. "Any way Miranda could punish 'em, she did. When she got bored with a guy, everybody in town all of a sudden found out he was sleepin' with her—married or not. Was her way of payin' 'em all back and gettin' at her father at the same time." Natalie took another short swig of beer. "She had a lot of contempt for men."

Natalie glanced around furtively then turned back to me. "But Miranda drew the line at guys like Vinny Caputo. Shit! What a slob! You know, Vinny goes about three hundred pounds now?" I couldn't help glancing over to Johnny who was himself easily over two-fifty. "Gut hangs over the top of his zipper. Guy's a greasy pig. No way Miranda was goin' that low.

"Vinny was always goin' around tellin' people he was just what Miranda DeCosta needed. How she needed a big bull's cock to keep her happy and how he had just what she was lookin' for. What a loser!" Natalie drank more beer as if bracing herself.

"The night it happened," she went on, perceptibly affected recounting her friend's death, "Miranda hadn't been drinkin'. Dorothy Ponder says she was stone sober, eatin' a burger when Vinny and a couple o' his buddies stumbled in. *They* was all drinkin' and makin' remarks…just loud enough to be heard all over the place— high school shit!

"I guess Miranda let it go for a while before she finally let Vinny have it. What I heard, Vinny made her a bet if she could even take what he had between her legs, she'd never be able to settle for second best again. I hear Dorothy said Miranda went nuts. Called Vinny every four letter word she knew."

Natalie leaned half way across the table before she whispered the next part of the story. "I don't think Miranda told nobody but me, but she was pretty sure she was pregnant with Duke Matta's baby."

I wasn't surprised at the revelation, but it stung my male pride all the same.

Natalie went on almost apologetically. "She was in love with him, you know? I think she was always in love with him. Problem is, Duke's more in love with Duke than anybody he's ever been with, including his poor wife. Miranda was only one o' the women Duke ran around seeing on the sly. He just calls and most of 'em still come runnin'."

I took another pull from my longneck.

"Duke's as big o' turd as he ever was," she said, "but Miranda just couldn't get him out of her system. He could get her back any time he wanted."

Johnny stirred for the first time in nearly half an hour. "We gotta go," he announced abruptly. "Gotta pick up the kids from my ma's."

Natalie didn't resist. Johnny picked up the tab then followed us out. The evening air was cool and fresh, scented with newly cut alfalfa. We stood for a while, awkwardly maneuvering our way out of the evening for a few more minutes before heading off in different directions.

****

Back in my room at the Trail's End, I went immediately to the shower to wash away the stench. I lay wide-awake on the bed, staring at the ceiling for a long time afterward. My thoughts rambled. Places like Divina are time bubbles, soap operas. Plots play out slowly, year in, year out. The stars of the show are always the same kinds of characters: you have your Duke Mattas, your Sal

DeCostas, guys like Frankie, Vinny. Even people like
Natalie and Johnny, though I found myself feeling sincere
sympathy for Natalie Silva. And, of course, there are
always the Miranda DeCostas of a town like Divina. There
has to be a star in the show, somebody with a bigger life
than all the rest. In Divina, the games they played became
the focus of their lives and informed the consciousness of
the entire population, just as Miranda DeCosta's life and
death had invaded the consciousness of Divina.

These people actually took themselves serious
enough to shut out the rest of the world as being below
their station, trapping people like me inside with them if
they could, then making certain *my kind* were kept in their
place. Maybe Divina was no different in that regard than
other backwater towns across America with different ethnic
bases, all sequestered in their tiny, bigoted, dysfunctional
cocoons, convinced they're somehow superior to the rest of
the world.

The irony, it occurred to me, was ten years after
high school, Miranda DeCosta thought she might be
pregnant by Duke Matta, who was married to somebody
else, and was screwing around like he was still the local
football hero. Things *really* hadn't changed much.

I was pondering the tragedy of Miranda's life when
I slid into deep slumber aided by the four beers Natalie
Bettencourt managed to pour down me.

CHAPTER 8

WHEN I WOKE Saturday morning, my body complained. I hadn't done any physical exercise in several days. I was stiff. There spun a matrix of mixed emotions inside my head, behind my eyes. What confronted me hadn't done anything to relieve that condition. Even before my two tours in Vietnam, I'd worked out regularly, running mostly. Running is my thing. Once I got back to the States, more than ever, I relied on it to keep myself centered and in shape. It's the perfect recharge, mental as well as physical. I could punish myself without inflicting visible damage.

While I wallowed in the warmth of the sheets, I thought I should pack up right then, drive back to my shack on the beach in Old Mexico. And if Natalie Silva hadn't poured those four beers down me the night before, I would have.

There was nothing in Divina to hold me. I'd come back to deal with an affliction from which only Miranda DeCosta would be able to liberate me. She was dead now— long before her time and under circumstances about as horrible as it gets. But I couldn't change things. Sticking around only aggravated other throbbing spirits working inside me.

I could accept the fact of death with a certain detached rejoinder, like a callous building up where a rub of constant irritation might otherwise create pain. It wasn't normal I should feel numb to the news of death, but that was what happened. There'd just been too much of it all around me and if I couldn't find a way to sanitize my psyche, I'd go insane.

Last night, talking to Natalie, had only served to complicate the deep-seated issues I had with Miranda. There was nothing to be gained hanging around, brooding about what could not be changed. But my body screamed for rejuvenation. What the hell was another hour here or there going to matter?

I slipped into my running shoes and a pair of jogging shorts. My reflection in the bathroom mirror showed the toll of the previous evening as I rubbed my hands across the shadowy stubble. The minimum I could get by with was brushing away the soured beer saliva taste in my mouth and splashing a little warm water into my eyes and onto my unruly hair.

The crisp April morning greeted my bare-chest inhospitably. The chilly dampness set me considering a shirt. But in a few minutes I wouldn't need it. Decided to rough it. I jogged past the Catholic church, then City Hall and the city park on my right with its tall cottonwoods and oaks; wet Bermuda grass beneath, long overdue for mowing. Across from the park I took notice of the Valley View Apartments. They were new, built after I moved away. According to Natalie, that's where Miranda lived.

Jogging north along Park Street, I turned right onto Farm Road Lane. From there I could run nearly all the way across the San Joaquin Valley unimpeded.

Even I couldn't argue with the panoramic view. The road fell away at a gentle slope as I left town, stretched like an attenuated ribbon across the valley floor until it finally was nothing more than an ephemeral dot. Above the haze, two hundred miles to the east, the highest peaks in the Sierra Nevada poked their brilliant snow-covered crowns above the clouds as if they were floating like islands instead of jutting thousands of feet into the clear blue sky from the earth's crust. The sweet smell of damp alfalfa, emphasized with fresh cow shit, continued to inform the olfactory sense of Divina. The tall wild grass covering the rolling foothills was like fur, still in deep shades of jade. Suddenly I felt inspired to run hard.

Worth noting, I'd be running uphill all the way back. A mile out of town I realized I was running along the northern boundary of the Caputo Dairy where Miranda's body had been discovered along the edge of one of its fields. I spotted a bright orange speck in the distance. Being alert to everything was so deeply embedded in my DNA I wondered if I'd ever be able to just relax with what was around me without being endlessly on guard.

Thinking about what Natalie told me last night, I picked up the pace. Miranda thought she might be pregnant by Duke Matta. Not that I gave a shit one-way or the other about Vinny Caputo. I barely knew the guy ten years ago and had no reason to feel anything one way or the other for him now—especially if he'd done what he was accused of. But if no one knew Miranda was pregnant, who would have known Duke could have a motive for killing her? Married guy messing around with the loose rich girl, his old high school sweetheart. Maybe she threatens to go to his wife, he gets scared the whole town is going to find out. Guy like Duke could never allow something like that to happen. But she was raped and brutalized according to Dorothy Ponder and Natalie Silva. Why would Duke do anything like that? Still...

The orange speck I'd spotted began to take human form. Another jogger? Good pace, too, considering how fast we were converging. My attention shifted to the runner. Who the hell in this town could be a serious enough runner to be clear out here?

We were closing fast, converging like two cars coming toward each other on a highway. Not until she was about to pass did I think I recognized Audrey Romero. We hadn't been friends growing up, but I knew who she was. She raised her left hand, but kept her eyes focused down on the asphalt in front of her.

I pulled up and turned, shouting, "Audrey! Audrey Romero? Is that you?"

The long auburn ponytail hanging down her back stopped bouncing as she slowed to a walk and turned cautiously. "I know you?" Her tone was not friendly.

My chest was heaving and I was sweating heavily by then. "Charlie," I shouted, breathing unevenly. "Charlie Caldwell."

"Charlie...Caldwell?" she repeated. "Where in the world did *you* come from?"

"You might be one of the few people who hasn't heard I was in town." I answered walking toward her.

"Probably right. I don't get out much." She began walking back to meet me, then. "Gosh, I hardly recognize you, Charlie," she said drawing close to me.

She stuck out her hand. Her long slender fingers wrapped around my palm firmly. Without releasing my hand, she looked up into my eyes and went on speaking.

"I would have kept right on going if you hadn't called out."

"That bad!"

"That isn't what I meant," she said, letting my hand slide slowly from hers.

Audrey was a sophomore when I was a senior. She was a pretty girl, tall and thin with hair more red than brown. I remembered her freckles. And the fact she dated older guys who owned cars. Locker-room talk had it she was easy as long as you met her prerequisites. I'd asked her out once, but she politely declined.

In front of me now was a truly beautiful woman; five eight, hundred twenty pounds, I guessed. Her reddish hair had turned a darker auburn color and almost all of the freckles were gone. Those remaining were lovely and very faint across the bridge of her nose. She had long tanned legs with well-shaped calves. The roundness of her rump was that of someone who worked to stay in shape. A narrow tube-top compressed her breasts under the thin bright orange tank she had on. She seemed completely comfortable dripping sweat.

"Come on, walk with me a minute." She pulled up the front of the tank to wipe her face. A flat, tanned tummy disappeared into her jogging shorts just below her belly button. "No good to just stop running when our heart rates are so high." Her chest heaved as hard as mine.

We walked a ways back in the direction of town.

"What are you doing back here?" she was finally able to ask in a controlled voice.

"Not sure," I lied. "Been ten years. Guess I got curious about the place—people—you know."

"Nothing much changes around Divina," she said, her tone perceptibly dissonant. "You ought to know that." She spun, skipped a couple of steps and was jogging again. "Come on, I'll jog back out with you."

She was instantly out in the lead, jogging at a slow, easy clip. I pulled up on her right shoulder and glided along with her

"Been running long?"

"Left my house around five—"

"I meant how long have you been a serious runner?"

"Guess it's been about five years now." She looked straight ahead as she spoke. "Ever since I got rid of that Nunez asshole. Remember him? Darryl?" Audrey glanced over at me. "What about you? Don't I remember you made the all-state track and field team junior and senior years?"

"You remember that?"

"I was on the girls track team. Doubt you guys even knew there was a women's team."

I wouldn't admit to her she was right about that.

"When did you start jogging?"

"Never really stopped training. Track was always my favorite sport. Just kept working out after I graduated. I thought a lot of things were going to happen that didn't. Then came the Army. Just as well I'd stayed in shape."

"You have to go to Nam?" Her tone changed, almost an implied apology.

"Yep." I kept my focus straight ahead intending to convey I wasn't interested in talking about it further.

We jogged in silence a while.

"Married?" she asked, trying to break the ice.

"Always too many disruptions. Hasn't been enough peace in my life yet to have anything to offer a woman." I grabbed my breath a few beats. "And I never found the right girl," I added, but didn't look over at her.

"Yeah." There was a sense of exasperation in the way she said the word.

A bit further along she said, "I was a genius. Darryl knocked me up my senior year. Never even graduated. Ten years later the sonofabitch dumps me for some honey over in Modesto."

"People make mistakes." I remembered what I thought was a relationship with Miranda DeCosta until the afternoon I saw what I saw.

"I scare you?" The question seemed to come from nowhere, as if it were a private thought coming out in stream of consciousness.

I looked over at her. It was impossible to tell her of the horrors it could take to scare me. "No, you don't scare me."

She glanced over her shoulder at me as if she could read my thoughts. "I didn't mean in that sense," she attempted to clarify the question. "I meant as in make you uncomfortable. You know, talking about stuff like my broken marriage, the dumbass mistake I made."

"Nope. Nice now and again to know somebody else feels the way I do about mistakes they've made. Nothing unattractive about a little self-deprecation. Unfortunately, about all we can do is learn from our mistakes and get on with life." That sounded so easy slipping off my tongue. So why did I have such a hard time putting into practice my own advice? "Easier to say than to live I'm afraid."

Audrey snickered. "Not the kind of reply I'm used to hearing around this town."

We went along in silence a ways. She seemed to try to digest what I'd said. Or maybe she was just trying to decide what to say next.

"I scare the hell out of the guys around here," she said finally, looking down at the gravel passing below her feet. "They come sniffin' around, lookin' for a stray piece of ass. I call their wives. Assholes."

I slowed and made a wide turn behind her, heading back toward town.

She caught up to me. "Shit! I didn't mean to offend you, Charlie. I get carried away." Her voice was softer as it trailed away.

"Had nothing to do with anything you said. It's uphill all the way back. You've already been out here once this morning and I'm burning off last night's beer. Unless you intend to carry me back, I gotta make the turn here."

"I doubt that," she snorted.

The energy expended to maintain the pace immediately increased. I kicked the tempo up a half stride. She handled the cadence with little effort.

"You in town long?" she asked, now huffing some as she spoke.

The truth was, I intended to grab a shower back at the motel, check out and put Divina, California in my rear view mirror. Forever. Suddenly, I didn't feel in any great rush to do that.

"Day or two maybe," I lied.

The uphill grade began to work on us, but every time I fell off a bit, she continued on, steadily leaving me behind. She had no intention of slowing.

"This too fast for you?" she shouted back over her shoulder.

I smiled at her thoughtfulness and became aware of the pleasant smell of her. If I smelled like soured beer, she had the good grace not to say anything about it.

"Staying at the Trail's End?" she went on shouting sideways toward me.

I surveyed the bounce of her round bottom as she ran. "Yes," I huffed out. "Classiest accommodations in town, I'm told."

"Not to mention your only choice," she pointed out.

I was caught back up to her. She looked over at me, smiled, gleaming straight white teeth.

"Like I said, high class." I grinned, staring straight ahead. "Want me to slow up a little?"

"No," she said, her tone a little hurt or annoyed, I couldn't be sure. "If this is too *slow* for you, I can go faster."

"No, thanks." I breathed heavily, but controlled. "I'm feeling the beer I drank last night." And I smelled of it. I couldn't see how she couldn't smell it on me, too. Still, she mentioned nothing.

We ran in silent rhythm to our heavy breathing most of the way back into town.

At the top of the hill she broke silence again. "You any good at barbecue?" She looked straight ahead as we continued to slow the pace.

"The best," I assured her. "You look up barbecue in Webster's, you'll find a picture of *me* right next to the definition."

"And will I find your mug next to *modest*, too?" she shot back.

We grinned.

Her face was flushed bright red and dripping sweat. There was a small twist in one eyetooth that left a tiny, barely perceptible gap on the right side of her upper row of teeth. It was one of those fine flaws that somehow enhances rather than detracts from beauty. Her green eyes twinkled and were lovely without makeup.

"Think you might be in the mood to barbecue this evening?"

My thought lasted a split second.

"You turned me down flat when I asked *you* out back in high school."

"Who says I'm asking you out?" I liked the smirk curling up her lips and the playfulness in her demeanor. "You never asked me out!"

"Sure I did," I insisted. "My junior year. You were a freshman. Dance right after one of the home games. Don't remember who you showed up with. Wasn't me."

"I think you're making that up so I'll feel bad." A guilty smile of recollection spread across her sweat-soaked face.

Of course she remembered.

"I don't remember you asking me out...ever." Her denial was playfully, emphatic.

I went with the flow. "If that's how you recall it, what can I say? Maybe it was somebody else who crushed me."

Finally, unapologetically, she said, "So, if I did turn you down, I'm willing to make up for it."

"Fair enough. You like red wine?"

She turned her head slightly and smiled mischievously through several strands of loose wet hair streaming across her face. "I'm willing to explore the possibility."

I liked the way she flirted with me. "Willingness works for me."

"Got a freezer full of steaks. Special request?"

"You decide. Want me to pick up anything besides the wine?"

"Grab a baguette, if you don't mind." After a few moments, she said, "Get two bottles of wine. I wanna hear what you've been up to all this time. How long's it been?"

"Ten years. Not so long a time—just the other side of forever."

"Ten years," she repeated, not picking up on the restive nuance in my words. "Should be a long story."

Suddenly we were back in town. The time had evaporated. We slowed to a walk in front of the high school.

"How am I going to find you?"

"Got a car?"

"Buck," I chuffed. The old `52 Ford pickup truck my father saved for me while I was away in Southeast Asia. But I was partial to it. I was also acutely aware of the effect the rusted heap could have on the unsuspecting when I pulled up in it.

"Buck?" Audrey echoed.

"My truck. Not fancy, but I'm attached."

"I see...Buck...your truck." She rolled her eyes. "Phone book lists the street addresses. I'm under Romero. You won't have any trouble. Four okay?" The smile said, don't be late.

"Saturday's my day off."

"Mine, too," she countered. As if to reinforce her invitation, she said, "Four?"

She broke into a slow jog heading further up Farm Road Lane toward Pacheco Pass Crossroad.

I watched her running away from me. I thought; *could that body actually belong to a mortal woman? And I'm going to spend an evening with her.*

As if she could read my thoughts, Audrey stopped and turned to face me. Her long, tanned, slender legs disappeared up the edges of her loose jogging shorts, the curve of her butt round and perky. The tummy was flat as a board and invited my eye to her belly button and the way the shorts slung dangerously low down on her hips. She looked like a model posing for a photograph. "Hey," she shouted, "don't forget...two bottles." She waved, spun and ran on.

I jogged south along Park Street, glancing over my shoulder, hoping to get one last sighting of her. The previous hour of my life was playing like a movie in my head. I'd been ready to lump everybody in this town into one basket, put a rock in it and drop it over the side of my boat. Then...

The horn blaring behind me startled me so badly I nearly fell charging for the curb. Jorge Olivera pulled alongside of me and hawked a luggie close to my foot. "Thought I told you to stay the hell outta my way."

"That's not funny, Olivera—pulling up on someone like that in a car."

"Wasn't meant to be funny, Caldwell. Meant to let you know I got my eye on every move you make. Saw you out the road with Audrey."

Olivera's stunt pushed me over the edge and I decided it was time to set a tone with the prickly deputy. I strode along the front fender of the police car to the door. His forearm leaned on the open window. He flinched sideways as I approached him.

"Jorge," I said in a soft, menacing tone. My inflection rose a bit on the last syllable. "I'm in town a few days. Doesn't have anything to do with you or your business. But if you think you're gonna push me around because the cops got away with that shit when I was a kid, you'd be wrong." I allowed my eyes to bore a hole straight through him. "You pull another stunt on me like this one and I'm gonna

58

pull your puny ass right through this window and pinch your fucking head off like a pimple, you prick. Got that?"

"That a threat, Caldwell?" Olivera challenged, guarding the side of his pocked face.

Fear was unmistakable in his eyes. I'd seen the same look on more than one Vietcong face…just before he died.

"That's a caution, Olivera. Don't threaten or harass me again. Even someone of your limited intelligence should be able to understand that. Now let's see if you're smart enough to stay out of *my* way." I stood straight and began walking down the street directly in front of the police car like a matador who'd just mystified an addled bull. I glared once over my shoulder, daring him to make a move before I turned my back on him completely.

He was bright red in the face and yelled at me from a safe distance. "Just who the fuck you think you are, you white trash motherfucker? I'll run your ass in just like Mendoza did your old man the old days you get in *my* face." But the deputy failed to leave the safety of his patrol car and waited until I'd crossed to the other side of the intersection before pulling up, making a right turn and burning the rubber off the tires as he peeled away in his squad car.

By the time I'd jogged back to the Trails End, I'd put Jorge Olivera out of my mind. But I could not clear the vision of Audrey Romero from my head. Four o'clock seemed a long time off.

Out of the shower, I threw on a fresh pair of jeans and a long sleeved khaki work shirt, ruffled my hair and called it good. My stomach growled for real food.

For the first time since landing back in this crummy town I didn't feel disoriented. My senses were sharp, the way I'd been back in the jungle. I was engaged. Probably the temporary euphoria of endorphin release from my workout. Partially, it was the mental image of Audrey creeping back into my mind's eye.

I'd found my way back to this grub-hole of a place because I'd learned the price of not confronting things in life that matter. The nagging questions about Miranda mattered. At least they mattered to me.

Audrey Romero? That was confusing. I wasn't in the market for romance. But I found myself not in as much of a hurry to put the place behind me. Life was complicated for me at the moment. The demons I was fighting were difficult enough to understand and I had no desire to talk about what happened to me. I felt a need to be purified, but I had no idea of how to go about achieving that.

CHAPTER 9

THE BIG ORANGE cat wasn't sitting in its perch at the front window to greet me when I approached The Sweet Shop. The heavy glass door gave way when I pushed inside. Two couples sat in booths. They looked up, then went back to eating. Nobody I knew. Dorothy Ponder acknowledged me the minute I cozied up to the counter.

"Hi, Charlie," she said, as if I was one of her regulars. "You gonna have something to eat today?"

"Eggs and bacon, if it isn't too much trouble?"

"How you like 'em?" Dorothy asked.

"Over easy'll do." I settled onto one of the swivel seats at the counter. "Couple pieces of toast would be nice."

Dorothy went on with what she was doing. "Glad ya decided ta drop back 'round." She hacked at something with a spatula on the griddle. "Wasn't sure ya would way I dropped that bomb on ya the other day."

"Wasn't your fault. The idea of her being...gone," I avoided actually saying Miranda's *name* and *dead* in the same sentence, "caught me off guard.

"Had a history—well, childhood history anyway—with the DeCosta's. For a while that last two years of high school, I was pretty serious about Miranda. Just me, though. She hardly knew I existed."

Dorothy was a notorious town gossip.

"Oh, I remember seeing you two kids together in here." She took my lead as if we were on a dance floor.

"Hard to believe she's gone. I keep having this vision of her smile. Still expect to walk around a corner and run into her." What I fed Dorothy Ponder just happened to be the truth.

"You're not the only one feels like that," she answered, her tone bent to genuine sympathy.

"Dorothy," I swiveled from one side to the other on the stool, quick glance over my shoulder, "you told me Miranda and Vinny had an argument in here the night Miranda was killed." I squinted over my shoulder again at the two couples having breakfast. Neither seemed interested in the conversation I was having with Dorothy Ponder. "You have the impression Miranda'd been drinking?"

"She had, ya wouldn't o' known it. Seemed sober to me." Dorothy walked around from behind the pass-through window and set a plate with two eggs, hash browns, bacon and two pieces of toast in front of me.

"What about Vinny?" I asked her.

"What *about* Vinny?"

"I mean was he drinking? Was he drunk?"

Dorothy leaned with both forearms on the counter in front of me while I ate. "Vinny was drunk enough to be feelin' real important. Know what I mean?" She went to the coffee maker and poured herself a cup. Worked her way back toward me. "Lookin' to impress the other two, Aguilar and Balthazar—Alvin and Ray. They come in with him."

One of the couples walked up to the register. Dorothy pushed herself away from the counter and walked over to take care of business.

When the couple left, she slipped back down the counter in front of me.

"I remember their names, Aguilar and Balthazar." I picked up where we'd left off. "That's about it. Police question them?"

"Sure did. Claimed they met Vinny here and left in their own trucks. Like I told Prado—you remember him— Chief of Police—'at's what I saw. All three of 'em pulled up in them big pickup trucks they drive...parked right out front. Fog was thick as cloudy soup that night. You know how it can get 'round here—up in the pass? Easy to see they all come in separate trucks 'cause them bright yellow fog spotlights lit the whole inside of the shop up when they pulled ta the curb. Might notta noticed hadn't been for that. No question, they all drove in and left separate."

"In their own trucks?"

"Yep." She took a quick sip of coffee. "After Vinny and Miranda got into it, Miranda went out the door just as casual as you please, holding up her middle finger at Vinny. Walked over from her apartment. Too foggy to drive even that far, she told me when she come in. She only lived a few blocks from here.

"Ray and Alvin, they pulled out 'bout five minutes later. Vinny stayed and finished his burger before he took off. He was hot under the collar. Talkin' to hisself. Called her a bitch. Said what she needed was a good, you-know-what, that 'F' word."

"Who found her?"

"One o' the hands out the Caputo place." Dorothy leaned a bit closer to me as if she was about to reveal a secret. "Like I was sayin' the other day...they was cuttin' alfalfa in them fields out east o' the mercantile...them big sections out passed the irrigation canal. There's a dirt road separates a couple o' sections. Way I heard it, tractor driver near run over her, found her stripped necked, like I told ya, at the edge of the field, right next to the road."

"Where'd they find Caputo?"

"Still sleepin' it off in his own bed." Dorothy screwed her face up into a disgusted mask. "Said he went out to a canal bank on his place, clear out the other end from where they found her and drank two more six packs after he left here. Claimed he didn't even remember gettin' home."

"Caputo claims he didn't do it?"

"What else he gonna say?" Dorothy countered. "'Got too drunk to know what I was doin'. Went to her apartment, beat her up, dragged her out in the country, raped her—forgot I dumped her body in one o' my fields?'" Dorothy stood full up and mindlessly wiped at the counter with a damp cloth, the animosity she felt toward Caputo was evident.

"He did it all right," she concluded. "This feud between the two of 'em been goin' on nearly two months. Wasn't the first time somebody like me heard him threatenin' her."

Dorothy began collecting the dirty dishes in front of me and dropped them into the large sink before heading out to clear the table vacated by the two kids who'd just left. The other couple seemed to take this as a cue and went to the register to pay.

Dorothy went on, her hands loaded with dirty plates. "Sal had Prado come down on Vinny two or three times over it. Vinny was always too mouthy. Bragged about how he told Prado to his face what Miranda needed, how one o' these days he was gonna give it to her. Never was real smart that Vinny."

"Didn't know him well." I took a sip of coffee, considered my next question. "Dorothy, did Miranda ever come in with Duke Matta?"

"Not in here. You know Duke's married?" she pointed out, shuffling dishes into the sink.

"I've heard. I just remember they went out a few times in high school. Wondered if they were still friends." The question was as benign as I could make it.

"Not as far as I know," she repeated her conviction, "but then, look at me. What would I know? I open this place at nine in the morning, close it nine at night and spend the next hour tryin' to round up Jeff."

"I ran into Jeff. Did he tell you?"

Dorothy's attention shifted seamlessly to her son, the fatigue in her life with him unhidden. "No," she replied in a demeanor that spoke to her struggles, "but you might remember how it is with him. Tends to only remember the moment, 'cept where them damn insects or reptiles are concerned." She shrugged and took a breath. "With that kind o' stuff, he's a walkin' encyclopedia, but he can't remember where he took his shoes off."

The woman deflated before me. She suddenly looked older and more bedraggled than a woman of her age ought to.

"Must be difficult."

"Have my moments." She wiped the side of her face against the back of her forearm. She didn't look at me when she spoke, just plodded along with what she was scrubbing. "Everybody seems to keep an eye out for him though. 'Bout two years back he scared the wits out of me. Lost him a whole day and night." She scrubbed a bit harder. Her breathing was heavy and audible. "Found him 'bout half way up Pacheco Pass along the creek looking for some kind of nymph was supposed to hatch any minute. Just forgot to come home."

Neither of us spoke for several moments.

"Any chance you'll be able to find a way to channel his interests into something that will lighten your load?"

She spoke into the sink, acquiescence the message from the droop of her shoulders. "I've looked into every county, state and federal program I could find. Nothin' People like Jeff don't exist...'cept to those o' us in no position to deny the reality." Dorothy scrubbed hard again on the object I couldn't see.

"He's got you, Dorothy," I pointed out. "He looks healthy...happy."

"Yeah," she conceded, a faint smile breaking across her face. "He's a handful to keep up with."

"Hang in there," I encouraged. "Breakfast was great. Thanks." I stepped toward the cash register. "Gotta get a move on. I'm on the hunt for a couple of bottles of good wine."

"Souza's Market," she predicted. "Even carries a few from Napa. Wine gettin' to be big business over there."

"I'll give it a try." I put down twice what the check would have been and told her I didn't need any change. "See you again, soon." I turned and walked toward the door. As I pulled it open, Simon charged through meowing, announcing his hunger or perhaps it was just hello. I reached down and scratched the big cat's ears. "Enjoyed the visit Dorothy."

I set off for Souza's Market. Dorothy was right about there being a decent selection of wine. I'd already bought one from the rack.

****

Midday was approaching by the time I settled on which two bottles of wine I wanted to share with Audrey later that afternoon. The labels appealed to my eye.

I locked in again on the flirtatious encounter I'd enjoyed with Audrey that morning. However improbable, meeting her was the perfect distraction. Especially considering where I found myself. It'd been more than pleasant for me, but I needed to keep it in its place. Divina, California was not in my future.

Breakfast would hold me until evening. That left time to dig up a few more details about Miranda's death. Maybe the authorities had it right. Caputo probably did do it. But if nobody knew about Duke Matta, except Natalie—Dorothy

Ponder didn't seem to know anything. And if the town gossip isn't prattling about a pregnancy like that, chances were nobody knew—they wouldn't have checked out Duke.

The precipitating event I'd witnessed that led to my break up with Miranda and leaving Divina was the driving force that brought me back. Resolving that mess with Miranda was obviously no longer possible. Was I pursuing this because of what I saw take place between Duke and her all those years ago? Could my meddling simply be about ego? Did I just want to get back at the guy? If I'm honest with myself, that probably was part of it. But it wasn't all of it. I genuinely wanted to know what happened to her, how *this* could have happened to her. There were, of course, a couple of glaring questions I *didn't* try to answer: Just what business of mine was any of it, and, how did I presume I had any right to pursue it? I suppose my contempt for Matta...Divina itself, maybe...was all the license   I   figured   I   needed.

CHAPTER 10

TWO BOTTLES OF wine nestled in a bag under one arm like a football as I headed for the City Library. They'd have back issues of the newspaper. Local news coverage was the place to expand my information.

An obese young woman named Beverly Ferreira introduced herself as the librarian. "Where would I find back issues of your local paper?"

"Enterprise, Merced Sun Star, Modesto Bee, down that aisle against the wall," Beverly said, pointing. "Copies of the Enterprise clear back to the first newspaper ever published here in Divina. You a reporter?"

"Just getting acquainted." The rows of bookshelves, reminded me I'd once attended Cub Scout meetings here when I was a boy. "Thought I'd peruse a few back issues. Get a feel for your town."

"Against the wall." Beverly shot out an arm with a finger pointing the direction. She returned her attention to the papers on her desk. "Enterprise is local. Merced's the county seat, of course. You'll see them hanging on the racks." She glanced up at me then. "Use any table you want. Not likely you'll be bothered."

Beverly was neither the friendliest librarian I'd ever encountered nor the most enthusiastic to assist. In this instance, that worked to my advantage. No questions about what specifically I might be looking for.

The date was April 28. Dorothy said it happened about a month back. I looked through the Enterprise first. March 10—nothing. March 17, maybe.

There it was in a column next to an update on the Watergate investigation - **LOCAL WOMAN MURDERED** - the headline ran. The picture must have been from her college days. Natalie was right. Miranda had grown more beautiful than I remembered. I felt a genuine pain rise up inside me. Seeing her face hit me hard. Even the black and white newsprint photo could not dull the twinkle in her eyes. They were the color of dark chocolate with flecks of emerald green. I always considered them one of her most striking features. Her dark brown hair was parted simply down the middle and hung straight and shiny passed her shoulders, just to the crest of her breasts. Her high cheekbones lent her a Cher Bono sort of look, but she had a much finer nose and a prettier mouth.

March 17, 1972
The nude body of Miranda DeCosta, age twenty-nine, was discovered Saturday morning, March 12, by field hands working at the Albert Caputo Dairy. Miss DeCosta, a lifetime resident of Divina, is the eldest daughter of Salvatore and Medora DeCosta.

Biography…I skimmed ahead.

Miss DeCosta was raped and strangled. The police have arrested Vincent "Vinny" Caputo in connection with the crime.

No details. It occurred to me Miranda had been found on the 12th. Probably too close to publication date to do more than report the gruesome event and some background.

I hung the copy back in the rack and searched for the next issue, March 24th. The rustling sounds of the pages echoed across the small library.

"Finding what you're after?" Beverly Ferreira shouted all the way from the front desk.

"Thank you, yes."

I ran my finger down the page, skimming over the lead-in. "Here we go," I whispered under my breath.

The nude body of Miranda DeCosta was discovered March 12th on the edge of a dirt road located west of the Central California Canal on the Albert Caputo Dairy. Police reveal Miss DeCosta was raped before she was killed. The autopsy indicates the cause of death was asphyxiation.

Chief of Police, Prado Mendoza, is conducting the investigation. State and County law enforcement agencies are assisting. In an interview with Chief Mendoza, it was learned there are no other suspects. The case against Caputo is, 'Open and shut,' said Mendoza.

Chief Mendoza went on to say that on the night of the murder it is believed Caputo went to Miss DeCosta's apartment in a drunken rage after an argument occurred between the two earlier in the evening.

Evidence suggests Miss DeCosta was raped in her own home, killed and her body later dumped near the dirt road where she was discovered the next morning by one of Caputo's own employees.

Caputo is being held without bail in Merced County Jail on charges of rape and murder in the first degree. County Attorney Grant Pederson, in a telephone interview, says Caputo will be arraigned within the next two weeks. The court is expected to set a trial date within ninety days.

The investigation is nearly complete. The evidence against him [Caputo] is overwhelming. There is no reason to delay the matter,' said Pederson, declining any further comment. If convicted, Caputo faces life in prison without the possibility of parole.

I leaned back in my chair and gazed up into the dark open beams of the ceiling. Miranda'd been a part of my childhood. As kids, when she was at Frankie's house, we played together. What came later occurred as we grew to be adolescents. Miranda and Frankie, cousins, they'd been close then.

When I broke it off with her our senior year, she put it in my face the only reason she ever went out with me was because her father forced her. Dating me was about keeping me in line to play football, make sure I didn't do some stupid teenage guy thing that could keep me off the team or get me hurt. There was my reputation for being a tough. The emphasis around football in Divina in the 60s was that absurd. That cut deep when she said it to my face. But it didn't cut as deep as what I'd seen take place between Duke Matta and her. The psychological scar that episode placed in me came back to haunt every relationship I'd had with a woman since.

It was an incident I never told her I'd witnessed. I'd held that secret and what it did to me inside all this time. There was no choice now but to bury it there forever. Learn to deal with it the best I could.

This occurred our senior year in high school. Early spring. Baseball and track season were getting under way. Old man Bannon kept me late after class for not having done my homework. I arrived late to the gym that day. Coach Woodhause would make me run wind sprints for being late. Everybody was already gone to the practice field and the place was empty, I thought. Then I heard muffled, giggling coming from a darkened hallway leading to the

71

basketball court. The hallway was never used that time of year. Figuring to catch some couple making out, I sneaked up to the corner to see who it was I'd be ribbing later.

About twenty-five feet down the dim corridor, Miranda, my girlfriend, I thought, was bending over to get a drink of water from the fountain. She had on her short cheerleading skirt and each time she went for a drink, Duke Matta would pull the back of her skirt up playfully and peak. Duke was the star quarterback on the football team. Actually, he was the star athlete in just about every sport at our school.

"Stop it, Duke," she said, giggling and slapping at his large hands.

"Come on, you ain't got nothin' under there I ain't seen before," he argued playfully.

"Somebody's gonna catch us," Miranda complained without much conviction.

"They're all outside. We got time. Come on." He slid his hard penis out from under the leg of his gym shorts.

"Jesus, you're so nasty." Miranda feigned protest, but that was not what her countenance told me. "Besides, you don't have a rubber."

Duke grabbed her and kissed her deep, rubbing himself onto her. Miranda reached down and took him into her hand and stroked back and forth. "Come on," Duke pleaded. "There's nobody around. We're wasting time." He slid his hand down the front of her panties.

"Okay, okay," she caved, breathing as heavily as he was. "But don't you cum in me. You hear me? I mean it, Duke."

"Stop worryin'." He spun her around and she bent over the water fountain. This time he slid her panties down almost to her knees and pulled his gym trunks to the bottom of his butt. Then he guided himself from behind and thrust deep into her. She held firmly to the fountain and pushed back and forth with him.

"Ooh...yes. Yes! Harder...harder! Come on. Fuck me, Duke. Fuck me harder!" She whimpered and rolled her head back and to the sides.

Duke pushed Miranda's short skirt up over her hips so he could watch himself sliding in and out of her. I could still remember vividly the clear view I had of her ass, a part of her anatomy I'd never laid eyes on before. I wanted to vomit, but I couldn't avert my eyes. It was like I was hypnotized by what I was seeing. They were both sweating and it made a slapping sound each time he slammed into her.

"I'm gonna cum," Duke moaned. "I'm gonna cum."

"Pull it out. Pull...ooh...it." Duke kept going, harder and harder, faster and faster. "Pull it out, Duke! Goddamnit, you said you wouldn't cum in me. Pull it out!"

But she made no effort to make Duke stop. In fact, she'd pushed and thrust and pulled and moaned just as hard as he had.

When Duke exploded inside of her, Miranda melted. "Oh, yeah," she cooed. "Pump it...pump it in me."

Finally they were still for several moments, breathing hard together. Only then did Miranda stand straight up, forcing Duke's penis to slide out of her.

"Goddamnit, Duke," she whispered angrily, looking up and down the hallway, giggling again. "You promised! You get me pregnant, my father will kill you...and me. You're crazy!" She kissed him quickly, pulling up her panties and scurrying off toward the girls' locker room.

Duke called after her, "What's your hurry?" He casually pulled up his gym shorts walking backward toward the end of the hallway, a cocky grin on his face.

Everyone believed Miranda had broken it off with me our senior year. They all thought the melancholy stupor I was in was because *she* dropped me. I never told her or anyone else what I'd seen. I allowed everyone to believe what they would. Those images of her remained seared into my memory.

Sometimes a person has to get back from an event to really see it as it is. After I left Divina I figured out Sal used Miranda as much as he'd used me. Putting physical distance between the place and me helped soften my feelings toward her enough I thought I could rid myself of the destroyed self-esteem I suffered over what I'd seen. I'd really needed to hear her tell me none of it had anything to do with any failing in me. My self-image, compounded by what I'd had to do to survive combat, was an issue I'd be forced to deal with some other way now.

No doubt about it, Sal manipulated and used Miranda for his own purposes, and in the end refused to let her into his world. No wonder she'd gone down the road she did. A wave of revulsion similar to what I'd experienced that first day when Dorothy Ponder revealed Miranda was dead washed over me again.

Maybe Sal DeCosta was about to use Vinny Caputo the same way he'd used Miranda and me while the real murderer walked away. These newspaper articles pronounced Caputo guilty before the investigation—if there really was one—was even completed. The finger had been pointed and that was good enough for Sal. Now he wanted Caputo hung from the highest tree. Why the rush to justice?

Then I remembered Frankie's words. How Miranda had become a *"pain in the ass"* to the entire family. How he wasn't sure if Sal was pissed over the loss of something he considered his chattel or whether Sal, as the grieving father, was the real thing.

I'd thought Frankie's indictments of Sal were disingenuous. How could any father, even Sal DeCosta, not have been torn to his soul over such a brutal and tragic death of his child? But I conceded it was not beyond Sal DeCosta to hang the first suspect without bothering with a minor inconvenience like a police investigation to look too deeply into his daughter's, *or his family's*, lives.

There were three more articles about her murder in the Merced Sun Star. They became repetitive. The theme was the same in all of them: Vinny Caputo got drunk, raped and killed her, case closed. The police, if not the town, practiced the same oversimplified thinking to this tragedy they applied with most issues.

I was surprised they weren't going easier on Vinny since he was drunk at the time of the murder, if, in fact, he really had done what he was charged with. But this was Sal DeCosta's daughter and if Sal had his way, and he might, Vinny would never see the light of day again. And he should count himself damn lucky he wasn't facing *Old Sparky*.

Outside the library a light breeze soughed in the tall sycamore trees. The air was warm. The bright sun was welcome as I strolled back to the Trails End. The fresh air and walk cleared the stupor I felt. Once more I invited the vision of Audrey Romero turning back to me that morning into my mind's eye.

CHAPTER 11

WHEN I ARRIVED at my room, I shaved and grabbed a quick shower. I hadn't brought a lot of extra clothing along. Already I'd remained in town longer than planned. The jeans I wore would have to withstand more wear-time.

I looked into the bathroom mirror at the image of myself and shook a small splash of Brut for Men into my hands, rubbed it vigorously onto my face and neck. There was a slight sting in my still open pores. My hair was slightly wet and I tousled it, said to the image staring back at me, "Sorry, Audrey, this is all I've got to work with." I collected the two bottles of wine and stepped out the door.

Beside Buck's driver's door I stopped a moment to take stock of the pitiful condition of the old truck. I'd meant to get around to working on his body. His engine, though, was in perfect condition. That continued to provide me with an excuse to procrastinate with the balance of the restoration.

Buck wore as much rust as he did paint, which was mostly an original turquoise blue enamel color with the occasional glimmer of black accent trim still visible in spots here and there. To my eye, the burnished hues of rust in combination with the turquoise and black weren't all that unpleasant. But that was just me.

Inside, I'd spread a bright blue and red and yellow Mexican wool *serape* to hide the worn-out vinyl seat covers. Across the top edge of the windshield I'd planted a prominent fringe of white cotton dingle balls. Buck seemed quite fetching down in Old Mexico. But up here…

At least I wasn't being faced with introducing Audrey to my one-room casita and Buck both at the same time. My beach hut appealed just fine to me, but I doubted it'd be met with the same appreciation by most women.

I hopped behind the wheel, drove to the north end of town and made a left turn onto Farm Road Lane; opposite direction from my run that morning. Several blocks further on I made another left onto Silverado Trail then a quick right put me onto winding Pacheco Pass Crossroad. The desk clerk at the Trail's End had given me directions to Audrey's house.

Divina's streets were originally laid out along a grid of east-west, north-south squares and rectangles. Probably something to do with the way the small sections of the original giant land-grant rancho were cut up before being sold off.

In the ten years since I'd been gone, the town limits had pushed west, higher up the rolling foothills of the Diablo range a couple of miles north of Pacheco Pass Highway. There the streets broke into quaint, roughly paved curving lanes where an abundance of cottontail rabbits and bevies of chubby plumed quail scurried about. The lots were pocked with huge lichen-covered granite boulders weeping russet and black patina and shaded by ancient oak trees only a few years younger than the venerable boulders themselves. The houses were large enough to afford privacy and preserve vast, sweeping views of the San Joaquin Valley, which lay roughly two hundred feet below the center of town and three hundred feet below the scattering of homes built in this new section.

Audrey's sprawling Adobe house appeared as a shock to me. It was one of those Spanish ranch-style homes built in a squared up "U" shape. The long main run of the house opened to a tiled courtyard facing east and sat imperiously above the town on a shelf of land with a massive outcropping of dark craggy boulders jutting out to form an overhang high above its roof. There were no homes larger than hers on the side of the hill.

A wide arching, circular driveway traced its gravelly upper limb toward a three-foot high stem-wall separating the driveway from the courtyard in front of the house.

Before I killed Bucks engine, Audrey strode casually out to the short wall to greet me. I wouldn't have thought it possible, but I found her more appealing at that moment than when I'd left her sweating and jogging up the hill earlier that morning. There's something about the unmade athletic female that charms me more than…the prepared, as it were.

She stopped on the inside of the wall, adjacent to my driver's door. "What a great old truck." She studied the spectacle of Buck from front bumper to tailgate.

"I keep meaning to do the body work on it, but…"

She grinned knowingly. "Maybe you should leave it? Looks pretty good just the way it is. Have any trouble finding the place?"

"Girl at the Trail's End pointed me in the direction." I reached back into the cab for the bag with the wine. "Thought you said we were barbecuing?"

"What makes you think we're not?"

"Pretty fancy outfit for a barbecue." The silk shorts and cream-colored blouse were classy.

She held her drink glass up and out from her body, peered down the front of her sheer blouse and knee-length silk shorts. Then she looked up at me, her emerald green eyes twinkling, "You like it?"

The grin on my face must have answered her question. Her beaming smile told me how much she appreciated my noticing.

She shifted toward the eight-foot opening in the wall forming the entrance to her courtyard. There the wall supported a massively framed double doorway topped with a wide arched single campanario in the center of which hung a traditional mission bell. Two huge, heavily weathered massive doors of august wood swung inward and drooped from their hinges under their weight; Spanish mission. She set her glass atop the squat wall and walked out the entrance.

"Here, let me take those." She reached for the bag holding the two bottles of wine. "Come on in."

I handed her the baguette. "I'll carry the wine."

Inside, the courtyard was capacious with clean lines. From the opening in the gate to the front door I calculated thirty feet. The back edge butted across the entire front of the house in a serpentine shape with patches of planter areas here and there. The bends were accented with small and medium-sized gray and brown granite boulders piled into mounded shapes to match the natural terrain around the house. In the south end of the courtyard was a fountain rising up, perhaps eight feet and spilling water back into a pond about ten feet in diameter. I made the front of the house to be more than one hundred feet wide. The place had to be five thousand square feet. I analyzed my cover and escape routes. The nightmare never goes away.

The courtyard was paved with fired stones. The eight by sixteen inch slabs seemed still molten with splashes of burgundy, ginger, copper, yellow, umber, olive and black. They felt alive.

Audrey snatched her glass from the wall. "Follow me." She extended her arm in the direction of the house.

"Huge house," I said. "Beautiful."

"I was thinking family when we built it."

She walked back toward me. "It's mine now." She turned, tracing the expanse of the sprawling structure with her drink glass held in hand. "Darryl never did anything on his own, but his father was loaded. He inherited everything when his dad passed away. You know the Portuguese— only son. He lives on his dairy, looks after his mother. This house, the land, all mine. My alimony and child support maintain it. I'm a regular lady of leisure. What that prick's freedom cost him."

Her auburn hair, no longer sweat-soaked, seemed lighter, tending to chestnut and denser than that morning. The base color was cut through, streaked with highlights of blond hues. When she spun, it flared like the lush mane of a young colt or the skirt of a twirling dancer.

She wore a cream-colored blouse of some sheer silky fabric. Black pearl-like buttons about an inch apart all the way down the front held it closed, starting where her cleavage would have been if she'd had any. The loose fit allowed it to be worn untucked. Her medium-sized breasts roamed freely inside as she moved. The fabric looked fragile, like it might dissolve simply at the idea of it. The bottom edge fell just below her narrow waist and was fringed in a sculpted lacey ribbon that encircled her slender curvy hips. The entirety of it was stunningly feminine. The wide-legged saddle-colored silk shorts she wore stopped midway on her thighs. The material glistened in the descending sunglow of the afternoon. The shorts hung from her frame as though they were clinging by the tiniest grip to her waist. There were no panty lines and her butt moved as freely as her breasts.

I stopped staring and caught up to her at the front door. "That's a pretty steep run up the hill from where I left you this morning."

R.P. McCabe

"Run it six days a week. Sometimes I go on long runs, ten miles now and then." She held the front door open, gesturing toward the kitchen.

"Lot of miles a week. You training for something?"

"San Francisco marathon," she said.

The earthy tile floors ran off in every direction of the house. There was no foyer per se. We stood immediately in a vast room with not a single item out of place and furnished elegantly. "This is a magnificent house, Audrey."

"How 'bout we get one of those open?" She pointed to the two bottles. There was an unforced sassiness about her I found utterly captivating.

"Wanna drink this white one first? It's Chardonnay." I pulled the bottle of white wine from the bag while I followed her to the island in the center of the kitchen. "Label says it's from Sonoma. We can have the red with dinner, if that's okay with you?"

She handed me a corkscrew. I liberated the cork and poured. We each took a test sip.

"That ought to do the job," she said. I wondered what she meant by that. Then she smiled at me. "Come on. I'll give you the tour."

The house was furnished in Spanish Mission style, as authentic as the massive front entry gates; spacious earth-tone rooms filled with unusual antique appointments.

"Where'd you develop your taste for the Mexican influence?"

"My cousin Lydia...lives in Santa Barbara. See her when I can. Love the homes down there." She moved down the hall. "This is Rachel's."

"Rachel would be about...ten, eleven, maybe?"

"Twelve going on twenty," Audrey quipped. "Very mature for her age."

There were three shelves of books on one wall. A pair of pink ballet slippers hung over a hook near the closet door. There was a full-sized canopy bed off center against

81

the opposite wall next to a large half-moon-shaped window extending outward creating a window seat furnished with soft colorful cushions. Just beyond the edge of the open door was a small desk with an orderly stack of schoolbooks.

"She's a bright kid." Audrey beamed. "Gets straight A's. I'm starting her on piano lessons, too."

"Where is she?"

"Wanted to spend the weekend with Grandma...my mom." She brushed past me, continuing down the wide hallway. The perfume of her entirety invaded my reason like I was drugged. The gravitational pull of her was overwhelming. "This is my exercise room," she said, pointing into another room. "Originally intended to be a bedroom." Exercise machines and a small rack of dumbbells filled the space.

"You're really committed to keeping in shape."

"Not a lot to keep me occupied around here. Works off some of my frustrations," she said sipping from her glass. "This is nice." She held the glass with the lemony-colored liquid up slightly. "I guess I got a little desperate after Darryl and I split."

She went on with the tour. "This is the den, family room, TV room...whatever. Rachel and I spend most of our time between here and the kitchen. The rest of the house doesn't get much use. Over here," she crossed the cozy room, "are two more bedrooms and just down here and to the right is my sanctuary." She walked around the corner and stood to one side of the double doors opening into the master suite, which amounted to a small apartment.

For several moments I stood there taking in the beautiful room, everything in its place. "You could stand military inspection. You might be one of the neatest people I've ever been around."

We stood planted in the doorway, looking directly into each other's eyes and drank deeply from our wine glasses. There was forceful tension growing between us. It was there the instant she walked back toward me that morning, precooked electricity. I sensed it radiating out from me then and I could literally feel it crawling across the ether between us.

Finally, she lowered her eyes, stared at her glass a reflective moment. "Follow me." She crossed back through the den, down the short hallway and into the kitchen once more. There she slid the arcadia door open, stepped out onto a winding brick path sloping slightly down the hill from the main house. The bricked walkway led through lush gardens to a small, detached building thirty yards away.

"Mother-in-law's quarters." Audrey pointed at the building. The bungalow looked as large as some homes I'd lived in as a child. "Darryl planned to move his mother here from the dairy after his father died. I'd use it for guests if I ever had any." She lifted her wineglass and drained the small amount remaining. "Pretty though," she went on, admiring the bungalow, "don't you think?" She shrugged, cocked her head to one side and appraised the small house one final time. "Seen enough?"

"Helluva place, Audrey."

I'd never known anyone my age who owned anything like what she possessed in this piece of land and house. It'd take a lifetime to accumulate the kind of money a man would need to afford something like this for his family. Actually, that's exactly what it had taken her ex-husband's father to accumulate the money to afford it. Deflating to contemplate.

"Come on," she said, perking up and clutching my hand. "You'll love the courtyard at sunset. Besides, you need to get the barbecue started." She smiled taking control, leading me back up the short path and through the open door.

As I drained the dregs of wine from my glass, I reached for hers. Topped up, I handed her glass back and we headed out the service door off the kitchen. The door led back into the courtyard.

Next to the grill several pieces of mesquite firewood sized for the barbeque pit were stacked along with plenty of kindling. This was the sort of thing I was good at. In a few minutes I had a flame going.

The quiet of the outdoors surrounded us while I worked. Audrey stood to the side and followed me with her eyes.

"Like the wine?"

Her gaze made me uneasy. There was just the hint of the cat about to jump the mouse.

"It's really good. Not too sweet," she said.

"You like tart or sweet?"

"This is working just fine." She smiled over the lip of her glass.

Silence

"You're a good looking guy, Charlie."

"And you're a good looking girl, Audrey."

She sounded giddy. From the wine or the moment, I couldn't be sure.

Good looking didn't really cut to what I was thinking looking at her. She was beautiful beyond words. What a husband to a woman like this could find more appealing in some other woman was beyond me. But I'd seen this before. Marrying your high school sweetheart sounded good, but rarely worked. And if the marriage came about based on an unwanted pregnancy…do the arithmetic on the divorce rate.

She walked up to me, stopped inches away. She was only slightly shorter. The mischievous smirk on her face gave her shiny brick-colored lips a sexy appeal. Her hair was haphazardly parted on the right side of her head, then pulled all the way over to the left side where it fell across

84

her right eye in an attempt to work its way back the other way.

"Look at this. Another empty glass." She held it up for me to take.

She smelled like jungle flowers after a tropical downpour.

"Where'd you learn about wine?" She followed me to the table.

I drained what was left in my own glass. "Moved to Denver after I left here. Made friends with some kids from New York. They were wine drinkers. Now I'm a wine drinker."

"What'd you do in Denver?" She turned down the heat a little. "Snows there, right?"

"Sometimes…winters. Plenty hot in the summers." I jabbed the burning wood. "Got lucky, I guess. Landed an on-the-job-training program with a savings and loan bank. Not very glamorous, boring beyond words, actually." I turned to poke the logs again. "They'll take a while. We need to get anything else going?"

"All in the fridge. Ready to go. What else?"

"What else…what?"

"Denver," she said. "Tell me the rest." She strolled across the courtyard to two fluffy chaise lounges. "Relax." She said climbing onto one, patting the seat of the one opposite her.

Audrey sat facing me with one leg tucked under her and the other dangling over the side of the chaise. Her full attention seemed focused on me alone. When she leaned forward the dainty blouse crumpled open slightly at the first button, revealing the tops of her naked breasts.

"Not much to tell really."

"You know, Charlie, I admit I didn't know much about you when you lived here. But I know *where* you lived. I knew *who* your father was. I remember the big flap that was made over that stupid football game your senior year, and I can tell you this much...there's a story somewhere, 'cause you aren't the same Charlie Caldwell I remember." She took another long sip from her wine. "And I like the *you* I see now. So, go on, tell me how you turned into the guy I see in front of me. I'm just curious," she said, curling a strand of hair around an index finger.

"Okay. Long story short. The kids I hung around with in Denver, the ones from New York, they all attended college—at least part time. So after auditing classes for two semesters, I enrolled in a couple myself. The bank I worked for picked up the tab. My new friends were all political. We got involved in SDS.

"What's that?"

"Students for a Democratic Society."

"You were a war protester?"

"We advocated for civil rights, too. It wasn't all about the war."

"I thought you told me you went to Nam?"

"I did. It's complicated."

"Then what?" She eyed me curiously over the top of her glass as she drank.

"I bumped along until my political convictions got in the way of the idea of becoming a banker."

The fire crackled and I dashed over for a quick check.

"Keep going," she encouraged the instant I sat down again.

"One of my New York friends, girl I knew, worked at a magazine.

"You have a girlfriend?"

The antenna was visibly extending out of her head. "Only in the sense she was a good friend and she was a girl. She put in a word about me when an opening for a proofreader came along. I'd never thought about doing anything like that as a job."

"Doesn't sound real exciting," Audrey said honestly.

"That was my reaction, too. I was wrong. I learned more about places and people and things in one year proofing than all of high school and the first two years after I moved to Denver. Mostly, I guess, I learned about myself."

"So, what was it you learned about yourself, Charlie?"

Her eyes were glued to me as though there was nothing else on earth she could possibly focus on. I wanted to reach out and touch her hand. But I didn't. There was no point in escalating something I had no intention of seeing through. I fully intended to keep it a nice, but controlled, evening. Holding her hand might not be the smart move.

"Well, the first thing I learned was I had an interest in things I never was exposed to growing up here. Some of that was because of my parents, I guess. A lot of it was growing up here. White trash kid like me didn't exactly warrant much extra effort from the school system, if you know what I mean." Audrey may have had her bitterness about life in Divina. I had my own. And as much as I was enjoying being with her at the moment, there was no point creating any illusions.

She looked steadily back at me. This was a woman who acknowledged things as they were. No icing. It didn't seem to matter to her whether it was her story or mine. Facts were facts. She continued to want to know more about mine and made no objection to my harsh judgment of her town.

"You still do proofreading?" she asked.

"Not exactly."

She lifted her glass again. "This really gets good if you give it a chance." She smiled into another sip. "The wine I mean."

I went to check the fire again. "Getting close to ready to cook on."

Enough darkness had settled it was difficult to see detail. Audrey stood and walked to a support post at the front of the house. Light came up slowly until the courtyard was bathed in a gentle blush of blue-green light.

"Exactly what then?"

I looked to her inquisitively.

"I mean, if you don't do proofreading, what is it you do?" This time when she approached me, she locked her arm into mine. "Look at the lights." She led me to the stubby wall at the front edge of the courtyard where we stood for several moments taking in the early spring evening with the last of the Chardonnay. "I love this view."

Below us the lights of Divina twinkled, which at night made the town appear to triple in size. Stretching out as far as one could see into the Valley below were small clusters of lights accompanied by silence that left only the peaceful sounds of crickets chirping.

"I'm thinking about becoming a writer," I allowed myself to utter, looking straight ahead.

"Now you're trying to impress me. You mean like books?" Audrey looked up at the side of my face.

"Not yet. I'm working at it though. Went to see my old boss in Denver right after the Army cut me loose. Told her what I had in mind. She agreed to give me a chance. I'm going to be freelancing for the same magazine I read for. Might get one or two assignments a year. Not much, but it'll pay for my place on the beach in Mexico.

"Between assignments I plan to work on trying to get my head right…baggage...maybe start a novel."

"You're serious." At that point I wasn't sure if she was mocking me or encouraging me. "Writer," she repeated.

Vocalizing my thoughts about becoming a writer made me uncomfortable. I had no credentials or even formal training except for my brief stint at *Past, Present & Future Magazine* before going into the Army. But I'd never

88

forgotten the words of advice given me by Stan Jones, one of their staff writers.

One blustery snow-driven afternoon we chatted. I'd just finished proofing one of his stories. He told me I didn't need any special education or license to be a writer, just the audacity to write good stories; honest, truthful. "If they work, you're a writer. If they don't, better keep the day job." Stan was a no bullshit guy.

"Oh, I'm serious, all right," I told Audrey. "But don't make too much of it. It's little more than a palliative pursuit for now."

She looked at me. "I don't know what that means. But it sounds like the most romantic thing I've ever heard, living on a beach in Mexico, writing magazine articles—"

"Eating fish tacos six nights a week to survive, and I'll probably never earn enough in a lifetime to afford what you already have here.

"Means I'm treating the symptom, not the underlying problem."

"What?"

"Palliative—means treating the symptom, but not the cause."

She smiled up at me, made no reply and dropped her head gently forward onto my chest. A few sweet moments passed while she nuzzled my shirt with her nose slowly. "Charlie," she said finally, "nobody could afford what I have here. And what I've endured to get it hardly seems worth it. I'd gladly trade positions with you." She looked up into my eyes. Her's were brilliant and shiny. "I'm hungry. How about you?"

I stopped to consider what she'd just said. It wasn't the first time I'd heard the conviction from someone about possessions and money not necessarily connecting to happiness. But that's an easy declaration to make when you have the money and the possessions. Having never had enough of either, I wasn't as certain as Audrey seemed to feel.

Everyone carries a burden of some sort, I figured. Was I wallowing too much in self-pity over mine? I thought about the families I'd visited over the last few months. Money wouldn't mean shit if they could have their sons back. Money...possessions...these were subjects worthy of more serious consideration.

CHAPTER 12

WHEN WE SAT down to eat I popped the cork out of the red wine. "Pinot Noir," I read from the label. "Saintsbury, Carneros Creek, full-bodied red wine with a spicy bouquet, excellent with red meat." We laughed easily.

"Just pour." She pushed her glass toward me.

The evening air was crisp, but not uncomfortable.

"Back up a ways and tell me about your time in the service." She lifted a fork full of salad to her luscious mouth. "Were you a Marine?"

"Army."

"And?" she encouraged, eyeing me over the top of her glass again.

"I did some time in Nam." I retreated into my own glass

"Can you tell me about it?" Audrey affected gentleness in her tone that sounded genuine. But it wasn't kindness I was looking for. The truth was I couldn't bring myself to verbalize what was inside of me about the horrors I'd seen, participated in.

"How 'bout another time?"

"Sure, Charlie." She seemed to sense the difficulty of the subject for me.

None of us who'd seen combat were being what you could call *welcomed* home. The protests I'd been a part of had begun in the early `60s with the Civil Rights Revolution. That movement morphed into a revolution against the government and the war in Vietnam. There was a heavy sentiment of resentment toward returning vets. People didn't seem to get it.

The Weather Underground was blowing shit up in protest. The underpinning sentiment toward those of us who hadn't burned our draft cards or gone to Canada was that we'd *allowed* ourselves to be used as pawns of the government. Images of the *My Lai Massacre* on the five o'clock news made it look like all soldiers were murderers.

Vietnam was a shit war. And it was a shit situation for draft age kids—country, conscience or jail. Guys like me got fucked either way we went.

Westmoreland and Nixon wanted me to believe I was a hero. Every time I saw a story about Bernadine Dohrn and Bill Ayers, I felt like a fucking sell out having allowed myself to be used in the war. But for me, going to Canada wasn't an option. And then suddenly they had me and it was out of my control. Do what I was told or face Federal Prison.

We ate quietly and sipped our wine.

After a few moments, I reached over and placed my hand on hers. "I saw a lot of action. It was brutal. Maybe I'll tell you about it sometime…just not tonight, okay?"

"I made dessert." She squeezed back and smiled. "What do you say?"

"Later?" I patted my stomach.

"Okay. Let's levitate ourselves back over to those lounges again?" Audrey slid away from the table. "Push them over here." She pointed to the opening at the front gate. "We can see the lights better."

We shoved the chaise lounges together to form a large double chair and set the small patio table to my side with the wine on it. "You're in charge of the wine," Audrey said, pointing to the side next to the table.

I looked at the setup. Audrey noticed.

"Okay?"

"Yeah…more than okay."

I settled onto the side closest to the wine as instructed and without thinking said, "Pretty terrible what happened to Miranda. Were you friends with her?"

Audrey tensed perceptibly and set her glass down. I was instantly sorry I'd raised the subject. "Everybody knew Miranda," she hissed. "She was a slut. Darryl was fucking her on a regular basis before he dumped her for that little bitch he finally left me for. Miranda was a piece of strange for a lot of married guys around town."

"I'm sorry," I offered. "I didn't—"

"No need to apologize." Her tone was dry, emotionless. "Not your fault." She tossed her head back running her fingers from her hairline over the top of her head through her thick hair. Audrey stared up into the night sky for several moments, seeming to search the vastness of space for an answer as to why things turned out the way they had for her.

"You still love him?" I asked this understanding there must always be something between two people who create a child together—love or hate, there was necessarily something. The two sentiments, I knew, were not that far separated.

She didn't answer. Only the crickets continued their serenade.

Finally, she lifted her glass and held it under her nose. "Label was right. Spicy," she said. "No, I don't love him anymore, Charlie." She didn't look at me as she spoke. A chill had frosted over the warmth I'd been feeling from her. "I'm twenty-eight-years-old, I have a twelve-year-old daughter and I'm stuck in a place where the odds of meeting someone I might be able to love again are somewhere between zero and none." She scooted away from me then. "And I'm a target for every local jerk who fancies himself God's gift to women. They think they know just what a lonely woman needs." She drained the wine from her glass and held it out to me mechanically. "I'm...bitter," she admitted. "Hell, that pig Vinny Caputo they arrested used to hit on me all the time, too. I don't know where these guys get the idea they're so wonderful." Audrey shook her head and reached to take her glass from me. "That slime-bag, Duke Matta calls me all the time, too." Her face contorted into a look of disgust. "He's married, that creep—not that it matters to him. He's such a loser. Fixed his ass though. I told his wife." She snickered softly. "You know that dumb bastard still comes on to me when he sees me." Her head shook incredulously.

It wouldn't have done for me to point out I thought I could understand Duke's ardor in her case. Continuing where this conversation led was the last thing I wanted to do, but Audrey's revelation about Duke was too much to ignore.

"Were Duke and Miranda..."

"How would I know? Could have been. I wouldn't be surprised, but I never heard about it. Haven't heard anything like that come out since she got killed." Her voice was cold, detached.

Another person who didn't know Miranda thought she was pregnant with Duke's child.

Duke and Miranda managed to keep the fact they had a real relationship secret in a town as small as Divina. Maybe Duke wanted to make sure nobody ever found out.

Seemed a good time to change the subject. "You know, when the magazine gets around to sending me on assignment, I could end up somewhere in Central or South America."

"Is that somehow supposed to be exciting to me...impress me?"

"I didn't mean to make you angry, Audrey. Maybe I should go." I set my glass on the table and pushed myself up from the chaise lounge.

"I should have known she was why you were here. You just wanted to know who she was fucking before she got killed. I don't know what I was thinking."

Audrey'd worked herself beyond anger by then. She sounded hurt, and for that I felt genuinely sorry. I owed her nothing and yet I couldn't bring myself to treat her callously.

"She *is* why I came back, Audrey. But not for the reasons you're thinking. We've all got our skeletons. I came back hoping to chase some of mine out of the closet. Something I've carried around way too long. Believe me, if she was still alive, I'd have already dealt with why I came back. You're going to have to accept it was not for the reasons you obviously think. We would've never met this morning. Even the brief moments of pleasure we've shared this evening would never have happened.

"I didn't tell you the entire truth this morning," I confessed. "When you asked me how long I planned to be in town. The real answer to that was as soon as I got back to my motel, showered and checked out. But I hadn't run into you yet when I made that decision. And when I did run into you..."

She looked up at me, tears leaking down the sides of her pretty face.

I walked toward the gate.

"Is that the truth?" she whispered.

"I'm a lot of things, Audrey. But I'm not a hurtful liar." I was nearly at the gate by then.

"Well, could you stop, please?" She struggled to get to her feet from the chaise, trying to avoid spilling the wine on herself.

I turned slowly in the entryway and waited.

"I like you, Charlie," she said.

"I like you, too."

"No, I mean, I like you and you're handsome and smart and interesting and I was fantasizing. I haven't been around a man I could actually see myself with in years. And then suddenly there you were...and then you asked about Miranda and I—"

By then she was standing right in front of me.

"Slow down, Audrey. Stop. Please. I didn't come back to be with Miranda. But I didn't come back to stay in this town either. I wasn't being fair to you...maybe to myself. But I certainly wasn't being fair to you. I apologize."

I turned and walked toward Buck.

"Please don't go, Charlie." My hand was on Buck's door handle as she spoke. "Please."

"I won't stay, Audrey. I hate this fucking place worse than you do and I'm sorry, but I don't have anything holding me here."

She walked purposefully toward me. When she reached me, she didn't slow down. Her arms went up around my neck, her lips found mine like polarized magnets and our bodies seized together as if a welder had laid a tight bead down the seam where we were joined. Her lips were warm and wet and soft. The tears that traced down the sides of her fine nose found their way into my mouth. Their salty taste mixed with the sweetness of her saliva as she let her tongue slide softly next to mine, created alchemy between our souls. From the sweet, humid softness of her breath, something escaped her and fused itself inside me. My knees felt weak. She held my head in her hands and kissed me long and deep and with so much passion it consumed the neurotransmitters in my cortex. It was as though she sucked the good sense right out of my brain. I knew what I should do. But there was no way I could do it.

My arms seemed like they could go around her lithe body twice, but there was no need, for she clung to me like my own skin. She was muscular, but soft, and when my hands drifted down over the turn of her soft bottom, she lifted herself to me so the mound of her womanliness pressed against my own hardness.

We remained locked together until neither of us could breathe.

"Please don't go," she whispered into my ear, holding me as tightly, yet as gently, as I had ever known.

Suddenly the sound of several small stones crashing onto the roof of the house startled us. We spun just as a larger rock pounded the roof shattering a tile.

"That happen often?"

"Little ones sometimes, but I've never had anything that large come down."

We waited and peered up into the darkness at the top of the craggy overhang. Nothing but shadows in the night. We didn't see or hear anything more.

Audrey took me by the hand. "Come on."

I let her lead me back toward the house. She slid her hand up the post near the kitchen and switched the patio lights off as we brushed by. There remained only the ocher glow from a single light burning in the kitchen.

"I won't stay, Audrey."

She tiptoed up and kissed me softly again. "Planning to leave tonight?" She said this to me wearing a sycophantic moue at the corner of her beautiful mouth.

I looked hard into her sparkling green eyes. "No, but—"

She kissed me again, long and deep and wet and delicious. A fire raged inside me that began to burn out of control. I cupped a perfect, delicate braless breast in one hand as I kissed her neck.

"I want you to kiss them," she said, her head falling backward.

I nuzzled the décolletage of her blouse aside with my nose and took her nipple between my lips.

A soft moan escaped her as she hit the switch on the wall, turning out the kitchen light. Then she took my hand and led me to her bedroom. Tiny night-lights glowed from unseen sockets taking a slight edge off the darkness.

Inside her bedroom, she stood near the bed and faced me in the muted glow. In torturously slow motion she unbuttoned the front of her blouse and let it fall open. Her nipples were smallish with pouty fawn-colored aureole encircling them in the center of perfect half grapefruit sized breasts; the kind of breasts you find in a centerfold of Playboy Magazine. Then she reached down and pulled the pretty bow at the front of her shorts allowing them to fall in a shimmering puddle around her ankles.

She reached up and slowly unbuttoned my shirt. The softness of our bodies together blinded any pretense of judgment in me. I laid her gently backward onto the giant bed and kissed her from her eyes to her toes. My tongue traced the length of her long slender neck to her breasts, alternating between them. It seemed I could suck the entirety of them into my mouth. First one beautiful, soft orb then the other as I listened to the mournful, fragile whispers of delight climbing out of her. Audrey clawed at my back pulling me firmer onto her. "Harder, baby," she pleaded when I pecked at her nipples. My lips traced down the center of her torso to her belly button and I felt her quiver beneath me. When I buried my face in the sweetness between her thighs she arched her back, spread her legs wider and ran her fingers through my long hair begging me not to stop.

If there is a fragrance for female pheromone, it was probably her perfume, because the only way I could define her taste, her wondrous scent, was simply...her; her femaleness. The taste of her turned perceptibly sweeter; she became wetter when she reached her orgasm. I savored the taste of her while she went on her journey. Only when she began to plead for me did I crawl up her body like I was stalking in the jungle, hesitating for a moment, poised to slip inside her.

She looked up into my eyes. "Gently, baby," she whispered. "It's been three years."

Her breath sucked in hard when I slid inside her. I understood immediately Audrey was telling me the truth. The tautness of her yielded to me begrudgingly at first, easing some the further we went. I didn't want to hurt her and yet it was all I could do to control the need to feel the inside of her. It had been more than three years for me, too, but I didn't want to admit that to her. We watched each other's eyes as I allowed her to pull the length of me deep inside her. Her fingernails dug painfully into my flesh. Finally she forced me to begin thrusting. Her whimpering voice, the trembling of her body under me drove me to a place I'd never known with a woman. What we were doing went so far beyond making love I'm at a loss now to describe what really did happen between us except to say; I doubted I'd ever be the same again.

CHAPTER 13

AT FIRST LIGHT Sunday morning, Audrey rolled over on top of me. She flinched when I reached between her thighs to touch her. "You okay, Baby? I don't want to hurt you."

"Didn't realize how sore I was gonna be."

I began to roll her back down beside me. "Oh no you don't." She pushed me back down. "I'm not that sore," she said taking my hardness in her hand, guiding me up into her. She settled down onto me slowly, taking me deep inside her, allowing us to fit together gently, naturally without force.

Feeling her engulf my manhood was an exquisite warm, velvety sensation. Audrey began to move up and down on me, drawing me in and out of her slowly, contracting her muscles as though she were holding me gently with her hands. When she sat up and threw her head back I reached up and grabbed a breast in each hand kneading her creamy flesh, squeezing her nipples gently between my fingers. With each thrust of my hips her whimpering became increasingly more urgent, her movements faster and faster, driving me once more to my physical limits to hold back.

"Oh God, I want you, Charlie."

In one savagely passionate roll I pulled her down under me, forced her legs wide and drove deep into her. Her moans turned to cries for me to do it harder.

I pushed myself up and looked deep into her eyes when I thrust into her the final time. The flesh of my chest tore where her fingernails dug into me when our energies began to flow together.

"God I never want you to pull out of me," she wept as our spasms went on together several times.

When we were completely spent, we collapsed into each other like a supernova in the cosmos; our cosmic energy and radiation released for all of eternity. But the entity particles that had once been individual, no longer held any identity. We lay together in stunned silence, holding each other until Audrey finally whispered to me, "I need to pee."

I brushed my palm across her soft bottom as she rolled off the bed. Watching her walk naked toward the bathroom was like witnessing the fine features of a lithe gazelle sauntering across the African steppe. When she came out of the bathroom I was sitting on the edge of her bed contemplating the blossoms in her garden and what had happened to me over the past sixteen hours.

****

"You sleep well?" she asked while she shuffled between the refrigerator and the stove. "Three eggs?" She held one up.

"Sure." I felt starved.

"You groaned and babbled a lot in your sleep. Were you dreaming?"

Sometimes I'd wake in a cold sweat sitting upright. "I can do that I guess."

When she rolled out of bed, she'd seized my shirt from the floor and slipped it on. She had her back to me as

101

she worked at the stove. The shirt covered her butt. The backs of her legs were shapely, sinewy and evenly tanned. When the bread popped up she reached toward the toaster.

"Can I get that?"

"Stay where you are," she said, juddering her fingers, having scorched them.

She flipped the eggs onto a plate with the toast and spun toward me. The shirt flew open. Audrey's naked flesh pulled all my strings.

"You're making it difficult to eat."

"You didn't have any trouble last night." She smiled, turning back to get her own plate.

When she twirled again to join me at the table, she left the shirt open. She seemed not to have an ounce of shyness about her nudity.

"I was having dessert last night."

"Well eat up, soldier," she said, smiling. "Maybe you'll get another helping of that dessert."

Audrey kept her word.

****

By mid-morning we'd showered and pulled ourselves together enough to be seen in public. She walked me to the gate wearing a bright yellow cover-up with nothing under it. The moment was excruciating for us knowing what was coming. Wispy strands of her thick auburn hair obscured a clear view of her face when she hung her head. But she made no plea for me to reconsider. She'd been an honest participant in our brief encounter.

Audrey seemed more capable than me of letting go what happened between us. The night hadn't meant any less to her. But she seemed possessed somehow of a resignation about the inevitability, like this was what would happen when she met any man who might come to mean anything to her. Our brief connection reached so deep into me it felt like I was ripping my guts out driving away. But I'd told her I wouldn't stay. I'd been honest with her.

"I—" My voice simply failed me. I stared into her pretty face.

"Go on, Charlie," she said. "If you hurry, they won't charge you another day at the motel."

When I reached for her hand she pulled away.

"No, you need to go now."

I hesitated before sliding behind the wheel of Buck and starting his engine. Audrey remained standing framed in the entrance gate to the courtyard. "Write to me sometime. Let me know what South America's like." Her eyes were brimming then, but she was one tough cookie, no sniveling.

I bounced my forehead on the steering wheel, looked up straight ahead and drove away. In my rear view mirror I saw her bury her face in her hands.

Instead of turning back toward town, I made a right at the bottom of the hill and drove up around the curve toward the outcropping of boulders hanging above Audrey's house. The lane skirted the rocky ledge a few yards off the road. A little way further up and on the opposite side was a shallow turn out where I could pull Buck out of the roadway. I parked and got out.

At the crest of the formation of boulders I looked down into Audrey's courtyard. Empty. But that wasn't why I'd wanted to see the spot. I was careful where I stepped. Checked the hard ground. There were no impressions. I surveyed the courtyard and approximated where I thought the sounds on the roof had come from last night.

That's when I saw them, the broken down plants and twigs. There was a wide finger of sand jutting into the boulders where something had laid down. The ground was disturbed all around and there still remained several small stones and a few larger rocks that, if molested, would easily have rumbled down onto the roof below. Could have been a coyote or deer. There were plenty of both around. No evidence of anything sinister.

The memory of the night haunted me while I stared down into the courtyard, the indescribable scent of her fresh in my mind. I stood there asking myself questions I was not prepared to address before returning to Buck and driving back to the Trails End.

CHAPTER 14

AUDREY'D BEEN CORRECT. They didn't charge me for another day when I checked out.

To tell you I was in a state of lugubrious turmoil would be to grossly understate what was going on inside me. My brain very nearly would not function. What I felt physically in my solar plexus was akin to the fear I'd had of being taken prisoner in Vietnam. It was that kind of dread, or craving for survival, I felt as I drove away from Divina. At a long distance back in my side view mirror, I tracked Jorge Olivera following behind me when I made the turn west onto Highway 152. As I headed up into Pacheco Pass I could see his black and white pull to the side of the road and stop. His brake lights told me he was spinning around, turning back.

I drove the two-lane windy road up into the Diablo Mountains. The tall wild grasses were still green. Sometimes this section of Highway 152 was called *blood alley* by the locals because of the head-on collisions common going over the Pass with or without the dense fog crawling up into it like some living thing. I'd seen fog so thick you could hold out your arm, your hand would disappear. That day was clear and beautiful and I thought only of her.

I'd acted the fool. I wanted nothing to do with Divina, California. Any reason to ever go near the place again had been erased by a horrific act I couldn't have stopped nor could I now do anything about. What had I been thinking to allow the kind of complication I now felt in my life?

From the moment she walked back toward me that morning we were jogging, something visceral took hold in me. What we had wasn't all physical and that was what I fought now. But what Audrey'd shared of herself with me last night would remain unforgettable the rest of my life.

So, besides what Vietnam did to me, and the depression I felt over what happened to Miranda, not to mention the turmoil I felt over the country I'd fought for ripping itself apart, I added the grief of leaving behind a girl I might really be able to love and who might be able to love me. That was a lot of shit to have bearing down on my unsteady mind.

I wanted the vision of her standing in front of me with her breasts peeking out from my shirt that morning to go away, vacate my brain, leave. And there was the sweet taste and perfume of her clinging to me still. I wanted it off of me and yet I never wanted to be free of it or have it go away. "Jesus-fucking-Christ, Charlie! What have you done?" I did what I could to console myself for letting this happen and drove on.

Around two in the afternoon I pulled into Casa de Fruita at the bottom of the west side of Pacheco Pass where Highway 152 splits and Highway 156 curves off toward Hollister.

The Zanger family fruit stand has stood there since World War II. My father had an Army buddy who lived in Salinas. When my folks drove over to visit, Casa de Fruita was always a stop. When I was a boy, it was a single wooden cart by the side of the road. Cherries.

All of this is to say, while I held onto deep resentment toward the town I grew up in, Casa de Fruita represented for me an oasis of childhood pleasure that followed me into adulthood. As much as I felt repelled by Divina, I felt rooted to Pacheco Pass and this place. Audrey confused and complicated the growing conflict in me over my place in the world I inhabited. I needed to belong someplace.

I pulled off and found a spot under a giant oak tree. Casa de Fruita was offering a lot more than a box of cherries by now. Hovering over the small bag of dried figs and mixed nuts I'd bought, I nibbled and brooded.

There seemed no way to erase her from my mind. Worse...I didn't want to. Neither could I erase Miranda DeCosta's memory. I considered the deep riffs in my psyche that drove me back to Divina in the first place and this new turbulence I felt. Hadn't I been explicitly taught tragedy awaits people when they don't confront those seminal events in a life that have the power to change us forever, leave us incomplete or perhaps to fill us with something extraordinary. Or maybe to live out the rest of life in a regretful existence? Another handful of nuts found my mouth.

When I wandered back among the colorful array of fruits and nuts and vegetables, I slung a straw shopping basket over one arm. I snatched mostly dried fruits and vegetables. But there was no way to avoid an assortment of candied nuts, three different kinds of fudge.

Walking toward Buck, I recalled how casually Audrey had accepted the beat up old truck without judgment. A smile coursed my lips while I shook my head and climbed back behind the wheel. "You're a fucking mental case, Caldwell," I told myself pulling out of Casa de Fruita and heading back over Pacheco Pass to more trouble than I'd bargained for.

****

107

The hour was near five o'clock straight up when I pulled up in front of her house. The garage door was open and the rear end of a white '68 Chevy Impala stuck out. I sat for a moment, took several deep breaths, collected my two bags of goodies before I slid from Buck's seat. I didn't slam the door just in case I changed my mind before getting to her front door and deciding to get the fuck out of there.

The giant doors at the front of the courtyard stood open as I imagined they did most of the time. I crept slowly toward the front of the house, believing I still had the option to change my mind and beat a retreat. It wouldn't have been the first time retreating might've been the smarter thing to do. I was still contemplating my decision when what would turn out to be the prettiest vision I could image besides her mother stepped out from a door on the opposite side of the courtyard behind me. She startled me when she spoke.

"You the creep made my mom cry?"

The little girl was a string bean; slender, straight up and down, tall, close to five feet. Her skin was the color of matte bronze. The hair was an absurdly thick profusion of jet-black curls. Not the tight, kinky type, but loose fluffy soft ringlets. They cascaded beyond her shoulders. Her eyes were azure and piercing. As much as all of that struck me, it was the confidence the child exuded that reached out and gripped me. There was exquisite assertiveness in her tiny mature voice.

I was so stunned I couldn't speak.

"So?" she insisted impatiently.

"You must be Rachel."

"Passion Flower," she shot back. "My mother misnamed me. She thinks it's Rachel. That was a mistake. She couldn't help it. Now she knows better and so do you. It's Passion Flower. So are you the creep?"

"Rachel, who—" Audrey stopped in her tracks as she came out the door to see who her daughter was talking to.

She had on a pair of threadbare short jeans frayed at the cutoffs and a white cotton blouse tied at the waist. It was obvious she wore no bra. Her hair was tied up in itself into a knot that dripped strands of chestnut wisps helter-skelter at the sides and front of her face. She was barefoot.

Rachel regarded her mother, then me. "Yeah, you're the one," she pronounced in disgust as she wheeled and went back inside. "It's Passion Flower," she chirped, annoyed as she slammed the door behind her.

Audrey looked to the closed door then to me. "I told you she was going on twenty. She's recently announced to me I gave her the wrong name. Supposed to have been Passion Flower…What are you doing here?"

"We need to talk."

"Why? You owe me nothing. You told me you were leaving. I had no right to expect anything else. I don't want you here. You get in that fucking truck of yours and go."

"Audrey, listen to me. Please. I did leave. Got all the way to Casa de Fruita. But I can't just go away like that."

"Why? You feel sorry for me? Guilty? Well don't. I fucked you! You didn't fuck me. I just let you go along for the ride."

"Stop it! Nobody fucked anybody." Audrey's words were harsh, but her demeanor didn't match. She was protecting herself. And why shouldn't she. We were both vulnerable and I understood that then.

We were silent for several seconds

"It was a pretty nice ride," I whispered.

Tears coursed her lovely cheeks, but she grinned. "You were pretty good, too. I loved you actually enjoyed going down on me as much as I enjoyed it."

"What can I say? Dessert. I couldn't resist."

"We can't talk like this," she whispered, walking toward me. "Rachel—Passion Flower—might hear us."

"Right." I looked toward the closed door. "Please, Audrey, come, listen to me." I took her by the hand and led her to the short front wall of the courtyard. We sat together quietly while I took a moment to collect my thoughts. Slowly I began to recite the preposterous idea I'd concocted driving back over Pacheco Pass. "So, look...I told you I wanted to take a shot at being a writer. There are some things about the murder of Miranda DeCosta that bother me." She turned her head away. "Please, hear me out. If you decide to give what I have in mind a go, I'll share the specifics with you. If not, it won't matter."

I waited for her to turn back. She crisscrossed her arms over her chest. "What?" The look on her face was not positive.

"Okay, so I don't have a lot of money. I received a good combat bonus when the Army let me go. Plus, I saved some of my pay while I was in Nam. Like I said, it isn't a lot."

"What are you getting at, Charlie? How much money you have or don't have doesn't matter to me. Is that what you think?"

"It might matter...if I asked you to rent your bungalow to me?"

She sat up, unfolded her arms and looked at me. "You mean like, rent it for you to live here?"

"For a while. If you think it could work? I could poke around the investigation behind what happened to Miranda. Maybe I could use what happened as the plot for a novel. It's a little out there. I know. But it would give us a chance to...give us a chance. Some time. Just to see."

"To see what, Charlie?"

"Jesus, Audrey, can't you see I feel the same way you feel?"

She didn't look at me. Her eyes remained focused straight ahead. "You mean that? Like, I don't want your pity or—"

"I mean it. And I'm not making any outlandish promises after one night of—"

"You were saying."

"You know what I mean."

"You don't have to rent the place, Charlie."

"Yes, I do. And we have to have some rules. I'm serious. You don't want my pity. I don't want your charity."

"It's not charity."

"Would be if you just let me live here."

We sat in contemplative silence for several moments.

"What kind of rules?" she asked.

"Well, for starters, we respect each other's privacy. If you decide to invite someone else to your home—"

"You mean like a guy?" She threw back her head and laughed then stopped abruptly. "Oh, I get it. Or you might want to have someone over, maybe?"

"That's not what I meant."

"Fine. Go ahead. Won't matter to me."

"Yes, it would, but that's not my point. Work with me here, will you, please? There's only one reason I'm here and I'm looking at it. If not to make this about us, I'd be driving down the road right this minute."

"You mean you want to find out if there could be an...*us*?"

"I think that's exactly what I would like to find out."

"And what about living in Divina? You know I can't leave here."

"For now."

"For at least another eight years."

"And you think that's a long time?"

"Isn't it?"

"Not if the *you and me* really turns out to be an *us*."

The smile that crossed her face gave me the hope I'd need to sustain me through this experiment. Audrey stood and smothered me with one of her long passionate kisses.

The front door of the house swung open and Rachel stepped out. "Does this mean I get to look in those bags he brought?" she shouted.

"Yes, Passion Flower," Audrey said. "And he'll be staying for dinner."

CHAPTER 15

THE TRANSITION FROM the contemplative stupor in which I was accustomed to spending much of my time to renter-secret boyfriend turned out not as simple as I'd envisioned. My idea of hours alone with Audrey...passionate lovemaking...proved unrealistic. What grew out of our new setup were two overheated adults, agonizing to find a way back to the unrestrained heat of that first encounter. Rachel—Passion Flower—was the factor I hadn't calculated, though obviously she would become our primary consideration. She sounded and acted mature, but she was just a young girl.

My shortsightedness was apparent from the moment we finished dinner. Audrey suggested she and Passion Flower get me settled into the bungalow. Everything between Audrey and me that had begun to feel relaxed suddenly felt awkward; that—we've crossed a bridge moment when something irrevocable has taken place. On the walk down the path, she apologized the place had been decorated for her ex-mother-in-law.

"Just make do for tonight," she said. "Tomorrow I'll make it more suitable for you."

"It'll be fine. I don't want you to go to a lot of trouble."

"It's no trouble for her," Rachel jumped in to assure me. "How long will you be visiting us?"

Audrey and I regarded each other.

"Sweetie," Audrey began, "Charlie isn't sure exactly how long he'll be staying."

"Daddy isn't going to like it," Rachel predicted.

Audrey stopped walking. She knelt in front of her daughter. "Charlie is a nice person, Rach—"

"Passion Flower!"

"Passion Flower." Audrey looked up at me briefly then back to her daughter. "And Charlie is our friend— yours and mine. It will be all right with Daddy because I say so. You understand what I mean?"

"No. He made you cry."

I listened, noting Rachel missed very little. She'd make me earn her friendship and trust.

"That was my fault, sweetie. Not Charlie's."

"You like him. It's obvious."

Audrey glanced down in contemplation. In a moment she raised her eyes to find me once more. Her attention shifted back to Rachel.

"Yes, Passion Flower. I like him. And I think you will too if you give him a chance."

"He has good taste in fudge. We'll see. Daddy's gonna be pissed."

"Rachel," Audrey started to object.

"Passion Flower," Rachel repeated, cutting her mother off. "He's pretty cute. Daddy *really* won't like that."

"I've warned you about your language."

"I'm only a child, Mother," Rachel argued. "I'm just repeating what I hear. You can't blame me for being impressionable. We gonna stand here forever?"

Audrey eyed me imploringly, then, "I—"

Rachel grinned and skipped on ahead of us.

Audrey closed her eyes, squeezed the bridge of her nose and exhaled a deep sigh. She shook her head and smiled up at me. "She's her mother's daughter. Come on." She took my hand.

Audrey's bungalow was a three-room cottage with a small bathroom and shower, a tiny kitchenette, which she voiced the hope I would not use much, and a spacious core. One end was bedroom, the opposite was living room-cum-make-it-into-whatever-your-needs-dictated. The area was startlingly generous, about thirty feet long by twenty wide with a queen bed on the end nearest the bathroom. Audrey fretted over how small it was. I thought bivouac, field tent with four cots, smelly balls and asses, one room shack in Mexico, eau de rotting fish parts a few feet away. She really had no idea.

The bed was covered with a pink duvet and piles of pillows in soft pastoral designs with matching towels hanging in the bathroom. The top of the dresser, the table the television sat on and the small end table with the lamp next to the chair were all covered in white crocheted doilies. The place reminded me of my grandmother's small apartment when I was a boy.

The end-wall in the living room space framed a large set of double French doors, which faced east and opened into a garden filled with zinnias, marigolds, trellised morning glory and rose bushes. There were two soft-cushioned club chairs nestled onto a smallish patio of flagstones with a short round wrought iron table between them. With the French doors thrown open, the place felt immense.

"I'll redecorate for you," Audrey promised.

"Not necessary," I said, sincerely pleased she would. "Sure didn't look this big from outside."

"Grandma, doesn't come and stay anymore anyway," Rachel added.

"It won't be any trouble. I've been meaning to do something different with the place. This gives me the perfect excuse."

"Besides, you make her all gushy," Rachel added.

I loved the precocious nature of this kid.

"Passion Flower, " Audrey beseeched.

I felt for her pain. Rachel was merciless—and perceptive.

****

The next couple of days went forward in a similar awkward cadence. We were all three adjusting to our new symbiotic existence. Between Audrey and me an uncomfortable reserve set up. Where there'd been an air of casual, playful interaction between us, there now existed a kind of formal caution. Intent had been stated between us and I think we both acknowledged and felt the responsibility of what that might imply for each of us.

Rachel on the other hand was having fun with her new situation. As soon as she was home from school she'd race down to my bungalow to see what I was doing. I learned quickly I needed to be mindful of this habit as she saw things in an informal light.

Happily for me, Audrey couldn't be dissuaded from the redecoration she'd promised. She dropped Rachel off at school on Monday and headed to Modesto to shop. I used the time to familiarize myself with the entirety of the place.

That first week was filled with adjustment. By Saturday the three of us were finding balance in our new relationships.

Rachel spent Saturday at a friend's house. Audrey and I went for a long run out on Farm Road Lane. These were our first moments entirely to ourselves since I'd spun Buck around and inched my way back over Pacheco Pass and into her life.

We were tentative. I was tentative. I wanted her so badly I ached. But I was also afraid of saying or doing the wrong thing, frightening her away, making her feel trapped or somehow obligated.

We stopped at the entrance to the courtyard. There were several moments of indecision for both of us. Uncertainty was palpable. Finally, as I'd become thankfully accustomed, Audrey took the lead. The assertive sassiness in her would remain one of her most endearing qualities with me.

"Come on," she said, heading toward the bungalow.

As we stepped through the French doors, she pulled her tank top up over her head and let it drop to the floor. Her medium breasts were beautiful. I'd only seen them in the subdued lighting of our first time together. The vision of her held me—paralyzed as if struck in the head. She stepped on the back of one heel and pulled her shoe off, then slipped out of the other, drawing her foot up behind her, pulling her footie off.

She looked up to see me watching her. "You gonna get in the shower?"

"Oh, yeah. I—"

"Have you never seen a naked woman?" She slid her jogging shorts over her hips, letting them drop to the floor.

I had no capacity to tell her how beautiful she was to me. I'd have been happy to stand there consuming her with my eyes forever.

She stepped out of her shorts, turned toward the bathroom. "Coming?" The roundness of her perfect naked butt left me gawking.

She had the water warm by the time I joined her. My male anatomy gave me away instantly. Audrey glanced down at me and smiled. "What's on *your* mind?" she teased lasciviously, running a soapy hand over me. She seemed to derive a good deal of pleasure from her ministrations so I stood and watched her touch every part of me, almost examine my maleness as she touched me gently everywhere. In a few moments she raised her eyes to mine and smiled. We spoke not a word.

I bent down and kissed her softly on the lips and pulled her warm, wet body to me. She pushed my manhood down, angling it to slide between her wet thighs while we kissed. Her mouth was as wet as our bodies, her lips as velvety soft as I remembered the inside of her to feel.

"Oh, how I've looked forward to this," she said running her hands over my shoulders, down my back, grabbing the cheeks of my butt and pulling me hard against her pelvis. "Tell me you want me, too, baby," she said.

"I couldn't hide it if I tried," I whispered, kissing her along her neck running my hands over her, squeezing the soft supple muscles of her bottom. I went back to her mouth and kissed her deep again, sliding my fingers into her from behind.

"Kiss my breasts, Charlie," she whimpered.

When I took her hard nipple into my mouth, I cupped her breast with my hand, bent her backward slightly and moved her under the warm water, letting it cascade over our joined bodies like the warmth of the emotions washing over our psyches.

Slowly she pushed me away from her, took me into her hand and stroked me several times again before she spun her back to me, bent from her waist and leaned with her hands against the shower stall.

The intention was clear and I needed no further invitation. I slid inside her from behind. She didn't seem as tight this time.

She threw her head backward, her wet hair slinging back across her shoulders and moaned huskily. "Take me, Charlie," she pleaded.

I held her hips in my hands, gliding deep into her and out, watching and listening to her cries of pleasure until I could delay no longer.

The water was running cold by the time we turned it off.

We were exhausted when we dropped onto my bed.

"I want you to do that to me every chance we get," she said, rolling on top of me.

"You inspire me," I confessed.

We kissed and caressed each other tenderly. Feathering the tips of my fingers over her shoulders, down the sinewy curves of her back to her coccyx, across the roundness of her soft bottom, gave her chills. Her body shuddered slightly.

"Oh my." She kissed me deep and tender. "I think you're inspired again." She took me inside her once more.

Late that afternoon I opened a bottle of wine and built a fire in the barbecue while she put dinner together in the kitchen.

When Rachel's friend's mother dropped her off, the woman lingered clumsily until Audrey finally offered her a glass of wine, which Geraldine accepted enthusiastically.

Audrey and I were aware Divina's rumor mill was working overtime by the end of our first week together. We'd been seen jogging out on Farm Road Lane. There was no missing the looks cast our way when we shopped for a few grocery items one afternoon.

Geraldine's curiosity at that moment was not unexpected. We'd have to let the nosey snooping run its course.

A few days earlier I'd caught sight of deputy Olivera shadowing me when I drove Buck down to fill his tank. The kid at DeMartino's filling station actually asked me if I was Audrey Romero's new boyfriend.

To that point, Olivera had kept his distance. I hoped he'd keep it that way, but once I began asking questions about the murder of Miranda DeCosta, I doubted he would.

CHAPTER 16

AUDREY AND I fell into a routine of running each morning after Rachel went off to school. Rachel seemed content and quite capable of getting herself out to catch the school bus. Nevertheless, we waited until she waived goodbye from her window seat before jogging down the hill.

We were finally beginning to relax with each other as my second week in residence began.

We left the town limits behind, jogging east early one morning. Audrey asked me about my plans to begin writing.

"New territory for me," I admitted, huffing along.

"I can't imagine where you start."

"Remember, I told you there were things bothering me about what happened to Miranda?"

Audrey bristled noticeably every time I mentioned Miranda's name. I needed to reassure her.

"Natalie Bettencourt...told me Miranda had confided to her...thought she was pregnant...Duke Matta's baby," I said.

"You're serious?" The revelation moved her.

I looked over my shoulder to her. "Serious."

"I've never heard a word...anything like that."

"You aren't alone. Nobody I've...spoken to seems aware of...that little bit of fact—*if* it's actually fact." Our heavy breathing had begun to affect our words but the conversation was important.

"How would you ever...find out...something like that was true?"

I wasn't certain about the answer to that question myself, but I had a few ideas. All of which I feared were sure to have negative effects on Audrey as well as me. There was an MO in Divina. If anyone became pissed off at me, Audrey would end up in the middle, guilt by association. The rumor mill was already churning with speculation about what was going on up in her house. Those were the mechanics of how it worked here and I felt certain it was going to get much worse.

"You have any idea...who Caputo's lawyer is?"

She grinned. "Remember Theo Azevedo?"

"Only recall he's...old attorney the Portuguese trust. Seen him...never met the man." I glanced over at her catching my breath. "Didn't even know...he was a real attorney. You're not telling me...that old relic...defending Caputo?"

Audrey huffed and spoke in short staccato bursts. "Careful, that...old relic...is one of my godfathers. Close...friend of my dad's. Promised my parents...he'd watch over me...day I was baptized."

"No disrespect...but that's exactly why...defending Caputo astonishes me. He was a crustacean...we were kids. Surprised he's...still alive."

"Hey!" Audrey objected. "Theo's a nice man. People trust him."

"Man's life on the line...capital murder case?" The revelation was preposterous to me.

When I figured we'd jogged about four miles, I made the turn to head back. Audrey settled into the tempo change before returning to the subject of Theo Azevedo.

121

"Theo might be...helluva lot tougher...than you think," she said.

"Not tough I was...thinking about."

We were both sucking air heavily by then.

"I mean...what kind of experience...can...this guy have doing wills and divorces or DUIs?" I hesitated a moment to catch my breath. "I don't know much...but I'd think Caputo would want...an experienced trial lawyer...working...to save his ass."

"Vinny's father...be calling the shots. Darryl's father...same way right up 'till...he died. How it works...our families. Old world."

What Audrey said was true. And the extension of that truth was at the core of their fear and bigotry and prejudices. They could call their mindset tradition or cultural ethos. In my book it amounted to fear and ignorance, resistance to anything different.

In fairness, it was no different in my family. We had our history, too. My people were just as guilty as any of clinging to the bullshit of legend that served neither them nor the kids they trained to be just like them. I was damn lucky I left all of it behind me. I was even luckier I landed among people who were thinkers with a social conscience and who were interested enough to encourage me to be a thinker as well.

"Theo graduated...some law school...New York," Audrey was saying.

"New York University?"

"Maybe...can't remember. His folks...poor immigrants. Spoke no English...like most of our families...they first get here.

"Dad ended up working...for the Mob. Driver...some bootleg operation. The old man...shot one night. Theo was a kid. According...to may father...some guys showed up...Theo's mom's house with...bag o' money. Took care o' both of them. Made sure...Theo went to college."

"After Theo graduated...law school...guy shows up...tells Theo, pack his bags...take his mother...don't come back. The mother had a cousin...living here."

"That a true story?"

Audrey pondered the question.

"Who knows? But...even if some of it's true...he might be a lot...smarter...than you think. Anyway...Theo's a nice man. I don't see...much of him...'cept at church. Mom talks to him once in a while."

"Maybe I should...go talk to him."

"Maybe..." Audrey agreed. "Tell him about...what Miranda told Natalie."

"Might be nothing. But I'll bet...nobody questioned Duke Matta...where he was or what he was doing the night...Miranda was killed."

Audrey abruptly stopped running and stared at me. "You saying you think...Duke killed Miranda?"

I stopped and faced her. "I'm saying...I'll bet nobody considered him...a suspect and no one asked...the questions."

"Holy...shit, Charlie!" Audrey bent at the waist, hands on her knees breathing heavily. Sweat dripped from the end of her nose. "You know...what you're saying?"

"Know exactly...what I'm saying." I was panting equally as hard and shining with sweat over my entire body. "And I know...I need to be damn careful...'bout who I say it to."

One thing was certain. Audrey was now able to talk about Miranda DeCosta without thinking my interest was motivated by some latent feeling I held for her.

"What are you going to do?" she asked, breathing some easier.

We began jogging again.

"Gonna introduce myself to Theo Azevedo for starters."

Thick Fog in Pacheco Pass

****

We cooled out walking the last quarter mile up the grade to Audrey's house. We kept walking down to what we were now politely calling, my place, stripped naked and climbed into the shower together.

I'd sought to simply put Audrey at ease talking about Miranda DeCosta. I'd gotten a good return on my effort. She'd become invested. We were partners. At least it had begun to feel that way. We were friends. That was a certainty. And if not quite in love just yet, it seemed we were headed in that direction. At minimum, we were in deep infatuation.

Cupping her bottom in my hands, I lifted her up. Audrey locked her long, smooth legs around my waist while we kissed and held each other until the water ran cold over our bodies and still the fire was not quelled. We fell into my bed and launched ourselves into each other again and again. I adored the way she caressed my hips and the sides of my body with the soft flesh of her inner thighs.

Though we both would've been happy to lie there all day, making love again and again, she finally drew herself up out of bed.

"I have things to do today." She stood fully naked in front of me. I loved the way she did that, not a self-conscious thought in her head. In fairness, anyone with a body like her's could afford to be like that. "And so do you," she reminded me, fishing out a pair of shorts and a fresh top from the drawer where she'd begun keeping a few items. She slipped into the shorts without putting on panties and wriggled them onto her hips, zipped up and pulled the top on braless.

Audrey smiled down at me still lazing in the sheets and crawled on top of me—reached down and gripped my manhood. I slid my hand up the leg of her shorts. My fingers slipped inside her. Her clitoris was as rigid as I was again.

"Get your ass out of that bed mister," she said playfully, removing my hand from her shorts and climbing off me. "You've got a story to write or had you forgotten that part?"

"You're a wicked woman, Audrey Romero."

She smiled sweetly at me, turned, picked up her jogging clothes before stepping to the door. "Good luck, Charlie."

I tossed the sheet back and lay totally nude on the bed, my intention standing prominently in obvious evidence.

"You cruel bastard." She smiled as she closed the door behind her.

CHAPTER 17

I SPENT THE remainder of that day making notes and organizing ideas. At least I had a notion how I might proceed to write the story of Miranda DeCosta's murder. What would come next, the prospect of how deeply I might get myself involved with people I'd rather avoid or, for that matter, the fabric of the town I wanted nothing to do with, didn't occur to me.

At four-thirty in the afternoon the long orange and black school bus pulled to a stop in front of Audrey's driveway. The accordion door retracted and Rachel jumped from the bottom step, hurling herself full stride. She ran past the main gate to her house and straight down to my place.

When I heard her coming, I set aside my yellow legal pad. "How was school?" I hugged her as she came bounding through the doors.

"Boring," she complained, wandering about my small sitting area, fingering items, taking everything in like a dry sponge. "What did you and mom do today?"

"Went for a jog this morning. Haven't seen her since."

"What's on this pad?"

"Notes."

"I'm probably gonna write my own book someday."
She skimmed my scribbled notes.

"You know, Passion Flower, I don't doubt that one
bit."

"Gotta go." She spun and raced out the French doors.

I'd begun leaving them wide open when I was
around. An open door was less awkward for everyone and
served to remind me Rachel could show up unannounced at
any time. Being around a kid, a young girl, was a new
experience. But Rachel was a great little human being.
There was no denying that. Smart as a whip with a sharp,
satirical sense of humor.

I followed her out. About a quarter of the way to the
main house she stopped, looked back and came running
back toward me. She stopped in front of me and hugged me
hard.

"What was that for?"

"Mom and I love you." Her face crinkled into a lovely
smile and she ran off.

I looked up to the house. Audrey watched out the
kitchen window. Our eyes met for several moments while
we watched her daughter gain the door.

For several days since moving in I hadn't been having
the nightmares or flashbacks that plagued me. I watched
Rachel dash through the door and hug her mother. Love, it
seemed, was a better image to hold in my head. Maybe I
was beginning to heal. At least I felt...more sound.

****

Theo Azevedo had a small office built off the side of
his residence. I pulled Buck to the curb in front of the place
and parked parallel. A large patch of lawn was split by a
cement walk that led to three wooden steps badly in need of
a coat of paint. The well-worn steps led up onto a large
wooden porch. The wood there was in only slightly better

condition. The house had a high gabled roof with clapboard siding and was painted white with dark green trim around the windows and doors. The front of the porch was edged with rose bushes in a profusion of red and orange and yellow and pink softball-sized blooms. At the left corner of the house stood a mulberry tree with a twenty-foot canopy shading the side of the home and office while its giant roots were destroying the foundation. The house was not fancy nor was what served as his office ostentatious in any way.

Audrey offered to call her godfather on my behalf, but I'd asked her not to. My intent was to keep her isolated from what I was about to initiate as long as possible.

There was a sign to the left of the entry door of the house with an arrow. It read: Law Office. I followed the arrow pointing to the end of the porch and opened the only door there.

The receptionist I encountered sitting at the desk was a middle-aged, morbidly obese woman. She either couldn't or refused to leave her seat.

"You need something?" she growled.

"Here to see Mr. Azevedo." I replied too much in kind.

"Got an appointment? I don't see no appointment here in my book." She glanced up at me. "Name?"

"Charlie Caldwell."

The grumpy matron maintained a blank look on her puffy face. "I'll see if he wants to talk to you."

The scene might have been funny if it wasn't so horribly pathetic. The beefy matron hit an intercom button on her phone and announced me to her boss while I stood listening and watching.

"I'll be out in a moment, Earline," Azevedo responded patiently.

"He'll be out in a minute," she repeated as if I hadn't been listening to the entire conversation. "Take a seat." She pointed to two straight back chairs against the wall of the tiny lobby.

I sat, as ordered. The gold shag carpet displayed a dirty footpath leading from the entrance door all the way under Azevedo's office door. So prominent was the wear pattern and soil I doubted it could be cleaned. The wood paneling buckled from age or poor installation in several spots. The place reeked of stale cigarette smoke while a filter tip burned away in the ashtray full of old butts atop the desk of the corpulent receptionist.

"Mind if I open the door?"

"Suit yourself," said *Miss Personality*, puffing on her cigarette like a steam engine.

Theo Azevedo's office door opened and he shuffled out into the lobby. Theo was big and droopy, made to look worse by his slouching posture. He stood roughly six-six on a hulking frame with a conspicuously large head and equally enormous ears, nose, hands and feet. According to Audrey, he had an even bigger heart. She claimed half his fees were received in eggs and vegetables, raw milk from struggling clients.

His clothes looked as though he'd just walked out of a steam bath. Even his arms hung a little too long, giving the impression they'd stretched along with the outdated suit jacket hanging from his dumpy frame like an oversized scarecrow. His jowls sagged at each side of his tired-looking face and the skin under his chin collected in folds. His hair, however, had not one gray strand showing, although it was sufficiently thin to see straight through to his shiny scalp. The bags under his large brown eyes dripped like a bloodhound's, displaying red irritation along the lower part of his eye socket. Theo was not a physically attractive man.

"Come in, Mr. Caldwell," he said in a deep bass voice. "Earline, hold my calls, please." He closed the door and pointed to a chair in front of his desk. "Are you the same Mr. Caldwell now living with my goddaughter?"

"I...I—"

"Come now, Mr. Caldwell," he followed up with a directness that stunned me. "Speak up."

"I don't live with Audrey, Mr. Azevedo. I'm renting her guesthouse."

"I see." He studied me carefully.

I don't rattle easy, but the man had immediately gained a psychological advantage over me. I didn't need to feel guilty, but I did.

"People talk. It's a small town." Clearly he intended to make me tacitly aware of the consequences of how I conducted myself in the eyes of his community.

"I'm renting her guesthouse," I repeated, recouping my composure.

He held me with an unnerving scrutiny. "How may I help you?"

"I wanted to talk to you about the murder of Miranda DeCosta."

"Oh?" His bushy eyebrows seemed to sweep upward to his hairline in surprise. "And how might that concern you, Mr. Caldwell?"

"Miranda and I were friends growing up. We were...close...in high school."

"I cannot discuss this case or my client with you. If that's why you're here, you're wasting your time and mine."

Audrey'd been more than correct about the old lawyer's toughness. He wasn't the least shy, nor did I suspect he could be easily intimidated.

"Like you said, people talk. I heard a rumor. And since I grew up here—let's just say, I don't have the greatest respect for how some things are done occasionally."

He didn't stop me so I went on.

130

"Like, I imagine from what I've heard, your client might as well get used to where he is because it sounds like he's already been convicted—by Sal DeCosta."

"What's your point, Mr. Caldwell?" There was no avuncular tone in his voice. He sounded tired and impatient.

He'd left me no option but directness. "Did you know Miranda thought she was pregnant with Duke Matta's baby?"

He flinched. I could see from his face what I'd just said was a revelation.

"I repeat, Mr. Caldwell," he said, recovering, "I'm not at liberty to discuss this case with you. And I think we both know there are people who would not take kindly to someone like you poking around where he doesn't have any business."

"Why I came to *you* with this. I thought you might be the only one in town who would be interested in that information."

"It's a rumor. What am I supposed to do with it?"

"Well, for starters, you might want to see if you could confirm it as a fact. Wouldn't that at least create a motive to murder for someone other than *your* client?"

Azevedo eyed me thoughtfully for a few moments, as though he was sizing me up. "You're either a gutsy young man or not very smart, Mr. Caldwell. Which is it?"

"Both," I admitted.

Azevedo smiled for the first time.

"Fair enough. Good answer. So, you think there might be something to this...rumor?"

He was giving me an invitation to discuss what was on my mind. "Duke and Miranda were an on and off item going back to high school. According to a friend, it was still going on even though Duke is now married." I gave him time to assimilate what I was inferring. "If that rumor is true...Duke's life was about to get messy. He might not have wanted to let that happen."

"I take your point."

"Something else you should know, Mr. Azevedo." I paused and looked directly at the man. "I've decided to write a novel based on this murder." Once more I saw surprise register in his caricatured face. "I can only imagine what's going to happen once I start asking questions around town."

"I'd be careful if I were you," he cautioned. "Important people will not take kindly to an invasion of what they consider their privacy."

"You mean Sal DeCosta." I was stating a fact, not asking a question.

"And others, perhaps," he replied evenly, settling back in his chair and folding his giant hands across his stomach.

"Duke Matta—"

"And Chief Mendoza and our DA, Grant Pederson. They all consider this case solved and closed. The trial will be a formality."

We were silent for a few moments and I contemplated the warning the old lawyer was giving me. For the first time in nearly two weeks, I flashed back to a dark jungle and muzzle flashes, gunfire coming from every direction. Men I knew, ate with, slept next to, were dropping around me. There was blood everywhere, body parts and the smell of cordite. Duke Matta, Prado Mendoza, this DA, Grant Pederson, even Sal DeCosta, none of them seemed overly threatening to me.

"I'll be alert to that possibility," I said.

"There's no *possibility* about it, Mr. Cald—"

"Any reason we can't use our first names?"

He unfolded his fingers, spread his hands slightly in a gesture I interpreted as ambivalence. "If that will make you feel more comfortable. What novels have you written, Charlie?"

"I haven't actually written a novel...yet."

"What *have* you written?"

I hated how this made me look. Every writer must have been faced, at some point, with a story being the first. This was going to be mine. Admitting I'd never actually written anything was the primary reason I never discussed my aspirations about writing. I tried to elevate my qualifications the best I could. "I work for *Past Present and Future Magazine.*"

"Ah. You write magazine articles."

"Yes. Sort of. It's complicated."

"Well, Charlie, are you a writer or just someone who wishes he was a writer?"

I was tired of being on the defensive. "Look, Theo, I worked for the magazine as a proofer before I went into the service. Now that I'm back, they've hired me as a writer. They're taking a chance on me. I'll be doing a couple of stories for them. We'll see how it works out.

"When I get my first assignment, I'll leave and go do my job. In the mean time, I'm going to begin writing the novel I told you I would. And I'm going to be asking the questions necessary to make sense of the story I intend to write."

Theo Azevedo remained stone-faced. I sure as hell would not have liked playing poker with him. He could have been dozing the way his eyes hooded. But he was mercurial in a way that let me know I'd underestimated him once more.

"You look physically capable of taking care of yourself, Charlie. How long were you in the service?"

"Couple of tours."

"You were in Vietnam?"

I shook my head, unwilling to go down that road.

"I see you're reticent to discuss that," Azevedo said, reading me accurately.

We sat in what, for me, was claustrophobic silence for several moments before he continued.

Suddenly, he leaned forward in his chair, placed his elbows on his desk. "All right then." His tone and demeanor changed abruptly like a cat that'd sat quietly waiting for an unsuspecting bird to come closer before it pounced. "Before you walked into my office this morning my client, frankly, didn't have a chance in hell regardless of his guilt or innocence," he said candidly and with more vigor than I believed him capable. "I'm not so sure this rumor of yours would change that. But I'm too old to be chasing around town attempting to find out who was fucking who."

"Who was fucking whom?" I said.

"What?"

"When the pronoun acts as the subject of the clause, you use *who*. When the pronoun is the object, you use *whom*. Who was fucking whom?"

Laughter erupted from his belly like thunder. A few moments passed before he was able to compose himself.

The intercom came on. "You all right in there, Theo?" the rotund receptionist's voice bleated through the phone speaker.

"Yes, yes, Earline. Everything's fine," he said into the intercom and clicked it back off.

He fixed his watery gaze on me once more. "I'm beginning to see what Audrey finds so interesting about you."

I wasn't quite sure what to make of the subject of that sentence, but his tone was friendly, obliquely complimentary, and it was implicitly clear he had a good sense of humor.

"Seems to me, Charlie, we are both about to stir the pot."

"Not sure I'm following you."

"We're both about to begin asking questions a lot of people are not going to like."

"We need to find a way to verify or debunk the pregnancy rumor," I said.

"When did this become a *we* arrangement?"

"I used the word euphemistically."

"Audrey's right. You use big words."

"You and Audrey have spoken about me?" That was the second thing he'd said that made me suspicious I'd been the subject of covert conversations.

The old lawyer ignored the probe. "If Miranda DeCosta was pregnant, it should've been stated in the autopsy." He slid a drawer open at the side of his desk and retrieved a manila folder. He sat quietly, ignoring me, leafing through pages—stopping to read here and there. "No hint of anything in this report." He looked up at me quizzically.

Suddenly, I was off balance. I'd been so sure I was onto something significant. "Why would Miranda have told her friend she was pregnant if she wasn't?"

"Perhaps she only *thought* she was pregnant. That happens. But unless you're accusing the ME's office of covering up the fact—"

"Is that a possibility?"

"Women frequently think they're preg—"

"No. I mean...could it have been covered up?"

"And why would they do something like that?"

I thought for a moment. "Sal DeCosta."

"That's a serious accusation, Charlie. Involves a lot of people and a very grave crime. It's called tampering with evidence, obstruction of justice. That's a severe offense. What would be the motivation?"

"DeCosta's reputation?"

"Clearly you don't think highly of Mr. DeCosta, but many people do, people in high places. I'd be very careful going down that path if I were you."

"So that's it? We just ignore what Miranda told her friend?"

"Something tells me no matter what I've said to you, you're going to pursue this."

I held his liquid gaze, but didn't reply.

His sad eyes remained locked to mine for several seconds. "Go ahead and begin asking questions, Charlie," he said finally. "You're a smart man. I can see that. Be thoughtful in how you proceed. I'll make a few discreet inquiries of my own. You discover something interesting, come and see me."

"You suggesting we work together?"

He took his time with the reply. "I'm suggesting you come to me if you stumble onto something interesting."

"What about you? What if you find out my information was more than just a rumor?"

"Lets take things one step at a time, shall we?"

Although Theo Azevedo had countered my suspicions with sobering argument, I could detect the glint of inquisitiveness in his manner. I'd posited questions he found intriguing. His client had nothing to lose and a good deal to gain by his asking the right questions. I felt confident I was not the only one about to make a few people uncomfortable. I figured any probing I did was certain to piss a lot of people off.

When Theo opened his door into the reception area, billows of cigarette smoke poured into the room like a rain cloud sucked right down to the ground.

"Good God, Earline," he complained. "How the hell can you breathe in here? Open the front door and keep it open if you're going to keep that up." In the nasty ashtray on her desk a freshly lit cigarette leaned against scorched stubs burning away. "And dump that damn ashtray!"

The foul brute of a woman fought her way to a standing position, grousing and complaining until she was upright. She rumbled across the wooden floor, which creaked and strained under the gargantuan load it bore. She heaved the contents of the ashtray, glowing embers included, into the wastebasket next to the door and shoved the door open all without one word. The toxic glare the vile woman cast toward her employer implied more than slight displeasure.

"Don't mind Earline," Theo explained. "She's perpetually miserable. Thinks the rest of us should be as well."

I watched the smoke curl up from the trash can where she'd dumped her ashtray, looked again at the dilapidated wooden structure of the office and knew she wouldn't make it the eight feet to the door to get out if a fire started as a result of her noxious behavior. "A Sad Tragedy" the newspaper article would read.

CHAPTER 18

THE MINUTE I stepped out of Theo Azevedo's office, I was greeted by the presence of Deputy Olivera. The miscreant half sat, half leaned on the front fender of his shiny black and white police car. He'd pulled up close behind Buck.

I crossed the porch and descended the steps.

Olivera was smoking one of his wooden-tipped Cheroots. "Plannin' on suin' somebody, trash?" he snarled as I approached Buck.

When I drew near, he slid around to the driver's side of the patrol car, putting solid metal between us. He pulled the cigar from his black mouth and spit toward my truck. All four of Buck's tires were flat.

My inclination was to go over the top of the hood of the patrol car and tear his head off. Instead, I kept my feet planted firmly on the sidewalk.

"You do this?" What had been trained into me took over as instinct. I assessed the prick...my situation.

"You gotta watch the vandals in the neighborhoods. Know what I mean, trash? Lotta property damage goin' around. Good thing I came along when I did. Might o' stole this piece of shit. On the other hand, maybe nobody but some dumb-fuck like you would want it.

"What are you doin' back in town? Thought I ran you out once already."

I moved the rest of the way across the sidewalk toward the rear of Buck. Stepping down from the curb I moved between Buck's back bumper and the hood of the patrol car.

Olivera opened the driver's door and climbed behind the wheel. "See you're shackin' up with that Romero bitch. She's got a reputation, that one. Seen the two o' you shagin' ass down the road like some kind of bullshit health fucks. Better be careful some drunk driver don't turn you into road kill." Olivera laughed derisively at his crude joke.

Calling Audrey a bitch were words I'd look forward to cramming down his spiteful throat sooner or later. The cowardly bastard had flattened the tires on Buck. But unless I was prepared to engage the punk, there was little I could do about it. It didn't look to me like this was the moment.

I walked to the driver's door of Buck and locked it. Never occurred to me that would be a necessity in Divina.

DeMartino's filling station was several blocks away at the south edge of town. The walk would allow me time to cool off, get my temper in check.

A few yards up the street Olivera pulled along side me as I walked. "Watchin' every move you make, trash. Step outta line once, your ass is mine."

I turned toward him and grinned. "Why not pull over and have a piece of my ass right here? No witnesses. Just you and me."

He hit the clutch and gunned his engine then popped it back in gear hard. The black and white jumped like a racehorse breaking from the gate, leaving a strip of burnt rubber stinking and smoking on the pavement. The tires of the patrol car squealed as he took the next corner dangerously fast and sped from view.

The kid at DeMartino's said it would be at least a couple of hours before he could help me. They had an old three-quarter ton Chevy with a compressor mounted on a flatbed. Just then the truck was in use out in some tomato field.

I told him where Buck was parked and he promised to go take care of it soon as the compressor was available.

From DeMartino's I walked up Main Street still pissed off at Olivera to the point of distraction. All I could do was try to shake it off.

It was past mid day when I walked into Souza's Market. I went to the cold box and clutched a Coke. Out front I found a shady spot on the top step at the corner of the building, sat down and leaned against the support post.

When I was a kid my buddies and I would steal empty deposit bottles from behind the store, then sell them back to old Mr. Souza, who was still alive then, for three cents each. The old man always gave us the money and the next time we went to swipe bottles, the same ones we'd stolen before had been replaced where we could easily get to them.

I'll never forget the day in later years, I must have been a sophomore in high school, when I realized Mr. Souza had known of my criminal activity all along, had abetted my ingenious scheme with the same bottles over and over again, making sure I could always get a bubble gum or a nickel Coke. There were some decent people in Divina. The Deputy Oliveras and Sal DeCostas didn't define the place. But I'd let them do just that.

A crack in my armor was beginning to widen. I thought I hated the fucking place. And I was pretty sure I did. Olivera and Sal DeCosta were reminders of just what fueled those feelings.

But there was also Audrey and Rachel, Natalie Bettencourt. Dorothy Ponder. And today, Theo Azevedo had turned out to be a pleasant surprise. The casual pleasantries around town over the last two weeks leached into my consciousness. Personal bitterness can be a highly debilitating force. That isn't to say I didn't believe I had justification for being bitter. But when you allow it to consume you, it can place a veil over your judgment that keeps you from seeing all there is instead of simply that which hurts and destroys a piece of you.

An older modeled green Chevy pulled to the curb and parked.

Natalie Bettencourt didn't realize it was me sitting on the steps. She fussed with her purse, checked her face in the visor mirror, brushed her bangs from her forehead and got out. I still thought of her as cute. Maybe that's how our minds preserve our lives for us.

When she stepped up onto the curb, she recognized me. "Hi, Charlie!" Sweet lilt to her voice.

I stood and walked toward her and we hugged.

"I heard you were still in town," she said.

"I'll bet you did."

She laughed softly. "You know how the gossip works."

The conversation turned awkward for a few moments. Finally Natalie couldn't contain her curiosity. "So's it true?"

"Is what true?"

"Come on, Charlie. This is me. Natalie. You and Audrey. You two together?"

"Depends on what you mean by *together*."

"Did you move in with her? That's what people are sayin'."

"Not exactly. I'm renting her guesthouse. Apparently that translates to shacked up together."

"You could do a lot worse," Natalie offered, a naughty smirk slipping from her lips. "I didn't know you two knew each other."

"We don't. We just accidently discovered we both liked jogging, got visiting about things. One thing led to another."

"Jogging? That's what you're calling it?" She was beating me up and enjoying herself. Her banter had a cozy feeling behind it.

"Jogging. Running. You know."

Natalie grinned. "I do know. Just never heard it called that."

"It isn't—"

"It ain't none of my business and it ain't nobody else's neither, Charlie." She touched my arm. "Hope it works out for ya. I gotta get movin'. Groceries, kid stuff. I hope I get to see ya again."

"Lets make a point of it. I'll ask Audrey."

"That would be fun."

"Natalie?" I looked both ways up the sidewalk and stepped closer to her. "I need to ask you about Miranda again."

"Axe me what, Charlie?"

"When you said she told you she thought she might be pregnant with Duke's baby," I looked around again, "how sure was she about that? I mean, was she unsure you think, just hoping maybe?"

"I don't think so. She told me she missed her period. Said she was feeling tired. That don't sound to me like hoping. And there was one more thing."

"What was that?"

"Her and Duke had a couple of arguments over it. When she told him her situation, he told her there was no way she could hang the kid on him. Everybody knew she was sleepin' around. Duke told her she was a whore and nobody was gonna take her word over his."

We were silent for several moments.

"He was always a sonofabitch," she said bitterly.

"Sounds like he still is."

142

"I gotta go, Charlie. Get in touch you and Audrey wanna get together." Natalie climbed the steps and disappeared inside the market.

I upended my Coke, drained the bottle, stepped inside and set the empty on the counter.

Outside, I stood contemplating the building up the street I knew housed Duke Matta's office. The squat two-story walk-up was flaking baby-blue paint like dandruff. His was the small office over the beauty parlor. Did I really want to do this? The thought was in my head.

I'd stopped thinking about my aggravation with Jorge Olivera and begun imagining confronting Duke with my suspicions. Theo Azevedo's words rung in my ears as I stepped from the curb to cross the street. I'd make it a friendly conversation. No point tipping my hand.

At the side of the blue building was a short staircase leading up. I climbed to the landing and walked to the end. Matta's was the corner office overlooking Main Street. The view out the front covered the main intersection of town. I could see everyone coming and going at Souza's Market, the bank and the post office. The balcony would've been an excellent vantage point for a sniper. Four-inch, white, stick-on lettering in the window read: *Accounting Services – Income Tax.*

The receptionist was high school age. "May I help you?" she asked, her squeaky voice high-pitched, mousy.

"I'd like to see Mr. Matta."

"He's playing golf this afternoon. May I tell him who was here to see him?" she asked, following the routine I was sure she'd practiced in a mirror.

"Charlie Caldwell. Just tell him Charlie Caldwell was here. I'll be back."

Too bad I'd missed him. I was in the right frame of mind.

****

When I strode up to Theo's office, he was standing out front on the sidewalk. The kid from DeMartino's filling station was just finishing airing up the third tire.

The kid glanced up at me from one knee holding the air hose and gauge onto the tube stem.

"Have her ready for you in a few minutes, Mr. Caldwell."

"Thanks." I realized I'd never asked the kid's name.

I stepped up onto the curb and walked to Theo.

"I didn't know this was yours until I heard Brian start his compressor and begin airing the tires. Came out to investigate. All four tires flat?"

"Deputy Olivera was waiting to greet me when I left you this morning."

"He did this?"

"If I'd been just a few minutes sooner leaving your office, I'd have caught him in the act."

"Why would he do such a thing?"

"Been harassing me since the first day he found out I was in town."

"He got some kind of grudge against you?"

"Punk syndrome. I've warned him twice now to leave me alone. He's beginning to push his luck."

"Hold your temper, Charlie. He isn't worth the trouble."

"I attempted to talk to Duke Matta," I told him.

"And?"

"Playing golf this afternoon. I missed him."

"That's it, Mr. Caldwell," Brian announced, stepping toward us. "Gonna be ten bucks for the service."

"Thanks," I said, going into my pocket. I pulled out a twenty.

"Sorry, no change," Brian said.

I turned to Theo. "Can't remember the last time I had change for a twenty."

"I'll follow you to the station, Brian."

"See you there." He headed back to his truck.

"Be careful, Charlie," Azevedo warned me once more. "You're already starting from a disadvantage. Don't give Olivera or anyone else a reason to take any action against you."

"Do what I can, Theo. But I'm getting tired of the abuse."

"Nice truck," Theo said sardonically. He grinned and turned to walk back to his office.

CHAPTER 19

A NOTE FROM Audrey slipped under my door greeted me when I returned home. She was picking Rachel up from school then having dinner with her mother.

After Peeling off my jeans, I kicked off my shoes and jumped into the shower.

I'd been scribbling notes for a couple of hours when hunger finally got the best of me. Nothing in my refrigerator sounded good.

I missed having dinner with Audrey and Rachel. Maybe I felt a bit shifted, lonely without them, the way you feel a vacuum of presence when you've had people around and suddenly they're gone. Cold silence. No movement.

Pizza from Tony's Hamburgers was a desperate measure. While I waited, I eyed Deputy Olivera cruise by twice. When it was ready I had them box it for me and took it home.

I'd polished off the pepperoni pizza and a half bottle of wine when I heard Audrey pull into her garage.

My clock said nine-o-five. I was in bed reading by then.

A half hour later there was a soft knock at my door. "It isn't locked," I said. Audrey opened the door and crept inside.

146

"You awake? Saw your light was on."

"Laying here reading. How was dinner?"

Audrey crossed the room and climbed next to me on top of the blanket. She nuzzled her nose into the crook of my neck and kissed the upper part of my chest gently. "I always enjoy helping my mom cook. 'Rach' did her homework. Mom and I gossiped. How 'bout you? How was your day?"

"Eventful. Went pretty well with Theo. Jorge Olivera let the air out of all four of my tires. Stopped at Duke Matta's office. Wasn't in. Almost forgot, ran into Natalie Bettencourt."

"Wait a minute. What the hell?" she said, rising up on her elbow to look at me. "Olivera let the air out of your tires. What did you do?"

"Walked to DeMartino's and had them go fill them back up."

"You should have called me to come get you."

"I used the time."

"How'd you know it was Olivera? You catch the prick?"

"He waited for me to come out of Azevedo's office so he could see my face and gloat."

"God, he's such slime," Audrey said, a look of disgust drifting across her face. "How's Natalie doing?" She worked her warm hand onto my bare stomach as she lay back down and snuggled into me again.

"She's fine. Suggested we all get together sometime."

"Fine with me if you'd like."

"We'll see. No rush."

"Smells like pizza in here. I should have made something for you and left it in your fridge." She slid her hand down to fondle me. "I think he missed me today." She teased my erection.

"*He* missed you and so did I." I pushed my book aside and lifted her face to kiss her.

Audrey ran her hand firmly down my shaft as though the action had no consequence while we talked. "We're an item around town," she said, cuddling closer to me.

"Apparently. Theo brought it up."

"So did my mom. My mother-in-law called her to complain."

"You have a problem there?"

"Not really," she stroked up and down on me slowly, almost absent mindedly, while we went on whispering to each other.

"You talk to Theo Azevedo about me?"

She slowed her occupation just slightly, but it was perceptible.

"Not directly. You asked me not to. But he called my mom and my mom called me. You know, all of them wanting to know what's going on." Her caressing was beginning to make me wet and sticky.

"What did you tell them?"

"The truth."

"And that is?"

"We're friends and you're renting the guesthouse for a while."

"How'd they receive that?"

"Cautioned me. Warnings. Rachel to think of—family concerns. There's no problem."

Audrey pushed the blanket back, slid down, took me into her mouth. The insides of her cheeks felt warm and soft. Her tongue traced every curve and ripple of me while she caressed and worked my testicles gently. She seemed to sense when I could hold back no longer and squeezed my stomach just as I tensed to let go. I ran my fingers through her hair, but she went on slowly and gently through my spasms.

When I'd exhausted myself, she went on touching me while she slid up to kiss me. "That was nice," she whispered between soft kisses.

148

"Didn't do much for you."

"Did plenty for me," she countered. "I'm gonna drop Rachel at school in the morning."

"Gonna miss our run?"

"I need to pick up a package I ordered over in Modesto. You be okay without me for the day?"

"No," I confessed.

"Good." She kissed me again. "I'll be home in time to get Rachel from school. I'll take something out of the freezer. We can do dinner on the grill." She finally let go of my flaccid man-part and crawled off the bed.

"Don't you want—"

"It was satisfying for me, too, Charlie."

Looking up at her standing beside my bed, I knew I loved her. But would it be enough to hold me? Could I get over the *Miranda effect*? Did I love her enough to stay with her in this town? As much as I loved her, there remained a jumble of conflict in my head.

I snatched my robe and scooted out of bed. "Let me walk you to the house."

"I know my way."

"I know." I pulled my robe together and knotted the belt. "I wish you could just crawl in with me."

"We can't do that, Charlie."

"I understand. Believe me, I understand." I put my arm around her shoulder and she slipped hers around my waist as we walked up the path to the main house. At the entry off the kitchen we stopped and kissed for several moments.

"Good grief you're hard again." She reached into my robe. Her hand felt warmer than normal holding me and sliding over my testicles. "We're gonna kill each other if we don't slow down soon."

"Of all the ways I can think of to go, making love to you would top the list."

She kissed me quick on the lips. "Go on. Go read."

A faint odor, like caramelized bourbon drifted on the night. "Smell that?" I lifted my nose to the air.

Audrey took a deep whiff. "No. What am I sniffing for?"

I wasn't sure what the scent was. Survival in the jungle taught me never to ignore my senses. You may not know what a thing is, but I learned to pay attention when something seemed out of place, like the faint odor of which I'd just caught a fleeting hint.

****

My run began early the next morning. There was no movement in the house, but I knew Audrey and Rachel had to be stirring.

Not until I crossed the railroad tracks at the east limit of town did the pong of cow shit assault me. It'd not occurred to me until then the foul odor didn't waft up to Audrey's house. There was a plus I could put in the *stay* column.

The oddly familiar fragrance from last night continued to puzzle me. I couldn't zero in on what it was. But I felt sure I'd encountered it before.

Audrey and Rachel were gone by the time I returned from my run. I jumped into the shower feeling cheated.

I poached an egg and made myself a cup of tea. While I ate I went over my notes.

Around nine-thirty I launched a search for the keys to Buck. My intention was to catch Duke Matta and satisfy the gnawing in my guts about Miranda being pregnant by the guy.

To be honest, I felt like a fraud. I wasn't at all certain the shift I was trying to make to dispassionate observer, inquiry without agenda, was without personal motive where Duke was concerned. There continued a deep sense of betrayal and resentment toward both he and Miranda. The memory of them—that day—assaulted how I thought of myself. That emotional damage had left an underpinning fear and insecurity in me about my manliness, even now, in spite of how things seemed at the moment with Audrey. I wanted to believe my focus on Duke was nothing more than objectivity. But in my belly, I wasn't positive about that.

I pulled in and parked in front of the unattractive blue building. Two older women were already inside the beauty parlor about the task of attempting to reverse the vagaries of age on their appearance. One sat beneath a device above her that looked like she was being sucked up by her head into a shiny chrome beehive. The other rested her head backward into a sink where her hair was being washed.

Taking the stairs two at a time, I climbed to the landing above and ambled toward Duke's office.

The prom queen was at her desk. She spun her typing chair around and stood, smiling. "Oh, Mr. Caldwell," she said, recognizing me. "You're back." The petite girl wasn't five feet tall.

"Caldwell!" came a booming voice from the inner office.

Duke Matta appeared in the open doorway wearing a blue print short sleeve sport shirt open at the top two buttons, a sparse crop of wiry chest hairs crawled up toward the gold-plated choker around his neck. He wore no belt with his gray spandex slacks. His loafers were black and scuffed. "Caldwell," he repeated, too enthusiastic—too familiar for our relationship. "Heard you were in town," he said, not necessarily friendly, but not antagonistic either. "Angie. This is the famous Charlie Caldwell. He was almost as big a football star as me," he said, a mocking sneer screwing across his face, his hazel eyes fixed on me.

"We met yesterday, Mr. Matta, when he stopped in to see you."

"Yeah, but did you know he was a football star from your very own high school?"

The young girl looked at him bewildered. She didn't have the slightest idea what her boss was getting at.

I'd caught up in size to Duke. He was slightly taller and denser now. The bulge of belly blubber in his spandex waistband publicized he'd gotten soft. But Duke still looked to be a powerful man.

In his senior year of high school he'd been a lean one hundred eighty pounder with a sculpted, almost hairless chest that drove the girls wild. In those days he wore his straight, thick jet-black hair trimmed impeccably around his ears and across the neck just above his collar. He parted it on one side and used a little Dixie Peach to slick it back. Now the hair was dry and razor-cut, long over his ears with bangs falling well onto his forehead. The shag at his nape hung past his collar. The total effect was a little like a mop planted neatly on his head.

When we shook hands, I was reminded by the time Duke was a freshman in high school he could palm a basketball. His hands were freakishly enormous. A football was child's play for him. He could heave the thing sixty yards in the air; deliver it to a moving target with pinpoint accuracy. His talent made the two of us a dangerous combination. I was fast enough to get to the ball. Or he could hit me in the flat and I'd outrun most defensive backs in our league. Mostly, we were unstoppable.

"Angie here answers the phone for me." He leered lasciviously at the tiny receptionist-in-training. "Gets a pay check and credits from her business class at school at the same time. Believe that?" He motioned me inside his office.

"Time for me to get back to class, Mr. Matta. Need me to do anything before I go?" Angie asked.

"Got it covered. Same time tomorrow. Right? Don't be late."

Turning to me, he said, "Kids! They want the job until it's time to show up. Have a seat." He pointed to a cushioned chair in front of his desk. As I settled myself, Duke shuffled behind his grey metal frame desk, dropped heavily into the swivel seat behind it and threw his feet up onto its corner. "Damn, Caldwell, you look good. Stayin' in shape, I see."

I shrugged.

"What the hell you doin' back around here?" Duke's words dripped with insincerity.

"Ten years. Long time. Got curious." Same story I'd told everyone else. That was what I'd stick to.

"Jesus, been that long?" He shook his head. "Seems like yesterday we were still in high school." He folded his hands together and rested his elbows on the arms of the high-backed chair allowing his long thick fingers to dangle just above his lap. I wondered if they weren't part of the fascination the girls had always seemed to have with him.

"Long enough for a lot of things to change," I said.

"Seen any of the guys?"

We might have been out along a canal bank with a six-pack of beer the way he carried on. If he'd recently committed a hideous crime, I couldn't read anything in his body language that would give it away. "Stopped by and saw Frankie DeCosta."

"Yeah...Frankie," he said derisively. "Fucker's set for life. Fix is in for him to take over that whole operation. You wouldn't believe the kind of dough that mercantile pulls down."

"Sal didn't save a top spot for Miranda?" I asked as innocently as I could manage.

"You heard about her?" Matta dropped his hands and looked down, flicking his two thumbnails together. The sadness he exhibited seemed authentic. The guy was confusing my expectations.

"I've heard," I admitted, observing every twitch, every facial manifestation, his breathing.

Nothing.

"Sal's gonna burn Vinny Caputo's ass, man." He dropped his feet off the desk forcefully and leaned forward. "I see him pretty regular. Sal, I mean. We play a little golf now and again. Talk about the old days." Duke had a fixed, wistful dullness in his eyes. "High school ain't had a team in any sport since we graduated. Sal lost interest once all of us were gone. Still calls us his kids, you know?"

Duke clung longingly to the glory days.

"I'm pretty sure Sal DeCosta doesn't refer to me as one of his kids," I countered.

"What the fuck you expect, man? You cost the guy twenty grand." Duke stood and glowered down at me. "You cost us that game, Caldwell. If you weren't such a pussy—"

"Grow up, Duke. Look around you. There's serious shit going on in the world. You're sitting around with your head up your ass, brooding over a fucking high school football game ten years passed?"

His face turned dark. "Fuckin' pussy!" He collapsed backward into his chair.

Life more than put the bullshit of the last football game I'd ever played into perspective. Only in a place like Divina could such insignificant history even be remembered. Here it would survive, festering like a boil needing to be lanced, lived and relived over one slobbery half-drunk retelling after another all the way into the dotage of the few participants who would never live more than fifty miles from the place until they would be planted unceremoniously two rows over from Miranda DeCosta.

For the first time in years, I allowed the memory of it to enter my consciousness.

We'd made it all the way to the end of the season without suffering a loss.

Jogging back to the huddle after the kick off, I didn't notice the middle linebacker coming up behind me. The forearm to the side of my helmet knocked me to the ground. It took a moment to shake the buzz. There was no call from the referees and our parents and school fans in the bleachers went crazy booing.

On every play it was a knee in the ribs, a thumb in the eye, one late hit from behind after the other and still no calls from the officials. Duke was taking a bad working over, too.

Just before the half, my helmet had been ripped off. Before I knew what was happening, I caught the gorilla linebacker's elbow square in the nose. My right nostril was collapsed and I couldn't breathe or see through the blood.

In the locker room, Doc Larson took a long-stick swab and pushed the cartilage inside my nose more or less back into place. I still have a slight twist in it as a souvenir. Then he used some chemical to cauterize it and stop the bleeding. Doc did what he could to patch me up enough to continue playing. He taped a metal bridge across my face to keep my nose from being smashed in again.

When the team came in at the half, Coach Davenport was cursing openly and threatening one of the officials. Coach DeGregorio had to restrain him. Sal DeCosta came in next. The ref, an attorney from a nearby community, took one look at him and slunk out.

I remember Davenport's words. "Caldwell, you gonna' be able to go?" Everyone turned to look at me. Black blood oozed onto my puffed upper lip. "I can go, Coach," I assured him. No one, including me, recognized the sounds I made as my voice.

The pounding continued in the third quarter. We tried to be alert after every play to make sure we didn't take a late hit. The huge middle linebacker walked up to me and spit bloody gunk on the front of my jersey. "You're dead, motherfucker!" He bounced the front of his helmet off mine, and his saliva sprayed inside into my eyes.

Early in the fourth quarter, while the officials untangled the pile of flesh, the ugly beast of a linebacker managed to stomp squarely on the back of the fingers of my right hand, breaking the middle two. Doc Larson soaked my hand in a bucket of ice water until it was numb, then pulled hard on each finger, aligning the bones. He splinted the two fingers together and bound them.

A roar went up from the opposite side of the field. I looked to the scoreboard to see it change; Jaguars 13 – Bulldogs 14.

Davenport turned to me. "What's it gonna be, Caldwell?" I didn't say anything to him. I slid my helmet on and tried to snap the strap.

Coach DeGregorio shouldered his way around Davenport and Doc Larson, grasped the strap and secured it over my chin. "Go do it, Champ." DeGregorio looked deep into my eyes.

Things grew steadily tenser as the quarter wore into its final minutes. The Bulldogs were stopping me from getting down field by outright tackling me at the line of scrimmage. The two-minute warning was issued.

The plan was to run three plays. Keep it on the ground. If we broke one loose, great. If not, we were to take every second allowed, running the clock down even if it included a call for delay of game. Duke was accurate from sixty yards. Five yards now would mean nothing and it might cause them to relax and think we'd given up.

On the final play, Duke warned us in the huddle there had better not be a single penalty. "Take the fucking pounding and don't raise a hand...for now!" he told us with a look that promised, on our own terms, out of sight of everyone, these miserable bastards would pay. "Caldwell, you *have* to break free downfield." Duke peered at me over his facemask from inside his helmet. "Under the goal posts."

I simply nodded.

The whistle sounded and the clock began ticking, 15 seconds, 14, 13. Matta went back. On the line they were biting, clawing, screaming. I slipped free. The side of my jersey was ripped by one desperate hand attempting to drag me to the ground. A split second was all I needed. 11, 10, 9...

Matta cocked his arm and let go with a perfect spiral. The stadium went silent. I had five steps on the closest defender. The ball floated gracefully, hanging there as if suspended by a wire. 5, 4, 3...

The nose of the ball began to drop. I sprinted hard, not looking back. I'd find it in the final seconds...2. I turned my head just as it struck me squarely in the facemask. The searing pain caused me to loose sight of it momentarily...1. The ball ricocheted up and in front of me. I dove. The scoreboard clock ticked to 0 while it bobbled in my slippery-bandaged fingers as my outstretched arms hit the ground. On impact the ball popped loose. My taped fingers simply would not yield a grip.

Most of my teammates were still on the ground or kneeling on one knee, watching me in the end zone. Duke stood alone, both hands on his hips. The anger on his face communicated to me from where he stood. He'd done his job. I'd failed.

The Bulldogs' middle linebacker jogged up to me, helmet in his hand, grinning. "You never had a chance, asshole," he said, and ran off laughing.

"What do you mean, I cost DeCosta twenty thousand dollars?" I asked Duke, returning to the moment.

"That's how much Sal bet on that game, Caldwell. Lot a people besides you got hurt when you dropped that ball. Sal, he don't forget things like that." Duke said this like he was surprised I hadn't known about the bets, the amount of money DeCosta had on the game. "And Sal ain't the only one."

I *hadn't* known about the bets. And now that I did, I had even greater contempt for Sal DeCosta...and Duke, too.

"You see, Caldwell. That's why you ended up such a loser," Matta said, now allowing his condescending attitude toward me to come through undisguised. "You never learned what, or maybe I should say, who, was really important."

"You're wrong, Duke," I assured him. "That's a truth I have learned. But I suppose if your financial well being is defined by Sal DeCosta, I guess you pretty much better be worried about how happy you keep him." I paused and grinned at him. "Of course, when you're your own person, the Sal DeCostas of this world end up being revealed for the lower life forms they really are."

Matta's face went red. "Who the fuck you think you are, Caldwell?" He jumped to his feet, coming around the corner of his desk.

I stood and braced myself. "I can tell you more accurately who I'm not, Duke." The grin on my face was daring him to make another move toward me.

He edged closer, calculating. For all Duke might have been, he was not afraid of anyone. We were toe to toe. The atmosphere between us was as combustible as a forest in drought with lightning strikes sparking all around. "Maybe you finally grew a pair of balls, Caldwell, but that don't cut shit with me. You watch your mouth around here or I might watch it for you."

"Watching my mouth, Duke, might be just the thing for you to do," I cautioned him. We stood nose to nose. There was a growing unsteadiness in his eyes. He was unsure, not of himself, but of me. "Calm down," I brushed his shoulder with mine as I pushed by him headed toward the open doorway. "Should watch your blood pressure."

"Get your ass out, Caldwell." He shook with rage. "And stay the fuck away from me."

"Be seeing you around, Duke," I turned toward the door. Just before I opened it, I spun back to face him. He stood in the doorway of his inner office. "By the way," I said, "were you still friends with Miranda?"

"What business is that of yours?"

"You think Vinny Caputo really killed her?"

"Everybody knows he did. What's *your* problem?"

"No problem. Heard she might have been pregnant. Wondered if you might know anything about that."

The color drained from his face. "Ho—how would I know anything like that?" he asked, trying desperately to control himself.

I eyed him evenly for several moments. "Don't guess you would." He'd just revealed he knew full well it was true and he was the unknown guy involved. "Just thought you might know something." I decided to keep what I'd figured out to myself for the moment.

"Don't know a thing," he lied again, his face completely ashen. "I'm married, you know."

"I've heard." I closed the door behind me.

There was no further doubt in my mind Duke Matta should, at the very minimum, be a prime suspect in the murder of Miranda DeCosta. But body language isn't evidence. It would take a good deal more than my suspicion to haul Duke Matta into the center of the investigation.

CHAPTER 20

ACROSS THE STREET at Souza's Market I bought a small baguette, a half bottle of Zinfandel and a hunk of cheese. I returned to Buck and drove to the city park. My legal pad sat next to me on a shaded bench while I commenced to tidbit lunch, stopping to scribble notes as thoughts came into my head.

Writer was a difficult title for me to call myself, but I'd actually begun the business of becoming just that. Though I was pretending to the label, it was an awkward fit. When I read books it seemed so simple the way authors would just start with a sentence and before you were even aware of it, you were in the midst of a story. That turned out not to be such an easy thing to do. My discarded notes attested to how many starts and stops I'd made over the last several days.

A glint of color that didn't belong, movement in a tall cottonwood tree at the far edge of the park caught my attention. My visual recon revealed no parked cars about. All quiet. As far as I could tell, I was alone.

There—clearly—movement high up in the branches. The disturbance of leaves was too far away to hear anything. I worked my way toward the disorder.

A shrill buzz from insects filled the park accompanied by the occasional ripple of leaves, as a hint of breeze played through the upper branches. White noise to me. I'd heard that sound so often growing up it didn't register. The buzzing was just there at times, particularly as early spring came on. By the time the blistering heat of summer arrived, it could be heard everywhere, all the time.

A dinosaur-scaly trunk supported the limbs I'd targeted. The cottonwoods had been around long before there was a park. There were lots of other, more recent plantings, along the streets around the park. But in the midst of them were the venerable cottonwoods. The ancient trees were huge with sprawling canopies; dense branches running out from heavy trunks with prehistoric looking bark.

The upper branches of the interior of the tree were thick and concealed the form. But my eyes and senses were confirmed. I was not alone.

"Hello," I shouted.

Jeff Ponder searched as if my voice had fallen from the branches or the sky itself.

"Down here," I shouted again.

He looked around, disoriented or puzzled or both. Who knew? Eventually he homed in and studied me for several moments. Without warning, he laughed. The sounds Jeff made weren't exactly a laugh, but that was his intent. I was reasonably certain about that.

"Heh, heh, heh," the sounds came. Guttural sounds. "Caldwell," he proclaimed, as though he was pleased to find me there looking up at him. "'Ole Caldwell. Heh, heh!"

We might have been having a long conversation, the way he bounded into his stream of consciousness. "Ever seen a seventeen-year cicada, Caldwell?"

The question was the same he'd asked when I spotted him in the tree at the high school, weeks earlier.

161

Jeff didn't wait for a reply. "There's one thousand five-hundred kinds of cicadas. Locust!" He paused. "'Ole Caldwell...heh, heh," A hand shot out, closed down swiftly onto the limb he was perched on. Drawing his cupped fingers slowly against the limb he captured another specimen. "Don't make fun of me, do you, Caldwell?" He examined the frustrated insect closely. "Black and green harvest fly," Jeff announced, holding up the fat bug by its minuscule legs while it buzzed in vain trying to escape.

He captured two more while I watched. There must have been more on his mind than the search for the seventeen-year cicada. "People are mean to me, Caldwell." Another poor cicada trying to mind its own business was nabbed and held horrifyingly close to Jeff's madcap eyes. "Don't like it—don't like it—don't like it! Mean!" He pronounced the words like a refrain in a song. "People over there," Jeff went on, pointing, "treat me real mean."

Across the street where Jeff pointed was the two-story building where Miranda had lived.

"Treat me real mean over there," he repeated.

Then he went silent once more.

"Good 'ole Caldwell." Another insect fell victim.

Jeff didn't speak again. He'd apparently moved on to a different place. Most likely there was no outside world there. But I thought I understood his struggle. His truncated world was destined to always be under attack from people who would not be content simply to let what was be.

****

The garage door was up when I pulled into Audrey's driveway. I glanced at my watch. She must have picked Rachel up from school and come straight home.

No one came running out to greet me. That was unusual, but I *was* beginning to be old news. Maybe that was inevitable. The truth was, when I'd said to Audrey I wanted to give us a chance to see if there could be an us, this was the time I was most interested in; when the shine of the new relationship began to burnish, become a thing with less glow, but maintained a sense of durability, I hoped.

When I walked into the bungalow Audrey and Rachel were bent over my desk tinkering.

They looked up at me, a pair of conspiratorial smiles. The combination of the two beauties together was striking. "What's this?" I asked.

"Mom bought you a present." Rachel kept no secrets.

"A present?" I edged across the room.

"Just something we thought you should have," Audrey said.

As I drew near, Rachel jumped aside to reveal a new IBM Selectric auto correct typewriter sitting on the desk.

I froze, staring at the new olive green machine.

"Say something, Charlie!" Rachel insisted.

But I didn't know what to say.

"You okay, Charlie?" Audrey asked softly, taking my hand.

"Yes." I moved my eyes from the new machine to meet Audrey's smiling face. She was pleased with herself.

Rachel studied us closely.

"This had to cost you a fortune," I said.

"But do you like it?" Audrey asked.

"How could I not like something like this?" I reached out to touch the typewriter for the first time.

"It didn't cost a fortune." Audrey slipped an arm across my shoulders as I bent to run my fingers over the keys. I hardly touched them and the type ball fired, placing a "k" on the sheet of white paper they'd rolled into it.

Instinctively I jerked my hand away. Audrey jumped in to rescue me. "It's all right, Charlie, look." She placed an index finger on the "x" and held it down. The typewriter rata-tat-tatted a row of "x" across the page. The speed seemed impossible.

"I've never used an electric typewriter," I confessed. "They had a few at *Past, Present & Future,* but people like me weren't allowed to use them. I don't even know *how* to type," I looked up at Audrey once more.

"You'll learn," she predicted. "You needed it, Charlie. You're going to be a great writer and you need it."

Rachel walked over by her mother's side and wrapped her arm around her waist.

Audrey draped an arm over her daughter's shoulder. "You'll learn to type," She beamed with pleasure over the gift they—she—had surprised me with.

I hugged them both for a long time standing there in front of the fancy green machine.

Not one ounce of shine had worn off our relationship. And in that moment at least, I wasn't much concerned about some Duke Matta-like character coming along to sweep Audrey and Rachel away from me.

CHAPTER 21

MY ASSERTATION I didn't know how to type hadn't been one hundred percent accurate. There was the typing course in high school. While I worked at the bank and at *Past, Present & Future Magazine* I had, from time to time, found myself in front of an electric typewriter. How to hover my fingers in the correct position over the keys...I knew the basics, understood the theory of memorizing where the letters were and training my brain to send the impulses to depress the correct key without thinking or looking at my hands.

While we breezed along on our daily run the next morning I told Audrey about all the things it would do.

"I take it you like it?" She grinned at me.

"I love it!" I reached over, took her hand and pulled her up slowly to a stop. We were both dripping. Our heaving, sweaty stomachs slid against each other when I folded her into my arms and kissed her long and deep and passionately. Taking her face between my hands, I held it inches from mine. "I love you," I said softly.

"Careful, soldier." She smiled demurely. "You could break a girl's heart with that kind of talk."

"I don't plan on breaking any hearts, Audrey."

We kissed again.

"Come on." She looked down at the front of my jogging shorts. "You need more exercise, big boy."

It was unnecessary, but I followed her eyes. "Dessert later?"

Audrey shook her head, jogged off. I caught up to her.

"What do you plan to do about that conversation with Duke yesterday?" she asked me.

"Nothing, immediately. Gonna confront Sal DeCosta. See if I can figure out what he really knows about things."

"Think that's smart? You need to be careful with Sal. He's got a lot more influence than you think."

"That's exactly what I do think."

"Not following you."

"Miranda was pregnant with Duke's child. There's not a doubt in my mind now. No way Duke could've covered up that fact. The only person with any reason and the juice to pull that off—"

"Sal DeCosta," Audrey finished for me.

"Bingo!"

We made the turn for home.

"If you're right," Audrey sucked air and went on, "Sal isn't going to like the fact you've figured it out."

She paused and looked over her shoulder. "And he isn't going to be happy at the prospect of having you bring it out into the open. You have to be careful, Charlie. You should talk to Theo."

"I will. Soon as I've had a little visit with Sal. For what it's worth, I know that's when the fireworks are likely to begin."

"Be careful," she cautioned me again.

The instant we were back inside the bungalow, shoes flew off with laces still tied. Pedi-socks were pulled off with running shorts bunched around our feet. We fought to hold our balance while we staggered toward each other. The salty taste and feel of her sweaty body naked against me, her wet hair clinging to my face and shoulders, set my

166

body to quivering. Animal desire is what I felt. I didn't want to just make love to her. I wanted to consume her, touch every curve of her, lick the small of her back, her round smooth ass, kiss every inch of her, rub my face on her, take her from behind, pull out of her and take her clitoris into my mouth, suck the folds of her pink flesh over my tongue again and again. The intoxicating scent of her was utterly identifiable as only her...Audrey. I couldn't go deep enough inside her. And I couldn't stay inside her long enough to satiate myself.

In the shower we took turns washing each other gently. I soaped her beautiful breasts, played her nipples hard. Then she hugged me from behind, rubbing her slippery, mushing breasts into my back and her soft warm tummy on my ass while she soaped and stroked my hard-on and balls.

"You like that, baby?" she whispered, her lips playing against the soft flesh of my back while she worked.

My hands slid behind me, up the insides of her thighs, spread her open and put my fingers inside her. I rubbed across her firm clitoris while she stroked me gently then harder and faster, slow again—my balls ever so softly.

The shower hadn't been enough for us. Audrey sat on the side of the bed and took me into her mouth, stroked me while she played her tongue over the head of my penis until I could barely breath. I leaned her back onto her elbows, took one beautiful ankle in my hand, held her slender tanned leg high in the air and let her watch while I drove deep into her over and over until we both went to a place from which there was no return.

And then we grew quiet—still. We lay side by side naked, spent, holding hands; our glazed eyes fixed in a near hypnotic trance to nowhere.

"I didn't know I could do that," I confessed.

"How many times did you come?"

"Not sure," I said. "You?"

"Lost count." She sounded dazed. "I didn't know sex could be like that."

"Me neither."

****

The secretary kept me on hold a long time. Eventually, Frankie DeCosta came on the line.

"Charlie?" I heard the dread in his voice. "Glad to hear from you." That was an out and out lie. "What can I do for you?"

"I need to speak to Sal," I told him, getting straight to the point.

"What makes you think Uncle Sal would want to talk to you?"

"Cut the bullshit, Frankie. I'm not asking permi—"

"Who the fuck you think you're talkin' to?" the unmistakable voice of Sal DeCosta broke in.

"Hello, Sal," I said.

"The fuck you want?"

"We need to talk."

"I don't have one fucking thing I need to talk to you about."

"Not exactly true." I confess, it was more than slightly gratifying talking to the man in this manner, knowing in the end he'd have no choice but to listen to me. "It's about Miranda—what happened to Miranda."

"What happened to Miranda ain't any o' your fuckin' business. Keep your nose out of it."

"I'm making it my business, Sal."

"You motherfuckin' low-life piece o' shit! You fuck with me, you're gonna find your ass in jail where you belong."

"I hope not. I hope not." Though my heart went out to this guy for the loss of his daughter, I'd had enough.

"Miranda was pregnant when she died and I know who the father was."

The phone went silent. I heard heavy seething on the other end of the line. "You're goin' too far you two-bit fuck." The words were squeezed from his thorax; a measured threat.

"Your choice," I said. "You want to talk to me or sit there threatening me?"

A phone was slammed down.

"Not very smart, Charlie," Frankie said over the line he listened in on. "Hold on a minute."

The phone went quiet.

Several silent moments elapsed before Frankie came back on the line. "My office. One hour—and don't be late," he said.

"An hour."

I went over my notes, reviewed in my memory the conversation with Theo Azevedo. The confrontation I'd had with Matta played in my head.

Maybe I was making a lot about nothing, but somebody concealed Miranda DeCosta's pregnancy. That was clear to me. There wasn't a word about her pregnancy mentioned in any part of the investigation thus far. Even to Azevedo, the defense attorney, it was a revelation. Because of this omitted detail, Duke Matta got a free pass. Only three people would've been affected by that pregnancy. Miranda obviously was no longer affected by anything. That left Matta and DeCosta.

Matta would've had no way of burying Miranda's situation.

Sal, on the other hand, knew his daughter was pregnant. But he didn't know who the father was. More and more it was looking like only three people knew the answer to the question of paternity: Duke Matta, Natalie Bettencourt and of late, yours truly. Natalie was oblivious to the significance of what she knew. Sal would've been just as hard on Matta as he was on Caputo or anyone else for that matter had he known. Conclusion: DeCosta didn't know.

Frankie's office, exactly one hour later, smelled thick of cigarette smoke, no air freshener this time. Frankie was seated behind his desk, puffing away nervously on a Marlboro. Sal stood and paced the room like a caged animal.

Sal looked disproportionately older than I expected to find him. He would've been in his late sixties. He still sported a full head of black wavy hair atop his bowling ball of a head and bloated face. The eyes were sunken and dark in their sockets with heavy bags beneath. His gut began at his chest and rolled outward like the puffed up breast of a fat rooster about to crow. Sal was a short, foul little man with the power to destroy or create people's lives in the bigoted little fiefdom he held sway over.

Easy to see how a man like that believes his invincibility.

"You ain't been around here in years and suddenly you show up claimin' you know stuff nobody else knows about my daughter," he said.

I let the tirade continue. Better he get the acrimony off his chest.

"I oughtta call Mendoza right now and have your ass thrown in jail."

"How did you do it, Sal?" I asked evenly.

"How'd I do what?"

"How did you cover up the fact Miranda was pregnant?"

He spun around and faced me. His fierce glare was venomous. Frankie looked sheepish while his uncle walked to the desk, grabbed the pack of Marlboros, rooted one out and stuck it between his fleshy lips. Frankie jumped to his feet with a lighter. Sal dragged hard, making the tip of the cigarette glow bright orange. "I don't know what the fuck you're talkin' about."

"I think you do. What you didn't count on was anyone else finding out about it. And since Miranda had obviously not confided to you, you have no idea who the father was, because if you did, somebody besides Vinny Caputo would be on the hot seat.

"I know you, Sal." He held me with a watery gaze resting somewhere between contempt and dismay. "You figured with Miranda gone," I gave him a beat to absorb the gravity of my words, before I went on, "there'd be no way to find out the prick who got her pregnant. The only people hurt by it coming out would be you and your family." Frankie looked to his uncle puzzled.

"How'm I doing?" I asked him.

No answer. Just a glare promising my indolent days in Divina were about to end.

"Pregnancy would've shown up in the autopsy," I said. "Since it didn't, it's a safe bet you paid somebody over in Merced to leave it out of the report."

"How the fuck you know what is or what ain't in that autopsy? You're makin' a serious accusation, Caldwell. I'd be damn careful with that, I was you."

"No accusation, Sal." I got up from my chair and walked to him. I towered above the man, standing in front of him, looking down into his beady eyes. "This is a *private* conversation. I'm accusing you of nothing. Just being straight with you about what I think I know. Goes no further...for now."

"I could make you disappear, Caldwell," Sal threatened.

"Uncle Sal!" Frankie shouted, jumping to his feet, coming out from behind his desk. "You pissed my uncle off, Caldwell. And I'm a witness you did it on purpose. You were trying to get him to say something like that."

I eyed Frankie for several seconds. "Family fruit falls close to the tree, Frankie. How does it feel to be a nobody?"

I turned my gaze back to Sal.

"You said you know who the father was," Sal said defiantly.

"Is he telling the truth, Uncle Sal?" Frankie asked, a look of confusion coursing his face.

"Keep out of it, Frankie. Well?" he demanded, turning back to me.

"Not so quick, Sal. Not only am I not going off making half cocked accusations about you, neither am I going to accuse somebody else in this mess without satisfying myself I'm right all the way around. But I promise you I am going to get to the bottom of it and when I do—"

"When you do, what?" Sal cut me off.

"When I do, I'll go to the proper authorities with what I know."

"You're lookin' at the proper authority, Caldwell."

I turned my back on the man who controlled so much of my life in my youth, a man who had the power to make or destroy me and he turned his back on me when he could have stepped up. He knew I'd given him everything I had to give as a kid and it wasn't enough. *Not good enough*, he'd declared.

I opened the office door, turned back slowly to face him. "Not anymore. Not for me anyway." I let my countenance serve notice on Sal DeCosta any power he might have once held over me was gone.

It was midafternoon when I left the DeCosta Mercantile. I climbed behind the wheel of Buck and drove to Theo Azevedo's office.

"Over to Merced," the foul receptionist, Earline told me. "Don't know what time he'll be back."

"Make sure you leave a message or tell him I must see him tomorrow...please."

Earline gave me an exasperated sigh as though what I'd asked was a major inconvenience to her. "I'll tell him," she agreed reluctantly. "He has an appointment in the morning. Be here at eleven." She scribbled my name into her appointment book.

"Thank you," I said. "I'll be here."

****

Rachel came charging through the open French doors of the bungalow, out of breath and full of exuberance.

"Whatcha doin, Charlie?" she gasped.

I spun from my desk where I was hunkered over my typewriter. "Hey, Passion Flower! How was school?"

"Still boring. What's that?" She pointed to the paper in the typewriter.

"Converting all of my notes to a manuscript. Know what a manuscript is?"

"Course I do! You think I'm a dumb kid or what?"

That was Rachel. Audrey was completely accurate about her precocious daughter; now twelve going on twenty or older.

"Sorry," I said. "Of course, you would know. Well, I've started converting my notes into a story."

"So this is your novel?"

"Will be."

"Can I read it?"

"That will be between you and your mom. But I'd prefer you not read it until I'm finished."

"Why?"

"Mostly because it really isn't much yet. I know how intelligent you are and I don't want to be embarrassed."

"You made that up so I can't read it."

I laughed quietly and reached out to her. "Give me a hug! Let's go see what's for dinner."

Rachel was a loving, smart kid. Nothing got by her. But she was not a petulant young girl. She reluctantly accepted she wasn't an adult.

CHAPTER 22

THEO LOOKED HAGGARD, as though he carried the weight of the world. And I suppose, in a sense, he did for the people who depended on him to see them through their troubles.

There could be little doubt about the burden he carried for the Caputo family. Personally, I had little interest in Vinny Caputo. But that wasn't the case for Theo. He knew Vinny's parents. Hard working immigrant people who grubbed for every cent they earned. All they wanted for their kid was a better opportunity and start in life than they had. And now they were faced with an unimaginable nightmare. The abusive slob of a human Vinny turned out to be landed him in this mess. If there would be salvation for them, it'd come through Theo Azevedo. Understandably, he felt the weight of the world on his shoulders.

"Matta almost vomited when I asked if he knew anything about Miranda being pregnant." I reported.

"Say anything incriminating?"

"Played dumb, but it was obvious. It's true. He's the one all right. I'm sure of it. Miranda *was* pregnant, with *his* child."

"Not good enough, Charlie," Theo said. "We need to prove it."

"I got a bit closer to that, too."

"Enlighten me," Theo said.

"Paid a visit to Sal DeCosta."

Theo was perceptibly disturbed by that revelation. "You should have consulted me before doing that, Mr. Caldwell. Sal DeCosta is an influential man."

"Understood. But if everybody treats him with kid gloves, allows him to continue to ride above the law, play by different rules than everyone else, we're never going to break through."

Theo was unconvinced about my direct approach with Sal. "How did it go? Did he tell you anything?"

"As much as told me he knew she was pregnant."

"Hear-say again," Theo pronounced, frustrated.

"He also told me he could make me disappear if he wanted to—or have Mendoza throw me in jail."

"Be very careful, Charlie. He could do both." Theo leaned forward onto his elbows and spoke down into the top of his desk. "Doesn't matter about right or wrong, legal or illegal. He has power here." He looked up at me. "He could make your life very difficult—Audrey's, too."

Audrey being persecuted by anything I might be up to was not something I was willing to accept. She was already a victim of the rumor mill. That was a given. But I'd never allow DeCosta or anyone else to take direct action against her to get at me.

Smoldering silence leached into me at Theo's caution. The guys I'd fought with in that jungle in Vietnam paid the ultimate price. I made it back. They didn't. I understood all too well someone else could be hurt while I might survive.

Across his desk, the old lawyer scrutinized me. Reflected in his face was the graveness I felt. "I'm nobody, Theo," I croaked in a near whisper, rage rising up in me like bile. "I don't give a fuck who in this town doesn't like me or what I'm doing. One thing happens to Audrey or Rachel, there will be no path to safety for whomever I hold responsible for that. Understood?"

He said nothing in response. For the first time I saw Theo rattled. The man saw in me the inescapable retribution that would rain down if Audrey were threatened in any way.

I brought my emotions back in check. "What did you find at the ME's office?"

Theo continued to measure me. "I don't know the ME personally," he finally said. "But I know the families of a couple of his assistants. I stopped in to visit with one of the women for whose parents I did some estate planning recently. She was very appreciative."

"Learn anything?"

"Asked her what she thought the odds were something like a pregnancy being missed in an autopsy involving rape."

"And?"

"And she asked me not to do anything for the moment. Said she knew the girl who prepared the report. ME and an assistant perform the autopsies and dictate a report. The notes get transcribed by one of two secretaries specially trained to prepare the formal document, the copy Pederson and I see. My friend admitted signatures in routine cases can get a little...perfunctory."

"Meaning?"

"I'm guessing she was telling me reports don't always get reread before they're signed and released."

"And if a minor detail was left out of a *routine* report, it might go unnoticed."

"Why don't we wait to see what my friend finds out?" Theo suggested.

"What's my role in all of this?"

"How do you mean? Thought you were writing a novel?"

"I am," I said. "But you know about Duke. DeCosta knows I know about the pregnancy. You've got someone looking into the autopsy report. I'd say I've stirred things up a good bit for you. Not sure I'm in any position to do much more."

Theo thought for a moment. "As you say, Charlie, you've stirred things up. Would you like to see this through?"

"I intend to do just that," I said, not understanding what Theo was getting at. "I'm going to work on writing my novel, developing a good relationship with your goddaughter and Rachel, sit back and wait for you to blow this investigation into what it should have been in the first place."

"Not what I meant." He reached into a drawer and drew out a file. "I meant, would you be interested in becoming my assistant on this case?" He slid the Caputo file across the desk in front of me.

I looked down at the manila folder.

Theo sat back in his chair, held me evenly in his soggy gaze. "I'd be quite surprised if you were allowed to disengage so easily, Charlie," he conjectured. "You've frontally challenged, and no doubt angered, people who aren't likely to just let it go. Why don't we make positive use of what you've started?"

"I don't follow you. I'm not engaged in anything."

"You and I know that," Theo explained. "But the players in this don't. You've gone right at two key participants who, up to now, were invisible. I'm guessing you'll be hearing from them before this is over."

If I understood Theo, what he was telling me was if Duke or Sal got dragged into the middle of the investigation, they'd hold me responsible. "They don't scare me. What are they going to do?"

"Officially? Nothing."

"Unofficially?"

"I have no idea. But human nature being what it is...one could imagine. At least if you were my assistant you could argue some legal rights in any confrontation with them."

"I have no credentials for being your assistant, Theo."

"Leave that to me. I can hire whomever I want and assign certain tasks. If you're my assistant, that means you're acting on my instructions when you ask questions."

"Think I get your drift."

"Do you?"

"I think so. You're providing cover for me."

"No, Charlie. I'm asking you to help me prove reasonable doubt for Vinny Caputo. I mean, I want you to act as a real assistant. As such, you'd have full access to the investigative files, interviews with all the witnesses. Everything the prosecution and the defense know about what happened. Probably useful information in the writing of a novel, I should think."

"You'd do that?"

He didn't answer my question. Instead, he asked me, "You love Audrey?"

"I do. But I'm not sure what that translates to for now. I've told you what happens should anyone bother Audrey or Rachel. And I mean that without reservation."

He held my attention for a few moments then began shuffling papers on his desk. "Treat her well, Charlie," he said in a tired voice. "It hasn't been easy for her."

I didn't attempt to involve myself in that line of conversation with Theo. Audrey and I were doing fine with our relationship in my view.

I stood, proffered my hand. "No way to know if what I brought you changes anything. But I admit, I'm more suspicious than ever this investigation was not conducted correctly."

"In the next day or so I want you to take the time to read everything in this file," Theo said, pulling the folder back. "Let me know when you have time. You can take it into my house next door. Quiet and private in there. You can spread things out on my kitchen table."

"I'll arrange to get on it immediately...boss?" I shook the giant hand of Theo Azevedo. "What do you want me to call you?"

"Call me Theo in private. Call me Mr. Azevedo in public, as I will use your name when referring to you."

****

When I pulled in to Audrey's driveway I had to pull around a black Ford pickup I'd never seen there before. But Audrey had lots of friends. I'd made it a point to keep a low profile any time she had company, unless it was inescapable.

I gathered my notes from the seat and began to slide out of Buck. Heavy, swift foot-drops pounding behind me were coming down the path from the house.

Audrey's ex-husband, Darryl, was scrambling toward me with purpose. She was close behind, a worried look screwing across her face while she barked at him to leave. "You better not touch him," she threatened him, referring, I was sure, to me.

Darryl'd been two years ahead of me in high school, class of `60. I didn't know the guy but I recognized him instantly. Him all right, coming right at me like a bull.

He pulled up in front of me and I braced myself. The guy was shorter than me, but he was stout; neither fat nor soft. If we tangled, he'd be formidable.

I found the black pupils of his eyes and bore into his psyche. "Back off," I ordered restively.

His bluster hadn't produced the response he needed.

I turned and set my notes back on Buck's front seat keeping Darryl in my peripheral vision, just in case he decided to take a cheap shot at me.

"I hear you're fuckin' my wife," he shouted into my face, jutting his jaw dangerously out in front of him. It made a perfect target.

"Far as I know, she isn't your wife."

I saw Audrey's mouth drop open. She drew both hands up over it, covered her face, all but her eyes.

"That mean what I hear is true?"

"That means whether I am or not, it's none of your business."

"Well I'm making it my business. I provide this house. My daughter lives here. I say who can be here."

Audrey jumped in. "That's bullshit and you know it, Darryl."

"Shut your fucking mouth, whore," Darryl barked. He swung back toward me.

My elbow caught his broad jaw just as he was half turned, feeling it disconnect at the back of his face. To his credit, he didn't scream. There was an audible thud as he landed full-weight on his back on the hard earth of the driveway.

"Oh, God!" Audrey cried.

She started to rush to him. I said nothing, but pointed to her. She understood I intended she stay back.

Darryl rolled to his side, holding his face. There was a small trickle of blood dripping from the corner of his mouth.

"Your jaw's broken," I told him, standing close, but not over the top of him.

Darryl got to his knees and I extended my hand. He stared at it momentarily before grabbing on while I pulled him to his feet.

"Never talk to her like that again," I said. "She isn't your wife any longer."

He wouldn't learn for a few hours it would be all but impossible for him to speak and be understood for the next eight weeks while his jaw was wired in place and all he could move would be his lips. He'd be shedding a few pounds on his liquid diet.

Audrey was crying openly. The incident scared the hell out of her.

I turned back to Darryl, on guard against any sudden attack, but relaxed. There was no intention of provoking the guy. "Look, this could have been much worse," I said. "Do yourself a favor. When you come here, which I have no doubt you have every right to do, understand that any abuse of Audrey is going to get you hurt. We're all lucky Rachel wasn't here to see this."

Darryl glared at me.

"I get it, Darryl," I said. "You hate me as much as you've ever hated anyone. That's as good a relationship as any between us for now. I treat both your daughter and Audrey with respect. You should follow my example."

I felt hatred ooze from him along with the trickle of blood at the corner of his mouth. "Go on. You'll need the emergency room at St. Kathryn's in Modesto to set your jaw. By the time you get there, you're going to be in a lot more pain than you're experiencing now."

I put my hand out to shake, but Darryl was not a man of honor. The odds were I'd get into it with the sullen prick again sooner or later.

"When Rachel asks, tell her you got kicked by a cow. Audrey and I will keep what happened between us."

Darryl drove away before I folded Audrey into my arms. She was sobbing. "I'm sorry," I said.

"*I'm* sorry, Charlie. He just showed up and he was so angry. He wouldn't listen to anything I tried to say. He was so belligerent wanting to hurt someone. Then when I saw you hit him so hard...I...I."

"I'm sorry that happened. But half measures in a situation like that will only get you hurt, Audrey. That could have gotten us both hurt. Better Darryl thinks hard about ever bothering either of us again."

"I'm not sure he's smart enough to just leave it alone. You watch yourself around him."

I kissed her softly on the cheek. "I'll be careful."

She wiped her eyes, getting herself under control. "I've never seen anyone hit like that. Where'd you learn that?"

"Just something I picked up."

"I thought his head was coming off," she went on. "I heard the bone in his face pop. Jesus, Charlie."

"That'll be in his head any time he thinks about me. He'll be less likely to threaten either of us."

"I still wouldn't bet on it."

"Then he's likely to get hurt again."

Audrey looked up into my eyes for several moments. "There's a coldness in you that scares the hell out of me," she said.

"Never gonna allow you or Rachel to be in any danger, Audrey." I averted my eyes because I didn't want her to continue with this line of discussion.

"But it's there, isn't it? You aren't afraid of anyone or anything. I can see it."

I ignored her probe taking her hand walking her back to the house.

"Theo made me a proposition today." I searched the refrigerator and pulled out a bottle of white wine.

Audrey's hand still shook when she pulled down two glasses. "What kind of proposition?"

"Wants me to be his assistant on the Caputo case."

"Is that a joke?"

"Why would you say that?" She stung my pride the way she said it.

"I didn't mean that in any reference to you, Charlie. Just—assistant to Theo in the middle of this mess? I mean...I don't get it. Thought you were writing a novel?"

"I am." We clinked glasses and I told her about my conversation with Theo and what we were on to.

"You know I believe in you, Charlie," she said. "If this is what you want, I'm behind you."

"But?"

"Well, I sort of thought you would be here most days...writing." She seemed confused.

"And I will be. You'll get Rachel off to school. We'll have our morning run—and shower." I grinned at her.

She swatted me gently, raised an eyebrow, took another sip of the cool lemon colored wine. "Promise me you'll be extra careful. Duke and Sal DeCosta are good friends."

"Until Sal finds out Duke was the father of Miranda's baby," I pointed out.

"I wouldn't want to be Duke when Sal finds out."

"Duke won't want to be Duke," I replied.

****

Dinner was perfunctory that evening. Rachel sensed the edgy dissonance between us. Underneath the aura of normalcy she attempted to convey, Audrey was still shaken by what happened.

It was not business as usual for me either. I'd spent so much time trying to reconcile myself to surviving my men, I never considered the other things I'd carried back home with me from that jungle: namely the ability to kill a man quickly and efficiently with my bare hands.

This is a reflex, an instantaneous response to a perceived threat. My reactions function counterintuitive to my personality just as being a soldier on the battlefield went against who I am. But survival is instinctual, isn't it? When it comes down to it, we all want to survive. In spite of the constant guilt I fought over surviving, I was good at it.

CHAPTER 23

OVER THE NEXT few days things seemed to normalize. I phoned Theo, explained what happened. "Give me a couple days to settle Audrey down, will you?" He hadn't said much, accepted my decision to change gears.

Audrey and I stuck to our routine most days. We didn't make love like the end of the world was imminent every morning, but it was close. We were drawing closer to each other. More than knowing it, I sensed us. Contentment, trust was taking hold.

She came and went while I worked transcribing my notes into a typed manuscript, which, in itself, became more comfortable. Typing proved an intuitive skill for me, though I continued my habit of making notes and scribbling ideas longhand. With the written word, there was no distraction between the process of thought and the mechanics of writing it. Tending the keyboard I still hadn't totally mastered proved a hindrance.

As to my living arrangement, I felt at ease shifting back and forth between the main house and the bungalow. But a realization came to me about the agreement Audrey and I had fallen into: we craved each other...in part because, though we were together, there were also several degrees of separation between us. When we were able to share our moments, they were special. We could never afford to waste them with pettiness. I didn't want that freshness between us to ever go away.

On a humorous note, Audrey was right. Some days it did feel as if we didn't slow down the sex going on between us, we were going to kill ourselves. And yet, neither of us could stop. We couldn't get enough of each other and I didn't want that to change. I became convinced what worked between us was in no small part due to our living arrangement, although we talked often about how nice it would be to crawl into bed together every night. Most couples think that's what they want. I thought it was what I wanted. But if you want something exceptional, maybe the relationship itself has to remain unique.

However Audrey conveyed it to me, I understood it to my core; no *Duke Matta*-like character, or anyone else, would move in to replace me in her heart. I believed her loyalty to me with all I was. I was moving beyond simply being *in love* with Audrey to *loving* the woman. And I loved Rachel, too.

A few days later Theo called.

"Your vacation is over," he said. "We have work to do."

Though I had been to Theo's office several times, Earline-the-chimney was no less surly toward me.

Theo stepped to his door, gave the rotund ogre a dirty look and invited me in, closing the door behind us.

"No one would give her a job," he said, shuffling around his desk.

"Why do you? She seems to hate you and your clients."

"She's been abused about her weight her entire life. Feels the world hates *her*. Her behavior is a defense. She needs this job." He sat down. "Received a call from my friend in the ME's office."

That brought me to attention. "What did she find out?"

"Something I haven't yet decided how I'll handle."

"And what is that?"

He fidgeted a bit before disclosing what he'd learned. "Sal DeCosta went to a young woman." He glanced at a note pad. "Mary Louise Parker, one of the transcribers in the ME's office. According to my friend, Sal found out she needed financial help. He convinced her it wouldn't matter to the investigation his daughter was pregnant. She was murdered. Newspapers would pick it up, destroy Miranda's memory, damage her reputation and his family's, too. He promised her if she managed to get the report and accidentally make a typing error, he'd take care of her money troubles."

"And why is that revelation so difficult for you to decide how to handle?"

"Charlie, it won't be Sal DeCosta who gets hurt in this. Other people's lives are going to be impacted, too."

"Well, what about the life of your client? He could rot in jail the rest of his life because Sal DeCosta didn't want anyone to know the truth about his daughter. And maybe, just maybe, somebody else had something to do with this."

"You don't need to remind me of my duty to my client," Theo said, looking up at me.

"Sorry, I didn't mean any disrespect."

"None taken."

"So what do we do?"

"If I take this to the DA, a foolish young woman is going to lose her job and maybe go to jail." He spun sideways in his chair, crossed his ankles out in front. "Sal DeCosta on the other hand." He gestured his hands wide apart. "Makes some calls, pulls in a few IOUs from the right people, receives a private admonishment not to do such things and goes on unscathed; life as usual."

"The wealthy have their privileges," I mused.

"And you should remember that well, Charlie. That's why I would have preferred you talked with me before you confronted Sal DeCosta with what you know."

"What do we do now? You just going to ignore this because the guy's rich?"

Theo smiled wryly. "Not quite. But think deeper. This *only* helps my client if we could show someone else had motive and opportunity to commit the murder Caputo's charged with. Potentially, *you've* uncovered such a person."

"Matta," I said.

"Yes, Mr. Matta. But before we ascribe to him these allegations and ruin his marriage, perhaps his life, should we not consider an investigation of our own to determine whether there's truth in any of this?"

"I don't get you, Theo. Who cares whether it's true or not? A lie was perpetrated that left your client standing out by himself as the sole suspect. You put what we know before the DA now and it seems to me they might just have to let Caputo go."

"And if what we know turns out to be anecdotal to what really happened?"

I didn't have an answer to that.

"They rearrest Mr. Caputo, refile the charges," Theo continued, "and we're right back where we started."

Theo's line of reasoning seemed crazy, frankly. But I was beginning to see canniness in the old lawyer that gave me pause to consider his ideas more closely.

"What do you want me to do?"

"You never confided to me the source of your information about the pregnancy. Who is this person? You positive he or she was in a position to know for certain Miranda was pregnant."

"Natalie Bettencourt," I revealed without hesitation. "She was Miranda's best friend. Miranda told her directly she thought she was pregnant. Duke Matta was the father."

"Now that, Charlie, is credible evidence. Still hearsay, but credible enough to make a lot of noise over. See how this works?"

Theo remained stone-faced. "She'd have to be willing to testify under oath. Your witness, Charlie. That's your new assignment." He began clearing papers from his desk.

"New assignment?" I asked.

"Your first is a complete review of this file." He handed me the manila folder containing the Caputo investigation. "And I suggest you get started on it right now. Your experience as a reader for that magazine you worked for is what I require in an assistant."

I looked up at him.

He grinned.

"I told you to let me worry about that."

"I can spend the rest of the day on it," I promised him. "What about Natalie? What do you want me to do with her?"

"She's comfortable with you. Explain to her how important her testimony could become. And *do not*," he emphasized, "under any circumstance reveal anything we've discussed here today."

"I won't, but what's the big deal?"

"Should things take a turn and we need her to testify to what she knew, I don't want to taint her testimony in any way, Charlie. Right now she has no agenda because she doesn't think any of what she knows will matter. She was Miranda's best friend. If she thinks Matta or even Sal DeCosta did anything to damage her best friend's memory, her motives for testifying could become suspect. DeCosta and the prosecutor would go after her very hard."

"You're a complicated man, Theo."

"One more thing—"

"What's that?"

"Don't reveal your source. Keep this between you and me. Sal or Duke get ahold of her, she could get hurt."

"What about you? What's your next move?"

"I'm going to invite Mr. DeCosta to my office for a private visit."

"You think that's smart...tip your hand like that?"

"I'm one of the few people in this town totally immune to Sal DeCosta. The way to serve my client is to prove he didn't kill Miranda. Sal DeCosta needs to stay on the sideline from here out."

****

By midafternoon I'd gone through the Caputo file. To call what had been performed an investigation was a joke. What was being called the investigation happened about as I suspected. *Vinny* was his own worst enemy. When the cops dragged him from his bed still asleep and half drunk the morning Miranda's body was discovered, he started off openly incriminating himself with one stupid statement after another.

He sounded vindictive and remorseless over the interactions between he and Miranda for more than two months leading up to the murder. Everything that came out of his mouth made his situation worse, but Vinny wasn't smart enough to shut up. He just kept talking. When his typed statement was placed before him, he signed it without hesitation, admitting to all manner of provocation and motive for killing Miranda. In this backwater town, nobody worried about rights of the accused. The irony of what one of those basic rights was called was not lost on me, but I doubted these local cops even knew what the *Miranda Warning* was. These were kangaroo cops, not trained professionals. There was nothing in the report showing clearly Caputo'd ever received those rights. I'd bring this important detail up with Theo.

Caputo's performance the night of the murder in front of witnesses at The Sweet Shop sealed his fate. As far as investigators, namely the Chief of Police, Prado Mendoza, and district attorney, Grant Pederson were concerned, Caputo all but confessed to the murder. The state cops pulled out of the investigation. The bit about being too drunk to remember getting home and into his bed was a little too convenient to be believable. In any case, if true, that would only alter the charge from premeditated murder to some lesser degree, which was where Theo was with the DA when I showed up with the new information.

By the time I'd finished scouring the investigation details, Theo was with a client so I left the Caputo file with Earline and drove to the city park. I'd come to relish an hour or so outside under the trees collecting my thoughts and condensing my notes.

The presence of Jeff Ponder crawling around the upper limbs of the giant cottonwoods was becoming a common encounter. We spoke frequently. He seemed in a time warp where I was concerned, as if in his mind we just went on being kids. And I was one who didn't torment him. There were days it seemed he actually waited, hoping to talk to me, if only briefly.

That afternoon he was at the far edge of the park across from the apartments where Miranda had lived. There's little doubt he was completely aware of my presence, though we had no conversation that day.

Deputy Olivera drove past twice, gunning his engine each time while mouthing the words, "Fuck you," at me before squealing his tires and driving away. No matter how I ignored the punk, he seemed always close by.

CHAPTER 24

TWO DAYS WENT by before Natalie Bettencourt could meet me. We spoke by phone and I tried to make our get-together sound as innocuous as possible.

My park bench became as good a place as any to hold court. Public as it was, it was quite private.

"So what's so important?" Natalie wanted to know right off.

I eyed her for a moment, considering my tack. "I'm working for Theo Azevedo."

That appeared to puzzle rather than shock her. "What's that got to do with me?"

"Maybe nothing. Maybe something. You told me Miranda told you she thought she was pregnant with Duke Matta's baby."

"That's right. What Miranda told me. 'Duke finally did what he's been tryin' to do to me since high school...pretty sure I'm pregnant with his kid.' I think those were almost her exact words."

"And you also told me Duke was not happy about it. Wanted her to get rid of the baby."

"That's what Miranda said."

Natalie was sticking to the original story she'd told, no added embellishments, no speculation. Obviously she couldn't see the significance in what she told me. There was nothing to be gained changing her thinking.

"Would you have any objection to testifying to what Miranda told you?" I watched her facial expression change as she considered my question. She was confused.

"Why? What difference would it make?"

"Don't know it would make any difference, Nat," I lied. "Just that I told Mr. Azevedo about our conversation and he wondered if you'd be willing to tell your story in court if he wanted you to."

"I won't do nothin' to save that pig Caputo," she declared emphatically.

"If it was to soften public opinion toward Miranda?"

"I'd do anything for her. You know that."

"That'd be the only reason I'd ask you to tell what you know, Natalie. You know how I felt about her, too."

She nodded. "I know, Charlie." Her tone was apologetic. "If that's what this is all about, you can count on me. I loved Miranda. You know that. I don't like how people talk about her." Natalie made the sign of the cross. "Don't see how me sayin' she told me she was pregnant with Duke's baby makes her look any better. But if *you* tell me it does, you can count on me to help."

"Might help, Nat. It just might help a lot."

"I don't know why, but I trust you," she said. "I know you got a good heart, Charlie. You need me to tell what Miranda said, you got it."

"Would you not mention to anyone we had this conversation?"

"What's the big secret?"

"No secret. Just the less Miranda gets talked about until this is all over, the better."

"Can't argue with that," she agreed. "Pisses me off how some people talk about her."

"We have an agreement?"

Natalie looked me in the eyes. "I wish she would 'o treated you better, Charlie. You would 'o been so perfect for her." She paused and looked across the park to the apartment complex where Miranda had lived. "Just never could get Duke out of her system."

When I got home I called Theo. We were making progress, but the wheels were grinding slowly. Sal DeCosta put off meeting with him another day.

Transcribing notes wasn't working for me, couldn't concentrate. All I could think about was Audrey. Finally I gave in to wanderlust and ambled up to the house.

She was on the business end of a large shaggy dust mop, running it across the tile floors. The scraping sound of the chair I'd pushed under the table caught her attention.

"Hey!" She smiled over her shoulder at me.

Her hair was haphazardly tied into an unruly knot on top of her head. An expediently quick do she often used without any apparent thought. I'd grown to love the way it cascaded in strands here and there around her face, down the nape of her fine neck. She wore cut-off jeans and a sleeveless white blouse tied at her bellybutton. I'd started calling it her uniform. I knew from experience there wasn't anything underneath.

"What?" She stood still as a deer in the headlights, watching me watching her. "Why aren't you working?"

"Couldn't concentrate," I admitted.

She spun the head of the shaggy mop and pushed the dust-bunnies back toward the kitchen. The handle hung up on the corner next to the pantry when she set it aside.

"Everything all right?" She shuffled up to me.

"Sure. Just one of those days." I folded her into my arms and kissed her softly on the lips. "Having trouble focusing that's all."

"Sorry I'm a little sweaty."

"One of my favorite flavors." I licked the tip of her nose. "Let's go for a drive."

"Just like that? It's the middle of the afternoon."

"You have any pressing engagements?"

"You're serious," she said, standing back, a quirky grin playing on her lips.

"Grab a bottle of wine, couple of glasses. Let's drive up Pacheco Pass Crossroad, find a shady spot, dangle our feet off Buck's tailgate..."

"You have it bad," she declared.

"Have what bad?"

"Spring fever."

She might have been correct. We'd moved deep into May. The days were balmy, but the nights were still cool. It didn't matter. Writing didn't seem to be at the front of my mind. I wanted to be with her, just have her close to me where I could see her and touch her and hear her soothing voice.

A half hour later we sat on a blanket doubled over to act as a cushion on Buck's tailgate. We'd found a spur of dirt road near the crest of the pass that turned off the main road, curved down the side of the hill about two hundred yards before it opened into a tight turnaround with two ancient oak trees.

I spun Buck around so we could sit under the shade of one of the trees looking out across the San Joaquin Valley.

Audrey poured us each a little wine. We toasted, smiled at each other and simultaneously took a sip.

Remote silence settled in around us. Buck's engine made popping noises now and again while it cooled. There was just the whisper of a breeze playing high in the leaves of the gnarled oak we sat under. Audrey sensed I just wanted her there close to me. Her perception was correct, though I also wanted her to be happy sitting there next to me, too.

We sat in silence for a long time, sipping occasionally from our glasses.

"Tell you a secret," I finally said.

She reached up and ran her hand across my shoulder.

"Probably sound corny—never missed the town after I left here, but I missed this place; Pacheco Pass." I scanned the terrain around me. "Anchors so many of the best memories from my childhood. The one physical place on this planet I feel connected to."

"I don't think that sounds corny, Charlie."

I smiled at her, wondered if she could read my thoughts about her. I wondered if she could sense how connected to her I'd become.

She leaned her head against my shoulder and held my hand. We sat in complete silence, listening to the gentle rustle of leaves dancing on the breeze through the upper branches of the old oak.

My mind coursed rapidly through images of Vietnam and my childhood that had ruled my life. Some of it still bore heavily on the wounds I carried. Nightmares about the war had become less frequent, but I was a long way from exorcising all the demons that haunted me.

The involvement with Theo and my writing was proving a worthwhile distraction. What was taking place was sending my life in a new direction. Catharsis was taking hold; validation I desperately needed to find. But the seminal change in my life sat right next to me. I could no longer see myself without her. But I still fought uncertainty over remaining in Divina.

"Passion Flower'll be home from school soon," she said softly after we'd been sitting for an hour or so.

"She has us trained," I said. "Nearly never slip and call her Rachel anymore."

"Persuasive, isn't she?"

We gathered our glasses and the blanket and headed home.

****

My hypnotic state was being abetted by the rat-a-tat of the electric ball of my Selectric. Focus jumped from one point to the next while I tried to convert what was in my brain to cohesive sentences that connected. I'd entered a trance-like state when the phone rang and I heard Theo's voice on the other end.

"Sal DeCosta just left my office," he began.

"How'd it go?"

"Pretty much as I expected." Theo sighed deeply into the phone. "Denied everything. Never had any conversation with Mary Louise Parker. A lie he accuses *you* started like all the other lies you're spreading about his daughter. Even if Miranda *was* pregnant, it's none of my fucking business, to use his vernacular. Faulted you for being the source of all the ugly bullshit that's starting to happen. No problems until you showed up and started asking questions, making false accusations."

"Sal still applies his unique sense of logic to things."

"Easier to blame somebody than take responsibility," Theo added. "But you're correct in your assessment. He knew about the pregnancy. And I let him know I had him nailed for it."

"How's that?"

"As I reminded him, the pregnancy was identified in the official recording of the autopsy. For now, a clerical error, I called it. Could have happened to anyone. Mary Louise made a simple mistake. Been caught and corrected...unless he wanted to make something more of it,"

"We're just going to let him get away with what he did?"

There was a brief pause.

"Charlie, if Sal is exposed, it's as I told you, he wiggles free. The only person who is going to be destroyed is that young secretary who made a horrible mistake. You ever made a mistake you'd like to be able to rectify?"

Theo's benevolence was why the community embraced this man. And Audrey had understated just how big his heart was.

"See your point."

"Sal's painfully aware I know the truth. He'll consider that before he does something else stupid. He can't be entirely certain I won't go to the DA with it. Let's allow uncertainty to work in our behalf."

"Think he'll stay out of the investigation?"

"He doesn't know I won't expose him."

"What about Mary Louise?"

"I've spoken with her."

"What did you tell her?"

"Scared the hell out of her. I spelled out what would happen if anything like this ever occurred in the future."

"Sal will go after her."

"Told her as much."

"What do you think she'll do?"

"If she's smart, exactly what I instructed her to do."

"Which was?"

"Make sure Sal gives her a lot of money to keep her mouth shut and make sure she records the conversation."

"How's she going to do that?"

"Think about it, Charlie. She works with recordings all day. It's what she does. She's a smart girl."

"Hope you're right, Theo. That's a big step to leave to a person who's already compromised herself."

"She's got a lot at stake," he asserted.

"What's next?"

"Not what. Who," he corrected me.

"Who, then?"

"Mr. Matta, obviously."

"How do you plan to deal with him?"

"Call him. Persuade him to come by my office. I intend to confront him with what we know and bluff him into admitting he was the father of Miranda's unborn child."

"Why tip him off we're onto him?"

"Because, Charlie, before I'm going to destroy a person's life, I want to be satisfied what I'm doing is justifiable."

"And you think Duke will just sit there and admit to you he did it?"

"No. No, I don't. But if he's lying to me, I'll know it."

"Not sure I'm following, Theo."

"If I'm convinced he's lying to me, I turn everything over to the DA."

"You think Pederson will act on it?"

"He won't have a choice. He doesn't reopen the investigation; I'll provide everything I know to the newspapers. Even Sal DeCosta's influence won't do them much good if that happens."

"And what if Duke convinces you he's telling the truth?"

"Then you'll have an alibi to confirm."

"And you think it'll be that easy?"

"No. But I have confidence in you, Charlie. And between us, we'll figure this out...do the right thing."

"Said it before, Theo. You're an interesting guy. You spend an inordinate amount of time trying to do right by people. I wonder if some of them deserve it."

"Everybody deserves that consideration, Charlie. I'm guessing you would appreciate that about as much as anyone."

And there I was, recipient myself of Theo Azevedo's largesse. There was no way to argue with the man's commitment to caring about people's lives, nor would I want to. The old lawyer was teaching me a valuable life-lesson. And the guy was turning out to be a crafty defense attorney, which was no longer surprising me.

"Fair enough," I said. "When will you meet with Duke?"

"Let you know.

CHAPTER 25

THAT WEEKEND AUDREY dropped Rachel off at her grandmother's. Rachel was to spend Saturday and Sunday with her father. Audrey usually went to pick her up around four on those Sunday afternoons.

Audrey and her mother went to Modesto for the day on Saturday. I worked at my new typewriter, which was growing on me as my manuscript grew. I'd rapidly reached a point I couldn't remember what it was like to write without it.

By the time she'd gotten back that afternoon, Audrey was ready for a quiet evening. We relaxed with a bottle of wine in the courtyard, held hands like a couple of teenagers, listened to the crickets, took in the lights out across the valley. I received a faint whiff again of that oddly familiar odor I'd smelled a couple of weeks earlier. Fusty must of some wild foothill plant, I'd finally decided. If the breeze was just right from the west, it was mildly detectable intermittently. Audrey seemed not to notice it at all. Most likely something she was so accustomed to smelling she no longer had any sense of it. I needed to relax. This wasn't the Vietnam jungle.

That night I slept with Audrey in her bedroom. Well, to be honest, sleep is not exactly what we did. It was more like a marathon. Every time one of us turned over in our dreamy slumber and touched the other, we ended up consumed all over again. There was something magic in the warmth of her soft, naked flesh touching me that reset my bio-vibrations. I wanted her non-stop. Still I couldn't get enough of her. She was no less ravenous herself, because if I snoozed too long between my attentions, I'd awaken to her already worked up and coaxing me back inside her.

On Sunday morning we awoke exhausted and in serious need of sleep. We showered together, which did little to rejuvenate us as Audrey clung to me, her long sensuous legs locked around my waist with me inside her once more.

When we couldn't go on making love any longer, we made breakfast together. We relaxed, ate leisurely.

"How's your book coming?" she asked.

"Finally has a beginning. Love the typewriter."

She smiled, her bare nipples peeking out from the edges of the open shirt she wore.

Audrey had chores around her house to get done and I needed to work. I helped clear the table, kissed and ran my hands over the landscape of her soft flesh, which threatened to cast us into another round before she pushed me away.

"Get out of here while I still have the willpower to fend you off," she said.

****

"Yeah," Rachel told us at dinner later that evening. "He said he was cleaning her utters and she kicked him in the side of the face. You should see it." She seemed fascinated rather than horrified by what she'd seen. "His jaw is wired so he can't move it. He can only eat liquid food he sucks through a straw. Yuck!" She made a face that caused me to grin. "He's really crabby all the time. Says it's going to be like that for a month."

Audrey and I said little, exchanged glances periodically while we listened to Rachel carry on about her father.

"You have homework?" Audrey asked when we'd finished dinner and cleaned the kitchen.

"Some reading," Rachel admitted.

"Off you go."

Rachel was well disciplined. She required no coaxing. Reading was one of her favorite activities.

Rachel was still reading quietly in her room when Audrey looked in on her.

The crickets seemed to chirp louder in the warm spring night. Lights twinkled bright up close—dimmer and dimmer the further out across the San Joaquin Valley they got, like stars in the universe. Audrey appeared next to me in the courtyard with two glasses of wine. After the weekends we sometimes shared, our Sunday night separations were a bitter parting for us, but no doubt contributed greatly to keeping alive what we had between us.

The following morning Rachel scurried out to meet her bus. Audrey and I ran out Farm Road Lane and raced back to a warm shower.

****

After we made love, Audrey curled up in one of the soft chairs outside the French doors of the bungalow with a book. The morning sun was warm, the flowers profuse in spring bloom. The vision of her sitting there did little to help my concentration as I tapped away on my typewriter.

Tuesday yielded a repeat of Monday morning but around two-thirty Tuesday afternoon my phone rang. It was Theo.

"Belligerent," he reported. "Threatening you, me, anybody who screws his life up for something he swears he didn't do."

"You believe him?"

"It's complicated. I don't want to discuss this by phone. My office, around ten in the morning?"

"I'll be there," I promised.

****

"What's up?" I asked Theo next morning after I'd negotiated Earline and her smoke chamber.

He sipped noisily from a cup of coffee that smelled and looked stale. "Wanted to discuss this with you, properly," he began. Theo's tone, the way his eyes shifted when he looked up at me was telling.

"You did find out something, didn't you? You think he did it!"

"Not what I said, Charlie."

"Yeah, but—"

"Yes, but nothing," he said. "It's as I told you. Complicated."

"How can it be that complicated, Theo? You think he did it?"

"When I told him what we know from the autopsy, he turned gray, as you would say. He began to sweat. Armpits of his shirt grew dark and he fidgeted in the same chair you're sitting in right now.

"He confessed he was the father of Miranda's child. Pressured her to find a way to make it go away. Those were his words, 'Make it go away.' But he swears he never would have hurt her and he did not kill her."

"And you believe him?"

"There's more." Theo sipped of the foul smelling brew in the stained cup before continuing. "He admits he was with her the night she was murdered."

204

I slid to the front of my seat. "I knew it. The sonofabitch killed her, Theo!" The words escaped me hissing like molten lava.

"Not so fast," he cautioned. "Think about this. If he did kill her, why would he so easily incriminate himself?"

"The jerk is trying to throw you off."

"Do you have some agenda here, Charlie?" Theo asked. "You've made it clear all along you didn't particularly like Mr. Matta, but it begins to look like there's something you aren't telling me."

"There's nothing, Theo. Just...I had a hunch about the guy. He has no honor."

"Being a man bereft of honor does not make him a murderer, Charlie."

"So you think he didn't do it?"

"I didn't say that. I said it's complicated."

"What else did he tell you about that night?" I asked.

Theo settled deep into his high-backed chair, fingers intertwined and locked together behind his giant head, studied me with those hound dog eyes for several moments.

"That's the part that's complicated. Says around eight o'clock the night of the murder, Miranda called him. Very emotional. Told him what had happened between her and Caputo. She was crying. Wanted him to come to her."

"Where was his wife?"

"According to Mr. Matta, sitting right in the room with him when he answered the phone."

"Okay. This is bullshit. How convenient. His wife hears him having a conversation with his girlfriend?"

"Hold on. Mr. Matta pointed out there was a thick fog in Pacheco Pass that night. It's true, there was. He told me he pretended in front of his wife it was a call about his office. Something needed attention. Told her he had no alternative but to go down there. She didn't want him to go—too dangerous to drive on a night like that. Claims he convinced her he had no choice. Had to go unlock the door to the place."

"Sounds flimsy you ask me."

"Gets worse," Theo agreed. "Admits he drove to Miranda's apartment. He calmed her down. Promised her he'd kick Vinny's ass, his words, next time he saw the guy."

"Sounds like Duke's idea of a solution." I didn't bother to mask the sardonic edge in my tone.

Theo studied me again for a few moments before he continued. "He confessed they made love. That's where he swears he left her. That was the last time he saw her. Says she was lying there in the bed when he walked out, got in his car and drove home."

"How convenient. His word against his dead girlfriend's."

"There is the call he took in front of his wife," Theo argued optimistically.

"You said he convinced her he had an emergency at his office."

"That's what *he* said."

"So what can she tell us except he received a call about his office and went out?"

"I find women have a sense about these things, Charlie. And let's not forget, Duke has a reputation. You think his wife doesn't know?"

"So she knows she's married to the biggest Casanova in the world. She can't tell us whether what he claims is true or made up."

"No. She can't." Theo sat up straight and scooted his chair back into position behind his desk. "But what she can tell us is what time Duke went out, what time he came home and if she perceived anything telling. As I said, never underestimate a woman's ability to divine things about her man."

"What makes you so sure?"

"Handled a lot of divorces over the years. Women know."

"So you want me to go ask Duke Matta's wife where he was the night Miranda DeCosta was murdered and if she could detect whether or not he killed her before he came home?"

"Don't be absurd. She's innocent in all of this even if it turns out her husband isn't."

"Jesus Christ, Theo! You're an attorney, not a fucking priest or social worker. When do you forget about this bullshit and go after this guy or Sal DeCosta for that matter?"

"I don't forget this bullshit, Mr. Caldwell. Because I don't like seeing innocent people pay for the mistakes of bad people. So I'll make the extra effort required to try not to hurt them further. That's how I practice law. You don't like that; perhaps you want to pursue this on your own."

Even in his exasperation, Theo found it in him to continue to be patient. But his vituperative outburst made me realize I did have an agenda where Duke was concerned. I had to admit it to myself. It was time to exorcize that demon along with others I was trying to shed.

I sat reflecting several moments.

"You're right," I conceded finally. "I don't like the guy and I'm allowing that to cloud my objectivity."

Theo went on studying me.

"So what do we do now?" I asked.

He was silent for several seconds.

"You're right on a number of issues," he granted. "I don't relish what I have to do next."

This time I held my tongue.

"I don't have any choice but to go to Pederson with this. It's a game changer. Short of an actual confession, I don't know how they prove anything. But _I_ can now prove reasonable doubt for Mr. Caputo."

"Think they'll let him go?"

"This investigation is so tainted now I don't see Pederson has much choice."

"DeCosta's going to go insane when he finds out his golden boy knocked his daughter up—may have killed her, too," I pointed out.

"I find no glee in that notion, Charlie." The weary look on Theo's face spoke of a man who'd witnessed human frailty and the pain it wrought on innocent bystanders. Mary Louise Parker, perhaps especially Duke Matta's unsuspecting wife.

"Go home," Theo said, standing. "Take care of Audrey and Rachel. Work on your novel. What comes next will happen behind closed doors. Any new developments, I'll be in touch." Theo shuffled out from behind his desk.

The floor on the other side of the closed door creaked loudly.

I looked up at him. "She tries to listen in sometimes," he said, a look of fatigue screwing across his face.

"You let her get away with that?"

"The door is solid wood, Charlie. She can't bend over close enough to get an ear against it. She couldn't hear anything even if she could."

Theo walked me out and stood on his stoop while we eyeballed Jorge Olivera gliding by in his police car.

****

From Theo's office I drove to the park, hiked out to my favorite bench. The revelations of the morning worked on me as I watched Jeff Ponder drop to the ground under a tree across the park. He moved on to find a different canopy the way I'd shuffled out to my bench, a known refuge. Jeff climbed up into the branches and disappeared.

I scribbled a few notes. Mostly I brooded about Miranda DeCosta's death, the disgust I felt for Matta, where all our lives had come to.

208

Even at that, I was learning valuable lessons from Theo Azevedo. Of course, he frustrated me. He was like a one-man guardian angel when I believed his own interests should come first. But I certainly couldn't argue with his selflessness for people around him. There was an example I could take from all of this. Phoebe Fillinger at the magazine had shown a similar kindness toward me when she helped me land the job. Maybe I'd shown up here feeling too full of myself, superior.

What happened in Vietnam manifested itself in my psyche in ways I hadn't understood, still didn't fully understand. To use Theo's euphemism, it was complicated. The issues I had would take time to sort out. Besides Audrey and Rachel, I sincerely liked Natalie Bettencourt. A number of Audrey's friends who'd come by out of curiosity over the gossip going around about her live-in boyfriend seemed nice enough. Theo taught impetuous behavior could unnecessarily hurt or destroy an innocent person. Wasn't that one of the very grievances I held so ardently?

To be clear, there were plenty of bad apples in the barrel. But there were a few good ones, too.

****

Around three-thirty I drove to the elementary school and waited near the bus-loading zone. When the final bell rang, gangly kids from tots to near teens poured across the schoolyard to climb aboard three different buses.

When I spotted Rachel I shouted to her. "Passion Flower! Passio—yeah. Over here."

"What are you doing here, Charlie?" she shouted, running to me, hugging me.

Mothers of kids exchanged looks with raised eyebrows—nodded knowingly to each other then made head gestures in my direction. Natalie Bettencourt caught sight of me and blew her horn. Heads turned when we waived to each other.

"Hey, Passion Flower. I was in town, ready to head home. Thought you might like a ride instead of sitting on the bus for an hour."

Rachel ogled Buck, glanced over her shoulder to her friends already aboard their bus and turned back to my rust-bucket of a pickup.

I eyeballed Buck myself, smiled at her friends. "Okay, you'd rather be with them." I nodded in the direction of her bus.

"Buck's kind of junkie," she said apologetically. "They're gonna make fun of me."

I had to admire her honesty. "He is junkie. Don't blame you. See you at home." I trotted off toward my old pick up. Buck's body really did need something done to it.

Half way to Buck Rachel caught up to me. She clutched my hand and turned to be sure her friends saw. "They won't make fun of me now," she declared emphatically.

"Why?" I asked, opening myself fully to the logic of a twelve-year-old girl. There were looks of admiration and giggling going on amongst Rachel's friends.

"You, silly," she said.

"Me?"

"They all think you're cute. And we're holding hands."

"Oh, Jesus, Rachel."

She scowled at me.

"I mean, Passion Flower." I tugged at her grip.

"If you let my hand go, Charlie Caldwell, I'll never forgive you."

This was Rachel Romero, Audrey's offspring; every bit her mother's daughter. I smiled for her friends.

Audrey sauntered out to satisfy her curiosity when I pulled in the driveway. "What's up with you two?"

Rachel ran across the courtyard. "Charlie gave me a ride home from school."

"I can see that."

"Finishing up in town. Thought she might like getting home an hour early."

Audrey checked Rachel through the window, opening the refrigerator. She turned back to me. "How was your day?"

"Interesting," I said. "Long story. Let's save it for later."

She smiled, tipped up on her toes and kissed me on the cheek. "I made lasagna for dinner."

Rachel was a chatterbox about school. Who said what about whom, which of her friends had a new boyfriend and which didn't. Mother-daughter interaction.

Abruptly, Audrey turned to me. "I saw on the news there was an attempted assassination on George Wallace today."

"Who's he?" Rachel wanted to know.

"Governor of Alabama," I said. "Was he killed?"

"News didn't say. He was in surgery. If he was, it wasn't immediate."

"We're at war in our own fucking country," I said into my plate.

The kitchen went stone quiet.

I looked up first to Audrey, to Rachel, back to Audrey.

"I apologize, Rach—Passion Flower. That came out without me thinking." I turned to Audrey. "Sorry, it jus—"

Rachel cut me off. "Daddy says it all the time. I've heard it before."

Audrey went red in the face.

"Well, I don't talk like that in front of you, Passion Flower. Thoughtless slip. Really ugly of me to use that language with you. Isn't okay and it won't happen again."

"I've heard Mom say it, too." Rachel lifted a glass of milk to her lips.

Now it was Audrey's turn. She set her fork down, laced her fingers together like a visor over her forehead and stared down into her half eaten food.

Rachel's fork clinked against her plate, punctuating the silence.

"Wanna go see The French Connection this weekend?" Audrey asked, finally looking up at me, total capitulation.

Rachel could have that effect.

****

The French Connection would have to wait. Darryl called Audrey cancelling his weekend with Rachel. They fought over his language in front of their daughter.

"You should have heard the prick, Charlie. *Fu foo!*" She mimicked the sounds Darryl made into the phone.

The three of us made a picnic on Saturday up in Pacheco Pass. I told Rachel the legend of lover's leap. How a young Indian girl and boy from different tribes that forbade their love—holding hands, jumped off the prominent outcropping of granite up in the Pass to their deaths so they could be together for eternity. Rachel didn't think it sounded like such a good idea.

CHAPTER 26

WHEN THEO'D COMMUNICATED the new evidence to the DA late last week, things remained eerily calm. Though none outside the investigation could have known what was about to take place, a hush fell around the subject of the DeCosta murder, as though the entire town could sense something prodigious coming. The weekend had passed. Theo and I spoke toward the end of the day on Monday. Pederson agreed to a meeting on Wednesday morning in Merced.

After Audrey and I went for our run on Tuesday, she cuddled up on one of the soft cushioned chairs just out the French doors of the bungalow with a book. The flowers were in a profusion of spring blooms and the air was sweet with their perfume. She lazed in the warm spring sun with her book while I wrote, glancing up to appreciate the sweetness in my life. Eventually she stood, wriggled my shirt off her shoulders and let it fall into the seat of the chair, seemingly oblivious to my presence. With me, Audrey never considered her nudity a thing of significance except when she decided to use it to incite me to make love to her. In that moment, she was simply being who she was, unaware even that I'd noticed. Her eyes remained glued to the book she'd become engrossed in.

My eyes were glued to every soft golden curve of her body; the gentle fall of her shoulders, the sinewy strands of lean muscle running down her spine to the dimpled indentation at her coccyx, the curve of her soft smooth bottom folding into the elegant crack of her round ass tracing to the confluence of the backs of her sensuous thighs and the secret place I knew if I slid my hand I'd find what made her a woman. She was a living sculpture of femininity and I adored her.

Writing for me, reading for Audrey consumed our day until early afternoon. She laced her sun-warmed golden nude body against me, held me gently, kissed me even gentler. "You get some work done, baby?" she asked, looking up into my eyes.

There was the suggestion of a smile, innocence, in her eyes. "I did," I told her.

She wiggled into her panties, pulled on her shorts and blouse. "You gonna take a break?"

My early afternoon meditations at the park were, by then, established routine.

"Want me to pick up anything in town?"

"Got everything, thanks. Fish okay for dinner?"

She walked with me out to Buck; we kissed and set about the balance of our day.

Jeff Ponder was usually either up a tree or molesting a shrub in hot pursuit of who-knows-what. Some days I talked to him. Others I didn't. Whether we actually interacted or not, it seemed to me he looked forward to finding me on the edge of his world. Sometimes when I gazed into his crossed eyes, I wondered if he was not lonely locked away inside a place only he could inhabit; a world devoid of meaningful relationship with another possessed of his own special intellectualization of things.

****

Theo called Wednesday evening wanting to fill me in on his meeting with the DA. "We discussed the *clerical* error, in the autopsy transcript."

"How'd he take the news?"

Theo grunted. "Not sure Mary Louise will keep her job in spite of my efforts."

"So I take it you didn't reveal DeCosta's role in it?"

"Would have only made things worse, even for Mary Louise."

"She did take a bribe, Theo. Actions have consequences," I pointed out.

He let out a sigh of exasperation. "They do."

"What's he going to do about Matta?"

"No way of knowing for now. But I can assure you; Mr. Matta is not going to receive the same consideration I would give him. I feel bad for the wife," he said.

"You know her?"

"No. She grew up in Modesto."

"They gonna drop the charges against Vinny?"

"Pederson didn't say he would. But face it...he has few options. My experience: let him handle it his way."

"You gonna keep me in the loop?"

Theo promised he would.

"How's the book coming?"

"Good," I said. "Progress is slow. Don't know the ending yet anyway."

****

Friday morning Audrey and I waited with Rachel beside the road for her bus. We'd decided to make an afternoon and evening of it in Modesto on Saturday. We'd have dinner, see The French Connection, stay the night in a hotel.

Forty minutes into our run we were jogging out east of town. At first I ignored the siren in the distance. Audrey heard it, too. We continued jogging, but the sound was growing louder.

I glanced back over my shoulder. The red light of a police car in the distance raced toward us. Scanning the road ahead, I detected nothing. A quick recon around didn't turn up any disturbance. Not much out here but Audrey and me.

Reaching for Audrey's hand, I slowed her to a walk. Standing at the edge of the pavement we looked back in the direction of the inauspicious sound. The patrol car was closing fast.

"What's going on, Charlie?"

"Don't know. But I don't see anything or anyone out here but you and me."

The Plymouth Fury, red light flashing and siren still blaring skidded to a stop. Jorge Olivera emerged from the driver's door and rushed around the front of the car with his hand resting on his holstered gun. "Step over here and put your hands on the hood, Caldwell," he ordered.

I dropped Audrey's hand, but didn't move. "What the hell is this?"

Olivera unsnapped the leather guard on his holster. "I ain't gonna tell ya again."

Audrey gripped my arm. "Do what he says, Charlie."

"Better listen to your girlfriend, Caldwell. Told you not to get in my way."

Reluctantly, I obeyed the prick...walked toward the police car. Zeroing in on Olivera's eyes, I drew a bead...placed my body between him and Audrey.

"What do you want, Jorge?" Audrey demanded. "He wasn't doing anything. Why don't you just get out of here and leave us alone!" Her hand tightened around my bicep.

A second police car raced toward us then. There were only two cop cars in Divina. In a few moments, for whatever reason, Prado Mendoza would be on the scene and I'd be up against the town's entire law enforcement team. I stopped at the front of Olivera's patrol car just as Mendoza pulled to a stop and stepped out. The chief of police didn't say anything—played the casual observer.

Olivera became emboldened with the presence of an ally. He reached up and grabbed the flesh of my bare shoulder, shoved me toward the car. "Put your hands on the hood," he ordered.

Audrey swung around me and shoved him. "You take your hands off of him."

"You bitch," Olivera yelled. His right hand fumbled with the leather strap as he drew his revolver.

In two quick moves I took control of his gun hand, folding the revolver around. At the same time, I pinned the wimpy bastard over the front fender of his patrol car. Olivera found himself staring straight down the barrel of his own gun. His wrist was twisted into a shape that felt like it would disconnect from his arm. He was screaming obscenities in pain.

Audrey was knocked backward.

"Let him go," Mendoza ordered, pointing his weapon at me. "Let him go, I said!"

Uncertainty was written in Mendoza's eyes, the muzzle of his gun as it pointed at me was unsteady. The situation was like a powder keg.

"Oh, my God, Charlie," Audrey cried. "What's happening?"

I reached up slowly, took Olivera's gun by its barrel, flung it across the pavement.

Mendoza was in a wide squatted stance, his dark eyes engorged with confusion.

When I relaxed my grip on Olivera's arm, the deputy made another critical error in judgment.

"You're ass's had it now, Caldwell," he belched as he shoved me back.

The punch he intended for my face came with a singing telegram. I parried the attempted blow, pasted the punk to the hood of his car again with my right hand clasped to his throat. Had any of them understood the detail, they would have seen it was the cartilage that protected his larynx, his Adam's apple. That was why he couldn't scream. All he could do was drool while his eyes bulged larger and larger.

The fool had no idea he was an eyelash from dead. I held him pinned down, gasping, flailing his legs like a puppet being dangled out of control by a marionette.

Mendoza held his weapon in both hands, but pointed it up into the air. "Let him up and step back, Caldwell!"

Olivera's face turned an alarming shade of red. I bent down and put my face directly into his so he could see my eyes. "You ever touch her again, even speak to her, I'm going to rip out your sleazy throat."

Without loosening my grip, I straightened, turned to Mendoza. "Ever kill a man, Prado?" Everything in the moment came from my guts. There was no conscious thought, just reaction. The blood behind my eyes must have conveyed the rage that had been incited in me. I could see Mendoza was scared shitless. He'd let whatever was going on here get beyond his control. I'd taken over at that moment and that was dangerous for me.

Olivera's face went from red to blackish-purple. Saliva bubbles drooled from the sides of his mouth. His legs had begun to move slower and slower.

Audrey sobbed. "Please, Charlie, you're killing him!"

I opened my hand, raised both my arms high over my head as Olivera slid down the fender of the black and white to a sitting position and began to cough. He rubbed his throat with both hands and the color gradually returned to his face.

The entire encounter had taken place in only a few elapsed seconds. There was no time to think. This was the very thing I'd been trained to do. Assess the threat to my life or anyone in my charge. Take decisive, preemptive action; control of the momentum. Confuse the gook before the enemy could think or react. If I'd detected any possibility Mendoza had it in him to actually shoot me, it would've been Olivera dead. Without hesitation I'd have shielded myself with his scrawny body.

"What's this about, Mendoza?"

"You're under arrest," the chief of police declared flatly, pointing to his patrol car. "Get in the car."

Olivera was on his knees, clawing his way to a standing position.

"Not 'till I know what this is about."

Mendoza was openly confused. Whatever *was* supposed to have happened here clearly hadn't worked out. He stammered. "Stickin' your nos...Interfering in my invest—get in the gotdamn car!"

"Why are you doing this to him, Prado?" Audrey was frantic by then. "Charlie hasn't done anything wrong."

Mendoza was collecting himself. He studied me intently for a flash of seconds. "Assaulting a police officer and resisting arrest," he declared flatly. "Now get in the car or I *will* shoot you."

"Audrey's coming with me," I told him, taking her hand, moving toward the back door of his car.

Mendoza didn't fight it. "Fine. Both of you get in."

"You okay?" I asked Audrey inside the car.

She shook her head. "Just scared out of my wits. What's going on, Charlie? You went crazy. You really scared me. I thought you were going to kill him. I—"

"Shush," I said gently. "It's okay now. Everything's okay." I stole a furtive glance at Mendoza and Olivera. "Don't say anything in front of Mendoza."

Mendoza was yelling into his deputy's face. The voices were muffled, but it was clear Olivera was getting a dressing down.

Mendoza slid in behind the wheel of his car.

"What do you want with us?" I demanded.

"Not her. You."

"Okay. What do you want with me?"

Mendoza ignored my question, spun a U-turn, turned off his red light and drove back toward town. The trip was short by car. Within minutes, he pulled to a stop in front of the jail. "Get out." He stood aside with the rear door open.

Outside the car Mendoza stood toe-to-toe with me. "I'm not that punk," he said, meaning Olivera. "You gonna make this easy or not?"

I stared him down for several seconds. An open fight with the chief of police wouldn't be a smart move.

"What do you want?" I asked again.

"Inside." He pointed to the front door of the jail.

"You locking me up?"

"Inside," he repeated.

Audrey was scared. Arguing with Mendoza was pointless and would have elevated her fear. I reluctantly moved toward the door of the police station.

The chief opened the holding cell and motioned for me to get inside. The instant I crossed the threshold of the cell, he locked the door behind me. Reaching up, I grabbed the two bars beside my face, locked my fingers around the cold, rough surface of the hard steel and demanded again Mendoza tell me what this was about.

Still he refused to explain.

Audrey became frenzied. "You can't do this. He didn't do a goddamned thing. You can't just lock somebody up."

"Go home," Mendoza told her as if dismissing a child.

Audrey looked from Mendoza to me. I saw the confusion in her eyes but there was little I could do at that point to calm her fears.

She crossed the small room and placed her hands over mine on the bars. "What do you want me to do?"

"First thing's first," I told her. "Go home, get into some dry clothes and bring me something dry to put on. I'm going to be miserable and chilled in a while."

"Jesus, Charlie. I can't just leave you here."

"We don't have a choice." I looked across to Mendoza who stood next to his desk fingering some envelops, listening to every word but pretending to ignore us. "Call Theo." I mouthed the words.

Mendoza looked up. "Do what he says. Doe wan him catch no cold in my jail," he mocked, half-chuckled. "Now get outta here." An ugly scowl drifted over his face.

Audrey backed toward the door. "I'll be back as quick as I can."

I nodded.

The place went quiet as a church after she closed the door behind her.

Several moments went by in claustrophobic silence.

"You gonna tell me what this is about?" I sat down on the edge of the single cot in my cell.

Mendoza dropped heavily in his chair, removed his hat and hung a boot on the corner of his desk. "You never was too smart," he sneered. "Keep pissin' off the wrong people."

"Who'd I piss off?" I asked.

The question was rhetorical. Who I'd pissed off was obvious. I was trying to get him to say Sal DeCosta's name.

"You can't just lock me up for making somebody mad."

"Just did," Mendoza shot back. "Now, shut the fuck up. Lucky you didn't get a bullet between the eyes."

There was no point in pursuing anything further with him. I knew the guy's life story. He was a hard case and he belonged to Sal DeCosta.

I'd heard DeCosta brag about his deal with Mendoza at more than one backyard barbecue; the happy days before I fell from grace with the DeCostas.

Mendoza's old man immigrated to the States when Prado was seventeen. They settled in San Francisco where father and son found work as crew on the fish boats out of Fisherman's Warf. Life there was hard for a kid. Prado learned to survive.

When he was about twenty-two he left San Francisco and moved inland to the San Joaquin Valley. Took a job as night watchman at the DeCosta Mercantile warehouse. When a position opened for town deputy, Prado went to DeCosta and offered to continue taking care of the warehouse if Sal would help him get the job.

Sal saw it for the sweet setup it was. Mendoza would be paid by the city while the Mercantile kept the same watchman for free. And DeCosta had the clout of a badge when he needed one.

Prado was a six-foot-two hulk, barrel-chested with powerful arms. His eyes were as menacing as an angry bull and his broad nose, pocked with deep, large pores, overhung thick, coarse lips. Broad, square shoulders were thrown back when he walked, amplifying his huge chest. One by one the local toughs tested him. Word got around. Mendoza punished his victims badly before he arrested them. In his youth, this was a small-town cop you didn't want to tangle with.

After the chief of police retired in 1952, Sal made certain the city hired Prado as the replacement. Now Mendoza had twenty years in the position and Sal DeCosta behind him. Prado Mendoza ran Divina as he chose.

Mendoza was still a powerful man. But he was an over forty victim of his genetics, bad diet and a sedentary job. His ass barely fit the chair he reclined in. I'd sit in his jail if that was what I had to do until Theo could get me out. But I'd made up my mind; Mendoza would do well to reconsider any notion of abusing me.

Audrey was back in under half an hour. She'd slipped into a pair of jeans and long-sleeved shirt but was still covered in sweat.

She rushed past Mendoza; ignored him as though he wasn't in the room.

He glared at her but did nothing to stop her.

She passed the folded clothing through the slot in the bars. "There's a sandwich and a coke, too. You need to hydrate and eat something."

"I didn't give no permission for him to get nothin' but some clothes," Mendoza growled.

Audrey spun like a cat. "I didn't ask for your permission." She spit the words at Mendoza so harshly I wasn't sure she wouldn't end up my cellmate.

"Let it go, Audrey," I said. "We don't need more trouble than we already have."

Mendoza stared her down but Audrey was defiant. She wouldn't back away from him. Mendoza must have decided engaging her wouldn't be worth his trouble because he stood and walked across the room to a door marked *Private* and went inside.

"Did you call Theo?" I asked quietly when Audrey turned back to me.

"Earline says he's out of the office. Went to see one of his clients or something."

I thought for a moment. "Listen, I'm fine. Don't worry about m—"

"How the hell am I supposed to not worry about you, Charlie? This is bullshit. You haven't done anything wrong."

"And that's why you shouldn't worry. They're harassing me and probably hoping you give them an excuse to use you against me somehow. You can bet Sal DeCosta is behind it. Theo will have me out of here the minute you let him know what happened."

"And in the mean time they have you in here and I'm out of my mind with worry."

"Calm down, Audrey. Trust me. I've been in worse situations. I'll be fine."

I reached through the bars and took her hands.

Her eyes teared up instantly.

"Go home and have a nice hot shower," I said.

She looked up at me and smiled.

"I know...won't be the same." I grinned back. "Do it anyway. Get to Theo as soon as you can. He'll take care of the rest. I'll be home for dinner."

Mendoza opened the door and came back into the room. "Visit's over." He crossed to his desk.

Audrey tensed and her eyes narrowed as words began to form on her lips.

"Go on, Audrey," I interrupted her. "Isn't worth it."

Audrey was fighting mad, but went along with me. At the door she stopped, turned toward Mendoza. "You're gonna get in a lot of trouble for this."

If the situation weren't as grave as it felt, I'd have laughed at her reprimand.

"Not from you I ain't," Mendoza snarled. "Get out...before I lock you up, too.

Not long after Audrey left, Mendoza pulled his hat onto his head, reached for his keys and walked out, locking the door behind him.

My sweaty body had dried—skin felt crusty so I rubbed down vigorously with the shirt before pulling it over my head. The clothes Audrey'd brought felt warm sliding on. The ham sandwich she'd made and the Coke were rejuvenating. The dank holding cell was familiar to me, but not since I was eighteen-years-old.

One Saturday night a bunch of us from the football team were out drinking beer when a crew of toughs from a neighboring town dropped by. They were looking for trouble and we did our best to give them what they'd come for. For our trouble that night we found ourselves run-in—locked together in the same cell—the cell I now sat locked in. Mendoza'd thought it was funny. By the time our parents got us out, we were shaking hands and declaring friendships. It was rare any of us were ever actually arrested over scuffles like that. We were kids, doing kid shit. They were pretending to be cops, pretending to perform cop duties. Not so different from what was going on right then.

My trip down memory lane was interrupted when I heard the door being unlocked. This time it was Olivera. Now I had reason to worry. I was a sitting duck behind the bars of the small cage.

"So you think you pulled some shit on me today, huh, trash?" He was puffed up, full of himself. But he kept a safe distance from the cell. "Now I'm givin' *you* the word, punk!" Deputy Olivera was working himself into a frenzy. Suddenly he pulled his revolver, pointed it at my chest while he went on with his tirade. "When Mendoza lets you outta there, you watch your back!" He was red-faced, out of control. "You and that bitch you're fuckin'! You both better watch your asses around me!" He jabbed the pistol toward me. "Last time I ever let you get close enough to put a hand on me! You got that, trash?" His black eyes blazed as he pounded his wimpy chest, did everything in his power to scare me. "You're dead you ever try that again!"

The prick tried to spit on me, but his mouth was so dry he couldn't produce saliva. When he stomped out I heard the key turn in the lock behind him.

Olivera'd known Mendoza was gone. Must've figured this was his chance to get at me. His references to Audrey hit home, made me anxious. Our relationship placed her in jeopardy with these people. As independent and tough as Audrey was, she'd be vulnerable without me there to protect her.

Around one o'clock she was back at the jail no doubt intending to fill me in on progress toward getting me out. But Mendoza was nowhere to be found and the door remained locked. Audrey went to the heavily barred window beside Mendoza's desk, shaded her eyes at the sides of her face and peeked in. We shouted back and forth, but it was difficult to make out words. The worry on her face was apparent and I understood she'd still not been able to reach Theo.

All we could do was wait.

The clock on the wall gave the time as four o'clock when the door opened next. This time it was Mendoza. Theo trailed him.

Theo walked over to me. "You okay?"

"Never better," I wisecracked. "Can you get me out of here?"

He didn't reply, turned back to Mendoza. "So why can't I make bail?"

"You know the answer to that," Mendoza said laconically. "Too late on a Friday afternoon to get the judge in chambers. He's gone for the weekend."

"You can release him in my custody. You've done it before," Theo pointed out.

"Can't do it. He attacked my deputy."

"Your deputy provoked him. He's been harassing him for weeks."

"So you say. Your word against my deputy."

"You planned this, Prado," Theo accused. "Sal DeCosta told you to shake Mr. Caldwell down and you planned this whole thing right down to no judge available."

Mendoza's grin was menacing. "Tell it to the judge, old man. Ten o'clock Monday morning. 'Cause that's when your boy here will go before him for assaulting an officer of the law."

I saw the ploy. Whatever they'd originally had in mind didn't matter any longer. I'd played directly into Sal

DeCosta's hands and Mendoza would put the hammer down on me for it.

"I'm representing him now. He's my client."

"Good for you," Mendoza said.

"I want to talk to him."

"Be my guest." Mendoza gestured toward me.

"Alone," Theo demanded.

Mendoza glared at him several moments. "Five minutes. I got tings to do." He went into the same door marked *Private* as he'd used earlier.

Theo turned to me. "You see what we're up against."

"Sorry," I said. "He shoved Audrey and went for his gun. Had no choice."

"They'll make it look like you started it. DeCosta will have the judge in his pocket by Monday morning. I need to move fast."

"What can you do?"

"I don't know just yet. Better to slow down and think this through. You need anything?"

"Olivera was here earlier. Threatened Audrey."

"Needling you. Knows you're helpless...sees how that'll work on your mind. Probably no real danger, but I'll make sure she takes Rachel and goes to stay with her mother this weekend."

"Thanks, Theo."

"Anything else?"

"Something to eat and drink. I've only had a sandwich and Coke since morning."

Theo did his best to negotiate with Mendoza to let Audrey bring me food and drink but he refused. Claimed he'd already made enough exceptions to the rules for me. No more. Said I'd get the same food and treatment any other prisoner would get.

Somehow food never made it onto the agenda that night. I drank water out of the tap of the tiny lime-encrusted sink mounted in one corner of the cell. Mendoza intended to make my stay as miserable as possible, solitary confinement, no conveniences.

CHAPTER 27

WHAT I LEARNED about how things progressed while I was locked up that weekend came to me in bits and pieces through Theo and Audrey over the weeks following my ordeal. The best I can do is guess at what actually took place—what might've really been said.

From the Police station Theo drove straight to Audrey's house. She was not the hysterical type, but when they'd spoken on the phone, he understood she was more than upset.

When he'd pulled up at her house, Audrey and Rachel raced out, expecting me to be in the car with him.

"Where's Charlie?" Audrey wanted to know. She and Rachel had been crying.

Theo did his best to calm them, explain the situation. "Mendoza's charging him with assaulting a police officer," he'd explained. "Let's go inside."

"That's bullshit, Theo," Audrey'd argued. "We were jogging. Minding our own business. Charlie didn't—"

"I don't have any doubt about that." Theo'd followed them in.

"Charlie didn't do anything," Audrey'd gone on protesting. "That creepy little bastard Olivera—"

"Calm down, Audrey. Let's have some coffee," Theo'd suggested, more as a means of distracting her than from any real need he felt for a cup.

She'd looked at him, stunned.

"Would it be too much trouble to brew a pot?"

Audrey was in a stupor. "No. No, it won't be any trouble."

While he'd distracted Audrey, Theo turned to Rachel. "How are *you* doing, Rachel?"

"Changed my name to Passion Flower," she'd informed him curtly.

"I see. Hadn't heard. How's school?"

"When's Charlie coming home?" Rachel's face had remained a mask.

Audrey'd turned to see how Theo would answer. "Soon," he promised, looking from one to the other.

Audrey finally calmed some. The coffee began to percolate. She sat at the table. "What's going on, Theo?" she'd asked.

"How much has Charlie told you about what's going on with the DeCosta case?"

"Everything, I imagine," she'd admitted.

"That's what this is about. Charlie followed up on his suspicions by coming to me...but not before he'd confronted Sal DeCosta. That led to other...matters...being raised that have made people all the way up the chain of the investigation angry. Caputo's likely to be released and the investigation reopened."

Audrey'd carried on in exasperation. "Well, if they have the wrong guy, what's the problem?"

"Not that simple," Theo'd explained. "A new investigation is going to reveal secrets that are making the people involved uncomfortable. Also makes Mendoza look like the amateur he is. Charlie's responsible for making a lot of people look bad."

R.P. McCabe

"They don't give a shit about the truth," she'd accused.

"Actually, I think they do," Theo'd countered. "But they're angry someone they dislike is exposing them."

"Why don't they like Charlie?" Rachel'd interrupted.

"Because he's smarter than all of 'em put together, sweetie," Audrey'd spat caustically.

About then, Theo'd taken a noisy sip of hot coffee. "Look, you and I know what's going on here," he'd gone on explaining to Audrey. "They're all taking their frustrations out on him. They don't want to admit they made a mistake. None of the people involved with this wants to take responsibility. Charlie's a convenient scapegoat.

"I'll get it resolved, but they're going to punish our friend while they can. And in the meantime, Officer Olivera seems out of control. Frankly, Charlie's worried, as am I. Who knows, he might just try to take his anger out on you and Rachel."

"He wouldn't dare," Audrey'd said defiantly.

"Charlie thinks you should pack a few things and spend this weekend with your mother. Let things cool down.

"I'll have him out Monday morning, Audrey. Your lives can get back to normal," Theo'd promised.

Audrey'd insisted Theo hear her out. "You should o' seen what happened, Theo. I mean, I thought he'd kill Olivera. The creep comes screeching toward us in his cop car, skids to a stop...jumps out with his hand already on his gun like he's gonna shoot us or something and starts yelling at Charlie how he'd warned him to stay out of his way. Was ugly right from the first. But then Olivera put his hands on me, called me," Audrey'd glanced to Rachel, "a name. I've never seen anything like it. Happened so fast not even Mendoza knew what was going on. Next thing I

231

know, Olivera's looking down the barrel of his own gun—Charlie has him pinned to the hood of the cop car.

"Then Mendoza pulls his gun and threatens to shoot Charlie if he doesn't let Olivera up. Scared the hell out of me, Theo. But Charlie just takes Olivera's gun by the barrel and tosses it over to Mendoza—lets Olivera go.

"Probably would o' ended right there, but Olivera tries to take a swing at Charlie. Same thing. What Charlie did was...so...fast...so...I don't know. It was—no one could stop him even if they tried.

"He held Olivera by the throat like he was a rag doll. The look on Charlie's face was—I can't even describe it. I really thought he was gonna kill the creep.

"Mendoza's threatening to shoot him if he doesn't let Olivera go. Charlie seemed hypnotized. He turns like a zombie or something to Prado, looks him right in the eyes, cool as can be, he says, 'You ever kill a man, Mendoza?' as though he'd killed a lot of men himself and he knew Mendoza could never shoot anybody."

The epiphany hit both of them in the same moment. Audrey'd turned to Rachel. "PF, how about you go pack a few things you'll need at Grandma's this weekend. Bring your homework and a book."

"I know what you're doing, Mom," Rachel'd complained. You just can't put anything by Rachel.

"I know you do, sweetie. I can never fool you. Gimme a hug and go pack."

Rachel'd accepted the admission from her mother and padded off toward her room.

"Got your hands full," Theo'd said.

"If you only knew."

"Pretty clear there are some things about your friend Charlie we didn't realize." Theo was starting to put things about me together. Intuition he'd follow up on.

"It's obvious when we talk," Audrey'd agreed. "He doesn't want to discuss anything that happened in Vietnam.

Scares me, Theo. The way he dealt with Darryl—what happened today. There's something buried deep inside him."

"Can't blame him," Theo'd mused. "When you see what's on the news these days. Couldn't have been easy for him. But it's more than that, Audrey. The look in his eyes...maybe Charlie wasn't any ordinary soldier. Whatever happened to him...well...I need to look into this.

"I didn't make the connection, but I saw it once in my office. Some reference to you being put in danger. This look came into his eyes, more like a predator about to take down its prey. Unnerved me, but I didn't make too much of it at the time. We need some answers...try to understand what's driving your friend.

"Did he say where he worked before coming back?" Theo'd asked.

"Said he was living on a beach somewhere down in Old Mexico. Waiting for a story assignment from some magazine he worked for in Denver. Told me he worked for them before he was drafted."

"Tell you the name of the magazine?"

"*Past, Present & Future Magazine,*" Audrey'd said.

"Anybody's name? Boss. Supervisor?"

"Maybe, I don't recall."

"Look, Audrey, it's pretty obvious Charlie can take care of himself." Theo'd wanted to reassure her. "We can't do anything until Monday morning. Mendoza's seen to that. Only make matters worse for Charlie, we antagonize the chief. Take Rachel—go to your mom's. Let me handle this."

"Not so easy for me." Audrey'd bowed her head and begun to weep quietly. "I love him," she'd confessed to her Godfather.

"I know how much he cares for you and Rachel, Audrey," Theo'd asserted. "Go to your mom's. Wait for my call. Noon Monday—I'll have him back to you."

"I wish I believed that."

"You can believe it. Go. Gather your things. I'll follow you to your mother's."

****

Theo continued making phone calls late into the evening Friday. He started with directory assistance in Denver, Colorado, searching for the phone number of *Past, Present & Future Magazine.* By early evening he reached an assistant editor who was working late. No, she didn't know of anyone named Charlie Caldwell, but assured Theo that didn't mean much.

By the forth call along the chain, he reached Phoebe Fillinger, the magazine's Feature Article Editor and my boss. Theo filled her in on what'd happened to me. Fillinger was appalled at the story Theo recounted. She began to run down for Theo her connection with me, what she knew.

She'd been an associate editor when I was hired at *Past, Present & Future.* You could loosely call us friends, though we weren't close. Acquaintances would be closer to describing our relationship. When I came back after Vietnam, she stepped forward to recommend her boss give me an opportunity. But not before making some calls, digging into my service record. Phoebe got Uncle Sam's version on me, which disclosed a fair amount about my combat record since the Army considered me some kind of hero. She managed to learn just how good at the job of soldiering I'd been. Learned I'd been part of something called, Special Forces. Phoebe went to bat for me with the magazine even though I had no experience as a writer. She was against the war. Knew I was against the war, too. The body count—it was survival. Phoebe'd been an ally and friend; one of the few I had. She wanted to see me make it as a writer.

234

Nearly a full hour after Theo'd managed to get her on the line, he thanked her and hung up.

He'd made three more calls, attempting to get Grant Pederson on the phone, but he was out for the evening. That was the closest he'd come to speaking to the DA.

Sal DeCosta'd hung up on him twice.

He'd tried both Pederson and DeCosta twice on Saturday without any luck. He'd finally exhausted every possibility of getting me out of jail before Monday morning.

When he spoke with Audrey Saturday afternoon, he left out what he'd learned from Phoebe Fillinger about me. But if he couldn't get someone of authority to call the nonsense off and release me, it could well be disclosed at my Monday hearing. In typical fashion, Theo'd concluded if I wanted my military record made public, I'd have been bragging about it from the outset. He was an odd sort in that regard. Just who the guy is.

CHAPTER 28

MY WEEKEND STAY at the 'Divina Hilton' was tedious. But when you're locked in an eight by eight cage you have few options. Mendoza was set on making me as miserable as possible and turned my incarceration into a form of solitary confinement. If he felt like it, I was fed. If not—at one point he brought me a cold hamburger patty on a bun that looked like it'd been sat on. Both the bun and thin patty were dry as paper. Though Mendoza didn't know it, I'd eaten a helluva lot worse. There was a lot Mendoza, all of them, didn't know about me—my advantage. The water I drank came from the tap at the sink by cupping my hands. I managed to wash myself some in the same fashion. DeCosta must have felt he was teaching me a real lesson through Mendoza.

Theo told me some time later he'd refused to let Audrey come anywhere near the police station. He'd made the right call.

By Monday morning I was eager to be hauled before the judge so I could make bail and go home. But mid-morning came and went without anyone coming to transport me to the courthouse. Something was wrong. Obviously, I had no choice but wait for what was to come next. Around eleven-thirty it came.

The front door to the police station swung open and men began pouring through trailing sounds of angry, heated babble. Three of the voices were recognizable: Theo, Sal DeCosta and Prado Mendoza. The forth was not. Olivera trailed in behind all of them, making five, but his mouth was uncharacteristically shut.

The unidentifiable voice turned out to be Grant Pederson, the District Attorney. His physical presence was as out of place as his name. Pederson was tall, six-four maybe, a big square man with wide shoulders. The kind of body type you'd call big boned. He was young, fiftyish. His ruddy complexion emphasized deep blue eyes and a head of full thick wheat-colored hair.

He was in DeCosta and Mendoza's faces the way I'd never imagined anyone would dare. The man was fearless. "I'm a Goddamn Marine myself," he shouted. "You don't go around locking up a combat vet with a Bronze Star hanging from his chest simply because you don't like him asking questions." He stuck his finger in Mendoza's chest.

He spun sideways, towering over Sal DeCosta. "And I'll tell you, Sal," he said a little less vituperative, "you're gonna cross a line one day with your meddling...privileged standing won't be able to save you."

The room was eerily quiet for a moment.

DeCosta didn't say a word in response. His face boiled a shade of red I'd only seen a couple of times in all the years I'd known the man.

"And you're goddamn close," Pederson emphasized, "with this little jewel of an idea."

DeCosta let go a rattling smokers cough, but no other sounds came from him.

Pederson swung back to Mendoza. "Now get him out of that cell," he ordered pointing to me.

Olivera stood in the background fuming but apparently sensing that while he was the object of the alleged assault, he was simply too puny to be a participant in what was going on. One word out of his mouth would be the end of his career as town deputy.

Mendoza fumbled to find the correct key and get it into the lock.

Theo stepped toward me. "You doing okay, Mr. Caldwell?"

"Yes, Mr. Azevedo," I said. "Thanks for asking."

Pederson stepped up alongside Theo and proffered his hand. "Grant Pederson," he introduced himself. "Sorry about this little misunderstanding, son. You okay?"

"No worse for the wear, sir." I recognized the bearing of a military officer immediately in Pederson.

He grinned at me. "Marines, 3rd Recon Bn, 1963. First combat unit on the ground in Nam; Major Pederson, XO. You?"

"Staff Sergeant, Charles Caldwell, Sir. 5th Special Forces Group, Airborne Rangers." Pederson was the first combat grade officer I'd run into since getting back stateside not wearing a uniform. I knew the history of the unit he'd served in. He put me at ease.

Everyone else in the room had fallen silent.

"Attached to intelligence when we began to transition the Civilian Irregular Defense Group to the Vietnamese Army," I said.

Pederson and I were the center of everyone's attention. Suddenly, I didn't feel like talking anymore.

"One of your counterparts was working both sides of the fence," Pederson said, filling in what I didn't want to get into.

When I turned to Theo, those droopy hound dog eyes of his revealed he knew my story, too. But as I scanned the others, it was equally clear they had no idea what Pederson was talking about. And that was how I preferred it stay. But Pederson continued.

"You took out a lot of gooks to make it back alive," he said empathetically.

"My squad took out the enemy, sir," I corrected him.

"I've read the official record, son. They were brave men. But so were you. I'm glad you made it home."

The room was as quiet as a morgue.

"And that's where I'd like to go, sir. Home," I said.

"Thank you, Mr. Pederson," Theo said, taking control. "This way, Mr. Caldwell." Theo indicated he wanted me to collect my things and follow him.

As the door closed behind us, I could hear muffled, loud voices. I didn't need to hear the specific words to know the dressing down Pederson was delivering to the three men remaining in that office.

The drive to Audrey's was a short one, of course. "So, does *everybody* know, Theo?" I asked, meaning specifically Audrey.

"No." Then, as if it was an afterthought, "But they soon will. Probably best to tell the story your way to the ones that count."

As Theo turned the corner I glanced across the lawn of the high school. My reticence to talk about what happened was never about keeping it secret. Retelling how my four-man team and I wiped out more than fifty battle hardened Viet Cong; a dozen of whom I'd shot at range so close I could see the surprise on their baby-faces as death took them; another five I'd personally dispatched to the land of Buddha with my bare hands, sent me immediately back to a place in my psyche I was doing my best to escape. The image of my squad seared into my brain. I fought to forget, but I never would. The best I'd ever be able to hope for would be a new image to push the nightmare far enough down so I could survive. I thought I might have that now. I felt how she consumed me even as I sat there contemplating my next move. No doubt this was a bridge I'd have to cross with Audrey, but it couldn't happen in that moment.

When Theo pulled into the driveway, Audrey ran from the front of her house. She jumped into my arms holding so tightly to my neck I could hardly breathe.

Theo didn't bother getting out. "Call me." He pulled away.

Audrey clung to me for several moments, saying nothing.

Finally, I whispered in her ear, "You okay?"

She shook her head.

"I need a shower," I said. "I smell like a goat."

She relaxed her grip on me and leaned back to look into my eyes. "I missed you beyond words, Charlie."

"I missed you, too."

Her lips felt softer on mine than I'd remembered. Amazing, how even a brief separation heightens one's sensitivities to things like that. I inhaled her warm, humid breath, allowed her passion to melt over me.

"Come on," I said. "I really need to feel clean again."

Audrey took my hand and we walked slowly to the bungalow. Inside, she pulled my smelly shirt over my head and ran her hands across my chest. She reached into the waistband of my pants, slid them down over my hips. No boxers. I shook the pant legs the rest of the way to the floor and high-stepped until my feet were free. There I stood, naked in front of her.

My usual instant response to her was slow to take effect. She seemed to understand there was too much on my mind for prurient pursuits at the moment. "God, you're beautiful, Charlie. Get in the shower. I'll make you something to eat."

The bathroom door opened and closed quietly just as I'd soaped down going for a second scrubbing. Audrey slid the shower door open, stood nude before me for a moment then stepped in. "Food can wait." We melted into each other like brilliant color on a white canvas.

I needed the sustenance Audrey was serving up as much as I needed food. But by the time we'd completed each other, food could not be put off any longer.

CHAPTER 29

JUST PAST TEN o'clock the next morning; I'd managed to survive Earline's nasty smoke chamber one more time. Theo looked as limp as a wet scarecrow. For a man who'd just received news the charges against his client were about to be dropped, he displayed little in the way of brio. Caputo's release was scheduled for later in the week.

"Appeared my goddaughter missed you," he began in that deceivingly distracted manner he could effect. "You gonna stay with her or break her heart?"

"You don't seem very happy about Vinny Caputo being released."

He probed me briefly with his eyes. "Pederson asked the State Police to lead a new investigation. Mendoza will be little more than an ancillary inconvenience. Pederson reserved the right to file new charges against Caputo pending the outcome."

"At least he's getting a fair shake. Caputo, I mean."

"Mr. Matta is about to be exposed." Theo glanced up at me. Dark pupils underscored by mucousy cranberry bags. "If you think you pissed him off before, I'd hold on to my seat," he warned. "And Sal DeCosta is a long way from getting out from under his shenanigans. He has no pull where the State Police are concerned. Both he and Mr.

Matta are about to find themselves on the hot seat. You should not be surprised they'll see this as your fault."

He appeared lost in thought a few beats. "You explain to Audrey you weren't an ordinary soldier, the tragedy that pinned that Bronze star to your chest?"

"There's no Bronze star on my chest."

"Perhaps not literally," Theo acquiesced. Dipped his head this way and that. "But it's there. Always going to be there, Charlie, along with a lot of other unpleasant memories, I imagine. You okay these days?" He brushed another glance in my direction.

For a moment I considered what Theo asked me. "I am," I replied. And I was telling the truth. There were triggers that could set me off, bring on reactions trained into me. Olivera was proof enough of that. But I was steadily gaining against the demons of combat and the tacit resentment against the government for subjecting me to that kind of horror. "I am okay. I was okay when I took Olivera down. I could have squirted his brains out on the ground like the pulp of a bad grape. Instead, he got a warning."

"A warning?"

"Audrey or Rachel." I looked away to the window then back at Theo. "I'm fair game, Theo. But one inappropriate move in their direction, it won't be just Olivera who gets hurt."

"You need to explain to her. And keep what you've been trained to do under control."

"I will and I will."

"When?"

"I will." I looked him in the eyes. We sat there, eyes locked, like a couple of mountain rams about to bash our hard heads in defense of our turf. "Soon," I said, softening enough to let him know I understood his point.

"You'll both be better off for it, Charlie."

"I'll talk to her. So what's next?"

He fumbled and fidgeted some. "Unless they recharge, things're in the hands of the State Police and Grant Pederson."

"Leaves me in a helluva lurch." I'd gone from inside the investigation to the sidelines.

"How so?"

"I have a novel with an unsolved crime and no ending."

"What about happily ever after?"

"Audrey and I will work things out the best we can. That's all I can give you."

He stared me down again with those watery, red-rimmed sags of his.

"Pederson knows your story," he said finally. "Admires you, obviously. Nobody's gonna throw you in jail for asking questions. And technically, you still work for me."

"So what are you suggesting?"

"Stay close to the investigation. Follow your instincts. Write your novel. Find the ending or at least be there when the State Police do. But stay out of their investigation. You come up with anything, come to me."

****

A quantum leap in my evolution had taken place. There are multitudes of psychological alleyways I could go down attempting to explain how things were different...changing, both within and outside of me.

The history I carried inside could either end up as tragic baggage that would eventually tear me down to useless as a human being, or I would find a way to turn those experiences, if we can reduce what I'd been through to that, into an asset. I was finally making the bend in the road. Not to say I was around the curve at that point, but I categorically believed I was on the right path.

And whether they liked it or not, the exchange between Grant Pederson and me at the police station had served to notify Sal DeCosta, Prado Mendoza and Jorge Olivera that the rules for engaging me had changed. Surely Olivera understood if he continued his harassment or attempted to take his wrath out on Audrey or Rachel, if he didn't end up in jail, at minimum, he'd be washed up. That last thought, I felt, would be an improvement the town could make immediately. A sleaze should never wield power over others.

Nothing much changed after my lock up; except for the first time since showing up in town I didn't feel the constant presence of Olivera as I went about my life.

Audrey and I got back to our regular routine of running for an hour most mornings, showering together after and making love as though there was about to be a ban passed for such pleasures.

Sooner or later our lust for each other had to slow down. A man and woman couldn't do what we were doing with each other that many times in one day—that many consecutive days without a break—but we were doing just that. And if the sex between us was about to slow down, there was certainly no sign of it. She was like an addiction. The more I had of her, the more I wanted and not simply in a prurient sense. She was developing an appreciation for my work. Audrey took me seriously as a writer even when I didn't. She seemed not simply to understand, but supported how I was attempting to reshape my life.

She made me feel like a real knight on a white charger. I was heroic in her eyes, which was totally different than being a hero of combat in the eyes of the Army. And I was scared shitless to talk about my nightmare for fear it'd change how she saw me, how she loved me. I mean, how would she be able to love me still after she knew the price I'd paid to survive? This was the bridge I was petrified to go over, but I couldn't put it off much longer.

Writing every day was beginning to embed itself in me. But it came after my attention to Audrey. My process was developing into a comfortable rhythm: run for an hour each morning, make love with Audrey, make love again...sometimes again. And when I say make love, I don't necessarily mean we always had intercourse. Sometimes it was just making out like a couple of teenagers, touching, caressing, playing. We loved seeing each other naked, tasting each other. Feeling our bodies come apart for each other.

Around three each afternoon I'd push back from my IBM. I couldn't imagine ever not having it by then. I'd drive Buck to Souza's Market and pick up a mini-split of red wine with something to snack on. Souza's became the hub where I ran into old schoolmates or friends of my parents. Gradually, I was assimilating back into the fabric of Divina. After those exchanges, I'd head over to the city park to unwind. Still no signs of Jorge Olivera, but Jeff Ponder was a near guaranteed encounter.

A palpable buzz grew up as word spread about Vinny Caputo being released. People, mostly women, with whom Caputo was patently unpopular, were incredulous. That I had any connection to what was taking place hadn't come out yet. At least I hadn't spotted any disgusted glares.

"What do you say to a barbeque Saturday afternoon?" Audrey asked as we got dressed Thursday morning. "Just a few people we went to high school with." She spun around, throwing her arms around my neck wearing only her panties. The warmth of her nipples against my bare chest made my groin go tight again.

"Socializing?" I kissed her, played her butt softly like a bongo drum.

"You could invite Natalie and Johnny Bettencourt. You've been talking about that. Give me a chance to introduce you to a few friends. Some of the guys you played football with if you want. They're all married and fat now." She giggled, squeezed my hard-on. "You wanna do it again?"

"Yes, but we're not going to. I need to get some work done. You're wicked."

"I love you. I can't get enough of you," she said working me into a frenzy.

"Stop that." I removed her hand.

But like I said, I couldn't get enough of her. Half-dressed and there we went again.

I agreed to the barbeque.

CHAPTER 30

BY THE TIME I was ready to set my writing aside Friday afternoon and head to the park, Audrey was gone. Running errands, I presumed. I loved what we had together more and more. Our independence from one another made our time together intense. I know it's cliché, but a little dose of distance and the heart growing fonder may have something to it.

When I pulled Buck onto Main Street and drove past the front of Souza's Market, I saw her white Chevy Impala parked out front. I drove to the closest space. Friday was a busy shopping day.

A creative thought jumped into my brain. Those fleeting gems could dissipate without capture and I was learning not to let them escape. For several minutes, sitting there behind the steering wheel, I wrote down what was in my head.

When I stepped up onto the sidewalk, scuffling the fifty yards or so to Souza's Market, I gradually picked up on angry shouting. Male, female voices. The source of the commotion was near. Audrey struggled between parked cars at the curb with a large bag of groceries trying to get her car door open. Duke Matta was ranting in her face about the motherfucker she was shacked up with ruining his life.

Matta was so in her face I doubt he saw me charge at him. By the time he looked up it was too late. The blow was a short jab that began with the fingers of my right hand curled half into my palm so the second row of knuckles formed a solid hard mass. You don't throw that blow. You step in close to your enemy, drive upward with your legs using the power of your shoulder to accelerate. You crush your target just below the sternum, pile-drive upward with all you have; enough to lift him off the ground, force out every ounce of air in his lungs. The victim will drop soundlessly to the ground unable to breathe or speak. In combat, you'd reach down and slit his throat.

Matta fought frantically to gain a brief gulp of oxygen. He wore a soundless panicked grimace on his face, a mime in terrified, silent agony. His color grew redder and redder. Spittle in white slobbery bubbles drizzled from the corner of his mouth while he clutched at his chest and twitched.

"You okay?" I asked, taking the heavy bag from Audrey.

"Oh shit, Charlie," Audrey cried. "You did it again."

"Did what?"

"Look at him." She was growing frantic. "He's dying. Do something!"

"He isn't dying." I looked down at Matta. "He just thinks he is." I set the bag of groceries onto the seat of her car and bent over Duke. "Relax. Struggling makes it worse." He was growing purple in the face by then. "Raise your hands over your head," I instructed him while Audrey watched. He reluctantly did what I told him. I rolled him completely onto his back, grasped his belt at the buckle and raised him slowly, let him back down gently, raised him again at the waist. In the next few instances he claimed his first breath since I'd put him down. His gasps rendered nearly as much relief for Audrey as they did for him.

Several more lifts facilitated the refilling of his lungs, like a manual hand pump. When his gasps turned to breaths and color gradually seeped back into his face, I pulled him to his feet and propped his panting hulk against Audrey's car.

"I'm gonna tell you this one time, Duke." I squeezed his slobbery chin and forced his tear-filled, bugged out eyes to look at me. "Don't ever go near her again. You see her on the street, cross over. You run into her in a store, leave. You have something to say to me, I'm not hard to find."

I removed my hands slowly and turned back to Audrey. "See, he's fine."

"Jesus, Charlie. We gotta talk." She was upset. Theo'd been pressing me to have this conversation with her and now I couldn't put it off any longer.

"See you at home," I said.

Duke stumbled across Main Street toward his office, but I imagined I hadn't seen or heard the last from him.

Audrey backed her car away from the curb and drove off slowly without looking to me. Following her straight home right then was not a thing I could bring myself to do. A crowd had gathered near the entrance of the market watching and wondering what was going on. Most stepped away from me when I went in, but I wasn't entirely sure two women were not about to try to claw my eyes out. Duke had his admirers.

With an eight-ounce bottle of Zinfandel and a small chunk of cheddar under my arm, I headed to the park. Explaining myself to Audrey, why I reacted to crisis situations the way I did, required a little preparation.

Instinctual. Resolute. Here was a by-product of training young men to kill nobody wanted to talk about. How do you *untrain* that in the same man? I *was* making progress. Duke Matta did walk away under his own power just like Olivera. Audrey's ex got off with a broken jaw. I was pretty sure I was making some improvement. They were all still alive.

The thing was, I didn't go looking for trouble. Frankly, I did everything possible to avoid physical violence. Unless it involved another combatant of my own skills, someone was about to get very hurt. But as you've seen, when violence comes at me, I take care of business first; deal with consequences later. Talking my way out of a fight, however, had never been one of my strong points even before the Special Forces turned me into a walking weapon. It's a flaw, I know. I'm working on it.

****

"Good `ole Charlie Caldwell." His face was hidden among the leaves up inside the cottonwood tree, but I knew the voice.

"How's it going, Jeff?"

The rustling of leaves...branches spread apart revealing him. "Nymphs hatched," Jeff announced as though he were an expecting parent. "Wanna see one?"

"Not today. Lots going on. I can't stay."

The leaves rustled under his movements, but we didn't speak further. He went on with whatever it was he was up to while I stood below, not really enjoying but consuming the wine.

After a few minutes, I drifted away without saying anything more to him. I doubt he had any awareness I'd gone.

****

When I got home, I avoided Audrey. Fear worked on me. Later, when Rachel came rushing through my door, I was in front of my IBM. That was an event I came to enjoy as much as the pleasures taking place with her mother each morning after she went off to school.

"Hi, Charlie." She collapsed a fierce hug around my neck.

"Hey, PF." I'd been granted the privilege to use the condensed version as well. "How was school?" Her answer was always the same.

She walked around my desk. Ran her fingertips over my note pad, the keys of the typewriter. An "x" fired and the letter appeared at the end of the last word I'd typed. "Oh!" She jumped. Turned to me. A look of distress. "I'm sorry—"

"Doesn't take much." I shrugged. "Just a light touch. Once you get used to it."

"Did I mess it up...your page?"

"No." I hugged her again. "Let's go see what your mom's up to."

"Mom said I could spend the weekend with my friend Stephanie," she told me while we strolled hand-in-hand up the path. "Daddy called and said he couldn't take me this weekend. Grandma's sick or something."

Audrey met us at the kitchen door. She ran her hand over the top of Rachel's fontanel, buried her fingers in the luxurious thick mop of curls. She leaned down and kissed her daughter on the top of her head. "Have a fun day?"

"Yeah," Rachel replied. "Can I eat at Stephanie's', please, please, Mom?" she niggled. "Steph said her mother said it would be okay with her if it was okay with you." Rachel's plea had clearly been thought out, perhaps rehearsed.

Audrey turned her attention to me. "Thought you were following me home from Souza's."

"I needed to unwind a little," I said.

"You unwound?" Her tone had attitude.

Rachel pulled away from her mother. "You two fighting?" She looked from one to the other of us.

"I'm not," I claimed instantly.

"I'm not either." Audrey tiptoed up to kiss me lightly on the lips.

"Good," Rachel said. "I'd hate to have to cancel my plans." She padded off toward her room. "I'll get my things, Mom. Can you take me pretty soon?"

Audrey grinned, shaking her head. "Twelve—"

"Going on twenty," I completed the refrain. "You want me to help with dinner?" I offered, intending to deflect what was coming.

"You okay?" Audrey asked.

"Yeah...good. How 'bout you?"

"We've had a few cancellations for the barbeque."

"Oh?"

"Natalie Bettencourt's at the top of the list."

Natalie was positive Vinny Caputo killed Miranda. She must have decided whatever happened with Vinny was in some way tied to my conversations with her. My fault he was about to be released.

"The guys from your old team, too," she added.

I turned, gazed out across the San Joaquin Valley. They were all still tight friends with Duke Matta. "Less work for us," I said, understanding fully lines were being drawn.

"Everybody in town knows what happened between you and Duke."

"Nothing happened between Duke and me, Audrey."

"Well yo—"

"Nothing happened between Duke and me," I repeated. "He was out of line...being aggressive. Let him know he can't get away with that...all that happened."

She looked into my eyes for several moments. "You broke Darryl's jaw. You damn near killed Jorge Olivera and got thrown in jail for the weekend."

"They were going to throw me in jail anyway," I pointed out, attempting a defense.

"I really thought Duke was going to die right there on the street," she went on.

We stood in silence a few moments. Audrey held me with her eyes.

"No one's ever loved me like you, Charlie." She put her arms around my waist and buried her face in my chest. "I don't want to lose you over some jerk mouthing off to me. I'm not fragile. You don't have to hurt people to protect me."

I caressed her hair and held her to me.

"If you two could stop making out long enough, maybe you could drive me over to Stephanie's." Rachel headed out into the courtyard with a small bag slung across her shoulders.

"Wanna drive us?"

I kissed her gently. "Let's have a talk after dinner tonight."

She kissed me back. "Let's."

Rachel was sitting on Buck's bench seat, waiting impatiently. "You two are gonna wear your lips out," she chirped as Audrey and I slid in sandwiching her between us.

Audrey worked her arms around her precocious daughter and buried her face in her riotous mop of hair. She made mommy sounds and Rachel giggled.

****

We were coming to the end of May. The days had warmed measurably. Many afternoons saw the high eighties, but it was still pleasant by early evening. The grasses along the foothills had begun turning from deep variants of jade to more burnished wheat colors that would ultimately give way to bright golden in late June.

Our quiet dinner was an hour behind us. We'd pushed the chaise lounges in the courtyard together with a half empty bottle of cabernet sitting on the table next to me. Audrey was curled into my side, one leg lazily draped across mine, holding me, her hand slipped inside my shirt resting on my bare stomach. I did my best in spasms of sentences to explain to her how it was I came to be so lethal under certain circumstances.

"During boot camp they picked me out instantly. Lotta those guys struggled to do simple shit. Everything came easy for me. I was already in good shape...figured things out pretty quick. If I went into the jungle with the bunch of guys I was training with, my chances of getting back were limited. I was scared...drill sergeants made it clear where our next stop was after their care and training." My memory seemed to float, out-of-body.

"After advanced infantry training they gave me the chance to join the Airborne Rangers. More training...tougher bunch of guys. Gung ho types. I was rationalizing, I think. After jump-school they called me in again...told me about a new unit forming. Special Forces they called them. These guys wore berets instead of standard issue headgear.

"To be honest, I thought the longer I stayed in training the better the chances I'd find some way not to be sent to combat."

Audrey sat up, laid across me, reaching for her glass and took a long sip before setting it back on the table, snuggling back into her warm spot. "Plan didn't work, I take it?"

I remembered when I first sensed I wouldn't be able to avoid a combat tour. "No. It didn't."

We lay silent for a time.

"It was a fucked up situation," I said, feeling the need, not for the first time, to defend what I'd done. "I protested against the Vietnam war along with thousands of other college kids. And then I woke up and found myself right in the middle of the damn thing. I hated it, Audrey, but I didn't want to die. It was a nightmare. Those Vietnamese kids didn't want to die either. But they were going to kill me or I was going to kill them. That's how war is conducted. Governments stick young warriors out in places and circumstances from which they can't escape and wait. The most resourceful survive...all there is to it. You find a way to survive the horror. If you do, you're some kind of hero. Maybe your side wins?"

"How many men did you..." She lifted her eyes to meet mine, but didn't finish the question.

"Too many, Baby. Got very good at it. But not good enough to save the lives of three men I loved like brothers and for that they call me a fucking hero, give me a Bronze Star and now I can go home."

"You're trembling," Audrey noticed, stating something I was all too aware of.

For a time I couldn't reply. She held me while I did my best to put myself back to the place I thought I'd managed to get. I'd been doing much better keeping my demons at bay. Hard to explain to someone that in the retelling of it I was reliving the thing.

The instant I heard the report I knew what it was. A bullet exploded the wine bottle inches from my left elbow and ripped through the padded cushion of the lounge just beside my knee.

I rolled across Audrey, away from the direction the shot had come. I drug her with me as I fell off the opposite side of the lounge. She was screaming in terror...tried to scramble to her feet. As I pulled her back down, I saw a trickle of blood from a scrape on her knee.

"Stop fighting me," I shouted into her face.

She stared back at me, stupefied.

The paving stones scraped her knees as I dragged her across the courtyard toward the cover of the house. The shot had come from over my left shoulder. Against the front of the house the field of fire was reduced. The sniper no longer had a shot at us.

At the kitchen wall I pulled her to a sitting position. "You okay?" I made sure I saw no gunshot wound.

"Yeah. You?" she was momentarily in control.

"I'm not hit. Get inside and call the cops."

"No!" she screamed. "You come inside and call the cops with me."

"Call the cops," I ordered and slid around the corner. From there I was under the crest of the rocky overhang behind the house. The delay between the exploding bottle and the report put the sniper about one hundred yards out. I guessed about where he had to be.

The craggy rock face was the way to attack. They never expect you to come at them frontally. I slithered myself onto the upper ledge and found a shallow undulation in the earth. The trough was the best cover I could find.

Surveying the general direction from where I figured the shot had come; I waited, listened and watched. No movement. He was either still there, hoping to get another clear shot or already gone. Dead's the confirmation you get for the wrong guess in a situation like that. I began crawling toward the high ground. Someone would be dead all right if the sonofabitch *was* still there and I didn't plan on it being me.

Gaining the area I estimated the shot must have come from, I found broken down scrub and crushed brush. Whoever it was had fled. Anticipating the sniper could have retreated and taken up a new position, I kept low. I rolled onto my side looking down the path of the bullet. Had to have been one of the worst shots imaginable. By all rights, I should have been down there right then with a hole in the back of my head, my face blown out. Any reasonably good shot wouldn't have missed.

Two possibilities: he meant to miss or he was just a bad shot. Anybody's guess.

Searching by grid across the terrain, I stayed low. Gradually, I felt certain whoever it was had escaped. Broken scrub and brush left a trail back toward the roadway.

"Charlie! Answer me!" Audrey screamed frantically from the bottom of the rock overhang. She was out of control, in a panic.

I popped my head over the edge so she could see me. "I'm here, Audrey. It's okay. I'm okay. I'm climbing down to you right now. Calm down."

"Oh, Ch..ar..lie." She was sub-sucking like a three year-old.

I dropped the last few feet to the ground and folded her into my arms. "It's okay, Baby. It's okay." She clung to me tightly.

Moments later I had her inside the kitchen, sitting in a chair, cleaning blood from the scrapes on her knees and elbows when I heard a siren coming up the hill. Then I heard a second siren. The first car skidded to a stop out front. We heard Prado Mendoza as he saw the scene in the courtyard. "Holy shit!" he exclaimed.

The kitchen door remained flung wide open. He saw me kneeling in front of Audrey, cleaning her wounds.

"You okay?" he asked her.

She shook her head.

"You?" he asked me less enthusiastically.

We all turned to look as the second police car slid to a stop in the driveway. I couldn't wait to add Jorge Olivera to this scene. He came running through the door with his pistol drawn.

"Put that thing away before you hurt somebody," his boss ordered.

Olivera looked bewildered while he holstered his weapon.

Mendoza turned to me. "What happened? You see anybody? Anyting?"

I showed him where we were when the shot came. "There was no warning. Nothing to alert us. No chance to see a thing."

"Too bad he missed," Olivera said under his breath.

Mendoza spun on him. I turned my gaze at him as well.

"Didn't mean that," he offered reluctantly.

Mendoza stared at him several seconds before he turned back to me. "Audrey said you went after whoever it was shot at you."

"Too late," I dabbed at the nastiest scrape on her knee. She winced. "I found where the shot came from. Not hard to locate. Whoever it was ran for it before I could get there."

Mendoza walked to the sliding doors looking out toward the guesthouse and the rock overhang. "Too dark to see anything up there tonight. We'll see what we can find first ting in the morning. And don't move nothin' in the courtyard. I want to see everyting just as it is in the morning light.

"I'd ask you got any idea who might o' done this, but the way you made friends around town be a waste o' time."

Olivera laughed and grunted.

All three of us turned to him and he withered like a cut flower out of water.

"Charlie and Duke Matta got into a fight today," Audrey said.

"Whole town's heard about it," Mendoza said. "Don't tink it's his style. Makes him too obvious, but I'll question him."

"I agree." I got to my feet. "Look Chief, I didn't have a lot of friends here when I showed up in town." I glanced down at Audrey, turned a brief glare directly at Olivera before looking back to Mendoza. "But I don't think anybody wanted to kill me. That I know of."

"'N in the short time you're back, you break this woman's husband's jaw, attack my deputy and today you blindside a respected businessman in our community."

Audrey jumped to her feet. "That is total bullshit! Bullshit!" she screamed getting in Mendoza's face. "Every one of them, and now you, are harassing him. He was just defending himself...and me."

"And you moved in with *her*," he went on with his accusation as if Audrey wasn't standing directly in front of him, "like you own the place. 'N just to let us all know how important you are, you get a rapist and murderer out o' jail."

I pulled Audrey back from Mendoza.

He cocked his head, lifted his hat and ran his fingers over the top of his head. "I can tink roughly more'n a thousand people might want to blow your head off." Mendoza smirked. "I'd still arrest whoever did it though."

The room went stone silent for several moments.

"I'll investigate the crime scene in the morning," Mendoza said and drew Olivera with him as he left.

"Sonofabitches," Audrey muttered as the two cops pulled away in their cars.

We walked back out to the courtyard, surveyed the mess. I looked back up to where the shot had come from. Mendoza had it right: too dark to see anything more tonight.

"We were lucky," I said.

Audrey held me tight. "We're sleeping in my bedroom tonight."

I didn't argue.

****

We walked down to the bungalow for clean clothes. I was splattered with red wine down my left side and covered in dirt and foxtails up my front from low-crawling across the ground. Audrey held tightly to my right arm, refusing to let me out of her sight.

We showered together in her master bath, but neither of us was in the mood for our usual activities. I leaned in under the showerhead, letting the warm water run down over my entire body. Audrey washed my back and rubbed my shoulders. We held each other and kissed.

After we toweled off, we slipped into our underwear and decided to have a couple of bourbons. Audrey put ice cubes in two glasses and I poured us each a double shot.

We went to her family room where I sat on the couch in my boxers and she nestled against me in her panties. We didn't talk. We just were.

Before we climbed into bed, I had her sit on the side while I applied a large bandage to her knee over the nastiest of her scrapes. "It's okay, Charlie," she said softly. "What happened over there."

I continued ministering to her knee.

"You did what you had to in order to stay alive. None of that was your fault. You had no choice." She reached down and lifted my face, looked deep into me. "I understand. And I realize now what happens to you when you feel threatened. Just as bad if you think I'm in some kind of danger. I see what you're capable of. Just promise me you won't kill anyone ever again." She smiled. "Please."

We slipped between the cool cotton sheets, snuggled into each other's arms and let the power of the alcohol do its work

CHAPTER 31

WE WERE UP and dressed, finishing breakfast when Mendoza pulled to a stop in the driveway around seven the next morning.

He didn't come to the door and knock. Instead, he walked into the courtyard and around the chaise lounges, glancing here and there and up to the top of the hill.

Audrey opened the kitchen door and shouted to him, "Cup of coffee?"

He looked up at her as I walked up behind her and put my hands on her shoulders. Mendoza stared at us a few moments. "No tanks. Gotta see what I can figure out here."

Audrey and I walked out to where he stood. The mess looked worse in the daylight. Red wine stains appeared like blood all around. There were green glass shards everywhere. Where the bullet tore through the cushion, cotton stuffing bulged out and hung. There was a gouge in the paving stone where the bullet ricocheted. Unfortunately, we wouldn't determine the caliber of the rifle. The slug went right through the front gate opening.

We walked him through our movements after the shot hit. The chief made mental notes and moved around the scene. "Come on." He invited us to ride with him in his patrol car up Silverado Trail to the spot where the shot was fired.

Below the spot where I said the tracks led off, he pulled his car to the opposite side of the road. "Don't wanna destroy no tire tracks we might find."

We walked across the crest of the rock overhang and looked down into Audrey's courtyard. "Pretty much see everything goes on down there from up here," Mendoza said casually. He glanced back up the slight grade leading to the higher ground, turned and looked back down into the yard below. The path I'd taken the night before crawling up the gradual slope was easy to follow. Mendoza led the way.

When we'd climbed to the spot, "Hold up here," Mendoza ordered. He searched every square inch looking for a shell casing or any other physical evidence that might give him a clue. He found none.

Mendoza ordered us to go back the way we'd come while he worked his way step by step through the broken down scrub and grass toward the road. We rejoined him keeping to the pavement. "Nothing," he announced as we met back up. "No identifiable footprints. No article of clothing or anything else dropped. You can see, no tire tracks. Ground's too hard. Too much gravel."

We walked back to the patrol car.

"You can clean your place now," he told Audrey. "Whoever it was knows you're on alert. Stay out of that courtyard at night, I was you." Mendoza looked at me. "Caputo's out tomorrow. I tink somebody's pissed off at you for that. Just a guess." He was pretty casual about the whole thing, but then he hadn't been shot at.

Mendoza moved to get into his black and white.

"We'll walk back," I told him. "No offense. We just want the exercise."

"Suit yourself." He climbed in, made a U-turn and drove off.

Audrey and I stood for several moments listening to waves of gentle breeze panting through the tops of the waving field of grass across the hillside.

"He's been watching us," I said.

"Mendoza?"

"No. Whoever took the shot."

"What makes you say that?"

"Instinct. Just a feeling." I took Audrey's hand and we walked slowly down the hill toward her house. "Remember the night of our first date?"

She grinned up at me. "You bet I remember."

"Not that." I ran my hand over the top of her shoulder, pulled her to my side. "The rocks crashing onto the roof of your house that night."

"Oh, Jesus, Charlie!" She stopped and stared up into my eyes. "Are you sure?"

"No," I admitted. "Like I said, just a feeling. Remember the night I asked you about the whiff of some odor I thought was odd?" I saw she understood my drift. "It's the sum of the parts. Nothing concrete. Just one too many coincidences and now this."

"What are we going to do?"

"Have our barbeque tomorrow. Go on as normal as we can."

"Oh, God, Charlie. I don't know."

"We scare whoever did this, we might never catch him."

"We don't scare him," Audrey argued, "he might really shoot you the next time."

"Like Mendoza said, we need to stay out of the courtyard at night."

"And how long do you think we can accept being prisoners in our own home?"

"Your own home."

"Our home, Charlie—yours and mine and Rachel's. Our home."

The significance in what Audrey said and how she said it lodged heavy in me. I loved her more than any person I'd ever loved, Rachel, too. But Divina...there was the rub; the way this scrubby little town still bore on me.

****

Jane and Anthony, Stephanie's mother and father, showed up at three Sunday afternoon. Rachel gave Audrey and me big hugs before she and Stephanie disappeared to her room.

Jane went with Audrey into the kitchen. Anthony snatched a cold beer and watched me build a fire in the pit.

"Wife says you're some kind o' writer or somethin' like that," Anthony ventured.

"Something like that." I smiled and grabbed several more pieces of mesquite.

He wasn't pushy, but he wasn't shy either.

"So what kinda shit you write?"

I smiled. "Shit I find interesting."

"Hey, I din't mean nothin'."

"Me neither."

The logs in the pit began to blaze and smoke. Two more couples arrived. Audrey made introductions. All of the faces were recognizable from years in my past. Some I'd run into at Souza's Market in recent weeks. Oddly familiar-feeling encounters.

Three more couples arrived. The longer the afternoon went on, the more I could place individual faces in my memory, much younger versions of these faces, of course. They had kids together, most of them. We didn't know each other and yet we did.

The men gathered around me with cold beers next to the barbeque pit. The women congregated with Audrey in the kitchen. Everybody'd brought something. Salads and casseroles were being set up buffet style inside on the table.

"Remember you was a helluva running back," one of the men said.

"Long time ago," I replied.

"Heard you was in Nam," a guy named Clarence added.

"Some truth in that."

A big guy named Bruce moved around the edge of the group. "Seen what you done to Darryl's jaw." There was no accusation in his tone. "Heard you goddamn near knocked the piss out of Olivera, too." The entire group of them took a long pull of beer in unison. "Ain't so sure was too smart what you done to Duke though." In this observation there was judgment.

They all went quiet waiting for my response. I ignored the jibe. "Duke and I are old friends. Played ball together all four years of high school. Wasn't anything. Little misunderstanding's all."

"Ain't what I heard," Bruce insisted, eyed me over the can while he took a long pull from his beer.

A short tubby guy named Joe—original, I know— spoke up. Divina was full of Joes, Joeys, Josephs; popular Portuguese name. "I heard was you that got Vinny out," Joe added.

They were a friendly enough bunch of people. Curious mostly. I couldn't blame them for that.

Guy by name of Al stepped over and poked the logs of the fire. "I'll give you a hand when the steaks are ready to go on."

"Thanks," I said. "Get any of you guys another beer?"

"I'll take one." A raised empty.

"You ever wanna go over to Moss Landing, get clams sometime, give me a call." Another unidentified voice chimed in.

"Deep sea fishin' out o' Monterey," a new voice interjected. "Makes me puke like a somebitch, but always come home widda good cetch."

266

R.P. McCabe

The evening ended in quiet conversation. Tiny pods of two or three or four people huddled close; kids, cows or crops, issues in front of the City Council. It was as if there was no war in Vietnam, no riots in the streets of every major city across the country, a bunch of burglars somehow tied to the White House hadn't just broken into Democratic Party Headquarters at a place called the Watergate and the Weather Underground wasn't blowing up buildings around the country to make a point. Or that Miranda DeCosta hadn't been murdered and raped in their isolated little town; the murderer still among them.

****

Monday morning I watched Audrey wiggle into her panties. "What?" she asked, catching me. It was the first time I hadn't been honest with her about my thoughts. Yet what I told her was the total truth. "You have a pretty bottom."

"You, too." She grinned approvingly. "You gonna write?"

"For a while."

Having someone taking shots at me was working on me. I didn't buy Mendoza's speculation somebody was pissed off over the release of Vinny Caputo or blaming me was at the root of it. People don't shoot at people over things like that.

In my novel, as in my life, I'd come to the murder of Miranda DeCosta. My novel couldn't go much further without a resolution and neither could my life

267

CHAPTER 32

GETTING PASSED EARLINE had become less of a challenge than it was merely distasteful. I'd come to appreciate Theo's affinity for kindness to his fellow man, but this woman was simply an uncouth bore. The smell of the office space she occupied made me want to regurgitate.

"I want to talk to Caputo," I told Theo.

"Why didn't you call me about the shooting?"

"Nothing to tell, Theo. Someb—"

"When people get shot at in a small town there's something to tell." His eyes were dark as he leveled them on me.

"Should've called you. I'm sorry. Mendoza found no clues and I don't have any either. Not even sure it has anything to do with your case. Plenty of people around here don't seem to have much use for me."

He shrugged. Tended the small stack of documents in front of him. "Caputo certainly can be eliminated."

"Not following, Theo."

"My client was about to do a life sentence for this murder and now he's out, in no small way, thanks to you."

"Your point?"

"Maybe it does have something to do with Miranda DeCosta. Maybe the real murderer feels you getting closer to the truth."

And if Theo's speculation was correct, whoever took a shot at me was a bad shot. He hadn't meant to scare me. He'd simply missed his target.

"You could be right."

"I am right," he asserted. "I can arrange a meeting with Caputo. But you won't learn anything about who did the crime. Vinny is, as they say, irrelevant. Just a loud mouth in the wrong place on the wrong night."

I left Theo's office with more mixed emotions than when I'd arrived.

My note pad nested on my lap as I sat in the city park, staring at the blank page when a bear of a man walked up and took a seat next to me. The guy had a huge head and a burley beard. A grizzly character dressed in a cheap suit.

"Bobby Dale Clarke," he said in a deep baritone voice, extending his hand. "Lieutenant, Bobby Dale Clarke. California State Police."

When I shook his hand, mine nearly disappeared in his mitt. "Charlie Caldwell," I replied. It was clear he already knew who I was.

Clarke leaned forward, elbows on his knees, folded his thick fingers together out front of him, scanned the park aimlessly.

We sat quietly for some time.

"You've stirred things up pretty good around here," he finally said.

I didn't reply.

"Pederson says you strike him okay."

"You won't get that from Mendoza," I assured him.

"He isn't about to become your new best friend, I'd agree," Clarke said. "But you got him guessing about you."

Silence.

"I'm gonna start over from scratch with this investigation. Looks to some people like you got ideas about this murder."

I thought about the conversation I was about to have with this cop. There was an aura about the guy. Somehow he put me at ease but I'd never laid eyes on him. "You a vet?"

"Korea."

"Combat?"

"Pussy," he intoned laconically.

"Pussy?"

"Got all of it I could get over there. Love Asian women. Koreans are nice. Little too big boned for my taste. Now take the Japanese. Went TDY in Okinawa once. More petite. Very feminine Japanese women...my opinion anyway. You?"

"Just combat," I said.

"So I heard. You like *boom-boom* with the *dink* pussy?"

I appreciated how he avoided getting into my service record. I'd been down that road enough over the last few days. "*Dinky dau*," I said.

He eyed me briefly. "Probably missed out. I'm told they're sexy. Tiny little things. Hold one up in your hand looks like to me. Wouldn't mind tryin' 'em. Kentucky boy myself," he went on, shifting gears without a stop. "Born and raised. You, me, probably got a fair amount in common."

"How do you figure?"

"White trash, just like you. Least that's the way we started out, ain't it?" He glanced over his shoulder at me. His smile was disarming.

"Is this going somewhere?"

"Could be," he said. "Ever visited where they found her body?"

When he asked me, I felt ashamed I hadn't. I think I was afraid that would have taken me too close to what happened to her. "No," I admitted.

"Got time to take a ride?"

Nothing in or around Divina is very far away. We were sitting less than two miles from where Miranda's body was found.

The car we got into was an unmarked white Chevy Belair, maybe a seventy model, with black numbers on one corner of the trunk lid and black-wall tires. Buck was a rust bucket. But he was a good looking enough old truck. Clarke's official State car was ordinary ugly.

He pulled away from the curb slowly. "What's your history with this Duke Matta character?" he asked almost immediately as he turned the first corner.

The answer he was looking for was something too personal for me to confess to anyone. "We went to high school together. Played football on the same team. I guess you could say we grew up together. All ninety-four of us who graduated in the class of '62 went from kindergarten through twelfth grade."

"One big happy family," Clarke said, deadpan.

"Everybody knew everybody if that's what you mean."

"All you guys got some of the same pussy."

"You know, I'm no goody-two-shoes, but what's the deal with pussy all the time?"

"Just getting to know you, Charlie. Guy talk. Locker room shit. No big deal."

I knew the location, more or less where Miranda's body had been found, but I hadn't paid attention just how near it was to the path Audrey and I ran nearly every morning.

From the city park it was no more than half a mile to the bridge over the big irrigation canal heading out of town. Clarke turned right onto the dirt road running atop its east bank. We continued another three quarters of a mile to a rickety wooden bridge used for farm equipment to move back and forth between fields across the canal without having to drive all the way out to the main road to get across.

Clarke turned right again for a distance of about half a mile. He stopped in the middle of the dirt road, which was little more than a rutted tractor path between the fields. A freshly mown field of alfalfa lay on the north side of the road. Earth had been disked in the field to the south for planting something.

Clarke got out of his car grasping a manila folder off the front seat. He stood at the hood, seemed to study the contents in the folder like he'd never seen them before. He looked to the east. The fields followed the general contour of the slope down toward the valley. To the west were the outskirts of town. He gave a quick look in both directions once more. "About here." He pointed to the edge of the plowed field where she would've been discovered.

"Pretty wide open area. Risky."

"They say it was foggy that night," I offered.

"What it says here in the report, too. That would do it. Gets bad around here. Like soup. Broad daylight you can't see shit.

"Says in the report there were no tire tracks owing to the tractors driving over this road that morning. Didn't find her body until after they'd made several passes."

Lieutenant Clarke seemed nice enough, but I doubted the guy knew what the hell he was doing. "And now...what...three months later? Whattaya think we're gonna find out here?" I asked.

He looked at me. Big disarming grin. Walked a ways back to the west. Looked back to where I waited next to his car. Like I said, he didn't seem overly sharp, just friendly.

He walked slowly back toward me, leaned against the trunk of his Chevy and folded his arms across his barrel chest. When he spoke, I didn't feel included. "Guy goes to this girl's apartment, rapes her in her own bed according to the previous investigation, but he feels compelled to drag her body out here and dump her. Why you think he'd do that, Charlie?"

He wasn't actually asking me a question.

"Brings her all the way here where her body's sure to be found in a short time." He unfolded his arms and scooted up onto the trunk of the car, pulled his heels onto the bumper, gawked out over the San Joaquin Valley. The smell of the fresh mown alfalfa was sweet and pungent. It almost made you forget the aroma of cow shit. In the distance we could hear the thrum of a crop duster's Doppler crescendos as it dove, leveled off and accelerated to climb again. "Why not throw her body into that big canal?" he asked, purely rhetorical. "No one would have thought to look there. Could have been weeks...hell, months...before she was discovered." He slid off the trunk. Ignored me further. Brushed his hands deep into his pockets and went on talking out loud, but more or less to himself, thinking in stream of consciousness. "It was foggy as hell that night. No street lights out here to find that tractor bridge." He turned to look back toward the narrow wooden bridge. "Complicated enough to find your way out here in the daylight much less in a full-on fog after you murdered a girl."

I thought then I might have rushed to judgment on Lieutenant Clarke.

"You know, Charlie, when a picture is supposed to look like abstract art, but it looks like bullshit? It's usually bullshit." With that declaration Clarke unleashed a belly laugh that could have rocked pillars. The man's voice was as booming and big as the rest of him.

When he finished laughing at his own joke, I said, "Duke Matta confessed to being with her, having sex with her at her apartment the night she was killed."

"He told you that?" Clarke spun quickly to face me. The anticipation on his face was short of astonished, but hugely hopeful.

"Not exactly."

He walked back toward me. "What do you mean, not exactly?"

"He didn't say it to *me*. He told Caputo's lawyer, my employer, Theo Azevedo. Theo told me."

"Okay. Hold up here. You work for Caputo's lawyer?"

"Chasing leads. Mostly my own. Or poking around where my instincts lead me."

"Like a private investigator?"

"Just asking questions. I'm a writer. I'm not a private investigator."

"But you have an obligation to a client?"

"Caputo, probably. Matta, no. What I stumbled onto would make him a suspect, in my opinion."

"You gonna share this revelation?"

My instincts, more than any understanding of what was happening between Clarke and me, told me to get as much concession as I could for what I could tell him. "You gonna share what you find out with me?"

He gawped at me, a broad, toothy grin spreading over his friendly face. Clarke was one of those Hollywood good-looking types. He pointed his finger at me slowly like aiming a pistol, paused as if to size up the situation. "Off the record until after this case is closed and goes to trial?"

"Deal." We shook hands again and I began to spill what I knew—or conjectured. "Duke claims Miranda called him at his home the night of the murder. She'd had the well-publicized argument at The Sweet Shop with Caputo. She was upset. Pleaded with him to come to her apartment. Says he did. Admitted to Theo he had sex with her, but swears she was lying in her bed when he left. You do know by now she was pregnant?" I added.

274

"Yes, the autopsy report has been corrected."

"Well, you're all about to find out Matta was the father."

Clarke looked deep into my eyes. There was gravity in his countenance then. "I'd like to keep this between us, Charlie. I can't afford to taint the evidence in this case. It's already been fucked up once."

"We never had this conversation, Lieutenant."

"You got some personal axe to grind with Matta?"

I'd dealt with that question often enough by then, I no longer questioned my motivations. "None," I assured him with confidence.

"Then why'd you knock him on his ass on Main Street in front of half the town?"

He eyed me carefully while I collected myself. "Had nothing to do with me having any axe to grind, Lieutenant. He was abusing a friend of mine. Pissed me off. You know, flash of anger. Gone in an instant."

"While he picks his ass up off the pavement." Clarke scrutinized me carefully as he made the summation. Then he relaxed a bit. "So let me get this—Matta goes to her the night of the murder—has sex with her—she's already knocked up with his kid—leaves her in her bed and what? Goes home?"

"What he claims," I said. "You should also know they fought at some earlier point over her getting rid of the kid, getting an abortion. Matta didn't want her to have the kid. Gonna fuck up his life, his marriage.

"That's gonna to be the least of his worries when Sal DeCosta finds out about all of this."

"Getting interesting," Clarke agreed. "Think it could have been Matta who took the shot at you?"

"You know about that?"

"Mendoza called Pederson right away. Pederson called the State. Asked us to move on this immediately. I got the assignment. So you think he could be the one?"

"Personally, no," I admitted candidly. "Doesn't seem like Duke's style. He'd have to know he'd be an obvious suspect."

"Don't be naïve, Charlie. Some of these guys do exactly the opposite of what you think they would do; counterintuitive kind o'. I'll be checking his alibi."

Listening to Lieutenant Clark made me begin to reexamine my thinking about Duke. At first I hated the guy for his betrayal back in high school. Once I was able to let go of that, I was more willing to imagine him incapable of hurting Miranda. But that's what he'd been doing all along, hurting her, lots of other women, too. "Why would the guy incriminate himself the night she was murdered if he did it?"

Clarke's response was the same initial response I'd had with Theo. We looked at each other and said it in unison, "To throw us off his trail."

"Look, Charlie, knowing it and proving it are two different things. Let's guard our suspicions closely. And you watch your back. I'll be staying at the Trails End Motel," Clarke said.

"Nice place. My former residence, too."

"You need me for anything...leave a message at the front desk. Room 7. Be around town until this is under wraps."

He pulled his car into the edge of the alfalfa field, turned in a large arc and headed back the way we'd come.

Clarke looked straight ahead while he drove. "I've been over your service record," he said. "Made a few calls. Sorry." He shrugged, glanced over conveying no actual apology. "Routine procedure," he explained. "Guys like you are the good guys, Caldwell. Don't let the small town shit get under you."

I listened, but felt no desire to have this discussion.

276

He pulled to the curb next to Buck. "Whoever took the shot at you figures you're onto him. Eyes to the front and behind."

Regardless of what Clarke said to me, I knew better than to keep our conversation from Theo. I drove straight to his office.

"Comes as no surprise," Theo said. "There's going to be a lot of, 'Caldwell said,' going on in this investigation. Whether it was your intent or not, you've inserted yourself into the center of this firestorm. You have no responsibility of confidentiality to anyone except Vinny Caputo. He's my client and you my research assistant. Just remember, everything you say or do is going to touch some innocent person's life, Charlie." Theo, the eternal guardian angel.

****

The town was getting into full swing with the buzz Duke Matta had become the new prime suspect in the murder of Miranda DeCosta. This time around I thought they were actually getting closer to the truth.

Whether it was some deep psychological need in me that wanted to see him punished I can't honestly say anymore. That line in the sand one moment seemed clear and in the next, blurred once more.

Lieutenant Clarke was impervious to local politics and prejudice. He could have cared less what Sal DeCosta or Mendoza, for that matter, anyone in Divina, thought about how he pursued his investigation. Several marriages began to suffer the scrutiny of Clarke's pursuit into Matta's extra marital dalliances.

Funny how the dynamics of a small town work. There certainly was no secret about Matta's being a horn-dog low-life, frequenting the bedrooms of many women around town. A washed out jock doing his best to relive his glory days, maybe some of the women he chased around with, too. And yet, there was the hush of disbelief when a specific bedroom would come to light. "Who would ever have thought Tillie would have done such a thing?" Husbands were wringing their hands and pulling their hair. Some women were offended they hadn't been included in Matta's circle of *close* lady friends.

With the uproar surrounding Duke, I called Natalie Bettencourt to try to mend fences. Natalie was one of the few people I thought of as a friend. The sadness I felt for having used what she'd told me without at least an attempt to help her understand its significance was sincere.

"Well, you can go fuck yourself, Charlie," she said to me on the phone. "Duke is a creep. But no way you convince me he killed Miranda. You used me to get the sonofabitch who did kill her out of jail. God is gonna make you sorry!" She hung up on me.

"She'll get over it," Audrey predicted when I told her.

****

A week after I'd been shot at, Audrey and I were finally seeing the French Connection. We booked a room in Modesto's hottest new hotel, the Clarion. Parts of it were still being finished. We ate an early dinner and caught the seven o'clock show at the State Theatre downtown. After the movie, we walked holding hands until we found a cocktail lounge. We chose a dark corner table. Scotch with just a splash of water for me. Audrey ordered a sloe gin fizz.

Her hand was resting on my hard-on when the waiter delivered our drinks. She let go of me long enough to hold her drink with both hands and suck long from the straw while she eyed me lasciviously. "Guess what I'm gonna do to you when we get back to the hotel?"

"That car chase was far out," I said.

Old Blue Eyes crooned, *One Note Samba,* in the background through the stereo speakers.

"All violence: kidnapping, killing, action, noise," she complained.

"Got best picture."

"'Cuz old fat guys decide that stuff. Girls want a little romance included." She slid her hand back down and squeezed me firmly. "Like that." She leaned to kiss me.

Why fight city hall, I decided, slid my hand up the insides of her thighs. "Jesus, Audrey. You don't have any panties on."

"Like that?" She grinned and spread her legs slightly, looking around the room to be sure we had our privacy.

Sinatra moved on to, *My Way.*

"You're soaking wet." I played my fingers gently inside her.

"Drink up, soldier. We're wasting time." She stifled a moan. "On second thought, leave the drinks. Let's get out of here." She gathered her purse.

"Damn, Audrey," I complained, looking down into my crotch. "Everybody's gonna see."

"Yeah." She smiled. "Let 'em see it'n weep."

The waiter came over. "Is everything all right with your drinks?" he asked, sensing we were about to leave half way through them.

"He has a ride waiting," she told the waiter while keeping her eyes on me. "Pay the man, Charlie. You don't want to miss that ride, do you?"

Audrey stood, didn't wait for me. The swing of her ass and the glance back over her shoulder turned every head in the joint, women included.

There wasn't much I could do. I took a long pull of the Scotch as though it was pure water and stood. Grins broadened around the room as I paid the guy and made my way out front to catch up with her.

She put her arms around my neck as I came out and pressed her body up against me. "Oooh," she teased. "Shall we jog back?"

"Can you give me a break, please?"

She smiled innocently, curled both her arms around mine and we strolled slowly off toward the Clarion with her gazing adoringly up into my eyes. By the time we'd checked out mid-morning on Sunday, that new room had been properly baptized.

CHAPTER 33

WEEK TWO OF Clarke's investigation intensified. Matta was no longer going to his office. His wife, it was rumored, packed her bags and moved back to stay with her folks in Turlock.

Staying out of the spotlight was my aim. Audrey and I jogged together every morning, showered together after and did things to each other that were life changing.

Each day I worked on my manuscript. My story was expanding from what I originally saw as a fairly narrow plot line. Yes, there was a murder at its core, but a romantically saucy love story was beginning to unfold as well. I enjoyed where the characters took me.

Bobby Dale Clarke sidled up next to me at the park one day in that second week. "He did it," he proclaimed. "Matta. Not sure what happened between the two of 'em, but he did it. Killed her after he got there that night. Maybe they fought over the kid. Could've been unintentional," Clarke speculated. "Happens. Who knows? I'm sure of it though. Realized his wife knew where he'd gone. Told me as much. She confirmed it. Probably why he dragged DeCosta's body out to the field. Throw suspicion in a different direction. Had no idea when he did it how convenient Caputo would turn out to be."

"You positive?" I asked him.

"Still can't prove it. But I got it figured out."

"What's next?"

He reached over and helped himself to a piece of the Gouda laid out on the butcher paper next to me. "Wish I had one of those." He pointed to my small bottle of wine.

I picked it up, extended an offer for him to take a hit. He glanced around, shrugged, took the bottle and helped himself to a taste.

"What's next?" I repeated.

"Gotta prove it. But trust me...this punk's under a lot of pressure. He'll crack. Make a mistake. See it comin'. He's told so many lies he can't keep track anymore. Just a matter of time." Clarke began to focus on movement in a cottonwood tree across the park. "The hell's that?"

"Friend of mine," I said. "Wanna meet him?"

We walked casually over the grass to the tree and searched up into its branches. "Jeff," I shouted.

There was rustling. Finally, his face peered out at us from above. He was immediately agitated and began apologizing, shinnying down out of the tree. "I didn't do nothin'. I didn't hurt nobody. I...I...I—" The thud of his dropping such a frighteningly long distance to the ground nearly knocked his breath out.

"Calm down, Jeff." I attempted to put my hand on his shoulder, but he pushed me away. "It's okay, Jeff. It's okay. This is my friend officer Clarke."

"I didn't do nothin'. I didn't hurt nobody. Don't tell my mother, Caldwell. Don't tell my mother."

"Jesus, a fuckin' loony tune." Clarke turned away.

"Hey," I objected and turned back to Jeff.

"It's all right, Jeff. We didn't mean to upset you. Nobody's gonna tell your mother. It's all right. Calm down."

"You promise, Caldwell? You promise?"

"I promise, Jeff."

Clarke jumped in. "Hey, look, I gotta go. I'll be in touch." He put his right hand up near his ear as he walked off doing screwy.

"Don't tell my mom, Caldwell," Jeff carried on.

"Don't worry, Jeff. I never tell, do I?"

Jeff thought—at least I assumed he was thinking—for several seconds before a satisfied grin broke across his face. "Good `ole Charlie Caldwell," he pronounced. "Good `ole Caldwell."

****

Audrey, PF and I, sat huddled together in front of the TV in the big house Friday night. The movie was Robinson Crusoe. "Who wants popcorn?"

"Me. Me," Passion Flower shouted.

"Does sound good." Audrey started to unwind herself from her daughter.

"No, no. You girls stay put." I slipped into the kitchen.

The oil heated and I watched the two of them sitting together there on the couch. They were my girls. My feelings toward both of them were so powerful it scared me. But between us squarely stood this town. Sentiments I harbored about the place hadn't softened enough to ease my convictions. And while I was handling myself better, my demons over Vietnam never seemed far under the surface.

Audrey looked up and caught me watching them. She climbed off the couch and came to me. She slipped her arms around my waist, looked up into my eyes. "What's wrong, Charlie?"

I kissed her on the nose. "Oil's taking a long time to heat."

"Liar." I'd come to realize how perceptive Audrey was and our intimacy had revealed a good deal to her about how I ticked. She was seeing inside me and I knew it.

The house smelled like the State Theatre when I went down to my own bed after the movie.

****

Mid-morning Saturday I was at my IBM when Olivera's black and white Plymouth came into the driveway too hot and skidded to a stop. He marched up to Audrey's door half trotting.

I'd walked out to the side of the bungalow to see what he was up to. Audrey turned and pointed in my direction.

Now what?

He came almost on a run toward me. I braced myself. But he stopped several feet away. "Chief needs you at the station. Told me to ask you nice."

Must have pained the prick to be civil. "What's this about?"

"Don't know. Called me on the radio. Told me to get up here right now and ask you to come down."

I turned to go back inside.

"You comin'?" he shouted after me with attitude.

"Putting my shoes on. I'll go in my own truck," I told him.

"Fine by me." The deputy spun and made for his patrol car.

Audrey was at my door. "What was that about?"

"Your guess is as good as mine. Olivera says Mendoza wants me to come to the station."

"I'm coming with you," Audrey insisted.

"What about Rachel?"

She turned, looked toward the house. "She shouldn't be around situations like this."

"I agree. I won't be long."

284

"Jesus, Charlie. Be careful. Don't let those assholes push you into something. Please."

"Relax. Olivera said Mendoza told him to ask me nice. Doesn't sound threatening. I'll be back."

****

Lieutenant Clarke's ugly State car was parked out front. Everyone looked up when I walked in. Inside the station house felt crowded. Standing around Mendoza's desk was Mendoza himself, Clarke and Grant Pederson. Olivera stood off to one side as he had previously. Behind the bars in the holding cell was Duke Matta.

"Sergeant Caldwell," Pederson said, addressing me like a military officer would. "Good to see you again under happier conditions." He glanced at Mendoza. "Come in, come in."

Lying on the desk was a thirty-aught-six rifle with a scope on it.

"What's going on?" I addressed no one in particular—all of them.

Pederson nodded to Clarke. "Mr. Pederson here obtained a search warrant," Lieutenant Clarke began to explain, "for me to have a look around Mr. Matta's house in connection with my investigation. In the course of my search, I found this." He pointed to the rifle.

Matta yelled from the holding cell. We all turned to look. "I told you I didn't fucking shoot at anybody. I was only sighting the scope. Tell 'em I didn't shoot at you, Caldwell. You know I wouldn't do that. Tell 'em I wouldn't do something like that."

Everyone ignored Matta's frenzied denial.

Clarke went on. "Been fired recent enough I could still smell burnt powder in the chamber."

"I told you I been sighting the scope," Matta yelled again. Still no one paid attention to him.

285

"Probably okay to sit out front of your house again," Mendoza added.

"Lieutenant Clarke has provided enough evidence," Pederson added, "in addition to the charge of assault with a deadly weapon, I'll be filing charges of second degree murder. You're here because you provided a piece of the puzzle that prevented a gross miscarriage of justice against Vinny Caputo and damn near got yourself killed for your trouble. Not to mention the other inconveniences you were subjected to." Pederson glared at Mendoza once more.

"I said I was sorry about all that," Mendoza countered plaintively.

"In any case," Pederson went on, "wanted you to hear this first hand."

The truth was, I was so bewildered by what was happening I really didn't know what to say to them. One minute there was so much speculation and uncertainty, in the next, proof positive of what we'd been thinking. I had to admit; Matta taking the shot at me while Audrey sat right next to me pissed me off.

"Appreciate your consideration," I told Pederson.

"You motherfucker," Matta yelled at me. "You're gonna just stand there and let 'em do this to me? Goddamn it, Charlie, we've known each other since we was kids. You think I'd fuckin' try to shoot you?" Matta's words were part pathetic plea, part belligerent recrimination. "I'd kick your ass, but I wouldn't try to kill you. Tell 'em. Tell 'em I wouldn't try to kill you."

Matta looked and sounded wretched. I could see how Clarke's notion of what might have happened could be. In a fit of rage, when Miranda probably refused to do what he wanted with her baby, he could have accidentally killed her, then panicked, dumped her body so he wouldn't be caught.

I started to tell Matta I hoped they put his ass away for a long time, then thought better of it. "Thanks for pulling me in on this," I said. The gratitude was meant for Clarke and Pederson.

"Sorry about that misunderstanding we had," Mendoza responded.

The room was quiet for a moment.

"History, Chief." I looked from one to the other, seeing the disgust etched in Olivera's face. But he was trapped. Any mischief toward me would cost the pestilent prick his job. "Anything else?"

"That's it," Pederson said. "You'll be on my witness list, of course...but that's down the road. Mr. Matta's gonna need a good lawyer."

****

Audrey was incredulous while I recounted the scene at the police station. "The sonofabitch shot at us?"

"They had his rifle right there on the desk," I told her. "He was denying it. Yelling about how he was just sighting the scope—"

"Sighting it right on your back," Audrey said derisively. "That bastard. Jesus, Charlie. Who would have believed this whole mess? And he killed Miranda?"

"Clarke thinks it might have been an accident."

"Well, she's just as dead as if he meant to do it."

"Miranda really loved him, I think. On some level...I think he loved her. And then it ends like this."

The outcome was worse than that for me, really. I felt ill. And I finally didn't want anything more to do with the murder of Miranda DeCosta.

CHAPTER 34

THE NEXT SEVERAL weeks rolled by painfully fast for me. The way time evaporates when something you dread is implacably coming at you.

Summer was in full swing. Rachel was out of school and home most days. Audrey and I jogged together intermittently. Our showering and playtime together was mostly a memory. We had the weekends when Rachel stayed with her father. There was just no way to do what we wanted under the scrutiny of a very bright twelve-year-old, soon-to-be teenager.

Audrey and I'd been together four months. Each time we made love it was like being stranded in a desert without water for both of us. We'd come to the oasis and drink until we were about to burst and then we'd drink some more. There was the occasional evening when she would slip down to the bungalow an hour or so when we would furtively play with each other. Sometimes, when neither of us could hold back, she'd allow me go down on her. But there was no way to let go the way we wanted. Rachel could have walked in on us at any moment.

The town split nearly down the middle on the subject of Duke Matta's arrest. There were those who believed he was being railroaded and just as many happy an arrogant womanizer like him was about to get his due.

Matta retained an attorney from Sacramento. He was maintaining his innocence about everything—murder and shooting. My updates on the status of his case arrived the same way most everybody received their information, from the Merced Sun Star or the Modesto Bee. Very few details were released. Pederson intended no mistakes in prosecuting his case nor did he appear much interested in publicity.

Sal DeCosta expressed no more affinity for me after Matta's arrest and the revelations of his being the father of Miranda's unborn child than he had from the very beginning. He unleashed his wrath on Matta, making certain his clients turned someplace else for their tax services. Even if Matta were to be acquitted, which seemed unlikely, he was washed up in Divina. Sal went right on playing the town tyrant, pushing his substantial weight around to suit himself. Frankie kept his mouth shut and enjoyed having it made as the future head of the DeCosta Mercantile.

The final touches on my novel were beginning to take shape. One of the most difficult decisions I would ever have to make in my life was about to confront me. I wanted to put it off as long as I could. The gravity of it wouldn't leave me. Ultimately the burden began to manifest its effect in the way I related to Audrey. No doubt she was feeling the turbulence within me. She was scared and I didn't blame her.

More and more I spent my time alone writing, driving hard to finish the book. My breaks every afternoon in the quiet of the park were a welcomed retreat. Some days I actually found myself avoiding Audrey and Rachel because I'd begun to see the realization in their faces that a moment of truth was near. They seemed resigned I would not stay and it tore at them.

****

Jeff Ponder sat on the curb along the north edge of the city park, staring across the street at the apartment building where Miranda once lived. I sipped my wine, tore off another piece of fresh baguette and separated a chunk of cheese. He animated like he was talking to himself.

After I'd finished my wine I noticed him still sitting transfixed, staring at the building across the street. Curiosity got the best of me. I crossed the grass to where he sat. "Hey, Jeff. Mind if I sit with you?"

Acceptance was never stated but neither was rejection. "Good `ole Caldwell. Heh, heh, heh," he said after several silent moments.

Unresponsiveness, I judged, equivocated approval and sat next to him. Several minutes elapsed in total silence. I couldn't help but wonder about his world. When it came to insects and reptiles, Jeff was idiot savant. In his case, that came about because he read ravenously on those subjects. One could not argue against his capacity to learn, for if he was so inclined, he could. But those skills existed as an attenuated focus within his truncated universe.

"Good larvae in that cottonwood," he said wistfully.

The giant umbrella of the cottonwood tree Jeff was talking about seemed to beckon to him. The bows of its highest branches overhung the entire east end of the two-story building, its limbs thick and healthy, lush with leaves. I supposed it was a haven for the insects he relished studying. "Don't feel like collecting today?" I asked.

"Can't go over there."

"Why not?"

"Mean lady's back."

"Mean lady? Who's mean to you over there, Jeff?" He was harmless enough, but there were always people not content to let him simply exist quietly in the realm he

290

inhabited. When I witnessed such behavior I couldn't help but wonder who was the more damaged.

"Miranda," he answered.

"Miranda?" I was bemused to hear him say her name.

"She's back all right—back. She's back, Caldwell. Not under the bridge. She's back. Mean. Always mean to me. Tells my mother every time she catches me in that tree."

Jeff was becoming agitated.

"Calm down, Jeff. I'm here. I won't let anybody be mean to you. Calm down," I said, gentling him the way you might a frightened horse. He was obviously having some kind of hallucination. "It's okay, Jeff. Miranda can't be mean to you anymore."

"She's always mean to me, Caldwell. Calls me names. Bad names. Mean, mean, mean." White balls of saliva formed at the corners of his mouth. "Not under the bridge. She's back. Can't climb that tree no more now. Tell my mother. Call the cops."

"What do you mean she's not under the bridge, Jeff?"

"Where I put her, Caldwell. Checked on her. Not there. She's back. Mean."

The hair on the back of my neck bristled at what he said. But none of it made sense. None of what he was saying connected to anything other than something in his confused mind. Whatever it was he was talking about, I needed to fully comprehend.

"Jeff," I said softly. "You trust me, right? I'm your best friend. I never tell your mother, do I?"

"Good 'ole Caldwell." He grinned. "Good 'ole Caldwell."

"Jeff, let's have a secret between us. You wanna do that? Have a secret just with me?"

"Don't tell nobody?" He looked at me with eyes that made me dizzy. His right pupil was like a black marble being continually replaced. The dark center of the orb kept rolling down to the corner of its socket as though it was looking at the side of his nose.

"That's right," I reassured him. "We won't tell anyone. Just between you and me, okay?"

"Good 'ole Caldwell."

I scooted a bit closer to him and whispered, "Why did you put her under the bridge, Jeff?"

"Don't tell my mother. Don't tell," he whispered like a child.

"No. No, Jeff. This is our secret. Only you and me. We won't tell anyone. Just you and me." I leaned closer to him and pressed him again. "Why'd you put her under the bridge?"

He looked around furtively, like a feral cat about to steal food. "I throttled her, Caldwell. Throttled her good. Mean to me."

The unfolding story began to scare the hell out of me. But none of it made sense. "Jeff, I'm confused," I whispered. "Why don't you tell me the whole story? So I can understand. Maybe I could make it so she won't be mean to you anymore."

We sat again in total silence for several minutes. I was beginning to doubt he'd make clear what he'd been talking about.

"Was up that tree," he began suddenly. "Seen 'ole Duke doing that nasty thing to her. 'Ole Duke...mean. Always mean to me, Caldwell. 'Ole Duke."

I felt the kind of fear coursing through me I felt back in the jungles of Vietnam. Something awful was about to happen.

"Go on, Jeff," I nudged him. "Duke was hurting her?"

"She was liking it," he corrected. "'Ole Duke, he was puttin' his pecker in her and she was liking it, Caldwell. Nasty. Nasty. Saw his pecker when he was puttin' on his pants, Caldwell." Disgust oozed from him as he spoke. "Saw his pecker. Nasty. Saw her, too. Nasty, nasty."

"Did you see Duke hurt her, Jeff?"

"Nope," he said. "Just puttin' his pecker in her. She liked it. Nasty."

"Did somebody else come into her bedroom, Jeff?"

"Nope, just Duke. 'Ole Duke. Mean. Nasty."

Jeff witnessed whatever happened to Miranda that night. Somehow I had to get a coherent recounting of what took place out of him.

"What did Duke do after he put his pants on, Jeff?"

"Yelled at her. Mean. Real mean."

"He didn't do anything to Miranda? He just left?"

"Yep." He closed up again.

"What happened after Duke left, Jeff?"

"She yelled, too. Real mean. She was real mean to me, Caldwell. Saw me in the tree. Called me bad names. Yelling and yelling."

"Jeff, are you saying Miranda saw you up in that tree watching them?"

"Wasn't watching 'em. Not watching 'em. I told her that. Just getting larvae. Cicadas ready to hatch. Just getting eggs. She called me bad names and yelled. She made me look at her naked, Caldwell. Nasty. Naked. She told me to take a good look. Called me names. Said she was calling the cops." He was close to hyperventilating retelling what happened. I had to force him to go on regardless the risk.

"Don't stop, Jeff. Don't stop. What happened after that?"

He wrung his hands, tears had begun to slide down his face. "Wouldn't stop, Caldwell. She wouldn't stop. Don't tell my mother. Don't tell my mother. She won't let me go out at night no more. Won't let me go out."

"It's all right, Jeff," I said, trying to calm him. "This is our secret. Remember? Our secret."

"Good 'ole Caldwell. Good 'ole Caldwell. Secret...right?"

"That's right, Jeff. Our secret. What happened next?"

"Throttled her, Caldwell. Throttled her good. Made her shut up. Stopped yelling. Stopped calling me nasty names. Mean. Mean."

At that moment he confirmed what I feared I was hearing. I understood the full weight of what Jeff confessed to me. He wasn't having a hallucination. He was merely trying to unravel some confusion he now had over what he'd done to Miranda DeCosta. I forced myself to push on. "You got down from the tree and went into her house, Jeff? Is that what happened next?"

Jeff went on wringing his hands. "Secret, Caldwell. Secret. She made me look at her. Nasty! She was calling the cops. Made her stop. I told her no, no, no. Don't tell my mother, but she kept yelling, calling me bad names. Picked up the phone to call the cops."

He stopped abruptly. I let him gather himself.

"Told her no, no, no! Don't tell my mother. She wouldn't stop. Yelled and yelled. Throttled her good. She didn't make no more noise. Heh, heh." He grinned, grotesque, ominous and then he said to me, "Throttled her neck like a chicken. Quiet. She didn't call me anymore bad names."

As sick as I was inside at what I'd heard, I understood I had to get it all out of him right then. Once I did what I would have to do, I was pretty sure there'd be no way of learning anything further from him. At that moment, there was no way I could deal with the betrayal this man would feel from me, but I believed no one would be likely to learn the entire story if I didn't root it out of him right then and there.

"You made her be quiet?"

"Stop calling me names. No more yelling bad names," he said.

"What did you do after that, Jeff?"

"Wrapped her in a blanket. Put under the bridge."

"Along the canal at the edge of town?"

"Yep. Carried her over my shoulder so I wouldn't hurt her. Made her be quiet. Told her not to tell. Don't tell my mother, I told her."

"You left her by the bridge."

"Real foggy. Wrapped her up. Left her."

How Miranda DeCosta really died was becoming horrifyingly clear, and at whose hands. What I heard could not have been manufactured. The feeling in my guts was exactly what I'd felt seeing my brothers die in battle. And knowing this man would now be caged the rest of his life was a burden I'd have to grapple with.

In many ways, Jeff Ponder was no different than many dangerous animals in the wild. Left alone, unmolested, they're simply part of the ecosystem. They live along side of us doing no harm, playing their role until there comes a day when they come face to face with the cruelty of man. And then they fight back to defend themselves, to survive. And the injuries they inflict are always considered unwarranted. They are never seen as the victim.

What had just come to me was so hideous I really didn't know how to react, what to do, whom to tell.

Keep him calm for now. That's what I thought first. Jeff, I realized then, was potentially dangerous if provoked. Jeff's situation was really no different than when we were kids, but as cruel as kids could be, obviously, some adults were no better.

We sat without speaking. In a while he began to calm down. "You want me to make sure she's not home over there?" I asked him.

"Good 'ole Caldwell," he replied.

"If she's not home, you could get up that tree and find those eggs, right?"

"Right, right, right!" Jeff was like a child being invited to go ahead and do something he'd been told he couldn't. Words erupted from him in exquisite anticipation.

295

His face fractured in a bent, toothy convolution I knew as ecstatic pleasure. "Right, Caldwell!"

"Okay," I told him. "You wait right here. I'll give you the sign if the coast is clear." This was a game I felt I had to play out with him. The safest way to keep him calm was to have him doing what was normal.

Once across the street and around the corner of the apartment building, I slumped against the wall. I felt physically ill. Matta was as innocent as he'd claimed. Why the hell did he take a shot at me? But for *that* stupid move, he'd be a free man shortly. Too much. Too much going on in my brain.

I collected myself, stuck my head around the corner of the building and called to him. "All clear, Jeff. She's gone."

He came lumbering across the street, heavy footsteps thumping the pavement. Anticipation registered in his gleeful animation. "Good 'ole Caldwell. Good man. Good man," he proclaimed.

"She doesn't live here anymore, Jeff."

He looked at me puzzled.

"She moved away. You won't ever see her again. You don't need to worry about her. Okay?"

Up the tree he climbed. "Good 'ole Caldwell," he shouted down to me. "Good 'ole Caldwell."

CHAPTER 35

THEO ASSESSED THE situation and called Grant Pederson immediately. By noon of the following day we sat crowded together in Theo's small law office. Pederson was there. Mendoza sat in a straight-backed chair in a corner behind Theo. Dorothy Ponder was provided the most comfortable chair Theo had to offer and sat next to Pederson directly in front of Theo's desk. She had no idea what was coming, but she knew it'd be about her son. And she knew it was bound to be bad—real bad. She didn't bother trying to hide the fear she felt. I sat at the end of Theo's desk.

Theo told Pederson everything I'd related to him earlier that morning. Pederson, to his credit, authorized Theo to organize what was coming next.

"Mrs. Ponder," Theo began. He stopped. Looked to Pederson. Let his head droop, giving even more of a bedraggled impression than normal. He raised his red-rimmed eyes to her once more. The dread in the room over where this was going was palpable. "Mrs. Ponder, Mr. Caldwell here," he gestured toward me, "had a conversation with your son yesterday."

"Oh, God, Charlie," Dorothy Ponder said, looking at me, tears already coming into her eyes. "What has he done? Can it be all this bad?"

Theo nodded to me.

Months earlier I'd sat before three mothers telling them the story of their sons' last moments in this life. The pain of it remained raw, like a festering wound. Those memories were some of the demons I fought. This moment was no less devastating and would begin to haunt me, too.

"Dorothy," I said. My voice broke slightly. "I..."

I glanced at Theo who stared deep into his desk, then to Pederson who chipped at the cuticle of a fingernail with a thumb of his folded hands.

All the details Jeff told me began to slip from my lips in a near whisper. My throat felt dry and my voice sounded hoarse even to me. Miranda had spotted Jeff collecting bugs in the tree outside the window of her apartment that night. The horrible way she'd berated threatened him, picked up the phone to call the police. "He was simply trying to make her stop tormenting him," I concluded looking directly into her eyes.

Dorothy buried her face in her hands, her shoulders heaving uncontrollably. Pederson, in an act that would forever endear the man to me, placed a hand compassionately on her shoulder, but said nothing.

Even Mendoza, as gruff a man as he was, hung his head.

"From the time he was a little boy," Dorothy Ponder told us, "I was afraid when he got to manly urges, he maybe do somethin' with a little girl. I was a scared about that. Know whata mean? Tolt him it was nasty to look at his self...anybody was necked. Drilled it into him ever time I bathed him when he was little. Ya know? I was so afraid some day...but kids tormented him over it. Come home terrified a bunch of boys was gonna make him show his...thing to the girls. Finally convinced the school not to make him shower after PE. The trauma it caused in him wadn't worth it. But I was mostly afraid about girls...ya know?"

In the grotesque quiet, Theo wheezed. In...out...in...out.

"He's a gentle boy," she went on. "If folks'd just let him be. He only cares about them stupid bugs and snakes." She stopped speaking for several moments. No one said anything. The room remained morbidly silent.

"But people won't leave him alone," she continued. "As though it's fun torturing him. Like he oughtta be punished for how he is, what happened to him. Like as if it was his own fault or somethin'. Ain't punishment enough what his life is."

The woman was drawn and enervated. We all knew what Dorothy Ponder said was the truth. And because of how her son had been abused, he'd be punished even more.

She collected herself. Felt as if she'd accepted destiny. "What's next?" she asked, wiping her eyes with her small handkerchief.

Theo looked up at Pederson.

Pederson shifted uncomfortably in his chair. "I don't have any choice, Mrs. Ponder," he said softly. "Under stress conditions, he's obviously dangerous. I have no doubt you're right about how gentle he is, left to his own world, but society isn't like that. People say and do things. This could happen again."

"They'll cage him up—like an animal—he'll die. You don't know." She began to weep again.

"Maybe not," Pederson offered. "I have to remove him from society, but I won't seek prison for him. State facilities for mentally ill people are not what they once were, Mrs. Ponder. There's a facility in Sacramento. He'll be treated humanely."

"But he'll be locked away," she predicted. "He'll die. Lives to be out in the air, climbin' trees...sniffin along a trickle of a crick. Never come home at night if I didn't make him."

"He'll receive treatment, Mrs. Ponder," Pederson repeated.

But I knew that was a euphemism for locked up and drugged, the very essence of palliative, so he wouldn't hurt himself or anyone else. Dorothy Ponder was right in her assessment, and there wasn't a thing any of us could do to alter the reality of it.

"What happens now?" she asked.

There was a welter of discussion while Pederson and Mendoza considered how best to handle the physical aspects of the arrest. At least it was clear no one, including Mendoza, wanted to see this man hurt.

Once again Pederson demonstrated his humanity. "May I use your phone Mr. Azevedo?"

"Use this one or you're welcome to go to the outer office if you need privacy," Theo said, pushing his phone to the front edge of his desk.

Pederson made arrangements for Dorothy Ponder to immediately go find her son, drive him to Sacramento and remand him to the authorities at the State Hospital.

"Appreciate that, Mr. Pederson," she said. "I'll make him think he has to go see a doctor. He'll understand that."

I offered to drive her.

Pederson stopped me. "Sorry, sergeant," he said. "I can't allow that." He turned back to Dorothy Ponder. "I know you'll do exactly as we've agreed, but I have no choice but to instruct Chief Mendoza to follow you.

"Go and find your son, Mrs. Ponder. The Chief will follow you in his patrol car to Sacramento. He is to ensure Jeff is safely delivered to the authorities at the hospital."

"I'm sorry, Dorothy, about all of this," I added.

She didn't reply. Dorothy Ponder lowered her head, accepting the loss of her son as surely as those other mothers had, and wept in dignified silence.

****

Pederson remained with Theo and me after Mendoza followed Dorothy Ponder out to her car. There was little doubt they'd find Jeff at the park.

"I'll prepare a deposition for you," Pederson said, addressing me. "You mind driving to Merced?" I shook my head, letting him know the drive wouldn't be any problem.

The mood in Theo's office was about as somber as it gets.

"I'm going to confer with the State's Attorney General on this. I'll try to find some way to give the kid the best situation I can."

Theo gestured his approval.

"We'll drop the murder charges against Matta," Pederson said, "but I'm going ahead with the assault prosecution. That was still attempted murder."

Most of the afternoon was eaten away by the time we broke up and went our separate ways. All I wanted was to be alone on a warm beach in Mexico. After what I'd been through that morning, I couldn't bear the thought of facing the fear I'd find in Audrey's eyes, too.

"How bad was it?" She had a bottle of wine open and we sat with our glasses out in the courtyard.

"Awful," I said without elaboration.

Silence.

"New ending for your novel."

"Yeah." I sipped slowly from my glass. "Pederson says I have to go to Merced to be deposed."

"What's that mean?"

"Answer some questions under oath," I said.

"What's gonna happen to Duke?"

"He shot at us."

An uneasy silence between us continued.

301

Audrey nodded. "Somebody named Phoebe Fillinger called today from *Past, Present & Future Magazine.* Asked me to tell you to call her. Has an assignment for you."

I turned to Audrey.

"Probably just as well," she said, looking me right in the eyes. "Now you can say you don't have any choice in leaving us."

The still red liquid in my glass offered no escape. I felt so much pain I couldn't bring myself to speak. I loved this woman with all my heart. But more than love has to be considered in life or life will find a way to destroy love.

The crushing silence lingered until Audrey, as usual, took control.

"Rachel and I are going to my mom's for dinner tonight." She pushed up from her chair. "Plenty left overs in the frig." She lifted her glass to her lips, paused, stared into it then sipped slowly letting her head fall backward as she deliberately drained the glass. "You'll find something." She walked slowly into the kitchen and closed the door behind her.

****

They didn't return home that night. I felt like shit looking for a sewer. There was no point trying to eat. My stomach was in such a knot I felt physically sick so I drank until I passed out.

I hadn't even had the courage to try to explain to her how complicated things still were for me, how much turmoil was still going on inside of me. In Audrey's mind it was an easy picture to look at. You love me. You stay. You don't love me. You go. But it wasn't that simple for me. I did love her and Rachel...but...sonofabitch! I just didn't know what to do with the *but*.

Next morning I slipped on my shorts and shoes and went for a run. When I crossed the bridge at the edge of town my mind was pulled back to Miranda. The wooden tractor bridge in the distance seemed an unfair place for her to be dumped like a bag of trash—as if there would be any acceptable place for a thing like that.

When I got home, Audrey's car was in the garage. I jogged straight to the door and stuck my head into the kitchen. She looked over at me. Her eyes were swollen from crying. Rachel looked up at me. "Creep!" she shouted and stomped off.

Audrey grinned and shrugged her shoulders. "Takes after her mother. You didn't eat last night."

"Audrey, we need to talk."

"Done talking to you, Charlie," she said. "I know, I know. You love me. Look, let's not do this. It was wonderful. Shit, it was a lot better than that, who'm I kidding. But you weren't gonna stay. I've seen it coming for some time. Let's not complicate it more than we have."

Audrey was tougher than me that way.

"Thought about things last night," she said. "You have to go do this thing with Pederson and then this is over. That editor from Denver told me she needed you to go to Cartagena, Colombia. You'll go. That's how it is. Somehow I knew all along that's how it'd turn out. You'd get a call...something...you'd pack up and be gone. That's what you do, Charlie. You move on. I don't blame you. Wish I was more like you in that way."

Tears had begun to trickle down her face. I started to move toward her, but she put up her hand to stop me. We stood there awkwardly for what seemed an eternity.

"Can't take that long for things to wrap up around here for you. Be easier if you moved back to the Trails End. Much easier for all of us."

My eyes began to burn and I needed to get out of there. "I'll go right away." I stood there before her, leaning against the kitchen counter, as if I was rooted to the floor. I was supposed to walk out, but doing it seemed beyond me.

303

"I have things to do." She headed toward her bedroom.

There weren't many accumulated things to load into Buck. Leaving the IBM would've been a slap in Audrey's face. On top of what was taking place, it would have been insult on injury.

Once I checked in to the Trails End, I climbed into the shower. The act broke my heart and I wept with a sickness I hadn't known since that night in the jungle.

Sleep didn't come that night. Run the misery out of your soul, I thought, abandoning the lumpy bed at daybreak. Secretly I hoped I'd run into her again and we could start all over. Maybe the outcome would somehow be different next time. Of course, I was irrational.

Running the route we always ran I was ridiculously hoping to see her and thinking again about Miranda as I crossed the bridge over the big irrigation canal. What I thought was—how right Audrey was about me. *That's what you do*, she'd accused. *You move on.* And she was right. I'd come up with a new and different reason this time, but I was doing the same thing I'd done in every relationship after Miranda DeCosta: found a way out. Guilty as charged.

Mendoza found me at the motel later that afternoon. "Pederson's ready for you to come to his office." He handed me a piece of paper with an address and phone number on it.

"How'd it go in Sacramento?" I asked.

He breathed deeply, lifted his hat slightly, ran his hand through his thick kinky black hair. "'Bout as good as you'd expect."

"I'll call Pederson right away."

Dialing the number Mendoza'd given me reached the DA's secretary. Pederson's office day after tomorrow and I promised to be there.

No matter how long I laid on the bed in my room and stared at the ceiling, I found no inspiration for solving the mess I'd made. Finally, I rallied myself upright and drove to Souza's Market. Along with my usual baguette and hunk of cheese, I bought four full bottles of Zinfandel.

From there I drove to the park, settled onto my bench and opened one of the bottles. The bread and cheese sat. I drank the wine straight from the bottle.

Funny how much emptier a place ordinarily empty can feel. There was no movement anywhere. The void in the place felt like I'd been plopped down in a ghost town. There was an aura of eeriness. No sounds. No movement— just the unnerving silence of a vacuum and the buzzing of those fucking cicadas to remind me of Jeff Ponder.

My head was spinning when I drove back to the Trails End. I was drunk and obsessing over everything in my life. What the whole fucking turn of events had done to me was even eclipsing my disgust at myself over what I'd done to Audrey and Rachel. Where was Jeff right then? What were they doing to him? What must he be feeling? What must this be like for Dorothy Ponder? Misery enough to go around. There was a lot to be unhappy about. The words to Jeff's story unfolded in my brain over and over. How he'd carried her across his shoulder, being careful not to hurt her, telling her what she'd done wrong.

Those were the last thoughts I remembered before passing out.

The disgusting smell of stale wine and my own body odor greeted me when I awoke midmorning. My head felt like it was being struck in rhythm with a sledgehammer. The image of myself in the mirror while I took a piss was all too familiar. Thought I recognized the unshaven face, the rumpled hair, bloodshot eyes—me all right, those first months stateside from Nam. *Full fucking circle.* I stumbled back to the bed.

My appearance at Pederson's office for the deposition forced me to pull myself together. "You look like shit, sergeant," Pederson said, motioning for me to have a seat in his conference room. "You okay?"

"Never better."

"That good?" Pederson asked.

A stenographer was setting up with one of those machines they use to take the transcript of a court trial.

"None of this was your fault, Mr. Caldwell," Pederson said conversationally. "All-in-all, things have worked out the correct way, haven't they? You should be glad. Proud you did what you did. It was the right thing."

"Was it?"

"You really need to ask?" Pederson scrutinized me. "You sure you're all right?"

"Fine. I'm fine," I said.

The deposition didn't take as long as I'd feared. Pederson led me through how the story from Jeff Ponder unfolded with a series of well-planned questions. We were finished in about an hour.

Gratefully he'd rushed toward the end because he was due in court. Saved by the judge, you might say.

The drive back to Divina was one of those aimlessly slow crawls with no purpose, nowhere to be and no need to hurry getting there; the kind of driver that pisses all the other's off slowing traffic on a two lane road in the middle of nowhere. I was finally free to pack my bags and get the hell out. Going ahead...actually driving away...guilt...fear...self-loathing. My emotional state was considerably worse than when I'd arrived. Nothing in my life had been resolved. Matters had only been made worse and I'd hurt two people I loved. Real hero.

As sleazy as I felt, I couldn't leave without saying goodbye to Audrey and Rachel and I couldn't let them see me in this condition.

That evening I went to the burger joint. I drank a Coke and went back to the motel. A morning jog would get the rest of the alcohol out of my system...shower, load

Buck. You ever stand on the edge of a cliff; the bottom so far down you couldn't see it? Feel that near irresistible pull makes you want to slip over its edge? The landing isn't what's in your head. It's that painless, endless, fully conscious drop toward eternity; the blinding light waiting for you at the end of the ride scares the holy hell out of you. Heaven or hell?

Quick...make it quick, I decided. I lay across the bed, unable to sleep, thinking again about Ponder, Duke Matta, the deposition, the entire mess I found myself embroiled in. What I'd done to Audrey and Rachel in the process was the lowest low I'd ever descended to in my life and I hated myself for it.

****

Darkness bled to gray dawn the next morning. The bleakness of the four grubby walls in the room crawled slowly through gray, sepia and finally muted pewter. My head was clear but I hadn't slept much. The whites of my eyes were red but not from a drunken hangover. Time to take responsibility for myself. My first assignment in South America awaited me. The rewrite of my novel was ahead, also. Phoebe Fillinger offered to help me find a publisher once we'd polished it into a real book. Life wasn't so bad. So why did I constantly feel the need to regurgitate?

Jogging had always been the answer for me, the first step to my emotional recovery. Shoes, shorts...no shirt necessary. It was already hot. Probably climb over one hundred by noon. Crops were in the fields and maturing. The summer sun was doing its job. I jogged past the park and thought for the thousandth time about the tragedy of Jeff Ponder and Miranda DeCosta.

When I came to the bridge that day I stopped, panting hard, leaned my elbows on the guardrail and gazed toward the wooden tractor bridge in the distance. *Wrapped her in a blanket,* Jeff had said. *Left her under the bridge.* I wondered again why he said he'd left her under the bridge. Probably just misunderstood him. My head was spinning in shock at the time listening to him tell me about that night. I was sure he'd said, "Left her under the bridge." And he was positive she'd come back because he'd gone back to check on her. That's what he said. *She wasn't there anymore. She's back.*

That's when it hit me. What if he'd told me *exactly* what he'd done with Miranda that night? What if Jeff wasn't confused? What if I was confused? What if he did put her under the bridge? What if he put her under *this bridge*? The thought screamed in my head.

At the terminal end of the guardrail I leaned far over. From where I stood I couldn't see much. Cattails grew eight feet high along the water's edge and heavy brush filled in up the steep embankment. I worked my way down until I could gain access beneath. It was not an easy spot to get at.

"Oh, fuck!"

I ran as hard as I could all the way back to the Trials End.

CHAPTER 36

"LIEUTENANT CLARKE," the voice on the other end of the line answered.

"Lieutenant Bobby Dale Clarke?"

"Who's calling?"

"Charlie Caldwell."

"Hey, Charlie," Clarke said, relaxing the police persona. "Whatcha up to?" He didn't wait for a reply. "Hey, nice catch with the loony tune even if it did make me look bad."

"Jesus, you know, Lieutenant, he's a human being."

"Yeah, I know. But he's a loony tune all the same. And he killed somebody."

I could almost anticipate his response to what I would say next. "Maybe," I said.

"What?" Lieutenant Clarke choked on the other end of the line. "What did you just say? I tell you this, Caldwell, you go to Pederson now and tell him you fucked this up, you're gonna be the one lookin' out from behind bars."

"I told Pederson exactly what Ponder told me, Lieutenant. But something's wrong. I need you here to help me. Like right now."

"The fuck?"

"You coming or not?"

He was silent for several contemplative moments. Finally, "Take me about two hours to get there."

"I'm at the Trials End. Hurry."

"Ho, ho." That booming voice of his rang. "Girlfriend toss your ass out?"

"Get here quickly and don't worry about me and my girlfriend."

"On my way. On my way. Don't get touchy."

****

An entire afternoon had passed by the time the knock at the door came.

"Thanks for coming, Lieutenant."

"This better be good," Clarke said, stepping into my room.

Two bottles of wine sat on the table. The room stunk of the two-day-old cheese and me. "Want some wine?"

"You invited me to take a two hour drive to drink wine with you in a smelly hotel room? What's this about?"

"Have a seat."

The story I related to Clarke was a shortened version of what Jeff Ponder told me. I confessed to Clarke my presumption Jeff had simply been confused about where he'd left Miranda's body, until that morning.

"And what happened this morning?" Clarke asked, his interest piqued.

"I translated his story literally," I admitted. "After Ponder was arrested, Mendoza searched under the wooden tractor bridge out near the spot her body was found."

"And?"

"Didn't find anything. Everybody figured it's just been too long for any signs."

"You're not making sense, Caldwell."

"Let's go," I said. "I didn't touch a thing. I want you to see this for yourself."

We climbed into Clarke's Chevy and sped toward the edge of town. When he came to the bridge over the canal he turned right onto the dirt road and stopped.

"Come on," I urged.

"Hold it," Clarke said. He slipped his sport coat off, tossed it into the back seat and grabbed a camera. "You didn't touch anything, right?" He slung the camera strap over his shoulder.

"Right."

Clarke followed me down the steep bank and across the side-hill under the bridge. Tucked up into the joint where the bridge sat atop the embankment was a pink blanket.

"Jesus, you called me out here for that?" he complained.

"Think about it," I argued. "Ponder said he wrapped her in a blanket and left her under the bridge. *Loony Tunes*, as you keep calling him, had no concept he'd killed her. He just made her be quiet and not call the cops. He came back to check on her after all this time, but her body wasn't here. In his mind she'd gone home. He was upset she was back. He couldn't climb that tree anymore because she'd catch him and tell his mother or call the cops."

Clarke had a perplexed looked on his face.

"Wrong bridge, Lieutenant. Don't you get it? Ponder didn't put her under the wooden bridge. He stashed her body here. What do you want to bet that blanket matches Miranda DeCosta's bedding?"

Clarke went silent. "And if it does?"

"What if she wasn't dead? What if he choked her until she passed out but she wasn't dead? After he dumps her, she comes to. She's confused, disoriented. Makes her way up the side of the canal and wanders around out here dazed and bare-ass naked, freezing to death."

311

"Jesus fucking Christ," Clarke said.

"Who admitted he was out here on the canal bank that night?" I asked, "drunk on his ass and drinking more beer, conveniently, all by himself?" I let that sink in and went on. "She stumbles up to his truck. He can't believe his good fortune, decides to have some of what was offered up. She puts up a fight. He rapes her. She's screaming and threatening him with what's gonna happen when she reports what he's done. He panics, strangles her for real this time and dumps her where they found her. He would have had no problem finding that road in the fog. He's out here all the time."

"Caputo after all!" Clarke deduced. "Okay, okay. That's a lot of speculation. But it ain't bad." Clarke shoved his hands deep into his pockets and turned in a full circle. "First things first." He unshouldered the camera strap and removed the lens cover. "Step back," he ordered. "If your speculations turn out to have anything to them, I gotta treat this as a crime scene." Clarke spent nearly half an hour shooting photos of the entire location from every angle and viewpoint. Then he searched every inch of the area for even the tiniest object that could have been considered evidence. I looked on learning a good deal about controlling my behavior around situations like this if it ever happened to me again.

"Okay, grab that blanket," he ordered. "We gotta get into DeCosta's apartment—confirm this blanket belonged to her. I don't wanna say shit to Pederson or your locals unless this is for real. Jesus. You know how many times this thing has been solved only to have *you* come along and say everybody's wrong? I tell you, Caldwell, you do this and your wrong, ain't just you gonna have his ass in a sling. And while I like you, I don't like you that much. Might lock your ass up myself."

"Worry about that later," I told him. "I got an idea how we might get in without breaking and entering."

R.P. McCabe

Back at The Trails End Lieutenant Clarke went to make arrangements for the room adjacent to mine. I went to the phone book and looked up Natalie Bettencourt's number. "No, no. Please don't hang up, Natalie. Please. Just listen a moment."

"I'm still pissed at you, Charlie. You mighta got the guy killed Miranda, but you still lied to me. Used me."

"Natalie, I swear, I had no intention of using you. Things got all turned around and backward."

"I told you no way Duke would kill Miranda. He's scum. But no way. I told you he wun't do that."

"Duke tried to kill me, Nat—with Audrey sitting right beside me." I let her chew on that a few moments. "But you're right. There isn't much I can say to you, is there?"

She didn't reply, but she was still on the line.

"I need your help again, Nat."

"You gotta be kiddin' me. You got some nerve, Charlie."

"It's important. Really important."

"Whatta you need now?"

I hesitated. Held my breath. "I need to get into Miranda's apartment."

"For what? Nobody's been in there for months. They got the guy did this. What more you want?" She didn't wait for my reply. "True you walked out on Audrey?"

I was washing out every friend I had in town. "No," I said. "That's complicated. Can you help me, Nat? This is important."

"I don't know how I could o' been so wrong about you, Charlie." She was silent, but again didn't hang up on me. "Don't know why the hell I should do anything to help you." I listened to her heavy breathing. Thinking probably. "I still got a key," she admitted finally. "When?"

"Right now?"

"You mean like this instant?"

"Can you?"

313

Another long pause. "I'll meet you there in twenty minutes."

"Natalie," I said. "I'm sorry. I—"

"Save it, Charlie. Twenty minutes."

When Clarke finished checking in, we got back into his car and drove to the park. He pulled to the curb across the street from the apartment building where Miranda had lived. Natalie pulled in beside him.

"Who's he?" she asked, instantly suspicious.

"Lieutenant Bob Clarke, ma'am. California State Police."

"What's this really about?" Natalie demanded.

"Loose ends, ma'am," Clarke said. "Just loose ends. Mr. Caldwell says you were miss DeCosta's best friend. That right?"

"Yeah, why?"

Clarke pulled the blanket from the back seat. "Just wanting to verify if this belonged to miss DeCosta or not. Mr. Caldwell here offered to see if you'd help me."

Natalie eyed me suspiciously. "Could be," she said. "That why you want in to her apartment?"

"Thought we might be able to match it against her other bedding."

Natalie looked from one to the other of us. "Pretty sure it's her's." She was obviously skeptical about our motives. "Come on."

Natalie led off toward the far end of the building across the street.

She opened the door and went in. Clarke and I followed her. The bedroom was on the upper floor. We trailed Natalie up the narrow stairway made two sharp ninety-degree turns before being deposited onto the landing at the front of the bedroom door.

Natalie and I looked at each other. It was difficult even then for us to be in Miranda's space.

Clarke held the blanket. The room appeared to be as it must have been the night of the murder. No one had come to do anything with it after the police investigation was complete.

Clarke laid the thin blanket across the bed. We didn't have to rely on its color to make a guess. The pattern along the edge of the lining matched that of the other bedding.

My eyes met Clarke's. "That's it, Mrs. Bettencourt," he said. "All I needed. Sorry to have troubled you for no more than this."

"How come Prado din't come let use in?" Natalie demanded. "You a real State cop?"

Lieutenant Clarke pulled out his badge. "Sorry for the confusion, Mrs. Bettencourt. It was something Chief Mendoza missed. I was trying to save him some embarrassment. Mr. Caldwell here figured you might be willing to help."

Natalie continued to study us. "You done?"

"Yes, ma'am," Clarke said.

"Good, 'cuz I gotta pick up my daughter."

At our parked vehicles, Natalie went to her's, opened the door and stood with her back turned to us a few seconds. She shifted, looked at me over her shoulder. "You should be ashamed, Charlie Caldwell." She slipped behind the wheel of her car and was gone.

"Jesus, you're popular around this town, Caldwell."

"Fuck you. I need wine."

"Me, too. Let's stop and get some food."

CHAPTER 37

LIEUTENANT CLARKE SAT slumped down in the wooden armchair in my room, his feet propped on my bed. A paper plate with hunks of hard Italian salami and sliced pieces of provolone cheese sat on the bed between us. We used the water glasses from the bathroom for the wine.

The headboard of the bed acted as my backrest with my feet outstretched and crossed. We were musing, trying to make sense out of how the investigation of Miranda's death kept unraveling. How I couldn't seem to avoid being at the center of it.

"Sometimes that's what crime solving is," Bobby Dale Clarke said. "Deal with it every time I'm assigned a case."

"You mean continually arresting the wrong person...finding out somebody else did it?"

"I'm gonna look bad on this one," Clarke conceded. "Won't do my career any good either." He took a sip of wine. "There's usually more than one suspect or at least potential suspect in a crime," he said. "People say dumb shit. Incriminating things. Take Matta. His own mouth had me convinced he'd killed her." Clarke reached for a piece of salami. "And then the idiot takes a shot at you.

Convinces me and everybody else the circumstantial evidence is true.

"Crime solving isn't easy, Charlie. Remember, the bad guys, and even some of the innocent suspects, don't make it easy. People hide shit because everybody feels a little guilty about something they don't want you to find out. Honest people hide things they're embarrassed about. Crime solving's a jigsaw puzzle. And yes, fitting the pieces together sometimes requires a little trial and error."

"Whatta ya think we got here?"

Clarke let his head fall backward, stared up into the ceiling for several moments before he leaned forward, took a long swig of his wine. "Well," he began slowly, still chewing a hard piece of salami, wiping his mouth with the back of his hand. "Got no choice but to follow up on what the blanket implies. Still, doesn't mean she didn't just wander out there in the dark fog and finally die from what loony tunes did to her."

"You need to keep calling him that? I feel sorry for him. Poor guy just wanted to be left alone and people couldn't do that."

"Sorry. You're right. I see so much of that shit in this line of work. Tired of dealing with them." Clarke took another healthy swig of wine, poured his glass full again, gestured toward me with the bottle. "Why I didn't go into social work." He belly laughed the way he could without warning at how his own wit struck him.

We drank in silence for a time.

"You think she could have just wandered around out there? Didn't run into Caputo?"

"Gotta consider it," Clarke said. "Gonna be hard to get Pederson to refile against the guy. Lot of reasonable doubt there. I mean all you have is a blanket and a theory. Don't get confused just because you have an idea that's necessarily what took place."

Clarke thought for a bit, guzzled more wine. "Know why I took you back to the spot they found her that day?" he asked rhetorically.

I looked over at him.

"Because when you stand there where it all happened, looking around, sometimes things come to you, things you didn't think of before. We're gonna go back out there in the morning. Fresh. Clear our minds and we're gonna wander along that canal bank the way she must have. See anything jumps up and grabs us. Trust me, we can't take what we got to Pederson. It means nothing."

Clarke's appraisal shocked me. But when I heard him voice his assessment, he made sense. And maybe that's the mistake I kept making. Each time a new suspect jumped in front of me, I jumped to the conclusion he had to be the one. It all seemed simple to me. I was looking at the evidence in front of me as conclusive. No other possibilities. I needed to expand the way I questioned what I saw and what I heard. You ever hear the suggestion, what you see and hear isn't necessarily what you saw and heard? I've heard that somewhere. Hearing Clarke explain, it was a game of what if. There are always a lot of 'what ifs' in life. I needed to do a much better job of considering all the possibilities.

CHAPTER 38

LIEUTENANT CLARKE PULLED his Chevy to a stop about where we'd parked on the canal bank the previous afternoon. The air was warm and reedy. The aroma of the Caputo Dairy split the morning air with fresh cow shit as it did most days when I jogged out along Farm Road Lane.

Clarke pulled off his suit coat and tossed it into the back seat, walked over to the edge of the embankment we'd shinnied down the day before and looked around in all directions.

I decided I'd try his approach.

He looked over at me. "You tryin' to get cute?"

"Taking your advice, Lieutenant." I scanned all around. "What are we looking for?"

"Don't know. Maybe nothin'. You'll know if you see it, might just be an idea or thought that comes to you...question didn't get asked."

"Humph. Question. Right...okay."

We turned and walked slowly along the dirt road. The morning was beautiful. Made me want to be jogging. I instinctively turned to look along the paved road to see if Audrey was out for a run. No sign of her. Off the side of the road at the edge of town I made out a black and white.

Almost a guarantee to be Olivera snooping. By now he'd have spotted Clarke's car parked at The Trails End.

My focus returned to the canal bank. We were near the wooden tractor bridge by then. The canal was on the west side of the dirt road. There was a sharp drop down the steep bank to the water and bulrushes. The rutted tractor path dropped away to the east more gently. There was a thirty-yard apron between the canal bank and the edges of the two fields to the east.

Clarke stood on the wooden bridge and looked out to the west where Miranda's body was discovered.

I stood and gazed eastward. The snowcaps of the Sierra Nevada were brilliant and clear. I looked back to the west in the direction of town, the Diablo Mountains behind. Clarke noticed.

"Spot something?" he asked, coming toward me.

"Not really," I said honestly. "Just noticing that a truck parked down there," I pointed to the flat along the edges of both fields. "Wouldn't be visible from town."

"So what?"

"Nothing. Just a good place to sit and drink a six pack, fog or no fog, day or night," I said. "Probably just toss your bottles out along the field, don't you think?"

I walked in the tire tracks, dropping down to the flat on the left at the bottom of the steep grade. Lot of dirt clods, nothing more. "Spin around spot." I crossed to the other side.

I'd wandered about twenty yards south along the edge of the field to the right of the tractor trail when an avalanche of raw certainty hit me squarely.

"Lieutenant, come on down," I shouted.

"What is it?" Clarke stepped lively down the canal bank. "Find something?"

When Clarke stood beside me, I pointed to the ground.

"The hell's that?" he asked, puzzled.

R.P. McCabe

"They're the wooden tips and half smoked carcasses of Cheroot Cigars," I said. "Hundreds of them, I'd say."

"At least hundreds," Clarke inspected the scattered mound of wooden tips more closely. "So what?"

"Guess who smokes Cheroots?"

"How the hell would I know?" Clarke looked up at me. "Who?"

"Deputy Jorge Olivera," I squatted down.

That was the moment I knew Duke Matta hadn't shot at me, and who had.

I picked up a recently discarded butt, ran it slowly under my nose. The evening I'd smelled the faint familiar odor at the kitchen door to Audrey's house flashed in my head. My mind went to the first day in town when Olivera had thrown one of the half-smoked butts at my feet and I'd crushed it, picked it up. The recognizable trace. Now I realized why that smell had been familiar to me.

"You aren't going to believe what I'm about to tell you," I said to Lieutenant Clarke.

Clarke picked up on what I knew then to be the truth. "It wasn't Caputo she stumbled onto. It was Olivera."

"That sleazy sonofabitch," I said. "Natalie Bettencourt told me Miranda thought Olivera'd raped her one night when he hauled her home drunk. I didn't quite believe that part of her story."

"Still not proof that's what happened. But we're onto something significant now. If we're going to nail this guy, we need to smoke him out. We need him to tip his hand. *If what we think happened, happened at all.*"

"What do we do?"

"I don't know yet." Clarke gathered a handful of the wooden tips and half smoked butts, wrapped them in his handkerchief. "Let's get back." He stood.

Gaining the top of the canal bank, I looked up toward town. The black and white I'd seen earlier was gone.

321

Back in Clarke's car we sat for several minutes while Lieutenant Clarke fabricated a plan.

"Here's how we play this. We pretend we have Olivera dead to rights...conclusively know he did it. He isn't very smart. Every time he thinks he's gotten away with what he's done, you come along and screw things up. He's got to be tired of that—tired of you. He'll know I'm in town by now."

"Pretty sure I saw him spying on us while we walked on the canal," I said.

"You didn't say anything."

"Hadn't found the Cheroots yet."

"We need Mendoza in on this." Clarke pulled onto the roadway.

****

We drove back to The Trails End. Lieutenant Clarke called and asked Mendoza to meet us in his room. Explained enough to ask the chief not to alert Olivera. Mendoza agreed. He'd park his car at The Sweet Shop and walk to The Trails End being careful Olivera didn't learn about our meeting.

An hour later Mendoza knocked on Lieutenant Clarke's door. We told him what we'd found. Told him about the blanket. Everything.

Mendoza was pissed Clarke had pursued the investigation with me, excluding him. "You fuckin' sneak into my town, pull shit like this without comin' to me. Who the fuck you tink you are?"

"Shouldn't of happened that way, Chief, I agree," Clarke said apologetically. "Don't blame you for being pissed off. But look, first, I had no idea anything this guy was sayin'," he jabbed a thumb in my direction, "was anything but bullshit. When it turned out not to be bullshit...look, Caldwell did the right thing. He just had no confidence going to *you*. It's done. And now you know everything we know."

"He's been watching me for weeks, Chief," I put in. "One night at Audrey's, rocks were knocked onto the roof from above the house. We paid no attention at the time. Another night I smelled smoke from this." I held up the collection of cigar butts. "Didn't make the connection that night but when I saw the mound of wooden tipped cigar butts out by the field, smelled them...wasn't hard to put two and two together. He's been following me around town since I showed up. Flattened all the tires to my truck one day. Threatened to run me in, I ever got in his way. This may sound like sour grapes, Chief, but I assure you it isn't. I can't prove it—"

"Yet," Clarke inserted, cutting me off.

Mendoza looked up at him. "This is all circumstantial," Mendoza said to Clarke. "You can't get Olivera to confess, you got nothin'."

"Agreed," Clarke said. "Why I called you. We gotta have your help."

There was a long pause.

"You in?" Clarke prodded.

Mendoza dropped heavily into a chair, tossed his hat onto the table. "I knew the sonofabitch was trouble for a long time now. Hear tings around town...you know?"

Neither Clarke nor I replied.

"How we get him to confess?" Mendoza asked.

"Scare him into thinking we already know. Play our cards right, he'll reveal himself," Clarke said.

"He saw us out at the bridge today," I told Mendoza. "He knows we were at the scene. Probably pondering what's up right now."

"I wondered where he went to hide from me," Mendoza said.

"He hides up along Pacheco Crossroad, too," I said.

The chief shook his head. "Whatchu want me to do?" Mendoza looked to Lieutenant Clarke.

"Give me your keys to the station," Clarke said. "Go back to your car. Give Caldwell and me time to get over to the jail. Call Olivera on his radio. Tell him to meet you there. I'm about to reveal who really killed Miranda DeCosta. Give him time to get to us before you do."

"What are you gonna do?"

"Lie to him," Clarke said, a smirk curling up from his lips, bushy eyebrows growing into impressive arches— baritone chuckle that suggested he rather enjoyed what he saw coming.

"That legal?" Mendoza asked.

"Doesn't matter," Clarke said. "You're gonna witness his confession and make the arrest."

"Jesus," Mendoza said through clenched teeth.

"Make sure he has no keys in his patrol car before you come in. Don't want him escaping on us."

"You sure about all this?" Mendoza asked.

Clarke thought for a minute, looked over to me. "Frankly, no. But we're out of options here. People are in jail. Things are happening. We need to smoke this guy out."

Mendoza stood, grabbed his hat and moved in front of me. "Sorry...'bout the bullshit," he said and proffered his hand.

We shook.

CHAPTER 39

CLARKE DROVE US to the police station. Inside he unfolded his handkerchief on top of Mendoza's desk and spread the cigar butts. "Let me do the talking," he said. "But keep an eye on the bastard. He's got nothing to lose once he figures out we have him."

We didn't wait long.

Tires squealed to a stop out front. "Hear that?" Clarke eyed me. "He's scared. Tell by the reckless driving to get to us." He glanced through the window. "Here he comes."

Olivera burst through the door, noticed the top of Mendoza's desk. "What's that?"

"That's what nailed you," Clarke said, hitting Olivera in the face with it, cold. Even I believed him and I knew it was a lie. "Come on in. We need to talk."

Olivera quickly checked out the door, let it partially close, but kept a safe distance from both Clarke and me.

"We know everything, Jorge. Might as well make it easy on yourself," Clarke said.

"You don't know shit." Olivera's face turned red; sweat broke onto his upper lip. "What the fuck's this all about, anyway?"

"Stop playing games," Clarke said. "We know was you the DeCosta woman ran into that night out on the canal. We know was you took the shot at Caldwell here."

Olivera eyed the Cheroot butts on Mendoza's desk. Anxiety was written all over him. "Fuck you. Those don't mean shit. So I take a little smoke break out by the levee now and again. No law against that."

"Law against raping and murdering a woman, and taking shots at people. I got your rifle."

"Bullshit, my rifle's—" Olivera caught himself, glanced at the door. Eyed Clarke and me suspiciously. "You motherfucker!" He pulled his service revolver.

"Whoa, Jorge," Clarke said. "Calm down. That isn't gonna help you now."

"Fuck you. I ain't lettin' no white trash motherfucker like him," he pointed the pistol at me then, "put me behind bars. You got no proof of nothin'."

"You shoot one of us, we're gonna have all the proof we need," Clarke goaded him.

The gun was visibly shaking in his hand. "Caldwell came at me," Olivera said smugly, gesturing at me with his pistol, crafting his story. "Tried to assault me like he did before. This time we struggled. You got hit with a stray shot from the struggle." He turned the revolver on Clarke "I had no choice but to kill him," he said in a febrile frenzy, "in self-defense."

"Why'd you do it, Jorge?" Clark prodded him. "Why'd you kill her?"

"That fuckin' uppity bitch put out for every guy in town. You'd a thought she was a fuckin' virgin the way she acted."

"Maybe she was just cold and scared, Jorge. Maybe she thought she stumbled onto an officer of the law who would help her, not rape her."

"Fuck you. She wanted it. She always wanted it. Just needed a little persuading."

326

"You raped her before?" Clarke said, feigning surprise.

"I never raped her. I mighta fucked her once or twice. Bitch was always shitfaced. What difference did it make? She didn't even remember the next morning. She was a fuckin' whore! Don't you get it? Fuckin' uppity whore. Nothin' more."

The door to the station opened slowly. Mendoza's bulk smothered all light from outside as he stood in the doorway. The shotgun in his hands was aimed point blank at Olivera's gut.

"Gimme one excuse, I'm gonna cut you in half where you stand." Mendoza's words were so ominous; seemed he might just go ahead and do it without provocation.

Olivera's revolver drooped, quivering worse now. Suddenly, he pulled it steady toward me again. Neither Clarke nor Mendoza showed much concern this unstable creep might actually shoot me.

"Go ahead," Mendoza said. "I'll let you shoot him first so it's real clear I was justified separating the upper part of your body from the lower. You'll be with him before he hits the floor."

There was that moment of pregnant silence...that split second in which you're never quite certain someone won't decide to go out in a blaze of glory.

Olivera dropped the weapon to his side, then to the floor. "They made me say that shit, Chief," he sniveled. "They trapped me into saying that stuff. None of it was true. I was just playing along."

"Shut up." Mendoza held the shotgun level. "Cuff him, Lieutenant."

Clarke spun Olivera around and pulled his hands behind his back, clamped the cuffs around his wrists.

"Now put him in the holding cell," Mendoza ordered.

When the door clicked locked, he pointed his shotgun to the floor.

"You hear everything, Chief?" Clarke asked.

"Every word."

"You recover his car keys?

"Right here." Mendoza dangled the key ring. "Why?"

"The way he reacted when I told him I had his rifle. Let me borrow those," Clarke said on his way out the door.

In a few moments, he was back holding a .30-30 Winchester.

"How'd you know he even had a rifle?" I asked.

"Didn't," Clark admitted. "But if he didn't, how could he have taken a shot at you? Best guess."

I looked at the weapon. It had no scope. "Fires low and to the left," I predicted.

"Lucky for you, you white trash motherfucker," Olivera yelled from the cell.

Mendoza, Clarke and me stood looking at the pathetic excuse of a man.

"Satisfied, Chief?" Clarke asked.

CHAPTER 40

LIEUTENANT CLARKE AND Prado Mendoza discussed police business. I stepped outside and waited. Summer was in full bloom. The fusty smell of fertilizer hung in the hot afternoon air. In the distance, cicadas buzzed from the branches of the cottonwoods, mulberries and laurel trees. Tomatoes were coming to maturity. Hundreds of acres of them give off a distinct smell as they ripen on the vine. A frontend loader somewhere molested the newest mountain of cow shit, releasing its fresh perfume. It was indeed Divina's identifying bouquet.

"Mendoza and I are going to take credit for this arrest," Bobby Dale Clarke said on the short drive to The Trials End Motel. "Our livelihoods, not yours." He looked over at me. "Maybe we get a little redemption."

"I can't claim anything more than coincidence anyway," I said.

"Figured you'd understand. We'll prepare a sworn statement for you in our reports—couple o' days. Pederson will need your testimony at trial." He parked in front of our rooms. We slid out of his car, awkward with what to say next. "You have a good eye for observation, Caldwell, pay attention to details, good instincts. If you're as good at writing it down as you are at figuring things out..." We shuffled toward our separate rooms. Clarke proffered his hand. I sensed an enduring friendship. "Wouldn't mind an autographed copy of that novel when it's published," he said and disappeared into his room.

My room was a mess and it smelled bad. The silence there was shrill...split my eardrums. I scanned the stagnant, pitiful landscape, my thoughts muddled and confused—so many complications—so much uncertainty.

But I'd finally had my come-to-Jesus moment and it wasn't in anybody's church. My life and my country were a screwed up mess at the moment, at least in the dead of the night, alone in the darkness of my tortured memories at the *hour of demons*. But there was one certainty I had no doubts about.

As quickly as I could collect my things and check out of The Trails End, I made the short drive up Silverado Trail to Audrey's house. I pulled to a stop in front of the courtyard gate and sat in Buck. The vacant spot at the end of the drive, which had been Buck's parking place over the last few months, looked forlorn in its emptiness.

The blossomed flowers around the bungalow I'd called home were still in profusions of colorful sweet-smelling blooms. I recalled how lovingly Audrey systematically transformed the place masculine in her image of me...just for me. Relived what we had together there.

The front door of her house opened tentatively. Audrey stepped out wearing her uniform. As adorable as I'd ever seen her look. She padded barefoot to the open gate, shoved her hands into her back pockets, eyed me. "Everything okay?"

"Yeah."

Silence.

Rachel stepped out the door on the opposite side of the courtyard wearing a mini-version of Audrey's outfit. They looked like twins except for the stark differences in

330

hair and facial characteristics. She crept across the courtyard to her mother's side. She was growing like a weed, long spindly legs destined to be beautiful.

"What's *he* want?" she asked Audrey, making it a point not to address me.

"I think he came to say goodbye, PF." They were having this conversation about me as if I didn't exist. "Maybe you should go back inside."

Rachel looked to me, a glare that conveyed pain, betrayal, disappointment. She turned to walk toward the house.

"Wait, PF," I said. She stopped and turned back.

"What, Charlie?" Audrey demanded.

"I want her to hear what I have to say."

"Why?"

Rachel glided silently back next to her mother's side. Audrey slid her arm up across her daughter's shoulders.

"Why, Charlie?"

"Because I love her, too. I love you both." I slid out of Buck and leaned against the front fender. My eyes wandered nervously. Presently, I began to recount what all of Divina would be buzzing anew about in the next few days. Those issues had no relevance in that moment, but it was easy to talk about.

"You're a hero again," Audrey said derisively. "That what you stopped by to share with us on your way out of town?"

I ignored the stab.

"You realize you can't smell the cow shit up here?"

"What?"

"Cow shit," I repeated. "The defining smell of this town. Smell of cow shit doesn't make it up this far. Almost like you don't even live in Divina."

"What are you getting at, Charlie?" Audrey sounded impatient, but less intransigent.

"You remember the afternoon we had the picnic up on Pacheco Pass Crossroad? We sat on the tailgate of Buck under the big oak. Told you how Pacheco Pass was the one place on this earth I felt physically connected to, how it anchored me to my childhood?"

Audrey didn't reply.

Rachel looked up at her mother, puzzled.

I went on. "I discovered something else I feel physically connected to right here on the edge of the Pass." Rachel wore a mask of confusion, but Audrey's body language exposed naked hope. "I have a place down in Old Mexico I can't just leave. And I have an assignment to do a story on Cartagena, Colombia. Not sure how long I'll be there. There's also the matter of my first novel to finish and try to get published." I read deflation in Audrey once more. "And I need therapy," I admitted. "There are things I need to deal with, resolve."

Audrey looked down at her feet.

"Thing is," I went on, "all that business could take a while to wrap up. What I was hoping was...what I was hoping was I could have a long-term lease on the bungalow," I said, nodding in that direction.

Audrey looked up at me. "Cut the bullshit, Charlie. Rachel and I can't deal with any more." Rachel made no objection to the sentiment or the use of her name. "Say what you mean."

"You're a hard case, Audrey."

"With good cause," she said defiantly.

"Do you really not understand how much I love you?"

Audrey and Rachel both stared hard at me but didn't move a muscle.

"Can you really not see what I want is to be right here with the two of you?"

Audrey hugged Rachel gently. "Define long-term lease."

"As long as you live here."

"And after that?" she whispered over Rachel's head.

I thought for a moment. "If we make it a lease-purchase, you might say I would earn equity."

"So you're interested in buying?" she asked.

"I've already bought, Audrey."

"What the hell are you two talking about?" Rachel demanded.

I almost laughed.

"Charlie's making us an offer, sweetie."

"Is he staying or leaving?" Rachel demanded.

Audrey looked up at me.

"I have obligations that aren't optional, PF. I'm asking you to wait for me while I go take care of those things. I want to move into the bungalow for good. I'll be gone a while. But if you let me, if you'll wait for me, I'll be home before you know it."

Like THICK FOG IN PACHECO PASS?
Don't miss the next Charlie Caldwell
mystery
SLAUGHTERED.
Coming 2014
Keep reading for an excerpt...

PROLOGUE

ON February 16, 1973, a beautiful young mother, thirty-one-year-old Sarah Louise Gammons was brutally beaten, then savagely stabbed to death, *slaughtered*, in the youth building of the Community Presbyterian Church in Gustine, California. Gustine is a tiny, ordinarily quiet, community located on Hwy 33 along the edge of the Diablo Mountains on the west side of the San Joaquin Valley.

Allegedly, Sarah Lou, as friends affectionately called her, was found lying on her back in a pool of blood by her husband, Rev. Kenneth P. Gammons.

Rev. Gammons told authorities he and Sarah Lou left their home at the same time earlier that morning. He'd run downtown to grab a few (things). He'd taken the couple's one-year-old daughter, Mitzi with him. Sarah Lou had gone on alone to the church to practice a hymn. Sarah Lou was the organist for the church choir.

Rev. Gammons claims to have been gone no more than about thirty minutes. He returned to find Sarah Lou lying in a pool of blood, her head resting near a scattering of bloodstained bibles and other papers apparently knocked around the room by the murderer.

The autopsy revealed Sarah Lou had been beaten unconscious, and then stabbed four times in the right eye and twice in the left. One of the stabs in her left eye penetrated to the frontal cortex of Sarah Lou's brain resulting in her death.

The California State Crime Lab, Merced County Sheriff's Dept., the Fresno, California Police Dept. and the California State Department of Justice aided Gustine Police in the investigation.

Investigators were baffled by the lack of motive or clues in the case. Robbery has been ruled out as the motive and the autopsy revealed Sarah Lou had not been sexually assaulted. A random act by a transient has also been ruled out, as the murderer obviously possessed intimate knowledge of the church grounds. No murder weapon has been recovered.

****

January 7, 1973

Dearest Audrey & Passion Flower,

Cartagena, Colombia is picturesque, but missing something vital without the two of you. Historically, it was the seat of the Spanish Main. For your information PF, the Spanish Main began at the mouth of the Oronoco River off Venezuela and stretched across the entire north coast of South America to the Isthmus of Panama. (Look that geography up PF. Very exciting!) 16th Century world history. I'm learning all about it doing this article for Past, Present & Future.

Taking lots of slides and can't wait to tell you all about this place. The next time I come here though, you two will be with me, because I will never leave you again! I miss you both more than words can tell.

*I know, Audrey, you must have had your doubts
watching me drive away as I did. When I get home...*

"Mom!" Rachel yelled from the other end of the house. "Some woman on the phone for you." Rachel stood holding the phone out at arms length as her mother glided past her into the kitchen.

"Who is it, Rach?"

"Will you stop calling me that?" Rachel feigned abject pain in her countenance, as though she'd been wounded. She seemed forever reminding her mother she should have been named Passion Flower. And as far as she was concerned, that's what she was entitled to be called.

"Hello?" Audrey said.

"Hi Audrey, Phoebe Fillinger—Past, Present & Future Magazine..."

"Miss Fillinger," Audrey answered in a sloe gin kind of way...and then, "Oh, God! Is Charlie okay? Did something happen?"

"Calm down, Audrey. Charlie's fine."

"Sorry," Audrey allowed. "Last time we spoke you were tracking him down for his assignment. Never heard from you again. Just assumed something—"

"He's fine," Fillinger broke in. "But I may have to deduct some of his pay for this story." She laughed lightly. "He writes as much about you in his communiqués to me as he does about Cartagena. Goes on and on about you and Rachel; how much he misses you."

Audrey didn't reply for several seconds. "I...we...miss him, too. How can I help you?" she finally asked.

"No, nothing. This is a personal call."

"But we don't—"

Fillinger cut her off again. "Charlie ever show you his manuscript? ...*Thick Fog in Pacheco Pass.*"

"No...everything all right? Something wrong with it?"

Fillinger chuckled graciously. "Hardly. Nice piece of work. It's a finished manuscript now about to be published. A couple of my senior editors and I just finished reading over it one last time."

"Oh?"

Extended silence.

"All three of us have decided we wish we were you."

"I don't understand, Phoebe. Why would you want to be me? Why would anybody want to be me?" Audrey chuckled then.

"Tell you what Audrey," Fillinger said. "When you finally read this novel, if you still don't know the answer to that, you give me a call and I'll explain it to you."

"I'm confused," Audrey said.

"You won't be after you read his book. I just wanted to say hello, let you know he's fine. He'll be home soon."

****

February 20, 1973

The doorbell rang. "Can you get that, PF?" No answer. "That kid..." Audrey complained under her breath leaning the dust mop against the counter, padding out the side door of the kitchen to see who was ringing the bell."

"I help you?" she asked, surprising the giant standing at the front door.

"Oh, hello," the man replied, twirling to find her. "Surprised me. Sneaking up on me, I see."

"Sorry. I was cleaning in the kitchen. Can I help you?"

"Bobby Dale Clarke, mam." Clarke was a big man; well over six feet with a full head of thick salt and pepper flyaway hair like a lion's mane, an even thicker full beard and bushy eyebrows that swept upward at the corners of his broad forehead. He reached inside the lapel of his cheap wrinkled sport coat and pulled out a worn leather business card holder. "California State Police," he said, handing her his card. His mien was that of a gentle giant.

"Charlie mentioned you," Audrey said taking the card from Clarke. "Something wrong?"

"In a manner of speaking," Clarke replied. "Seen the newspapers last couple of days?"

"Not following you..." Audrey glanced at the card again, "Lieutenant."

"Murder over in Gustine—Sara Louise Gammons."

"Come on, let's go into the kitchen. Get you a coffee—anything?"

"Nice place you have here," Clarke said eyeing the layout. "I could do with a half cup if it's no trouble,"

"No trouble," Audrey said taking down a mug. "Yes, I saw the newspaper. Doesn't matter, it's all over the television news, too," she said. "Everybody in town's talking about it. Horrible!" she filled his cup.

"You in touch with Charlie these days, Mrs. Romero?"

"It's miss—Charlie in some kind of trouble?"

"Sorry—No. No. This murder. It's...not your ordinary variety murder case. I thought he might like to kick some ideas around with me."

"You mean work with you?"

"No...of course not. But Charlie and me...we hit it off pretty good on that DeCosta case last year." Clarke sat back in his chair, ran a hand over the top of his head through his profuse hair. "I was thinkin'...Charlie ever actually write that novel he was talking about?"

"*Thick Fog in Pacheco Pass,*" Audrey said. "Just received an advance copy from a friend of his works at his magazine yesterday."

Charlie has a good head," Clarke said. "Sees things. Pays attention to details. Look forward to reading it myself." He sipped noisily from his cup—

CHAPTER 1

ON a drippy wind-chilled March morning in 1973, I guided Buck, my newly painted `52 Ford pickup, off of California Hwy 152 into the parking lot at Casa de Fruita. The fresh produce market and candy shop I've loved since my folks began stopping there when I was a kid in the `50s, sits near the bottom edge of Pacheco Pass along California's Diablo Mountains. I wouldn't dare show up where I was headed without a bag of fudge. I was still feeling awkward seeing Buck's gleaming turquoise enamel and shiny bright black trim glistening instead of the rust-bucket it had been only a few weeks earlier. I'd made the decision to keep the fringe of Mexican dingle balls hanging from the upper edge of the windshield. Some kind of statement. I just don't know what it says.

The cool, damp morning air was redolent with the aroma of thousands of acres of garlic growing in the fields all the way to Gilroy. In another two months it will be a full year since I was last here. How a life changes the way mine has in that amount of time is difficult to imagine; lotta water under the bridge to quote an oft-used cliché.

The war in Vietnam rages on, seemingly without an end in sight. Nixon, it appears, is up to his ass in this Watergate thing and America remains in a state of protracted inner turmoil. Don't get me wrong, it all means as much to me as it always has; the political landscape of the country, I mean; social equality and justice—the lie I know in my heart the Vietnam War to be.

The difference up to now...I'd put all that ahead of any personal relationships I started to develop. Well, these realities and the unfortunate incident with Miranda DeCosta my last year of high school. But I've put that behind me, too. The scars combat left in me...I'm coping. I'm learning those memories are never going away. I'm getting better at controlling my demons. I haven't treated anyone to a near-death experience in months. I know that's progress.

Uncle Sam cut me loose more than two years ago now...after they'd used me to their advantage in Nam. That's a history I was trying to put behind me when I went to see Phoebe Fillinger, Senior Editor at Past, Present & Future Magazine in Denver two years ago. I'd asked her for a job as a writer. I had no credentials for the position but I'd been a proofreader for them before I was drafted and held a little hope.

Phoebe went to bat for me with her bosses. She talked them into taking a chance on me. More than that, she gave me time to try to get my head together before sending me on my first assignment.

That's how I ended up back in Divina, California, the tiny San Joaquin Valley town where I grew up and went to high school. I came to write my first novel, *Thick Fog in Pacheco Pass,* based on what I found there. It's been out a couple of months now. Probably too soon to know what people are going to think. Phoebe loves it. That's something.

Odd how things develop. I'd held the town of Divina in contempt for so long I'd forgotten there was any good in the place. I'd brooded for ten years over what I'd decided was a conspiracy against me. When I'd reached the point I was ready to confront that baggage and wipe the slate clean...well, look...if you're really interested in what happened when I returned to Divina to set my life on a corrected path, you'll want to pick up a copy of *Thick Fog in Pacheco Pass.*

After flipping the vendor a five, I climbed back into Buck with my bag of fudge. In less than an hour I'd be standing before the treasure I'd discovered in Divina a year ago.

****

Soon I was turning onto Pacheco Pass Crossroad. This was the most direct route back to Audrey I could take. When I came to Silverado Trail, I made a right turn. In the lane of the deserted road I pulled to a stop. For a moment I panned the stunning cinematic view of the San Joaquin Valley, drinking in its breathtaking beauty. The valley floor lays a few hundred feet of elevation below the Crossroad. The broad expanse of the San Joaquin from here is back dropped by the majestic snow-covered peaks of the Sierra Nevada a couple hundred miles distant. There were patches of ground fog covering the fields of crops and orchards of almonds and walnuts as far as I could see.

The knee high grass coating the Diablo foothills like a well groomed puppy was in deep shades of yellow-green, punctuated by black-green patches. Those darker places are the ancient oak trees, which for more than a century have stood sentinel over this place. This setting has moved and anchored me since I was a boy. Today, for better or worse, I planned to make a homecoming. I felt like a tortoise, the few odds and ends constituting the sum of my possessions were snuggly covered in Buck's pickup bed.

Nudging the accelerator, I guided my old Ford down grade approaching her driveway. My heart was beating like the pistons inside Buck's engine. I turned left onto the tiny pills of santan gravel that protected the circular drive. The stony riprap crunched under the weight of the pickup's tires. When I pulled to a stop, Buck's driver's door opened to the wide, heavy antique doors that guard the courtyard of Audrey's sprawling Spanish ranch-style home.

The bungalow which, a year earlier, had been my home, the place where I'd fallen in love with Audrey and written *Thick Fog in Pacheco Pass,* sat thirty yards away with its vines and flowers and Spanish tiled roof gleaming like I'd left it only yesterday; as inviting as it was the first time I'd seen it.

Pushing Buck's door ajar, I slid off the seat. The front door of the house opened slowly and there she was, peering out tentatively. I could see in her face Buck's new image had addled her. Rachel stepped out of the door on the south side of the courtyard and stared like a deer in the headlights. They were expecting me. Just weren't expecting what they were seeing.

Audrey had on a pair of tight fitting jeans that defined her long sensuous legs. Her auburn hair seemed longer and was tied back in a ponytail. She wore a simple sleeveless green blouse with sandals of a similar color. A beaming grin spread across her face in slow motion as the realization struck home.

Like me, Audrey's a runner. She broke like a quarter horse from the starting gate. At full speed she raced toward me leaving the front door wide open. "Charlie!" She sang my name at the top of her lungs—flung her arms out as she drew near. From five feet away she leapt at me, arms and legs groping and finding my body, nearly knocking me to the ground. I staggered backward with her clinging to me, legs wrapped around my waist, arms around my neck, her face buried into me shouting my name between kisses and holding to me so tightly I couldn't speak.

"My turn, my turn!" Rachel was shouting, jumping up and down like a pogo stick. "My turn!"

But Audrey was not letting go. Her weeping turned to inconsolable sobs. I held her as tightly and tenderly as I could. "Hey," I said softly. "It's okay, sweetheart—it's okay. I'm home," I whispered.

Our world went silent except for the soft sounds of women weeping.

"You two gonna be okay?" I ventured finally.

Audrey shook her head in the crook of my neck. By then Rachel had wormed her way into my side and had her arms around her mother and me both. She shook her head, too.

In time, breathing began to return to normal but Audrey had me locked up like a wrestler in a ring.

"I missed you, Charlie," she finally managed.

"Me, too," Rachel agreed.

"I missed both of you, too."

Audrey took a deep breath and spoke to me. "Your back hurting yet?"

"No," I lied.

"Good," she said, "cuz I'm not ready to let go."

"What about my turn, mom?" Rachel complained. "And she won't let me read your book, Charlie!"

At Rachel's grumble, Audrey lifted her head from my neck. Her face was streaked with mascara; her emerald eyes twinkled with moistness. "Do you realize this entire town has read that book? My mother, my mother-in-law, Darryl...all my friends...all of them...everyone everywhere is reading it."

"Did you like it?"

The passion in the kiss she smothered me with took my breath away.

Audrey's legs turned loose and she let her feet reach for the ground slowly while she hung from my neck and shoulders. Standing on her own, she finally let go and stepped back. She looked up into my eyes. "That how you really feel about me—PF, too?"

"That and more."

"Then why can't I read it?" Rachel groused and wedged her way in between her mother and me. "I missed you, too, Charlie. All my friends are talking about what their mothers are saying about you and mom."

I hugged Rachel to my stomach. She seemed a foot taller but I doubted that was possible. It had been too long since I held her.

There was no way to answer the flap over the book. I knew what the uproar was about, though these repercussions had not occurred to me during the writing of it. I looked down at Rachel back to Audrey then down at Rachel once more. "I didn't think about any of those people reading the novel when I wrote it. I was simply writing how I felt about you."

Audrey looked deep into my eyes, tiptoed up over her daughter sandwiched between us and paused. "Yeah," she whispered sensuously and kissed me softly on the lips. "Leave your things. Hungry?" she asked. "Let me make you some lunch."

"Hold on," I said, reaching back into Buck for the bag of fudge. "Here PF, picked this up for you."

"What is it? Let me see," Rachel said excited, scrambling to get her hands on the bag. She looked inside. "Vanilla-walnut! You know that's my favorite." She grinned up at me, her adorable blue eyes glowing like aquamarine gemstones against her prefect cappuccino complexion, framed by a thick mop of black ringlets draped luxuriously across her shoulders.

****

We were getting through the awkward baby steps of reintroduction like astronauts just back from the moon while we ate the tuna sandwiches Audrey put together.

"I dusted the bungalow," she said. "Things are just where you left them, pretty much."

Other than the occasional interjection, it was quiet while we ate.

"I stocked up on wine," Audrey suddenly announced. "I can open some if you want."

"Maybe later."

Rachel looked from one of us to the other, clearly anticipating something juicier between her mother and I than she was hearing.

A few more moments went by before I spoke. "I can't live without my typewriter," I said.

Audrey smiled. "Best investment I ever made."

Rachel watched.

I reached over and held Audrey's hand. "Nicest gift anyone has ever given me."

Rachel couldn't continue with the nonsense. "All my friends' mom's know you two are having sex. Stephanie's mom says—"

"PF!" The color came slowly up from her green blouse. Audrey looked from me to Rachel.

"Good grief, mother," Rachel said. "We're all grown ups here."

I wanted to burst out laughing but when Audrey buried her face in her hands I judged that was not the appropriate response.

Rachel was finishing her sandwich. "You guys want a piece of my fudge for desert?"

There was no reply.

"Suit yourselves. I'm having some." Rachel sat back in her chair eyeing the hunk of creamy fudge she held delicately between her slender fingertips.

Audrey still hadn't spoken. Finally Rachel said, "I think you two need to be alone." She pushed her chair back and stood. Thirteen going on adult, I thought grinning at her. "Thanks for the fudge, Charlie."

Audrey peeked between her fingers as her precocious daughter retreated.

"I see she still doesn't give you much of a break," I said.

"Much of a break? She gets worse by the day!"

"She's adorable."

"Lucky for her!" Audrey declared. "Let's get you moved in and settled. I've pulled out some steaks for dinner. You in the mood?"

"Sounds perfect. We'll pop a bottle of that wine."

"And I'll send my woman-child to her room early because there's no way you're crawling in that bed tonight without me," she said, looking me right in the eyes. "I've missed you so badly, Charlie."

As we kissed she welded her body to me so tightly I could feel her heartbeat. If Rachel had not been in the house I'd have taken her there on the kitchen counter.

****

Rachel came out to help when I pulled Buck down close to the bungalow, my new home...for the second time.

There were only a few armloads of clothes, some books and files. I carried the IBM Selectric Audrey had given me as a gift the year before. My most valuable and treasured possession, it had ridden in the front passenger seat next to me.

"You get my message about that cop, Clarke, came by here?" Audrey asked.

"Gave him a call," I said.

"That Gammons murder is still all over the news. Everybody's scared," Audrey said.

I hesitated before going on. "Might make another interesting novel," I said.

She wasn't surprised. "I knew the minute Clarke showed up asking about you what would happen," she said.

"You gonna be okay with it?"

"You're a writer, Charlie. It's what you do." She smiled across the room at me. "See that stack of newspapers?" She pointed to a spot on the floor near my writing desk. "Collected every article I could find for you, right from the first reports of what took place."

"How'd you—"

"Read your novel, remember?"

"And she won't let me read it!" Rachel chirped breaking her long silence.

"And you're not going to read it young lady until I tell you you're old enough."

"And when will that be? When I'm an old woman?"

"When you're grown up enough not to say things to me like you said at lunch and like right now," Audrey responded, surprising both me and her daughter.

The room went quiet for several moments.

"Sorry, mom," Rachel said finally. She paused and went on. "I didn't mean to embarrass you. But I know you and Charlie have sex, okay. I'm not a child. He doesn't have to live out here in the bungalow. He can live in the house with us."

"Okay," Audrey said. "You aren't a child. I know that. But you aren't old enough to be thinking about those kinds of things either. And Charlie is going to live out here in the bungalow because that's what he wants."

"And you agree, right?" I added quickly.

Audrey looked up at me, took a breath. "And I agree."

Rachel contemplated the conversation several moments. "Okay, if that's what you guys want. But just so you know, I know you're having sex."

I kept my mouth shut, doing my best to conceal the grin attempting to creep across my face.

Audrey hung her head in exasperation. Finally I could feel capitulation in her demeanor. "Okay, PF. So you know. I love him and we are adults—"

"More like it, mom," Rachel said cutting her mother off. "Just let me know when you need me to get lost."

"Oh, God, Rachel could you get lost now before I die of mortification!"

Rachel scowled. "You know I don't like that name, mother." She stomped out the French doors.

"You have your hands full," I said crossing the room to take Audrey into my arms.

"*We* have our hands full," she corrected. "You're in this too. I don't need a fair weather—" she looked at me, "lover."

We held each other a long time. The deep feelings we'd shared right from the first time we met began to well up in both of us.

"Can I be your muse from now on?" she asked me softly, angling her pretty face upward in a coy gesture, rocking back slightly in my arms to look into my eyes.

"You've been my muse since the first moment I looked into those lusty green eyes of yours."

She slid a hand down over my ass and massaged my butt. "I mean for real: talk to me about what you're writing...maybe let me see what you've written sometimes." She slid her hand around to the front of my jeans and rubbed the hardness in my pants. "There's no telling what I might inspire in you," she said squeezing my manhood firmly. She maintained her grip, pressed her body close to mine, edged up onto her tiptoes and kissed me softly. "Like if I had to make a guess...I'd say your creative juices are flowing right now."

"Jesus, Audrey."

"Oh...I don't think He's gonna do you much good." She stroked me firmly over my full length. "Close those French doors and pull the curtains," she said softly. "And lock it. I'll get the back door and the window drapes."

When I turned back to her from the far end of my room, she stood beside my bed in the muted light, gazing wantonly back at me, her fingers slipping one button after another of her green blouse open. I watched her work agonizingly slow in silence for several moments until the bottom button pulled out of its eye and she brushed the flimsy cloth open for me to see her soft breasts.

She looked down at them, cupped them gently in her palms, peered out the tops of her bright, promising eyes at me. "You joining this party, soldier?" Her nipples peeked out at me from between her fingers.

Pulling my shirt off as I crossed to her, I bent to kiss her naked breasts while she fumbled with my belt and the heavy metal button at the top of my jeans. I pulled her's open effortlessly and slid them down over her hips while I held a firm nipple between my lips.

We stood in a nest of crinkled jeans around our ankles, Audrey in her panties, me in my boxers and kissed ardently, pressing our not quite naked bodies against each other, recalibrating ourselves to the familiarity we'd known with each other before I'd left nine months earlier. It didn't require much effort.

Sliding her panties down over her slender hips in one fluid motion, I laid her back across my bed. When I pulled the lace from her ankles, she pulled her knees up, spread her legs lazily and touched herself, inviting me to do with her as I pleased. "Come here, Charlie," she whispered, barely audible.

The smooth landscape of her flesh was one solid unbroken pallet of honeyed velvet. Her bellybutton has an endearing tiny cleft to it that drew my lips like a powerful electro magnet. The ethereal softness of that part of her body fried the neurotransmitters in my brain. I let the tip of my tongue trace every inch of her torso up between her breasts and to her beautiful mouth.

She was drawing each breath with labored effort, whispering for me to just take her. Her lips were moist and supple. Inhaling her expelled breath was like swallowing a sweet tropical breeze. She reached down and took my manhood into her hands, caressing me gently, playing her fingers over every curve and nuance of me. Then she cupped my testicles gently in one palm, twirling them around like marbles in a velvet bag. "Please put it in me, Charlie...please."

Touching her, tasting her, feeling her beneath me was like arriving at an oasis in the desert after nearly dying of thirst; I needed to drink her in slowly or I might surely burst. I let my tongue slide down over her cheek, along her fine slender neck, teasing her ear lobe, tasting the unidentifiable uniqueness that I knew to be her and only her. I took each nipple into my mouth again and again tracing her aureoles with my tongue, holding her nipples gently between my teeth. I could feel every fiber of her body tremble beneath me when I kissed her belly button.

She reached up and ran her long fingers into my hair and pulled me to her. The tone of her whispers rested somewhere between pleading and panic. When I let my tongue slip down between her thighs and into the downy softness of her, she cried gently, arched her back and held herself up, inviting me to taste all of her.

By then I was completely consumed and now I wanted to consume her. Her perfume drove me to a visceral place as I let my tongue slide inside her, out of her, tracing everything that made her a woman. Each time I brushed the tip of her clitoris she arched, whimpered and dug her fingers deep into the flesh of my shoulders.

I was doing my best to hold off, but that much time apart was taking its toll on both of us. I wanted to do everything with her, but the urgency I felt at that moment couldn't wait any longer. I raised my self from between Audrey's thighs, permitted several moments simply to adore her lying there. Our eyes met and locked together, understanding what was coming. Audrey didn't take her eyes from me, watching me push my boxers over my hips, letting them fall to the floor. I crawled up between her soft thighs, my eyes still locked to hers, hesitated before I gently let just my tip slide inside her.

She was tight. I remembered how it had been for her our very first time together. There was little reason to believe it would be any different after nearly a full year. She sucked in a gasp of breath and whimpered. "Oh my God, Baby." A tear trickled from the corner of her eye but our eyes remained wide open, locked to each other. Neither of us wanted to miss one tiny emotion of our moment. I didn't thrust hard into her. Instead I pushed into her slowly, allowing her to swallow me inside her gently until our pelvises met. Finally, she closed her eyes and contracted herself closing tight onto me holding me like her prisoner. When I withdrew to thrust into her, her moans turned to begging and pleading for more and harder and deeper. When my thrusting began to go faster and my own breathing began to increase, she opened her eyes and gazed lovingly into mine. "Yes, baby," she said. "Don't stop. Harder," she pleaded, digging her fingers into my chest. "Harder," she moaned urgently. By then our voices combined like the rest of our bodies in a chorus of ecstatic realization. We saw deep into each other's souls when my energy flowed out of me and into her.

There is the difference of darkness and light between having sex and making love to the woman you love as life itself. We spent the next two hours experiencing the latter. In the afterglow, we lay silent, spent in each other's arms. Finally, Audrey whispered drowsily, "You gonna be alright living in Divina again?"

"Not gonna live in Divina," I replied.

In that moment, it was as if a bucket of cold water had been poured over her. She shot upright to a sitting position and glared at me.

I smiled up at her. "Easy, Bright Eyes," I said, sliding my arm up onto her shoulder. "I'm gonna live here with you, up along the edge of Pacheco Pass. I'm not going to live in Divina." I could feel her muscles relax as she simmered down and collapsed back to cuddle with me again. "It's a rationale."

"You think you can make that work?"

"Got you, got Rachel." I chuckled softly. "I've never smelled cow shit up here—not once."

We lay holding each other for a long time.

"I love you, Audrey," I whispered. "I love you. We're going to live a unique life together. But I love you and Rachel, and if you love me, too...

She felt the commitment I was making. I could feel it in every muscle of her warm naked body plastered against me. There was no need to finish what I was trying to explain. "I'll take the rest of the week," I promised, "to get settled; for us.

"I'll call Lieutenant Clarke next week. I'm anxious to get to work on my new novel."

"Got a working title yet?" Audrey asked, her nose nuzzled into my neck, her warm thigh pulled up onto my leg, her knee resting on the lower part of my abdomen. She stroked my chest softly.

"*Slaughtered*," I said.

"Graphic," she replied.

"You've seen the papers—the TV news." We lay quiet for a time. "Who the hell could do that to another human being?" I posited.

Audrey hugged me with her thigh and arm.

Also by R.P. McCabe

Betrayed

http://tinyurl.com/chcvzdo

ABOUT THE AUTHOR

After a successful entrepreneurial career, R.P. McCabe turned his attention to his long-held private aspiration of writing. During the '90s he was a featured writer for Enterprise Magazine.

In 1996, after several unfinished attempts at novel writing, he entered a two-year creative writing program with the Long Ridge Writers Group. R.P. studied under several different writing coaches before completing the curriculum. His debut novel, *Betrayed*, garnered national attention, earning him the focus of interviews on nationally syndicated radio shows and feature articles in major publications such as AOL Finance, Kiplinger Review and Business Insider Magazine, along with many small market media.

Mr. McCabe's novels are journeys filled with drama and suspense, deepening relationships, exquisite passion and personal growth, guaranteed to ignite your own imagination and passion.

Mr. McCabe enjoys hearing from his readers and can be contacted through his website, www.novelistrpmccabe.com, Facebook, and Twitter.

Made in the USA
San Bernardino, CA
17 August 2013